The Victorian Detectives
89, Manning Place

J.B.Bass

*'Welcome to the very beginning
of our extraordinary 'journey'.*

'With love and fondest wishes.

J.B.Bass

*Dedicated to **Connie***
My inspiration, my mentor, my life...

*To my dear friends **Tiberius** and **Pandora**...*
*and to '**The League of Ghosts**.'*

'Autumn 1898 – I'

~ Present Day ~

In a moment of private contemplation James Bass gazed into the middle distance of beautiful late autumn browns, reds and oranges which became a blurred artist's palette of ruby and ochre created by the motion of their train as it transported himself and his colleagues back to London. He reminded himself in this rare moment of unhindered tranquillity that this was his favourite time of year.

To both himself and his wife Constance the colours of autumn illuminated by the low, bright sunshine bridled with the crisp, chilly mornings that bite the face and numb the un-gloved fingers and the clarity of a clear blue-sky canopy overhead as they stole a private moment together strolling arm in arm by the Serpentine or visiting the animals in Regent's Park were welcome and comforting diversions, brief moments of stolen normality and a necessary occasional respite from the dangerous, squalid streets of Whitechapel to which Bass knew full-well that he, and his trusted colleague of long standing, Alan Tiberius Blackmore, must now return in order to seek out and lay to rest once and for all a malevolent ghost from their distant past.

"A penny for your deepest thoughts, husband" were the words Constance Bass chose in order to break the silence of the last few minutes that had passed between them.

Without at first turning his head away from the perfectly framed picture of autumnal beauty so created by the window frame of their train carriage, Bass began to speak...

"Forgive me, Connie, the cascading hues of late autumn as they flit by our carriage fill my heart with an overwhelming gladness the like of which I haven't felt for some considerable time."

"And pray forgive me if you will, my beloved, for I believe that my metaphorical penny has only been half spent" was the immediate reply from Constance.

"The remarkable events of these few months past have given you just cause enough to be reflective about a great many things, not least of which how we must all accept and assist you to deal with the raging conflict that burns within your soul. We have now witnessed first-hand the wolf spirit turned loose and we see that the powerful, human essence of you, James Bass, remains intact and shines forth ever brightly. Regardless of what you become in a physical sense, it comforts us to observe that you retain control of that spirit and return to us the man you've always been. I had no doubts as to the validity of both your strength and resolve in being able to face this – for want of a better word – affliction, James, and we shall continue onward together, loving and supporting each other as we always have done."

Bass turned his head inwards from his idle country gazing to face his wife and noticed a tear making its way down her right cheek as she spoke. Taking her hand and gently caressing it within his own, he spoke with all the tenderness that his hardened soldier's heart was able to muster...

"My dearest, sweet Connie. Weep no more for I am here. Stronger, wiser and able to love you more with every passing day as I always have, and always will."

As he continued to speak he patted his heart forcefully with his free hand...

"The wolf is here within and this is where I fully intend for it to remain until absolute necessity demands its release. I am now and always will be James Bartholomew Bass and I do so love you, my beautiful Connie."

Chapter 1

'8 Months Earlier... A lifetime Ago'

London throughout the nineteenth century was a metropolis of constant, swift and not always pleasant change.

For many years revered as the major capital of world trade, industry and commerce, the city stood as a shining example to all of the rapid development in industry; the constant introduction of new machinery and the vast improvement of transport links both at home and across the globe helped not only the city itself to become a respected world capital but also the British Empire, its rich history, traditions and impressive military forces, to be the envy of governments the world over.

Towards the end of the nineteenth century, however, London was a city in steady decline. New York, Paris and several other world capitals began to develop formidable industrial and political arenas for themselves until they eventually rivalled, even in some cases bettered, London as relevant and influential world powers in government and global leaders of both industry and trade.

The old aristocracy sustained by its inherited wealth, people with the richest business interests and most politicians became corpulent and bloated on the riches and power respectively that they amassed while the poorer people of the Tower Hamlets borough on the east side of the city suffered the worst form of oppression and poverty imaginable.

It was back to one such London East End Tower Hamlets district, namely the grim, poverty stricken and often mortally dangerous streets of Whitechapel, which detective inspectors Alan Tiberius Blackmore and James Bartholomew Bass returned after the successful conclusion of their latest case in the Midlands county of Derbyshire.

Taking a hansom cab from Liverpool Street Station onto Bishopsgate, the two detectives traversed street after cobbled street in the most direct route their chosen cabbie knew in order to reach the Leman Street Police station house, where the two exhausted companions knew they could rest awhile, take stock and ready themselves for whatever task may be sent to test them next.

"These cobbled, tired, filthy, mean old streets, my brother," began James Bass.

"I wonder, for all our travels and travails, taking into account the great many wonders of nature's beauty that we've seen that exist outside of this menagerie of filth, corruption and degradation, why sometimes we even bother with the notion to return here at all," he continued.

Tiberius Blackmore took a long pull on the clay pipe he smoked, usually when relaxing or when deep in concentration, and answered thoughtfully between puffs of sweet-odoured Hindu Shag brand tobacco, with good and carefully considered reason.

"We return here because we are compelled to, James.

"We two were raised on these streets. Brought up hard workhouse lads through harsh fortune of birth, pressed young to take the Queen's shilling over a life of dock work or possibly even transportation to the colonies for our past sins and return once again, decorated for valour, and the pair of us made honourable men by experiencing and dealing with worse atrocities than we ever thought that we could here.

"We are these streets, my good friend.

4

"They are within our very souls and they keep us sharp, right on the very edge of acceptable, lawful conduct. Exactly where we need to be in order to function with the guile and, indeed, on more occasions than one might care to remember, the brutality that we must constantly utilise in order to 'copper' as we do; and my heart is kept strong and true by the way in which we choose to go about our business."

His words tapered away with the wisps of smoke from his pipe as they spiralled beyond the boundaries of their hansom cab and into the late morning London air.

"Wise, well considered words as always, Tiberius," answered Bass.

As he gazed out of the side panel of their shared hansom cab that offered a fleeting glimpse of the familiar sights of London's East End unfolding before them, James Bass' final sentence was as poignant as it was so very true:

"These accursed streets, Tiberius. Rancid, filthy, corrupt, deadly... HOME!"

Chapter 2

'A Familiar Homecoming'

The two colleagues entered their oak door and window framed glass fronted office that was located at the very back of the Leman Street station house and offered a welcomed sanctuary from the menagerie of organised chaos that ensued on a daily basis outside, closed the door behind them, and, in what might be perceived as a well-rehearsed, synchronised movement to the casual observer but that in reality was a repeat of one such movement practised many times over, flopped into their wing backed Chesterfield chairs that sat behind a pair of large solid oaken, leather topped desks.

"Will you take a brandy and a 'stogie', Tiberius?" questioned Bass, knowing full well what the answer would be.

"Aye, Brother, a large one if ye please, and a pipe full of 'Hindu shag' to smoke awhile I think" was the expected response from Blackmore.

"It seems that upon reflection, then, we must ultimately believe that because of what we have recently learned through our latest experiences that indeed more instances of the supernatural may well occur to test our resolve even harder," continued Bass.

"One would suggest further that we should therefore remain open minded to any possibility with regards to the outcome to a case, however improbable it might at first seem, may indeed be the plausible and indeed the correct conclusion that we seek.

"I would add further that during these rapidly changing times in which we now live with the free and more readily available transport links to all points across the globe truly enriching our own culture and traditions with a multicultural vibrancy that enhances communities, adds also the darker spectre of the metaphysical and spiritual unknown. The imported customs and evil shadows from other lands that we have yet to fully understand."

"Agreed, James," began Blackmore.

"The very idea of someone born with the gift of extra sensory perception, as was my own daughter, or indeed the ability to shift freely within the fourth dimension of time, as do our colleagues the Aston family, would seem outwardly to all the very idea of fantasy and science fiction.

"I wonder if Mister Herbert George Wells had any such plausible notion of the physical possibility of these phenomena occurring in our time when he penned his popular work of fiction 'The Time Machine'," Blackmore concluded.

Bass answered with thoughtful silence and generous, long puffs of grey Indian 'Rajah' 'stogie' smoke.

The peaceful aside of the two detectives was all at once shattered by a loud rapping on the office door. The newly promoted detective sergeant Marcus Jackson entered...

"Begging your pardon, sirs," he began.

"A body 'as been found down by Saint Katharine's East dock. Horribly bloody and mutilated beyond recognition by all accounts," he reported.

"The street calls to us and so we must answer," mused Bass in a somewhat distant tone that hinted of an almost exasperated resignation.

"Muster a half dozen squad of our finest and true if you please, detective sergeant, you to command," Bass requested of Jackson.

"A full ten-foot cordon around the body and site, none to loiter close by and we two shall make all haste to attend the scene.

"Also, please to inform my good lady wife doctor Constance Bass to attend, bearing her full forensics and photographic bag of tricks, for I have a notion that her talents in both of those fields of expertise shall be required on this day."

Chapter 3

"This isn't the work of old 'Crafty Jack'"

A nd so, the scene was set.

On a late autumn afternoon in October an early evening mist began to rise from the river Thames making visibility increasingly difficult for the investigating officers gathered at St. Katharine's East dock, Whitechapel. As Blackmore and Bass arrived, they were pleased to witness the precise efficiency detective sergeant Jackson had shown in the way that the crime scene area had been organised in readiness for their arrival.

"That lad has done well by all accounts since we have recently been occupied out of town," began Blackmore with a hint of almost fatherly pride apparent in his observation.

"Looks as if he was well worth the recommendation for promotion we submitted to the Chief Super on his behalf."

"He's a good, enthusiastic lad, right enough," answered Bass...

"But?" retorted Blackmore. "I sense a 'but...'"

"But indeed, you old smoke blower," countered Bass matter-of-factly.

"He'll be right enough, do good things, even great things as may be the case, but in order to achieve anything at all he's got to stay alive and, in this business, on these foul streets as you well know, my good friend, that one thing is truly an ask of great proportions, a fact of that we are both all too well aware."

"Optimist you are, James. He'll be right enough with us awhile," retorted Blackmore.

"Realist with a hint of pessimist perhaps, cynic for sure, cyclist occasionally with chief raconteur and the merest hint of enthusiastic horticulturalist tossed into the cooking pot for good measure, I'd like to think of as a more astute observation of my capabilities and seemingly rapidly expanding skills set aye thang yew, sir!" added Bass with a hint of sarcastic wit and a mock doff of his weather beaten black homburg hat in the direction of his companion.

"Add to that list of self-serving parody if it pleases you, sir, crack-shot, smart arse 'stogie chomper'!" was the simple sarcastic retort from Blackmore.

The situation to which the two detectives were presented was not one of a pleasant nature. The body of a man lay face up on the cobbles, close to the river facing wall of one of the many ramshackle warehouses that were built all along the eastern side of Saint Katharine's dock.

His face was all but gone; his chest rent open, the rib cage split to expose a selection of bodily organs, haphazardly arranged both inside and outside of the chest cavity, and there were copious amounts of blood sprayed about the area for perhaps an eight to ten feet radius around the corpse.

"Not a pleasant sight to be sure," observed Bass.

"Last time we witnessed anything approximating this level of brutality was 13 Miller's Court, some ten years past. That poor wretch Mary Kelly, God rests her soul."

"This isn't the work of old 'Crafty Jack' though, brother," offered Blackmore thoughtfully.

"This reeks foul of something else, something quite hideous. A phenomena as contrary and primitively savage to anything we have ever witnessed before, I think," he continued.

"What first impressions have you garnered, if indeed any at all, from your preliminary investigation of this unfortunate soul, my love?" Bass asked his wife, the highly respected and well renowned forensic scientist doctor Constance Matilda Bass, who had been meticulously working the crime scene a few minutes before the two detectives' arrival.

"One's first instinct on examination not half an hour yet past is of a white male body, indigenous to this area or near abouts anyhow judging by his workmanlike attire and stevedore rough hands. This man displays all the signs of being torn to pieces by a large animal, or at any rate before further analysis, something of extreme size and power.

"The random trajectory of the blood splatter pattern up and along this wall hence and indeed all around this unfortunate soul suggests that rather than a precise fatal cut to any major artery, said arteries, bones and flesh were ripped apart with no apparent medical or butchery skill utilised.

"Nor is there apparent any contrived direction of blade or discernible signs of finesse displayed whatsoever. More than likely perhaps the savagery of this attack, coupled with the configuration of the wounds, appear as those that might occur in a purely random, mad feeding frenzy of sorts," Dr Bass answered.

"I shall photograph the scene in great detail and submit copies to our esteemed colleagues at the office of Metaphysical, Paranormal, Supernatural and Psychic phenomena, for I feel we will need to employ their expertise in assisting with the solving of this case," she concluded.

"How so?" asked Bass of his wife.

"What have you observed here that we have not, Connie?"

Dr Bass continued:

"Here, as I was examining what remains of the victim's larynx, across the throat area embedded inside the decimated jugular vein, I found what appears to be a claw, I would approximate to be about two inches in length.

"Judging by the organic matter around its base I'd surmise that it was torn from whomsoever, or indeed whatsoever creature it belonged to during the attack and was not placed thusly in order to offer us a false perspective on the possible causes of this atrocity.

"I shall investigate further and hopefully should be able to determine as to what species of animal it belongs."

"Excellent work, Connie," said Blackmore.

"Please keep us informed on a regular basis of all developments relating to the forensics reports concerning this case, however trivial they may seem to you.

"Also, if you could get copies of your images and a report of your findings onto the desk of Professor Jefferson at the O.M.P.S.P.P. as soon as possible it would be of great use to us to learn of any tangible connection with the supernatural that might exist here, for this situation certainly does appear to be exhibiting concerning traits that all point to this being a distinct possibility," he concluded.

"Just so, Tiberius and with the greatest of urgency," added Dr Bass.

"One more key point of interest for you to consider, gentlemen," she continued.

"I noticed what I at first perceived to be unshod footprints steeped in blood and thus leaving behind a very clear imprint, leading away from the carnage in a northerly direction inland away from the docks for a short distance then turning left along East Smithfield towards the West dock, and mark this well, gentlemen, after further brief investigation I observed that the prints were most definitely not of human making.

"I would need to be made absolutely certain through further research, but I'd say they were made by a large biped, possibly a bear or some similar sized creature on hind legs, but upon first instinct and if my memory of a long-ago study of animal pad types and configurations serves me as well as I fear it might in this case, the prints were more than likely made by a very large wolf!"

Chapter 4

'The Whitechapel Hotel'

The mortuary room situated within the hospital buildings just off the greater Whitechapel Road was the place where a good many of the cases of wrongful death that came to the attention of Blackmore and Bass were in fact solved with the aid of the rapid advancements being made in the study of medicine, human anatomy and in the constant development within the science of forensic investigation, being utilised on a more regular basis by the police as a reliable source of information to determine the outcome of a case beyond all reasonable doubt.

The space was of an open plan design, about forty feet square, its white tiled walls on three sides reaching three quarters of the way up to a high flat ceiling.

Lead framed, heavily frosted glass windows were set along both the north and east facing sides high into the final third of the walls so as to add natural light into the room and to discourage potentially inquisitive eyes from seeing within.

Gas lamps fitted equidistantly around the room offered ample artificial light when needed. A portion of the fourth wall was set aside as a storage facility for corpses under current investigation by the forensics team. Comprising a series of steel latched compartments, refrigerated by a concealed 'ice corridor' to their rear, three feet high, three feet across and eight feet in length with a sliding bench within on which the body lay, this revolutionary new method of storing corpses on site, albeit for relatively short periods of time, meant that vital case work could progress swiftly and without hindrance.

Along the centre of the room were situated five porcelain benches of approximately eight feet in length where post mortems and other examinations of bodies took place.

On one such bench lay the latest 'sleeping guest' at what had affectionately yet still somewhat macabrely become known as 'The Whitechapel Hotel'. Dr Constance Bass, the two inspectors, detective sergeant Marcus Jackson and Professor Florence Elizabeth Jefferson were present and discussing the progress they had made thus far.

"What news of our new 'guest', Connie?" Bass asked of his wife.

"The claw that I removed from the open wound in the neck area has proved to be of great significance," began Dr Bass.

"Upon further analysis I have discovered that the organic matter removed from the base of the claw is actually a marriage between two separate types of tissue."

"The victims and the owner of the claw, one would surmise," interjected Blackmore.

"Not conclusively so, Tiberius" was the unexpected reply from Dr Bass.

"I was able to isolate and ultimately separate all tissue types from the source and fully expected the results to favour what I would have expected to be the obvious two types of tissue present just as you have surmised, Tiberius, specifically those of a human male and that of our as yet unidentified assailant.

"Imagine, then, of my surprise to learn that here in fact are three types of tissue present, one of which, if one applies all the possible logical scientific thought processes to these proceedings, really should not exist.

"The forensic evidence proves beyond all reasonable doubt that the claw belonged to a creature with the tissue types of both human male and wolf, not haphazardly mixed together as might occur in a random act of violence, but rather intertwined precisely as one could possibly find when two or more separate strands of deoxyribonucleic acid might meld together to transform into the one entity. Thus, one being miraculously transforms into another but still retains enough of its own original DNA characteristics to make the argument tangible," the doctor concluded.

"The scientific evidence gathered thus far might well be more significant to this case than we yet realise," Professor Jefferson began.

"Let us consider for a moment documented facts that exist within the files belonging to the institute for Paranormal, Spiritual and Psychic Phenomena explaining in great detail the existence of a 'man-wolf' or to use its more familiar old English reference 'wer-wulf'. Often believed to be a mythological or even folkloric human, possibly a disaffected, spiritually compromised person in some way, an outcast from the accepted normal rules of society or even a mentally troubled individual unable to control the brutal, feral and savage urges forced upon its tortured soul by this affliction of the mind, infected by the bite or scratch of a werewolf and thus themselves becoming afflicted by the curse of lycanthropy.

These lycanthropes or 'lycans' have the proven ability to alter their appearance, or indeed to 'shapeshift' from their original human form into that of a muscularly enhanced, extremely physically powerful and unpredictably dangerous wolf-like being.

"All sense of human reason and decency lost to the savagery and carnal instincts of a wild animal, werewolves kill for food alone as would any normal carnivore in the wild, but to survive the attack of a werewolf is to contract the affliction oneself and thus, during the cycle of every full moon, to transform and succumb to the curse of lycanthropy."

"Thank you, Connie and Florence, for your insightful analysis delivered as always with clarity and flawless logic" came Blackmore's grateful reply.

"Once more we find ourselves facing a physically real and deadly phenomenon, as proven to be so by our esteemed colleagues, albeit on this occasion from within the pages of ancient folklore and superstition.

"Sergeant Jackson, deploy men to the docks and seek out any tangible information from both official and unofficial sources relating to all new merchant sailors, navy personnel and of generally embarked persons alike who are recently berthed..."

He was interrupted by Professor Jefferson...

"Pardon the interruption, Tiberius, one more key point of interest that I omitted to divulge earlier.

"Both yourselves and your officers should be aware that the phenomena we seek is quite real, very deadly indeed and if not confronted directly in its transformed state has a sign by which it might possibly be recognised whilst inhabiting its human form.

"Concerning all things associated with matters appertaining to folklore, psychic and paranormal entities. There is a great deal of colloquial superstition involved that is taken extremely seriously by the people of communities directly affected by these strange entities that we are now all too aware of exist within our midst and should no longer be dismissed lightly by us as mere conjecture and hearsay.

"The sign you should be wary of is that of a five-pointed star or the pentagram as it is known. A talisman of sorts, made of blessed silver, which is given by sympathetic locals to an unfortunate wretch known to be afflicted by the disease as little more than a form of comfort for the troubled soul, usually in the form of the five-pointed star or indeed, as the cycle progresses further and the spiritual resolve of the hapless victim to remain human grows weaker, as the wolven instinct becomes dominant over all, a clearly visible mark somewhere upon the skin; the 'mark of the werewolf'."

Chapter 5

'Mark of the Werewolf'

"The full moon cycle usually lasts for about fourteen lunations over which full moons vary in size and age. This probably leads to the suggestion that a larger, more powerful moon exerts more of an overtly dominant influence upon the weakened will of a troubled soul," continued Professor Jefferson.

"Lunation?" asked Bass quizzically.

"Indeed, James," answered the professor.

"The moon's orbit around the Earth is elliptical in its path, thus as a consequence at its perigee is nearer to the Earth than at its apogee half an orbit later.

"The period of the moon's orbit from perigee to apogee and back to perigee is known scientifically as the anomalistic month. This time period of approximately one month is known in folklore as 'the moon of the wolf'. We should therefore expect more random attacks during the remaining nights that this cycle of the moon has left to run."

"Might we also expect the werewolf attacks to remain constant within a specific area, as with an animal upon marking out and claiming a territory for itself?" questioned Blackmore.

"We should indeed, Tiberius," answered the professor.

"The werewolf is a creature that exists purely by instinct and habit. A feral, wild beast driven on by its most basic carnal desire to feed. Therefore, it follows that if food is in abundance and resistance to any attack is weak from the indigenous population upon which it has chosen to prey upon then…"

"Carnage!" exclaimed Blackmore.

"Random, merciless, brutal carnage. Might one ask how this unfortunate victim of nature's folly might be stopped, Florence?" he asked.

"Lycanthropy, for all the random savagery that is inflicted upon hapless innocents by the affected soul during the full moon cycle, is not a form of controlled evil as such and so remains a condition that can be successfully managed," answered the professor.

"The affliction is spiritual, a disease that causes an almost cataclysmic rift within the very depths of the soul, but if the afflicted 'Lycan' is in possession of a strong, disciplined constitution and has the full support, understanding and most of all the deepest love of both friends and family, then there is a real possibility that, providing all points relating to a successful management of the condition are adhered to precisely, a relatively normal life can continue.

"In this particular case, however, all the evidence gathered so far would suggest that we seek a lone, extremely troubled individual.

"Taking into account that just one attack has occurred thus far during this 'wolf moon cycle' we might reasonably believe that the perpetrator is indeed as was surmised earlier newly acquainted to this city and is developing a free feeding territory here in the Whitechapel dockland area, as would any carnivorous feral animal in the wild.

"Also, expect more attacks soon. Quite probably multiple, random attacks on a nightly basis and beware of those who survive an assault by a werewolf, for they shall indeed become afflicted and succumb to the curse themselves."

"And if we should need to terminate our mark at once with extreme and lethal prejudice, Florence?" asked Bass.

"Bullets or blades made from blessed silver have proven to be a most effective form of weapon against this particular phenomenon," replied Professor Jefferson. "A weapon made from a spiritually blessed source used to cleanse a malady of the human spirit. An exorcism of sorts, one might conclude."

Chapter 6

'Brandy and Bullets'

Both Blackmore and Bass were in pensive moods while engrossed in deep conversation as they sat at their usual table in the corner of one of the smaller back rooms of 'The Brown Bear' public house on the corner of Scarborough Street and Saint Mary's street situated at the heart of their Whitechapel 'patch'.

The pub was a mere stone's throw from the Leman Street police station and provided a welcome retreat for the two detectives when they felt the need to leave the often cloying and occasionally oppressive confines of their office in order to discuss the more 'delicate' matters of a case while sampling more than a few 'snifters' of their favourite Del Vecchio brandy that was especially imported for them from Italy.

Seated with their backs turned always to the wall with one solitary frosted glass window allowing the dull remaining light of Whitechapel to seep into the room during the rapidly diminishing daylight hours, blue smoke from the clay pipe of Blackmore mingled with the subtle, grey 'stogie' smoke of Bass' finest Indian 'Rajah' cheroot that helped to create an ambience of jealously guarded solitude around the two old battle hardened warriors, an ambiance which only the select few people who knew of their whereabouts were welcomed to join and even then were loath to disturb unless absolutely necessary.

On the table before them was the usual array of assorted firearms which were in the process of being re-loaded with various calibre bullets that were strewn about randomly, a half-finished bottle of 'Del Vecchio' brandy, hip flasks, two crystal shot glasses, an opened case of the finest imported Indian 'Rajah' cigars and an as yet un-rubbed brick of 'Hindu shag' tobacco.

Blackmore picked up the brick of virgin 'baccy' and began to rub it gently between his palms until it broke into small enough flakes, part of which he proceeded to load generously into his clay pipe, the remainder of the strong yet alluringly sweet-smelling flakes being deposited into the leather pouch that was always carried in his inside coat pocket.

"We need as a point of urgency to ask Phineas if he'll knock out a run of silver bullets, cartridge and shot for us and the men, six hundred rounds of each cartridge type and calibre I would suggest," alluded Bass as he casually dropped another conventional round into an empty chamber of his .44 calibre Smith and Wesson Schofield revolver.

"Though how we propose to write this particular expense off onto the department budget is going to prove most interesting when the monthly expenses are tallied, I would surmise," he quipped.

Taking a long pull on his freshly lit pipe and draining his glass in one gulp, Blackmore answered his colleague, at first with a flash of the customary humour with which they punctuated most of their private conversations, possibly as a lifting tonic with which to diffuse the seriousness of the words to come but most definitely as part of the unique language that the two detectives had developed between themselves over the course of their friendship in order to communicate beyond the ears and understanding of any random gossips or covert enemy agents that might be loitering in their vicinity.

"We'll ask both the Chief Super and Judge Alderman if their good lady wives will cough up their best Sunday silver in aid of the cause," he began.

"Failing that I'll get Phineas onto his crooked contact at the Royal Mint. I'm certain that someone owes him a big favour that's ready and ripe for a timely collection, no questions asked."

"Consider this potential disaster as it unfolds: no more Sunday lunch parties for the Chief Super and the Judge. A tragic scenario to be sure. Don't know how they'd manage. I'd sooner fence the silver off up West for a bit of extra coin than waste a potential tidy profit on bullets tho'," quipped Bass dryly.

"Or perhaps we could stab our werewolf with the good lady Alderman's best carving knife, it being made of the finest silver of course. Result!"

"It's at that precise point in the proceedings that I'd rather have bullets made from the mint silver to rely on," answered Blackmore.

"How so?" questioned Bass as he spun the full chamber of his revolver, laid it on the table and began loading his second pistol, his trusty old Army issue Webley mark one service revolver.

"That precise moment of direct contact when you'd find out that our esteemed donor's silver is in fact plate, not solid, and definitely not blessed by any one truly holy!" said Blackmore with a sigh of indignant resignation.

"Of course, the silver must be pure and blessed in the eyes of God!" exclaimed Bass.

"I'll enquire with Florence Jefferson about the possibility of tapping up the clergy for our raw material this time. One would assume that the prof. has a better than average chance of convincing the holy powers that be of our spiritual need for copious amounts of blessed projectiles."

"And there goes hence over the hills and far away forever any slight chance of fencing off the boss' family silver!" added Blackmore mischievously.

As the two colleagues continued their private conclave they were joined at their table by Commander Don 'The Undertaker' Blackmore, son of Tiberius Blackmore and celebrated London private detective recently recruited into the service of 'The League of Ghosts'.

"What latest news from the mean streets, son?" asked Blackmore Senior of his son.

"Plenty, and all relevant to our case I think," answered the commander.

"I've had agents sifting through the dregs of all waterfront inns, brothels and every God forsaken pisshole we'd expect any merchant seamen, visiting malcontents or even high-born west end 'toffs' out for a crafty 'spit and polish' and wishing to remain anonymous from detection to gravitate towards.

"There, as we made our enquiries from place to place and street to street, I noticed what can only be described as a putrid cloud of superstition and fear enveloping the whole area.

"There was one sordid little hovel in particular where our enquiries finally bore the fruit that we sought to harvest. An old dockers' inn named 'The Merchant's Stoop' just on the corner of East Smithfield and Cartwright Street, which seems to consistently attract a fair number of merchant stop overs, malcontents and ne'er do wells through its grimy portals on a regular basis. Almost akin to a sanctuary for the scum of Whitechapel, so to speak," he said.

"A veritable orchard of ripe fruit for the picking. Please divulge your findings in detail, Commander," added Bass.

"I began asking around casually at first about any new bloods in town who seemed set on keeping to themselves and holding their affairs close to and private like, as if to avoid direct contact with anyone they thought might arouse any kind of interest in their business," began Commander Blackmore.

"A few complimentary rounds of the finest quality 'mother's ruin' bought to loosen willing tongues offered up a fair old crop of your 'ripe fruit', James," he continued.

"I got to talking with a working lady of questionable morals who takes rooms regularly above the inn – 'Big Nosed Kate' is the name she is commonly known by.

"Turns out she's been visited by a Russian merchant seaman several times this past couple of days, calls himself Yuri Tokalev and is, to explain Kate's appraisal of his carnal desires in the briefest and most modest way possible, insatiable in his appetites, one might suggest animalistic even!

"I checked crew manifests for all vessels docked these past two days and a Yuri Tokolev shipped in on the Ukrainian freighter 'Lubliana' well within the parameters of our timeframe. Also, having seen Mr Tokalev up close and personal, so to speak, Kate observed that he had what she perceived to be a tattoo on the underside of his right wrist.

"She states that he wore a substantial leather vambrace that covered this mark over but upon removing it when they went to bed is when she noticed the mark clearly. It is that of the five-pointed star, the pentagram that we seek."

"Then it seems that we have our man!" exclaimed Blackmore.

"So it may seem, Father," answered Commander Blackmore.

"One more thing of note that should be considered. Whilst searching these several premises from rafter to foundation as is part and parcel of our method when set to task by 'The League', I came across another example of the very mark that we seek. It was in the root cellar of 'The Merchant's Stoop', scrawled roughly into the plaster on a wall and flanked on either side by two tall and burning candles. A five-pointed star, the pentagram."

The three detectives' conclave was interrupted by the sudden appearance of Detective Sergeant Marcus Jackson.

"Beggin' your pardons, sirs," he began.

"There's been another one, discovered this last few minutes further west up above Tower Hill in Trinity Square. Same 'orrible mess by all accounts," the sergeant reported...

Chapter 7

'Within the Darkest Shadows of the Mind'

Night time had cast its dark, forbidding cloak over Whitechapel as the three detectives had continued on with their deep conversation.

The 'wolf moon' was still at its perigee, almost Jewel-like in its stately mid-autumn hugeness, rather like an all-knowing, wise old face casting its expansive gaze down upon the whole world yet offering no comfort to those who chose to seek it within its cold, always intently staring façade.

"Same procedure as before with regards to perimeter boundaries and forensics deployment, sergeant Jackson, if you please," requested Blackmore.

"In addition, we need to locate and apprehend one individual named Yuri Tokalev. A Russian merchant seaman, we think, believed to be rooming at 'The Merchants Stoop' inn on the corner of East Smithfield and Cartwright.

"Be aware and under no illusion, Jackson, this man is potentially lethally dangerous to all and might well only be able to be restrained during the daylight hours. If you should happen across this man during the night time under no circumstances are you or your men to attempt taking him into custody.

"The reason will be immediately obvious should your paths happen to cross. You will not be able to restrain this man using conventional methods or terminate this man using standard issue ammunition. However vague my instructions might appear to be, please adhere to them implicitly and without question. Your very lives may depend upon your diligence in understanding and following this advice I now give to you," ordered Blackmore.

"I will accompany Jackson myself and brief him and his men further on the importance of the task that lies before them," said Commander Blackmore.

"I will then go street side with the police and assist them in organising the search for our mark, also attempt to keep them razor sharp of wits and extra vigilant."

As Commander Blackmore and Sergeant Jackson left the room there seemed to pass what could best be described as a brief moment when time appeared to inexplicably stop, as suddenly as would the movement of an unwound clock, and all senses were numbed to a state that could be likened to that of a waking stupor.

Upon regaining consciousness from their temporary trance, the two detectives were greeted by the appearance of Captain Pontius Maximillian Aston, Beatrice Juliette Aston and their son Professor Leopold Byron Aston, Time Enforcement agents and members of the secret organisation named 'The League of Ghosts'.

"Our profound and unreserved apologies for intruding upon your current investigations uninvited," began Captain Aston, appearing genuinely perturbed by his own and his families' unscheduled arrival.

"This case in which you find yourselves currently embroiled bears no threat to the security of any timeline past, present or future, so we risk much by even being here and discussing its outcome in any capacity with you both," he continued.

"Once more you face a phenomenon the like of which you never have before," interceded Leopold Aston.

"As you are both now well aware, the creature that you seek, a werewolf, does indeed exist within the parameters of this reality and should no longer be regarded as a mythical spirit from inside the faded pages of the parchment tomes of folklore and legend.

"We can offer no more advice as to how you might triumph over this unfortunate, troubled soul than Professor Jefferson, who would seem to possess all of the necessary, relevant and correct information that you require to hand. We might just add that if you have no alternative but to end this hapless creature's existence, please regard any termination with extreme prejudice as offering a merciful release from a hellish existence to a tortured and troubled soul not borne of its own choosing on a path to its damned course, a soul that needs to be put to rest and given everlasting peace."

Beatrice Aston continued...

"I would offer my own constantly unfolding experience of managing a soul in perpetual turmoil. Torn between a life of selfless service to the T.E.A. and to The League of Ghosts, hounded constantly by the torment of a tortured spirit enslaved to the nightly urge of feeding the insatiable 'blood lust' that is within me.

"Please make every effort to offer this lost soul the slender olive branch of hope that remains a viable option. Try with all possible vigour and compassion to explain that there is a way to keep his seemingly overwhelming animalistic and wild urges in check and under control. With care, compassion, guidance and the love and support of family and great friends there is a pathway back to the light," she concluded, her voice almost faltering with emotion.

"Gracious and the saints preserve us; time on this day is our enemy. We must leave at once," aluded Captain Aston with a seemingly startled timbre rising in his voice.

"We risk a paradox of untold proportions within the fourth dimension should we remain in this time period a moment longer without official sanction from the agency."

Directing his next words specifically at Bass, he continued:

"James, a word with you in private if I may."

James Bass and Pontius Aston left the room and retired to a table in a quiet corner of the adjoining bar, next to an inglenook fireplace where a well-kept wood and peat burning fire crackled away in the hearth and gave an earthy aroma and a warming comfort to the room on this chilly mid-autumn evening.

"So, 'The Industrial Dandy' has, albeit for the briefest of visits, has returned to our town, indeed, to our time," began Bass.

Eyeing the tall, slim frame of Aston up and down he continued by first commenting in a somewhat wry fashion upon the rather eccentrically inclined yet still sartorially elegant outfit sported by his old Army companion.

"The attire you choose suits you, old friend. Part the swashbuckling buccaneer, part Victorian gentleman and part eighteenth century dandy melded together as one provides a striking figure for the eye to behold for sure.

"I don't recall such flamboyant personal style being wholly apparent as we strove to survive the killing fields of the Crimean campaign or even during our service together at the forlorn hope at Sebastopol, the first Boer conflict, or indeed even whilst engaged in the Afghan and Egyptian campaigns," he continued.

"I shall endeavour to explain the concept and the ethos of 'Steampunk' and the bearing it has on my personal and my family's appearance at a later, more appropriate moment, James, but may it please you to be aware that there are more relevant and pressing matters for discussion that command your undivided attention. Matters of such keen importance that your very life might depend upon the method of your logic and the outcome of your actions during the next few days."

"My life?" responded Bass quizzically.

"I get the distinct impression from your tone that the signs of a favourable, indeed an unscathed, or possibly even a much worse outcome to this particular caper might be a distinct possibility for me."

Pontius Aston continued: "A possibility yes, a probability perhaps not. Alas, and the risk of a major rift occurring within the timeline be damned, I have most probably divulged too much information already.

"Please accept these two trinkets of blessed silver. Wear them about your person as the talismanic amulets of protection they are purported to be."

"Pentagrams!" exclaimed Bass with an almost indignant air of incredulity present in his voice as he answered...

"You've given me the five-pointed star in a bid to ward off ghouls, ghosts, goblins and perchance, werewolves?

"Best just to offer me a generous cache of blessed silver ammunition to prepare the only real harbingers of retribution I've ever required in the face of insurmountable odds, namely Messrs. Smith and Wesson and Webley respectively," spat back Bass with more than a little venom in his words as he brandished both of his pistols from concealment and slammed them hard onto the table before them.

"Our friendship, nay our brotherhood is such that my family and I risked much inconvenience to us and possible disruption of the timelines by the ripples our unscheduled visit might cause in order to pass on these amulets and deliver the information that we needed to," imparted Aston incredulously.

"Indeed," answered Bass, his agitated demeanour calming.

"I am ashamed. I ask your pardon, Pontius and stand well and truly rebuked for the harsh tone of my words and the severity of my immediate and ill-conceived actions.

"I meant no disrespect to either yourself, or to your family, for your offer of advice is truly sound and well-meant, your obvious concern for my wellbeing is graciously accepted as a selfless gesture made by loyal and true friends, and I fully appreciate what you have each risked in order to pass on your report to me.

"You are well aware from countless incursions past shared and in the face of seemingly impossible odds of the way that yourself, Phineas, Tiberius and I always found the pathway necessary to triumph over adversity. Always found a way, no matter how improbable the outcome or impossible the task seemed, to save each other's lives times over when confronted by insurmountable odds and always managed to choose the correct options in order to survive and ultimately to win.

"This current situation in which we find ourselves embroiled is no different to those of harsh exploits past, my brother. Admittedly a new and potentially deadly adversary we face, of that I am no longer in doubt, but once more we shall summon all of the courage, the strength, the fortitude, the guile and tenacity our wits can muster and once again we shall be victorious; and besides, these pentagram baubles will make a pair of fine watch fobs.

"Might even be worth a pretty penny sold on to a West End pawnbroker I shouldn't wonder," concluded Bass with his usual flourish of tension-relieving humour.

"Same old James Bass," retorted Aston, a wry grin forming on his skeletal-like, white bearded features.

"A rapier keen wit that has often been a well-chosen tool used to defuse even the most potentially volatile of situations on many occasions. If humour were able to be used as a lethal weapon, then both you and that other malcontent Tiberius Blackmore would each possess an inexhaustible cache that would never need to be replenished.

"We have taken the liberty of providing Doctor Jefferson with the necessary quantity of blessed silver ourselves so that he might proceed immediately with the manufacture of the rounds of ammunition that you require in order to complete your task effectively.

"The moment we became aware of matters as they unfolded within this timeframe we were able to arrange this several weeks ago. Your men should be receiving their allocation of ammunition this very hour, post briefing as to its purpose, of course."

"So much to be said for not being able to aid our cause," quipped Bass somewhat dryly.

"Might one ask how a most substantial fortune in silver came to be readily and somewhat conveniently at your disposal, you old pirate?"

"One might indeed ask" was the deadpan and only reply from Aston relating to the subject.

"Be very careful, old friend, and be especially mindful of both the unexpected anomaly that lurks in the darkest shadows and the element of random chance that might prove too costly a price to pay.

"Please remember that as sure footed as you might perceive yourself to be, the path that you choose might not always be the easiest or safest to tread."

All at once, without fanfare or fond farewell, the Aston family faded away into the hidden corridor of the fourth dimension as silently as they had arrived.

As his senses began to ease into a semblance of normality, Bass was aware of a lilting melody wafting through the muffled, smoke-tinged ambience of the bar to the comforting warmth of the fireplace where he sat. As he remained at his fireside haven, comfortable and warm, lost in his own thoughts as to what to make of the conversation that had just taken place, he became aware of the words that were being spoken, as would a piece of poetry be recited, over the ethereal music being made by a group of musicians playing what he perceived to be a lute-like, multi-stringed instrument of some description, a harmonium, a violin and a boron that added an almost sympathetic rhythmic pattern to this sombre, yet in some way still totally mesmerising piece of musical poetry.

'Under the sun, under the moon two souls entwine as one,

In trance as to one's earthly course, yet you shall know me soon, my friend, you shall know me soon....

Not knowing of this eternal fight, one's feelings torn between,

Even one with the strongest heart, becomes at one with the shadows of the night, my dear, at one with the shadows of the night.'

Bass listened intently and was overcome with a feeling the like of which he had not experienced for many years, not since the darkest of days when he and his comrades experienced the true, first-hand horrors of open warfare during the living hell of their many shared campaigns together. He was encompassed by a sudden fearful chill that cut him to the very core of his soul, giving him an unprecedented sense of vulnerability and, possibly for the first time in his life, made him feel quite alone.

"What covert verbal idlings and back room dark, under-the-table dealings did Pontius want to discuss with you that was so private a matter as to not allow your old protector to be party to?" questioned Tiberius Blackmore, just arrived by his still entranced colleague's side.

"Ah Tiberius, my very dearest friend.

"Nothing of great importance other than the Astons arranged for our cache of silver to be delivered to our good brother at arms Doctor Phineas Jefferson's Gunsmith and Weapons Emporium up on Wilkes Street, Spitalfields, in order for him to fashion us the ammunition that we require," reported Bass truthfully.

"They ordered it a month ago and so it follows that the consignment should be arriving at our station house on Leman Street as we speak. Clever, very clever and quite useful this dimension jumping malarkey..."

...His words tapered off into silence as he gazed into the embers glowing comfortingly in the stone hearth, possibly searching for an answer somewhere in the hypnotic movement of the diminishing flames, to the conundrum he had just been teased with by Captain Aston, an answer that he knew for all his searching within the enticing movement of the dancing fire wraiths would not be there.

"Do you hear the music, Tiberius?

"Such lilting, comforting sounds that warm and soften the hardest of hearts as do these embers, with words that reach deep into the relentlessly perambulating wheels of the mind, touch the very fibres of the soul.

"Do you hear it, Tiberius!?"

"There is no music to these ears, James, only the music of the orange flames dancing on the peat and wood in the inglenook before us," answered Blackmore, now with more than an air of concern openly shown in his voice for his obviously troubled colleague.

Chapter 8

'A Soul in Torment'

The Leman Street police station house was a hive of activity as the two detectives entered the building on what was becoming a bitterly cold autumn evening. Flecks of light snow began to fall, leaving an effect on the cobbled street as would a delicate icing sugar frosting atop a newly-baked cake.

"This'll settle and freeze overnight I'd wager," observed Blackmore as he pulled his old overcoat onto his broad shoulders.

"Keep those pistols of yours well-greased, James, and your bullets warm else they'll freeze in the chamber when you least expect them to in this cold," he continued.

"Just like the old Remington .32 calibres we used to in the Crimea. Nearly cost us dear on more than one occasion they did. Proper poor kit those Remingtons proved to be right enough."

"So, they did, Tiberius, and indeed they were," began Bass.

"Thank providence then for my trusty Smith and Wesson and Webley pair and a fine, sharp sabre that proved to be our salvation times many."

They were greeted almost immediately by a buoyant Detective Sergeant Jackson:

"A pleasant evening to you both, sirs.

"'The Undertaker', er, begging his pardon, Commander Blackmore, is briefing the men about how to use the shiny new bullets that have just arrived courtesy of Captain Aston and Dr Jefferson. Very nice indeed, real silver by all accounts and..."

His words were halted mid-sentence by the forcefully delivered commands of a clearly agitated and somewhat testy Bass...

"Relay these instructions to your men immediately, Sergeant. You should by now have been made aware of our mark, one Yuri Tokalev.

"You should also have been made aware that we know him to be an extremely dangerous individual, proven to be our killer, whose physical appearance might not be what one would expect it to be. If either you or any of your men are confronted by, for want of a better description, his alter-ego, show absolutely no hesitation in using your nice, shiny ammunition and bring him down without question or remorse. Extreme prejudice, Detective Sergeant! Do you understand? Extreme prejudice!"

"Y...yes...sir, sorry sir, I...meant..." stuttered the hapless Jackson.

"You meant no disrespect to Detective Inspector Bass and was just about to re-join your men at the briefing in order to claim your allocation of ammunition," interjected Blackmore in a most timely fashion on Jackson's behalf.

"On your way and, Jackson, one more thing for you to consider if you will. Should I or Detective Inspector Bass become aware that any of those nice, shiny, real silver bullets have gone across the counter in any posh pawnbrokers up west, I shall personally nail both the fence and the seller's sorry, thieving backsides to our office wall by their balls and I take no responsibility whatsoever as to what dire alternative fate awaits you if my irksome colleague should apprehend the miscreants before I do. Please make this abundantly clear to your men, Detective Sergeant Jackson."

"Y...yes s...sirs, s...sorry, sirs, begging your pardon, sirs..." Jackson spluttered as he left the office.

"He's a good lad, James," offered Blackmore in defence of the hapless young sergeant.

"Go easy on him and the other men for the good lord above only knows what unimaginable peril they, and indeed we, might face on this night. They require and have every right to expect our unwavering and true support, our strength of will, calm guidance and stoic leadership more than ever before and we need in return their unwavering loyalty and trust."

"Indeed, my brother," Bass said.

"Once more, Tiberius, your flawless logic and good common sense prevails as it always has.

"I will make amends with the boy later. I respect and value his continued selfless efforts on our behalf wholeheartedly. He will make a fine Detective Inspector one day soon, of this I am certain, and on that day I shall rejoice as if feeling an overwhelming pride for my own kin. Perhaps we two shall even call him sir in time, but now I must digress to a moment earlier in the evening as I conversed with Pontius.

"I stood rebuked and ashamed for my lack of tact and for my harsh tone in response to his obvious concern for my future wellbeing. Twice this day have I faltered and failed with regards to my professional and personal conduct towards both a brother and a colleague, and twice have I been vexed and frustrated for lack of an answer as to why such a blatant flaw in one's character could be so openly exposed."

Just as Blackmore was about to answer his now obviously troubled colleague, Bass continued...

"Will you now join the chosen men, Tiberius. See to it that the remainder of their briefing is precise in its content and requisition our cache of the ammunition if you please. I must retire to our office for a moment, but I shall join you all shortly."

"Just so, my old friend," answered a perplexed and now more than a little concerned Blackmore.

As the two detectives parted ways and repaired to opposite ends of the old station house, a young constable entered the lobby of the building and sprinted up to the high oak front desk. Out of breath and sweating profusely from obviously running at pace for a fair distance to deliver his report as quickly as possible, he began to speak to the desk sergeant on duty...

"Beggin' your pardon, Sarge, and with the greatest respect, I needs to speak to either Inspector Bass, Blackmore or both of 'em.

"Either or each it makes no mind. It's about this Ukrainian merchant sailor geezer they're wantin' to collar. I knows where he is."

"Alright, son, steady down a piece. Detective Inspector Blackmore is takin' a meetin' at present. Detective Inspector Bass is down that corridor in his office," instructed the duty sergeant.

Before he could offer any word of courteous thanks to his elder colleague, the young constable set off at pace down the corridor indicated by the desk sergeant and tore towards the closed office door of inspectors Blackmore and Bass. Knocking loudly on the door before entering without invitation, the young constable began to deliver his report to Bass before any rebuke or greeting could be offered.

"Apologies for the intrusion, sir and meaning no disrespect to your privacy at this moment, I knows where he is; the sailor fella you are lookin' for. He's..."

"Calm down, son. Steady yourself a moment and clear your thoughts before you continue," said Bass in a reassuring tone. "In your own time..."

Taking a moment to catch his breath and compose himself, the young constable began his report.

"The sailor geezer you're looking for, sir. He's in The Brown Bear, in the public bar just down the street."

"I know the place. How did you ascertain his identity, Constable?" Bass enquired.

"Well, he got involved in an altercation with another gentleman, sir; over who should receive first bragging rights over the courtship of a certain lady of the night, so to speak. Matters got quite heated, names was bandied about…"

"Names?" questioned Bass. "What names, try and be specific, Constable."

"Profanities, sir.

"Lots of random and crude profanities and names of little consequence to anyone other than themselves and a few debt collectors or whoremasters to be sure, sir," continued the young constable.

"But amid all the shouting and rawping one stands out proud above all the others. A foreign name, Eastern European sounding; Tokalev, it was, Yuri Tokalev. An' that's not all, sir. During the affray that ensued the leather vambrace on Tokalev's right wrist was torn off and I observed what I perceived to be a tattoo on the underside of his wrist, plain as day it was. A star, a five-pointed star."

"A pentagram!" exclaimed inspector Bass.

"We have him now!

"Top drawer work, young man, very nicely done indeed. Please join the briefing in the conference room at the corridor's end, invite Detective Inspector Blackmore and his men to attend me at The Brown Bear where we shall conclude our case post haste on this very night."

Without a moment's pause, despite desperate protestations from the young officer to first muster direct assistance from his colleagues, Bass left the station house with some considerable urgency in the direction of The Brown Bear public house.

His lungs still aching and fit to burst from his initial exertions, the constable ran as fast as he was able down the corridor Bass had indicated and burst into the briefing room. Without excusing himself to the assembled group of officers present for the manner of his entrance and on the cusp of total exhaustion, he began to speak…

"Excuse me, sirs... Detective Inspector, commander, sirs... Detective Inspector Bass...he's...he's gone."

"Gone where, boy, SPEAK!" was the stern riposte from Tiberius Blackmore.

"Gone to 'The Brown Bear', sir. Gone to snare Tokalev at 'The Brown Bear'," the young man spluttered whilst attempting to catch his breath.

"Holy Mother of God!" Blackmore exclaimed. "He's not yet requisitioned his silver ammunition.

"He will be ripe pickings and helpless prey for the beast, make no mistake. Damn the man, damn his pride, damn his arrogance, damn his raw courage and damn him for being the man we'd all aspire to be!" Blackmore exclaimed in both a tone of outright frustration whilst considering the potentially lethal folly of his partner's decision to apprehend Tokalev alone and unmitigated admiration for the courage displayed once again by his fearless brother at arms in order to protect the greater good in the face of seemingly impossible odds as he had done so on many countless occasions in the past.

"Chosen men! Lock and load your weapons and let us spare no effort to prevail in our immediate task should we hope to lose the best of us on this night" was the order from Blackmore.

Chapter 9

'A Grave Error of Judgement'

The cold night air bit sharply into the face of James Bass as he quickened his pace towards The Brown Bear public house.

It was becoming increasingly treacherous underfoot due to the steady, even snowfall that was now beginning to settle into a crisp, unspoiled carpet of white that covered the cobbled street, the kind of virgin snow that was always satisfying to leave one's footprints in first, and in that fleeting moment a distant memory of an innocent, brief instance in time came to mind, fondly remembered from a childhood long passed.

As he rounded the corner of Cartwright Street onto East Smithfield, Bass noticed a lone figure leave a side exit of the Brown Bear, stooping forward slightly, as if distressed and in some kind of physical discomfort, seemingly making for an un-named alleyway that led out towards the eastern dock and the sanctuary of an intricate labyrinth of jetties, recesses and 'rookeries' where one could evade detection with some considerable ease known locally as 'the maze'; instinct alone told the detective that this was indeed his mark and that he needed to act quickly in order to prevent his quarry reaching the relative safety of this darkest and most dangerous part of the dockside landscape.

Bass quickened his pace to intercept his man, whom he had the distinct impression was now slowing down considerably and stooping even lower to the ground, thus making the pursuit somewhat easier in the rapidly thickening snow. A feeling of almost triumphant elation buzzed through every nerve fibre within Bass' body when he realised that his man had turned into a cul-de-sac from which he was certain no exit existed.

'I have him now' he thought to himself as the figure ahead of him was halted in his progress by high brick walls on three sides, a fortuitous trap with no foreseeable means of escape.

As Bass moved to within eight or ten feet of his mark, he noticed that Tokalev's outwardly dishevelled appearance was that of a person who had suffered the most savage of beatings. His clothes were torn, his head badly bloodied from the blows that he had received, his hands and knuckles broken and scarred from the retaliatory blows that he had obviously administered in kind to his anonymous assailants.

He also seemed extremely agitated, murmuring to himself in what Bass perceived to be his native tongue and quite unaware that he had been followed, right up until the very moment Bass began to speak. With both of his pistols drawn, cocked and aimed squarely at his man, Bass began to deliver the official warning so required by the law, just as he had done so many times in the past ...

"Tokalev, Yuri Tokalev. Stand fast in the name of the law! Turn yourself to face the wall, put your hands behind your head and drop to your knees, do so immediately or suffer the inevitable consequences!" was the clear and concise order given by Bass as he edged further forward.

Tokalev continued to mumble inaudibly in some undecipherable Eastern-European language until all at once he became aware of the detective's presence in front of him. He began to speak in English, albeit broken English, his command and delivery of the language however being much better than Bass had thought that it might have been...

"You...cannot be here.

"Not here... Not now... Not in this moment...

"Please...I beg of you...go away... GO AWAY POLICE MAN!

"Far away to be with your own safety...far away... please..."

"We know of your troubles, Tokalev," Bass began, showing a hint of the compassion Beatrice Aston had reminded him to offer.

"We know of your great suffering, your intolerable pain. We can help you. We can teach you to deal with the devil that wrests for control of your mind, entwines itself around your soul.

"We can..."

Bass was interrupted abruptly in mid-sentence by an increasingly troubled Tokalev...

"No one can help. I am slave to the moon god. See how he looks down and gives power and life to the wolf," he pleaded as he tore at the shirt covering his chest.

"I warn you, police man. I warn you for own sake but now too late, too late for you... I..."

His last words tapered away into nothing as he looked directly into the full glare of a moon at its maximum perigee and became contorted by what seemed to be a sudden and crippling fit of agony. Bass could only look on in silent, bewildered curiosity as to what was beginning to unfold before his eyes.

He was not afraid anymore, merely stunned at the macabre spectacle of horror that was unfolding not ten feet in front of where he stood. He heard, amid Tokolev's screams of agony, what he perceived to be the cracking of bone and sinew as he became acutely aware that a bizarre metamorphosis had begun.

From man to wolf, he immediately surmised. He observed fingers pop from their sockets and grow to well beyond their normal length becoming lethal, flesh ripping weapons as nails were pushed out to become dagger like claws. He watched in perplexed silence while bones shattered and re-set as limbs were elongated to accommodate the larger and more powerful body of the beast. Clothes were torn away as the final remnants of human flesh were discarded, as one would discard a tired, ill-fitting old suit, to reveal the tall, powerful body of the wolf, and then the face; The front of the face elongating to a snout, teeth becoming terrible, salivating fangs and Tokalev's final, blood chilling human screams of agony becoming the full-blooded howl of a wolf, a werewolf.

Bass hesitated not a moment longer. Pistols raised, he began to unleash his own kind of retribution upon the great black beast that was rapidly moving towards him but, all too soon and too late, he realised that his standard issue ammunition would have no effect on the huge iron body of the wolf bearing down on him all too swiftly.

The beast was now upon him and too fleet in its movement to be avoided or outpaced. As the huge right hand of open claws of the hell spawn scythed downwards, shattering the helpless detective's collar bone and tearing on through rib and sinew across his chest, cracking open his ribs in one powerful blow, he became vaguely aware of several volleys of muzzle flash occurring firstly behind, and then over his prone body.

He heard desperate commands barked out loud to colleagues by his brother at arms Detective Inspector Alan Tiberius Blackmore; "Chosen men, send that monster back to the Hell from where it came"; and he realised in his last waking moment that if he were to survive this latest most intimate conversation with the angel of death that his life, and the lives of the ones he held most dear to him, would never be quite the same again.

Chapter 10

'A Wolf in Detective's Clothing'

As the brief cacophony of pistol fire came to an end and barely noticing that the massacred body of the werewolf had changed back into its original human form of Yuri Tokalev, the group of detectives and police officers proceeded to attend their fallen comrade.

"Too late, a moment too late," began an openly distressed Blackmore.

"How could he not remember to requisition his silver bullets and why, after all these years of watching out for each other, keeping each other alive, did he choose to corner this mark alone?"

"Sir, he's breathing! He's alive!" exclaimed an almost gleeful Marcus Jackson.

"God and all the saints above be praised" added Commander Don Blackmore with a mixture of emotion present in his voice that encompassed equal amounts of zeal and relief.

"Such carnage as this I've never witnessed on nought but a dead man, but I do so swear. God and all that's in Heaven be praised twice over!"

As the two Blackmores and Jackson celebrated openly an air of restless uncertainty, consternation and increasing fear began to ripple through the agitated conversation taking place within the group of six officers who had made up the remainder of the supporting task force.

One of them was heard to say over the confused gibberish of all the others:

"If we are to believe the facts of the briefing as gospel he'll change and kill us all. Better to finish him off now so as to avoid any more carnage."

"Aye, aye finish him now" added another. "Best for him, best for us all...Aye, best for us all."

Having heard this openly blatant and potentially life-threatening plotting towards what little might remain of his fallen comrade's life, Blackmore instinctively and with all the speed and stealth of his military training still very much in evidence, proceeded to scoop up his stricken colleague's pistols from where they had been randomly discarded as the wolf struck and round on the now obviously terrified would-be assassins in one lightning fast manoeuvre.

Levelling the pair of pistols into the midst of the now openly petrified group of officers he spat out a stark warning that none of them was ever likely to forget for the rest of their lives.

"Any one of you so called 'Chosen Men' so much as breathes a whisper to any third-party hereafter of how our fallen comrade was cut down or makes the slightest movement to end his life here in this cesspool of a place, or at any other time in the future, mark these words well: I'll kill you all myself.

"Chosen Men!" he exclaimed with scornful, almost raging disdain and expressing a mounting venom in his words that convinced his two trusted colleagues that he might decide to shoot them all anyhow regardless of any warning given.

"Not chosen by any ballot set by mine or my colleagues here! More like 'chosen mice!'

"Now get you all away from here post haste, muster aid for our stricken brother and keep your mouths tight shut. As far as you're concerned, he's fallen from a hansom and got mangled in the tac and hoof as he's gone to ground.

"Commander Blackmore will accompany you and mark these words well as if they be the last you ever hear in your miserable lives; 'The Undertaker' is not renowned for his patience when having to deal with disloyalty within the ranks nor is he tolerant of the merest whiff of treachery or deceit from within a supposedly trustworthy unit. For his part remember this well; 'The Undertaker' by name, 'The Undertaker' most definitely by nature and deed! Now get out of my sight and pray that our paths never cross in anger again."

Turning his attention at once to Jackson, almost without pausing to draw breath Blackmore continued to speak.

"Marcus, please get word with all urgency and speed to doctors Bass and Jefferson and have them prepare private quarters at the Whitechapel Hospital, to be guarded by a rotating eight-hour shift pattern over twenty-four hours by loyal and trusted retainers. Be sure and use all compassion and due respect when you inform Dr Bass that the admission is to be her husband."

Buoyed by the fact that a man he had respected for most of his short working life had just this moment for the very first time returned that respect in kind by referring to him by his Christian name, Marcus Jackson gave but a short, concise two-word answer in reply:

"Yes, sir" and was in this moment comforted in the knowledge that as for his professional career aspirations he was finally being allowed to walk amongst those he revered and regarded most highly as a trusted equal.

Blackmore then turned his attention to his stricken colleague and began to speak in the hushed, sympathetic and compassionate tones of a man realising that he might well be offering a few final, comforting words to his dying brother...

"Rest easy, my friend.

"Help is close at hand. We'll soon have some bandages and poultice on that sorry excuse for a wound you've picked up. I've got to be honest; I've seen a lot worse" was the part-lie that he offered to his colleague.

Just as he was about to continue his attempt at a 'barely adequate' bedside manner, to his utter astonishment Bass began to speak...

"Tiberius. Even though eavesdropping on another's conversation is a truly deplorable act, I couldn't help but overhear what you said to the boy," he began, coughing away copious amounts of blood and spittle as he spoke...

"A fine gesture in recognition of the trust we now place in both his service and friendship and so I shall endeavour to do the same when next we meet, to make amends for my earlier indiscretions on his part."

"James, as I live and breathe, is there anything that exists on this Earth that can properly do you down!" exclaimed a somewhat startled, yet very relieved Blackmore. "I perceived that on this occasion your time had finally come."

"Would that it had, old friend, then perhaps we might all be spared the potential horrors that may yet come to call on us very soon," replied Bass. "In hindsight perhaps your 'Chosen Men' were correct when they suggested ending my time on Earth here in the snow," he concluded.

"Easy, James, rest easy now. Help is close at hand: Look yonder, here are Connie, Florence, Phineas and my Pandora to take you away and tend to your scratches," observed Blackmore as a covered waggon drawn by two great Lancashire shires crunched through the thickening snow towards them down the alley.

"How are you feeling, you old warhorse?" he queried, realising immediately that the question he had just asked was quite ridiculously stupid in the scheme of things and deserved to be rebuked soundly for being so. The answer given by James Bass to his colleague's question, therefore, was all the more unexpected and took Blackmore completely by surprise...

"I feel... better..."

Chapter 11

'A Force of Nature's Folly'

A month on from the attack found James Bass convalescing in private quarters at the Whitechapel Hospital. He was attended by his wife Dr Constance Matilda Bass and his trusted colleagues and League of Ghosts members Tiberius Blackmore, his wife Dame Pandora Scarlett Blackmore, Professor Florence Elizabeth Jefferson, her husband Doctor Phineas Theodore Jefferson and Captain Pontius Maximillian Aston.

"Am I to understand that your music tour of Vienna and the Italian cities went well, Pandora?" began Bass.

"I regret that recent events occurring in the city rather unexpectedly forced my absence from the Vienna concerts, both of which Constance and I should greatly have loved to attend. I believe the Paganini pieces featured greatly in the programme this season with your virtuoso lead violin solo pieces providing the standout moments of each night's performance."

"Just so, James, just so," replied Dame Pandora.

"The reviews thus far have proved to be quite favourable but the concerts and the adulation that follows them for my personal gratification are of little consequence when such a dear friend and valuable asset to both the Metropolitan Police force and The League of Ghosts as yourself is in such mortal peril.

"Would that I was present before your impetuous actions were conceived to crack that thick skull of yours and hopefully knock some common sense into it!" she exclaimed brusquely. "YOU MIGHT HAVE BEEN KILLED, YOU...YOU IMBECILE!"

"I stand well and truly rebuked as I was by my Constance a while ago, but I assure you, sweet Pandora and all of you here gathered, my dearest brothers and sisters, that I am well and fit for duty," stated Bass confidently.

"My constitution is uncommonly strong and my scars are almost completely healed, as are my bruised ribs and broken bones. Only my pride and dignity remain somewhat tarnished, mercilessly battered and mislaid somewhere back on those cobbles where I lost them in the snow merely a few short days ago; but rest assured, my friends, they are things that can be readily located, repaired with ease and replaced quickly.

"Might one ask, Tiberius, how did you manage to navigate the labyrinthine passages of 'the maze' in time to thwart the wolf and cease what even I had convinced myself in that fleeting moment would be its fatal, life extinguishing attack?"

"We heard a howl first of all, what we perceived to be the werewolf and such a sound I would hope never to hear again for the rest of my days," began Blackmore.

"Only Hades' dark halls could despatch a creature with a call so hideous as to turn a man's warm blood to ice and test the very fibre of his resolve and courage to their limits. As we rounded into the cul-de-sac where you were in conference with the beast, your futile volley had already begun but we were still too far out of range for our own weapons to prove effective and thus too late to prevent the maiden assault by the feral monster in our midst.

"By the time we were within adequate range to dispatch the hell spawn back to purgatory, as its second attack commenced my heart was beating cold for in that moment, I thought you were lost to us forever, my friend."

"Yet here I stand, Tiberius. One month hence and my wounds are all but healed," said Bass. "My senses are sharper and I feel of both sound mind and body, far better than ever I have in point of fact, in ruder health than I deserve to be."

Pontius Aston broke his silence.

"Yes, James. To all intents and purposes your body is better than it ever was. Your human body, that is, for you are now more than human. You have become Lycan.

"Your being has reached the point where two spirits totally foreign to each other clash in a constant struggle to be the one true master of not merely your physical being but also vie for possession of your everlasting soul.

"Our plan is quite a simple one in principle.

"Beatrice, Constance and myself shall take you far away for a time, to a covert location in the high White Mountains of Tibet, and together with my colleagues of the Time Enforcement Agency and with the love and compassionate care you will undoubtedly require from your family and all of our trusted brothers and sisters from The League of Ghosts, we will teach you how to be master over the lycan spirit that resides within you; but be under no illusion, my dear friend, the road you must take will prove to be a long and painful travail.

"Fraught with danger and rife with an almost unbearably overwhelming feeling of loneliness and despair, these emotions will envelop you as you spiral deeper into the dark maelstrom of the unknown abyss that you must explore. The pressure and power the entity now resting within you bleeds into every fibre of your being and will be almost overbearing on what remains of your human soul, but your natural inner strength, your unflinching resolve and your fortitude will ultimately prevail. You shall return to us a stronger, more effective force of nature than ever you were before."

"Force of nature's folly more like," countered Bass.

"And did you not omit purposefully from your impressive array of words just spoken, dear Pontius, that I would also return to The League as a more effective weapon too."

"Undoubtedly so, if your recovery proves to be absolute," replied Aston.

"The advantages to both the League and the Time Enforcement Agency by investing the time and effort needed for your successful and effective rehabilitation and training by far outweigh the disadvantages and the prospect of failure in this case. The opportunity to utilise your great power, to understand the mystery that surrounds it and to channel its energy so as to help preserve and aid the greater good is most apparent here; the alternative for you, alas, is quite obvious."

"Plainly spoken, Pontius, and as always a flawlessly logical presentation of the facts on your part," reasoned Bass.

"I am under no illusion as to what I have become, I wear the mark of the pentagram here on my wrist; even on the night of what transpired to be my re-birth I perceived that if I were to survive any attack by the wolf I would undoubtedly become Lycan myself and as circumstances have unfolded before us thus has it been proven to be just so as fact.

"I shall therefore travel willingly with you all, Pontius. I will commit to the training of my mind and body all the fortitude, strength and courage that is in my power to muster, and be assured, my family and very dear friends, that I will ultimately prevail and be of effective use to our cause once more very soon; this I pledge with all my heart."

"Indeed you will, James, indeed you will. Of that fact there is no doubt," agreed Aston.

Addressing the entourage selected to join Bass on his journey, Pontius Aston continued...

"When your affairs are in order, my fine companions, please pack for a harsh winter climate. We shall then leave immediately thereafter."

As the group began to disband, Bass turned towards Blackmore, and addressed his old colleague directly:

"I am in no doubt that you will cope without my hindrance and unpredictability for a while, Tiberius, of this I am certain.

"Place a good amount of trust in the boy Marcus and make room for him within our inner circle of confidantes, for I believe that his actions during the unfolding of this case have earned him the right to be properly tested. Above all else, though, teach him how to survive."

"I'll teach him how to shoot too!" exclaimed Blackmore.

"Couldn't shoot the eye out of an eight-foot werewolf from six paces at the moment. Absolutely abysmal show to be sure!"

"One question, Tiberius, before I take my leave, if I may?" enquired Bass.

"Might I enquire about the conduct displayed by the group of six officers consigned to your force, the so-called 'chosen men'?

"As I lay prostrate and, to all intents and purposes even in my own mind at the time, dying at your feet, I overheard what seemed to be murmurs of rising and quite disturbing dissention within the ranks. Of spontaneous plots being hatched to end my life at that moment. Is this true?"

"It is true, James," answered Blackmore, and I must confess, old friend, that for a fleeting few seconds I considered their proposed final fatal action against you might indeed prove the feasible option, both for your own eternal peace and for the future safety of a great many others."

"Indeed so, Tiberius" was the considered reply from Bass.

"Perhaps theirs might yet be proven in hindsight to have been the correct course of action, but nevertheless, for even the thought of ending my life in that moment, should all of this training that I am to be a party to goes to the Devil of course, I shall probably endeavour to hunt down and feast on them first when I return."

"And what cruel fate awaits then those three loyal comrades and true who stood over you and preserved your life in that moment pray tell?" questioned Blackmore with a quizzical eyebrow raised in the direction of his partner.

"Oh, in due consideration of the fact that in my helpless state you three stoic gentlemen did indeed proceed to protect me from further harm by endangering your own lives and offering all the heartfelt gratitude to you that is undoubtedly deserved for your selfless actions on my behalf, with all the newly acquired resolve and self-control that I should indeed be capable of upon my return, I shall resolve therefore to eat you three fine gentlemen last of all," quipped Bass with a knowing wink and a crafty grin aimed in the direction of his colleague.

Chapter 12

'The Strange Case of Doctor Clavel'

The violent electrical storm raged above his laboratory with a savage ferocity that Clavel could scarcely recall ever having witnessed before in his entire lifetime.

He took a brief moment to marvel at the potentially cataclysmic force of nature that was unfolding above him, and reminisced for a few seconds about the fascination and respect that he'd always held since his days as a young medical student at the world renowned Leipzig University for this most wondrous phenomenon of natural occurrence and how someday he would utilise this great power in order to further his own fantastic ambition.

The now vertically falling torrents of rain he didn't require for this particular experiment, precious natural resource though it undoubtedly was, on this particular occasion was no more than a mere encumbrance and of no use to his work in any way. Nor were the constant, almost deafeningly loud cracks of thunder, courtesy of the mighty Thor's hammer Mjolnir, or so he allowed himself to romantically believe was the source of such a sound, that signified to him that the storm was now at its zenith and directly overhead.

It was the evenly spaced bolts of lightning in between Thor's legendary anger that he coveted. Tens of thousands of watts of nature's own electricity that was ripe for harvesting, providing all the equipment that he had invented and constructed by his own hand over a period of many months, ably and loyally assisted by his one trusted colleague referred to only by the single name of Heinrich, and at great cost to his own personal inherited fortune, functioned in the manner that he hoped, and prayed, that it would.

"This is our time, Heinrich!" exclaimed Clavel with an almost maniacal zeal.

"All of the personal and professional sacrifice on my part, all of the physical pain and suffering on yours, my great and trusted ally and one true friend. Every last vestige of the underqualified and uneducated ridicule that I've had to endure from my so-called peers and colleagues, all of the scorn and bile from my many detractors, will be swept aside and forgotten in an instant after the glorious triumph of the actions that unfold on this most wondrous of nights are made public. Now open the roof portals, my loyal retainer and prepare the batteries to accept the ultimate power of the Gods!"

Chapter 13

'Autumn 1899'

Number two platform of Liverpool Street Station to the east of the sprawling and ever rapidly expanding metropolis of the city of London was a mass of humanity going about their daily routines on this normal and most uninteresting of mid-September afternoons.

As they alighted from their train carriage onto the busy platform, Detective Inspector James Bartholomew Bass checked one of the two silver timepieces that he kept in each pocket of his waistcoat, glanced up at the old station clock above the ticket office, turned to his wife Constance and began to speak.

"Damn and blast that old clock," he scolded.

"Four sides to it and not one of its faces ever tells the same time!"

Joining them from their carriage were Captain Pontius Maximillian Aston and his wife Beatrice. Pontius Aston proceeded to speak first:

"Forgive me, Constance, if I might answer our testy companion's observation.

"Time, my dear James, is the flame in which we all burn. The two constants that occur within all four dimensions remain predominantly the same; the passage of real time is a certainty and so is, ultimately, death. A faulty old clock is of no consequence in the grand scheme of all things considered," he reasoned.

"Just so, Pontius," offered Bass as an almost half-interested response to his colleague's logical observation as he checked his second timepiece in his usual habitual manner.

"But does not time as it passes on its fleeting, insistent passage throughout this dimension that we inhabit remain the true enemy of each and every one of us, my friend?" he questioned.

"That it does, James, that it does indeed and I compliment you for such an astute observation," conceded Aston almost wistfully.

As they continued to converse the three companions were barely aware of the arrival at their side of two more trusted colleagues belonging to the 'The League of Ghosts', namely James Bass' brother at arms for many years Detective Inspector Alan Tiberius Blackmore and his wife, the world renowned musician and covert operative in the service of The League of Ghosts, Dame Pandora Scarlett Blackmore.

"James, by all the Gods it does my heart proud to see you looking fit and well again," began Blackmore as he enveloped Bass in a hearty bear hug, barely able to contain his joy at being re-united with his colleague once again.

"We've recieved no word of your progress other than the fact that you were well and would return to this station platform by the Time Enforcement Agency, on this specific day, at this appointed time," he continued.

"Welcome home, James," began Dame Pandora as she kissed Bass with the affection of a beloved sister on each cheek.

"Providence, a strong tail wind and this truly wondrous, newly completed trans-European rail service have seen fit to deliver you back to us safely, recovered from your trials we all hope and all the better we shall be for it," she continued with true affection apparent in her voice.

"Thank you, Pandora and you, Tiberius, for the unflinching support and love that you have shown me throughout this ordeal and for your patience whilst having to deal with the lack of information that has been forthcoming as to my progress.

"I assure you both that I am well, very well as a matter of fact, quite possibly more rude of health than I have ever been in my entire life and ready to resume my official duties immediately", gushed Bass buoyantly, half hoping that this would be an end, at least temporarily at any rate, to any thoughts of being expected to recount a thorough explanation of his past six months away being given at this moment. His hopes were immediately dashed by his erstwhile colleague's immediate and relentlessly insistent questions...

"James, please, if I may ask..." began Blackmore earnestly, barely aware that he had subconsciously reverted to his official role of Detective Inspector in suspect interrogation mode, though he would never normally have thought to do so whilst enquiring of his closest of friends' wellbeing.

"Your 'ordeal' as you refer to it as having been, must have affected you spiritually, changed you physically even in some way, and those dark spectacles you now wear. What of those?"

"Dear Tiberius, yes I have changed but how could I not when considering what form of creature attacked me and that I survived the assault," answered Bass logically, displaying no hint of consternation or any outward signs of frustration towards his great friend's insistence on persevering with his enquiries.

"I shall offer a full briefing as to my 'condition' and how I propose to manage it in due course and as for the spectacles I find that my eyes have become sensitive to the normal light of day so I cover them thusly in order to facilitate protection from the usually acceptable level of ultra violet light that burns daily above and around us; and besides, I think that they make quite the stylish fashion statement in some dark, melodramatic, even gothic kind of way. Do you not agree?

"Now please, without further hindrance and with the permission of our beloved wives and our dearest friends, may we away to our back room at The Brown Bear where I crave several fingers of Del Vecchio brandy and a stogie or two to ease my constitution back into some kind of familiar and recognisable routine."

"How nice to observe that your rakish humour was not tarnished whilst you were away, my brother, and for that blessing alone I am made eternally grateful," answered Blackmore with his characteristic knowing cackle that had been cultivated whilst imbibing copious amounts of brandy and smoking Hindu shag tobacco since before a time both of the detectives could barely remember.

As the group of colleagues began to make their way to the exit that would take them out into the bright mid-afternoon bustle of Liverpool Street, Blackmore turned and engaged his colleague in brief conversation once more...

"By the by, James, a piece of news that had all but slipped my mind during the course of our fond reunion. In your absence we were both promoted to the rank of Detective Chief Inspector in recognition of our continued and unwavering services to the Crown that have greatly exceeded the call of duty on numerous occasions past. Up for a medal and a commendation from Her Majesty too, so I'm informed by the top brass."

Bass eyed his colleague from behind his dark spectacle lenses and offered a shallow, wry smile upon receiving news that at this moment in time he considered to be quite trivial in its content when taking into account the greater scheme of events recently passed, and of those that were undoubtedly most definitely to come. He paused for a moment to contemplate his answer...

"Detective Chief Inspector werewolf of Leman Street, Whitechapel. That distinguished title has something of a unique, distinctive and slightly surreal ring to it, don't you think my old comrade!" he responded dryly.

Chapter 14

'Detective Chief Inspector Werewolf'

T he two re-united and newly promoted Detective Chief Inspectors settled themselves into the familiar surroundings of their private back room at The Brown Bear public house that was situated a mere stone's throw from their Leman Street base in Whitechapel.

It was here where they could shut out the world around them for a few precious moments of privacy, a place to gather one's thoughts, plan complex strategies or just a welcome bolt hole where two old friends could reminisce and re-bond whilst enjoying copious amounts of their favourite brands of tobacco and brandy.

"How I have missed these moments of self-indulgence, Tiberius," began Bass as he took a long pull on one of his finest imported Indian 'Rajah' cigars and blew expertly formed grey rings of smoke into the air, one after the other.

"Even a lengthy period of forced abstinence from such sweet and self-defiling vices could not quell my appetite for these most agreeable of the devil's many temptations," he continued, exhuding an air of self-satisfied contentment.

"Speak to me of your time away, James, if it pleases you?" asked Blackmore.

"Six months seconded to a monastery in the high mountains of Tibet. The tales that you have to tell of your ordeal must be like few others ever heard."

Bass took another long pull on his cigar, drained his glass and poured himself another generously sized tumbler of brandy before he settled himself and began to recount his fantastic tale in a measured and controlled tone.

"The last portion of the journey to our final destination was a long, arduous hike on foot up to a monastery built precariously onto the peak of a mountain top in the high white mountains of Tibet. I feared not for myself, for as I stated clearly before our departure, I was feeling in as finer health than I possibly ever have in my entire life; rather my chief concern then was primarily for the wellbeing of my three stoic companions, namely Pontius, Beatrice and my own sweet Connie.

"I needn't have worried on either score, however, as each one of my heroic colleagues were as well matched to the physical hardships of our hellish travail as I.

"What transpired for the next few weeks was, as I can best describe the process in layman's terms and in no way wishing to undermine your keen intelligence in any way, Tiberius, a total deconstruction of my human construct.

"My constitution, physical strength and mental resolve were tested to their maximum limit and beyond in order to first understand the troubled spirit that wrested for control of my soul before we could then master and control that spirit and eventually perhaps use it to achieve our own ends."

"And what then of the wolf, James?" pressed Blackmore further.

"How in the name of all that is holy can you even begin to deal with the intense trauma of metamorphosis from man to wolf? The physical pain of dislocating joints, the breaking and re-setting of bones, the re-alignment of internal organs. The toll it must take on your body must be excruciating, the agony immeasurable and almost too much to bear!" he exclaimed.

Bass pondered his companion's question for a moment and shifted in his chair as if momentarily in some discomfort.

"Indeed, my friend, the agony of metamorphosis is almost beyond explanation and far outside the parameters of human comprehension, but the overall feeling when fully turned to the Lycan spirit is one of great power and exhilaration and yes, my brother, before you ask the question, I am aware of every waking moment of the experience, both the euphoria of the power and strength that I possess and the excruciating agony of the metamorphosis.

"Ultimately, that is why I am able to control my thoughts and actions when the wolf inhabits my soul because I remain aware of the great chaos and harm to others that the beast could wreak and, coupled with the intense training that my mind and body has received from the monks and the retention of my own inner strength and fortitude, thus enables me to cancel out random appearances by the wolf during certain key lunar cycles and possibly to even be able to call on the wolf at will to aid us, God forbid, should ever the need arise."

"So the wolf retains command of your key human traits, namely your self-control, your compassion and your ability to make momentary, split-second decisions?" asked Blackmore.

"Rather the opposite Tiberius. My highly disciplined human senses retain command of the wolf.

"I have my intense military training and experience, coupled with my exploits as your colleague over many years to thank for that," Bass answered as he removed his spectacles using his left hand. As he did so he then proceeded to raise his free right hand as if to rub unwanted fatigue away, thus momentarily keeping his eyes purposefully shielded from Blackmore's view.

"If it were not so then I would be no better off than the unfortunate wretch that you were compelled to retire with extreme prejudice in 'the maze' a few short months ago. I believe that is the extent of what I have to divulge at this point with regards to my condition.

"The last words I will offer on the subject before we go to work are ones of advice and please heed them well, my dear old friend. Promise me to keep about your person at all times a cache of blessed silver ammunition. Though I remain confident that I will retain the mental discipline required to hold the wolf spirit in check, there may come a time when I falter and that a final, fatal action on your part is necessary. Promise me, Tiberius!" exclaimed Bass as he lowered his hand fully exposing his eyes to Blackmore's slightly startled gaze.

Blackmore looked deep into his colleague's now exposed eyes and noticed that the whole area of both eyes, whites and all, were as black as the darkest pitch.

"Your eyes, brother, both as black as the darkest night!" he exclaimed.

"Yes, my great friend, the wolf spirit is strong inside me this night" was the stark, cold answer Bass gave that sent an icy chill straight to the core of Blackmore's mortal soul.

Considering the words of his colleague for a few seconds Blackmore then proceeded to offer the only logical answer he thought possible under such circumstances:

"I promise you, James, that if the time is ever upon us and absolutely no foreseeable or logical alternative is apparent to me in that moment, that it shall be by my hand alone that your spirit will finally be laid to rest in peace," he answered, realising full well that the unpredictable nature of his tortured friend's spirit might well one fateful day force such a last resort action on his part.

"Good, then let us dwell on this potentially depressing topic not a moment longer and away to our work in the all too familiar sewers of

Whitechapel, my good Tiberius, where I might find some solace, even comfort perhaps, in the intrigue of a challenging case," reasoned Bass in a manner which gave the impression that he welcomed a return to his law enforcement role on the brutal East End streets of London with relish.

Chapter 15

'Prometheus, By Any Other Name'

A s the two Detectives entered by the front entrance of the Leman Street police station house, they were greeted immediately by trusted aide detective sergeant Marcus Jackson. Before he could open his mouth to utter any sort of greeting to either of the two detectives, James Bass himself began to speak...

"Marcus, my good fellow, I trust that I find you in good health and not too put upon with keen and perilous task in my absence by this old 'smoke billowing assassin'," he quipped, taking the young sergeant completely by surprise as to the unexpected familiarity shown towards him by Bass.

"Y...Yes, sir, I'm in the rudest of health and the hefty workload is always to my liking, thank you kindly, sir; and might I add that it does my heart proud to see yourself back on Leman Street and looking fit and well," said Jackson, showing genuine affection and deep respect towards Bass in the tone of his voice.

"I am not unaware of the major role that you played in assisting Tiberius on the night I was taken down, Marcus. Both of the Blackmore boys and your good self-stepped up and saved my life, thinking not of the potentially lethal risk to your own wellbeing, and for that action alone you have earned my eternal respect and trust. This I shall not forget," pledged Bass honestly.

"Now let us three away to the confines of our office for I sense that you bring word of our latest case," he surmised.

The three colleagues entered the office of Blackmore and Bass, closed the door behind them to shut out the usual cacophony of the busy station house and Jackson proceeded to deliver his report.

"Over the course of the last three months, a total of six corpses have been discovered in certain different, seemingly random parts of the river, particularly of note in this area around the east and west docks and even further up west inside the river entrance to Traitors Gate," he began, whilst referring to the areas in question on a detailed map of the Whitechapel area laid out on the desk before them.

"In what condition were the cadavers found, Marcus, apart from the obvious signs of death of course?" asked Blackmore with a raised eyebrow betraying an all too often hidden humorous side to his character.

"Three of the six were decapitated, sir, four had various arms and legs removed from differing joints and two were just the torsos" came the reply from Jackson.

"Might I continue, Detective Sergeant?"

Joining the three detectives at their briefing, Dr Constance Bass had entered the office and began to speak.

"I have this past two hours been made privy to the detailed reports prepared by Marcus and my own forensics team regarding the condition of the unfortunate souls of which you gentlemen now speak. I have also been able to examine all of them myself in greater detail and my findings offer something of a conundrum as to the possible motive any alleged murderer might have harboured in committing these crimes and quite possibly if the act of murder was actually committed at all," she said to the obvious puzzlement of the three Detectives.

"How so, Connie?" questioned a mystified Blackmore.

"All six bodies are male," she continued. "Each of them had been in the water approximately forty-eight to seventy-two hours, judging by the relative lack of bloating one observes when a corpse has been water bound for longer periods of time, so it is likely that they were all cast adrift from the same place at approximately the same time. The clean and precise lacerations made to remove each limb and appendage suggests that expert knowledge was applied to complete this task, so I would therefore surmise that you should direct your enquiries towards seeking out an educated, quite possibly even a medical person.

"Also, I would further add that I believe that these surgical procedures were carried out post mortem, thus alluding to my earlier assertion that murder might not have been a motive for, or indeed the cause of these actions."

"Sounds very much as though you might have an idea to whom we might pay our first call, Connie," said Bass to his wife.

Constance paused for a moment, as if to gather her thoughts before revealing what she surmised might prove to be a somewhat startling revelation.

"As James is aware, fifteen years ago I was lecturing on the subjects of several new, potentially ground-breaking methods being introduced into the advancement of forensic science and my own contributions to the development of revolutionary new photography techniques designed to be used primarily in conjunction with scientific and forensic investigations at the University of Leipzig in the federal state of Saxony in Germany.

"One of the other lecturers on the staff roster, whose area of excellence was in the multiple fields of medical and neuro science, in addition to the relatively new studies of heart and brain surgery, went by the name of Dr Henry Uriah Clavel.

"Already a brilliant medical doctor and surgeon by reputation, he constantly pushed the boundaries of what was ethically acceptable by perfecting the practice of transplanting organs from one body to another and, not satisfied by the constraints that the conventional and acceptable progress the board of surgeons guild put upon him, and feeling that he was being held back by inferior, backward thinking fools, he was rumoured to be even in the process of creating life from death itself.

"He had also become a willing member of a small group of people who believed that huge currents of electricity harvested from either a controlled torrent of water, or from a raging electrical storm, could be utilised in the re-animation of immediately deceased people, or indeed to stretch the boundaries of tangible, formulised ethics to the limits of acceptance and moral decency, of corpses pieced together from the limbs and organs of other deceased cadavers.

"They referred to themselves as galvanists, their practice adopting the unofficial title of galvanism.

"I recall this case," began Blackmore as a distant memory stirred within him.

"Reports of a raging monster running amok in the Austrian town of Bergstadt, some twenty years or more past."

"Rumours abounded even then locally of a creature fashioned from dead corpses given life by a modern-day Prometheus, or so the story was recounted by the superstitious townsfolk, but his name eludes me."

"I remember this well, Tiberius," interjected Bass.

"Were we not to be seconded to local law enforcement agencies with a view to tracking down and apprehending this beast and its alleged creator...doctor... what was his name?"

"Indeed, we were, James, but before we were able to embark for Austria word arrived that the trail of the elusive Dr Clavel had gone cold and our proposed marks had disappeared without a trace," answered Blackmore.

"Prometheus; the Titan who stole life from the Gods of Ancient Greece and gave it to man," remarked Constance.

"Both creator and created disappeared seemingly into thin air during the furore generated by the hunt for them and have never been seen or heard of since, until now perhaps."

"You believe that the one we seek is one and the same man, Connie?" asked Blackmore.

"I'm very much afraid that I do, Tiberius," she answered bleakly.

"What's more, I believe that he has sought to continue his work into the re-animation of self-constructed bodies utilising the practice of galvanism once more within this very city and now I recall his name, his true name," she continued.

"He is of old Austrian aristocracy, born into privileged wealth, educated to the highest level at the best medical universities and establishments in Europe.

"He was disbarred of his medical and surgeons' practitioners' licences, ostracised and publicly denounced by his peers as un-Godly and a blasphemer for his insistence that death should not be the final moment in a person's existence. That the life-force could be re-ignited if not in the original worn out body then why not in a newly constructed, stronger unit because, after all, is not the human body merely a shell that carries the mind and soul? I believe that the man who has been calling himself Dr Henry Clavel this past fifteen or more years is none other than Baron Victor Josef von Waldheim."

"Von Waldheim!" exclaimed Bass.

"Of course, a highly respected, world-renowned authority on both surgery and anatomy and a keen endorsee of the practice known as galvanism which first came to light publicly as a fiction within the pages of Mary Shelley's celebrated and somewhat disturbingly controversial work 'Frankenstein'.

"It seems as though he might well have used this rather disturbing gothic fairy-tale as something of a reference manual in order to assist in the furtherance of his own personal ambition.

"Tiberius and I had been made privy to an extensive file and a possible authentically scribed journal of personal scribblings concerning the man, his experiments and his alleged atrocities, but for him to be here, in our city and practising galvanism once more is almost beyond comprehension, yet if proven to be the case must be regarded as being a stroke of good fortune on our part in so much as we may now finally have an opportunity to apprehend our man."

"I believe that when you locate Dr Henry Clavel, then you locate the elusive Baron von Waldheim for they are indeed one and the same man, of that I have no doubt," said Constance.

"And what is more, I believe that, taking into account your recent grim discoveries in the river, his latest raft of vile experiments have already begun," she added.

The meeting was interrupted by the arrival of a runner bearing a message for the assembled colleagues.

Tiberius Blackmore took a neatly folded piece of paper from the young man, offered a generous tip of two shillings which the lad accepted gratefully, scanned the text briefly and then began to speak.

"This concerns you too, Marcus. It's from Pontius Aston," Blackmore announced first before he began to read its contents aloud.

"To all concerned and gathered herein:

"The Time Enforcement Agency has been aware of the questionable practices one Dr Henry Uriah Clavel has pursued for some considerable time and, because of the possible catastrophic ramifications that his actions might have in affecting a possible future should his work be allowed to continue unchecked, the Time Enforcement Agency would like to call on the assistance of The League Of Ghosts in order to bring this man to justice and cease his experiments indefinitely."

"Time then once more and without further delay to assemble The League of Ghosts," concluded Blackmore.

Chapter 16

'The League of Ghosts'

D eep below the Tower of London, beneath a maze of catacombs and secret chambers that were thought to have been built during the Roman occupation of Britain in around AD 80 by the Emperor Trajan to serve primarily as a fortified underground base of operations for the ongoing conquest of the island, lies the secret location that the League of Ghosts chose to make its headquarters and covert base of operations.

Circular in layout, as if its design were conceived in homage to the great Pantheon in Rome, the four levels of a most spectacular of all oak-shelved libraries could be accessed by climbing any of six ornately forged iron spiral staircases spaced equidistantly around the circumference of the central nucleus of the room.

Upon these impressive shelves, which stretched out to all points of the compass and for some considerable distance back into the vast tunnel excavation, were to be found books, parchments, relics and other priceless artefacts belonging to the pantheon of history, including examples from pre-documented periods in time; all thought to have been lost or never even believed to have physically existed at all, every piece gathered together in this remarkable place by the Time Enforcement Agency, who in so doing became the custodians of all the World's entire documented, and non-documented history.

The large round oak table that was placed at the centre of the deep, multi-levelled library had been made ready for conclave. Bass and Blackmore, their wives Constance Bass and Pandora Blackmore respectively, plus an open mouthed in wonderment and rather perplexed Marcus Jackson were greeted by the already present and seated Dr Phineas Jefferson, his wife Professor Florence Jefferson, the Blackmores' siblings 'The Undertaker', his sister Alanis May Blackmore, Lord Ragnar Thor Olafsson, his wife the Lady Anna Freya Olafsson, Detective Chief Superintendent Frank Abilene, and another new addition to the group, Dr Grace Henrietta Blake.

Initial pleasantries and fondest greetings were exchanged among colleagues who had not been in each other's presence for a number of years and in that moment, realising simultaneously that the Olafssons being called to attend this meeting of 'The League' in person bore truth to the fact that their assistance would have great bearing on this case, Bass was the first one of the assembled group to speak.

"Forgive me, Tiberius, for I assume that our immediate questions will be alike, if not the same; Lord Ragnar, Lady Anna, it gladdens our hearts to welcome you once more into 'The League of Ghosts'.

"Might one ask for what purpose your immediate presence is required here in London?" enquired Bass.

"It has been too long a time away for us from 'The League', James," began Lady Anna. "All that we are able to divulge at this precise moment is that we were to be present at this location at the appointed time at the urgent behest of the Aston family."

"Of course, and might one be so bold as to ask if any person here present knows of the whereabouts of the Aston Family?" questioned Tiberius Blackmore with more than a hint of first sarcasm, then frustration present in his words.

Lady Anna continued: "They are hereabouts, Tiberius and at this very moment perusing the library shelves that surround us for a particular journal that might have a significant bearing on investigations appertaining to our case, Tiberius."

As the general conversation between recently re-united colleagues and great friends continued, the familiar vocal tones of Professor Leopold Aston rang out from three floors above them from where his natural speaking voice was naturally amplified to spectacular effect by the remarkable acoustic capabilities of the chamber.

"Fondest greetings once more to 'The League of Ghosts' and please accept our immediate and heartfelt gratitude for the haste of your arrival to this most important of gatherings," he began. "Mother, Father; I believe that I have located the journals that we seek" was the message that he relayed to his parents who were searching in other areas of the library.

In what seemed like but a few short seconds the assembled group were joined at the round table by Professor Aston and his parents, Captain Pontius Aston and his wife Beatrice Aston, agents of the Time Enforcement Agency and honourable members of The League of Ghosts.

"Are we to assume that the mark we seek is of special interest to the T.E.A.?" questioned Bass.

"That he is, James," answered Aston.

"But please permit us to digress a moment and recount the whole saga of Professor Henry Clavel and the bearing that his actions and experimentations might have on one possible future if allowed to continue." Aston took in a deep intake of breath and paused for a few seconds before he continued on with his tale.

"Professor Henry Clavel first drew the attentions of the T.E.A. some thirty years past when he was secured as a private tutor to a more than promising young medical student and research scientist from the town of Bergstadt near the Austrian city of Leipzig.

"This student bearing an affluent Austrian family pedigree had surpassed all of the required academic and practical expectations of his lecturers and mentors at the world-renowned University of Leipzig. When he began to question the very foundations and ethics upon which modern medicine and surgery were taught and practised, such was the superior power of his intellect, he even had the audacity of suggesting to his so-called peers newer, more radical methods to further develop and potentially greatly enhance and advance the trusted, and one might suggest tired, staid and stubbornly steadfast parameters set by years of traditional study and practice.

"He even went so far as to blatantly showcase his remarkable arrogance by publicly denouncing his detractors thusly as, and I quote, 'intellectual minnows to a man' and 'all should be regarded as mindless, backward thinking insects to be swat aside accordingly and without recourse or remorse to allow genuine, progressive thinking science to prosper over all' unquote."

"And might well we guess the student's name, Pontius?" asked Blackmore, fully aware of the answer he was about to receive.

"His name, as you might rightly surmise, Tiberius, was Baron Victor Josef von Waldheim the third of the Royal Austrian house of Von Waldheim," replied Aston.

"Working together both Clavel and Von Waldheim, now becoming an equally adept colleague of Clavel rather than the eager student thirsting for knowledge, began to move their area of study towards the possibility that a person's life, including the very essence of the human soul, the life force if you will, could be preserved close to the moment of death and transposed into another body constructed from various pieces of other lifeless corpses using advanced surgical and neurological techniques invented and perfected by the two brilliant scientists, thus enhancing their belief that the human body is merely a vessel of transport, a temporary shell of flesh, bone and sinew born of nature in order to protect the universal life force, the mind and the human soul."

Leopold Aston continued the thread.

"Work began initially within the confines of the university campus at Leipzig where the two scientists could utilize the impressive cache of equipment situated within one of the best laboratories in Europe and with exclusive access to the extensive library facilities at their disposal proceeded to develop and hone their skills and to broaden their field of expertise far beyond the accepted parameters of science .

"Upon discovery of their somewhat radical experiments, the unproven areas of study that the two scientists chose to explore, and questioning the ethical ramifications of such ungodly ideology, the campus faculty denounced the pair to the world as heretics, ostracised them both from the medical fraternity and banished them from the University, forcing them to seek refuge and a new secret base of operations in the Baron's ancestral home town of Bergstadt.

"With his somewhat considerable inherited wealth at their disposal, Victor, being orphaned some ten years previously while still a young boy and being the only child born to the previous Baron, was made sole heir to the substantial family fortune and to extensive property and land portfolios that were situated all around the World. They could afford to build and equip the finest research facilities money could buy and all of their ambitions could now be achieved far away from the meddlesome interference of their so-called peers, or so they believed."

"Indeed, their tireless labours initially bore positive results and through many months of toil the two brilliant scientists were on the verge of a great scientific achievement until tragedy struck," continued Beatrice Aston.

"A key and extremely hazardous factor in the process of reanimating their lifeless, pieced together corpse, procured either from the newly deceased wretches from local workhouses, or recently executed criminals cut from a gibbet so as not to arouse any unwelcomed attention from the authorities, was the ability to harness and control the great electrical energy produced by the most violent electrical storms.

"Having designed and constructed bespoke equipment to enable them to carry out this part of the process one such storm manifested itself before they were able to properly test their equipment and ratify any problems that might occur whilst attempting to harness and channel such a vast amount of electrical energy into such a narrow conduit as was necessary in order for the re-animation process to succeed.

"The resulting explosion and fire cost Clavel his life, with Von Waldhein receiving serious third degree burns to his hands and face, but though initially grieving for the loss of his great friend and mentor, Von Waldheim was instantly inspired and motivated now by blind obsession to attempt the transfer of Clavel's superior brain, mind and life force into their empty, lifeless corpse."

"Then we know now for certain that their experiment was a success," interjected Bass.

"The person calling himself Henry Clavel is in reality the Baron Victor Josef von Waldheim and his companion Heinrich is the result of their work on that fateful night and all that remains of the mind and life force of Henry Clavel. Quite remarkable," he concluded.

"Indeed. Would that this situation might be resolved by simply apprehending and incarcerating the pair to prevent further such atrocities occurring, but alas, not so" was the stark reply from Aston.

"The Baron von Waldheim is now driven to the cusp of insanity by his overwhelming obsession to advance his work at any cost, now including the capital offence of murder as part of his plans, in order to obtain the raw materials that he needs. Heinrich, or Clavel as we now know him to be, is the unwilling, hapless participant in all of this madness. Confused by his outward appearance and quite probably driven to the verge of insanity himself upon realisation of what von Waldheim has done, also having to deal with the constant anguish of a continued existence inhabiting the misshapen vessel that they created together."

Turning directly towards the two detectives, Aston delivered his final, damning sentence:

"Be under no illusion whatsoever, my friends, that these two rampant megalomaniacs, brilliant though they are, must be stopped at all costs with extreme prejudice and any notion of a continuance with this abominable work eradicated and sent to the grave along with them; do I make myself abundantly clear?"

"Perfectly clear, Pontius," deadpanned Blackmore.

"Both James and myself need to be made aware of only one more thing; where they can be located!"

Leopold Aston continued:

"As you are both aware from recent unpleasant discoveries made in the river locally, von Waldheim and Clavel have most definitely been working in the area. One can only assume that overriding arrogance has clouded their judgement and caused them to be very lacklustre when disposing of their corpses and showing a total lack of respect and awareness for the rapid advances in both surgical and forensic science techniques now available to the authorities that have led to the conclusions that surgeons were responsible for the atrocities that they have committed."

"Or they are, in fact, long past caring of the consequences that they might incur as a result of their actions," added Dame Pandora.

"Doctor Clavel, who we now know for certain to be Baron von Waldheim, has attended quite a number of my concerts over the last few years. Having been introduced to him formally on several occasions I got the impression of nothing more than a charming, genteel individual somewhat characteristically displaying the slightly arrogant demeanour inherent to the higher born aristocracy one would now assume to be quite correct in learning his true identity, with two outstanding features becoming immediately apparent. Partially covered by a full greying, well coiffured beard was a heavily scarred face and his hands were covered by black leather gloves that were always worn in public, obviously masking the sight of his badly scarred hands – both, one would assume, were a direct result of the fire that took the life of his colleague Clavel."

"We too have had cause to be wary of the Baron von Waldheim and his unsavoury activities in our own land many years before we became aware of Henry Clavel," began Lady Anna.

"The von Waldheim dynasty has cast a long, dark shadow across the Balkan lands, as far to the east as Japan and throughout several Scandinavian countries for the dubious business acumen applied in amassing their considerable family wealth. Suffice to say that their ethical approaches and applications have always been explained at best as being questionable."

"Indeed," agreed Lord Ragnar.

"Five years past, in our southernmost Icelandic town of Vik i Myrdal, is when we became aware of the so-called Doctor Henry Clavel when he purchased a remote property in the southernmost area of Vik, close in proximity to the Myrdaljokull Glacier. We thought very little of this at the time other than in the positive sense that a medical personage of such wide repute should choose to live and practise in one of our towns. A benefit to both the town and our country as a whole, or so we believed until the shocking truth of the matter began to unfold."

"Just so," continued Lady Anna.

"The Doctor was accompanied by a tall, misshapen and ungainly looking companion who became known to us by the name of Heinrich.

"Those few locals who came into close contact with Heinrich reported of a badly scarred facial complexion, partially hidden by long black hair that hung lankly well beyond his hunched and uneven shoulders and over his face, possibly the result of some extensive surgery he underwent to repair serious injuries and the hugest pair of hands that too seemed to have been surgically grafted onto a body to which they did not originally belong, judging by the prominent scar tissue that existed around the circumference of both wrists.

"Dr Clavel was rarely seen but Heinrich was prominent in his frequent movements to and from their property, supervising deliveries of all manner of what turned out to be bespoke laboratory and heavy engineering equipment specially commissioned and privately built in order for them to construct their new facility.

"Each piece of apparatus was cleverly procured from different locations around the world and shipped to various, seemingly random European ports so as not to arouse suspicion of their true purpose or eventual destination. Heinrich proceeded then to collect the packages utilising various bogus transport companies and, using false processing and customs documents, proceeded to ship them to their new laboratory. Quite a brilliant scheme and one which I'm now certain that they have employed many times before."

"If it were not for the seven clinically dismembered male corpses, each one with either their arms, legs or head removed by what seemed to be an uncommonly skilled hand that were discovered purely by chance during an archaeological dig and laid to rest in shallow, un-consecrated graves to the southernmost secluded part of Vik, suspicions as to the unethical and quite unsavoury practices being perpetrated within Clavel's property would quite possibly never have been aroused," added Lord Ragnar.

"Realising immediately that our first line of questioning should as a matter of extreme urgency be directed towards both Dr Clavel and Heinrich, them being involved at the highest level of the medical profession and relatively new to the area, we hastened with all the speed that we could muster to interview the pair directly at the doctor's laboratory, hoping that the element of surprise would still offer to us a solid advantage."

"I sense an 'alas' that is inevitable at this juncture of proceedings, Ragnar," interjected Bass.

"Alas this was indeed the case, James," continued Lord Ragnar with an air of resignation apparent in his voice.

"Made wise to the discovery of said graves at the archaeological dig site, possibly by local agents handsomely paid for undying loyalty to their masters' cause; they had made good their swift and obviously meticulously planned escape into northern Europe and then on to England which is where our Scandinavian agents lost the trail."

"A trail that is once more opened out clear and wide before us by our latest grim discoveries in the Thames," added Blackmore.

"Thanks to the exemplary work of the forensic detection service led by our esteemed colleagues doctors Bass and Blake, we have been able to ascertain that all of the corpses floated downstream on the swift tidal flow from Greenwich.

"The ensuing thorough search of several properties constructed on high ground bore precious little ripe fruit until our searches took us to the old Greenwich observatory building that overlooks the river. Marcus, your briefing if you please," Blackmore enquired of his young colleague.

Jackson cleared his throat and took a sip of water, merely first presentation nerves he quickly thought to himself, and began to speak...

"My boys and me searched the whole area in and around the observatory building, room by room then brick by brick, but found no traces of any laboratory-type facility or any evidence of either surgery or galvanism ever having taken place on the premises.

"In the cellar area below the main building, however, we discovered a labyrinth of tunnels similar to these Roman ones that are above us here in the Tower. Many of these passageways stretching away to all four key points of the compass and a good many more in between had obviously been opened up and used recently as we noticed some of the oil lamps set into recesses within the walls of each one still burned brightly.

"Taking this as a sign of good fortune I proceeded to divide my squad of twelve into groups of three and we took a passage each.

"My own explorations took me in a north westerly direction, back towards where I supposed the border of Bethnal Green and then Spitalfields beyond might be, judging by the distance that we'd already travelled. I reasoned that we'd walked for about a mile or so until we came upon a recess within the passage wall on our left-hand side. Resembling a curved apse, like the ones inside a church or the safety arches in the walls of railway tunnels, the recess went back a good ten to twenty feet before the dead end of a solid and seemingly deep of foundation brick wall forced us to turn directly to our right and ascend a set of extremely well-worn, very steep stone steps upwards."

"Might one be correct in the assumption that the steps led you directly to a concealed area behind the primary pump room of the Greenwich pumping station, Marcus?" questioned Bass.

"That they did, sir, are you familiar with this place?" was Jackson's somewhat surprised response.

Bass remained in silent, quite obviously sullen contemplation. The young detective sergeant's question was eventually answered in part by Blackmore.

"Indeed we are, Marcus," he began.

"This labyrinthine maze of tunnels that could well lead to the very portals of Hell itself was used by the infamous Whitechapel ripper a decade ago to conceal his movements from the net we had cast for him above ground. James and I had the murdering bastard within our sights in close proximity to these very tunnels but for..."

His words petered out into nothingness when his eyes met the dark, withering look that Bass shot in his direction, a look that reminded him in an instant of the reluctant pledges of silence that the two younger detective inspectors were forced to make to a higher authority many years previously in order to protect the guilty. One day the tale would be recounted to all in full, but not today.

Blackmore returned his colleague's look and responded simply with a knowing nod of his head, the only communication that was necessary between the two detectives in order to diffuse the current thread of conversation and immediately move on to more relevant concerns.

"Please continue, Marcus," asked Bass of the young detective sergeant.

Jackson continued...

"We came to the top of the stairs and were confronted by what seemed at first to be a dead end. Another solid wall of stone before us until I noticed that a very narrow gap was visible to the left side of the wall.

"I decided to pass through this passageway alone, that after a few mercifully short yards opened out into the main engine room of what I surmised to be the recently abandoned Greenwich pumping station. All the machinery was still in place but on closer inspection I could see that it had been modified and indeed added to in several ways to facilitate a function other than the pumping of water."

"Might one assume that the modifications included large electrical generators, copper conduits, conductors, electrodes and batteries? Paraphernalia conducive to the practice of galvanism perhaps?" was Blackmore's question.

"Yes, sir. The roof space had been altered so as to allow for it to be opened in order to facilitate the raising of the large electrode present high above the roof of the pump house, one would assume to harness and collect the charge from an electrical storm and much evidence of surgical practice was also present within the room.

"An operating table, a very well-equipped laboratory similar to the one at Whitechapel hospital and lots of new surgical instruments that seemed to have been recently used," answered Jackson.

"But no sign of either of our elusive miscreants I'll wager?" asked Bass.

"Alas no, sir, they were both long away, but we did discover a trap door that when opened revealed a steep sided shaft that dropped a good forty or so feet into the river below. I'd surmise that our dismembered corpses were disposed of down this shaft and made their way to our bank of the river via the strong tidal current upstream," added Jackson.

Congratulating the young detective for his efforts Blackmore began...

"Quite an outstanding piece of police work, Marcus."

"Was there any indication left at all as to the proposed destination of our quarry?"

"None at all, sir. At that point is where our trail ground to an untimely halt," Jackson concluded.

Professor Florence Jefferson began to speak.

"If it might be possible for me to visit the pumping station there may well be a very good chance that I could at least ascertain the direction that our miscreants took and perhaps even the very place where they intended to go to," she began.

"How so, Florence?" asked an inquisitive Blackmore.

Professor Jefferson continued...

"After a person leaves a specific place there remains a certain residual amount of psychic energy left behind from deep within that person's inner psyche. If the trace amount of energy present is sufficient it is possible to read this energy and interpret it as one would garner information from the pages of a book but we need to make all haste to the scene.

"The longer the energy is left to tarry in one place the weaker the energy becomes until it eventually evaporates into the air and becomes totally useless to us."

"One of the several functions of which this box that I wear on my belt is capable is to collect and interpret the code of residual psychic energy left present in a space, to then convert it into a language that we can all understand and so potentially give us the information that we seek. We named this device the 'box of souls.'"

"Then without further hindrance Tiberius, Phineas and I shall accompany Florence and Alanis to the Greenwich pumping station and attempt to gather the vital information that we seek, and pray to God that we are in time," stated Bass flatly.

Chapter 17

'The Box of Souls'

The engine house of the recently disengaged Greenwich pumping station remained a testament to solid, functionable and somewhat imposing, yet traditional neo-Gothic/Georgian architecture.

Cast iron pillars were set at equidistant points along the wide-open floor of the building and sprouted up from the flagstones like the imposing, dead straight trunks of great iron trees to meet the intricately fashioned iron joists that ran across the ceiling space as would the joists and bosses of some monolithic industrial cathedral.

In between this man-made forest of pillars, the dormant machinery still gave off a strong odour of oil and grease, as if being carefully maintained either to be called back into its mechanical life immediately or to be moved on to resume that life elsewhere.

As the companions entered this space Phineas Jefferson was the first to speak...

"Observe immediately the physical evidence all about us. A conductor hangs from the converted roof space. Large batteries over here for the collection and short-term storage of huge quantities of electrical energy. Over here, recently used surgical equipment and electrodes, presumably used as a means of transferring that energy into a body perhaps. Galvanism has taken place here for sure," he stated with knowing authority.

Jefferson continued with an air of unflinching zeal present in his voice.

"This equipment, if utilised and perfected with a view to establishing a feasible and sound avenue of study, could be revolutionary in the advancement of certain revival techniques. At present in the infancy of development, it could be refined immediately for primary use during resuscitation procedures after seizure, surgery or heart murmurs. It could literally be used to save lives! The inventor is a true innovator and undoubtedly a remarkably gifted genius of the scientific community and as such I offer my utmost respect and acknowledgement of that fact."

"Just so, Phineas," began Blackmore. "But remember well, that in this particular instance the 'inventor' as you describe him has been tainted, possibly even driven completely insane by what could be best described as God-like delusions of grandeur and as such must be apprehended at all costs or terminated with extreme prejudice before any further unlawful and wholly inhuman atrocities are committed outside of the controlled and acceptable context of true progressive science."

Blackmore at once turned his attention to both his daughter Alanis and Florence Jefferson. Before he could speak Alanis said...

"The residual psychic energy remains very strong in this place. Two people were here, two months past, up until one week ago. They lived here, worked here tirelessly, obsessively even, using this equipment to achieve the ends to which we are now familiar and left in great haste upon being discovered purely by chance by a hapless group of vagrants who randomly and quite innocently sought a dry haven for the night."

"Vagrants, of course," began Blackmore.

"That would explain the reason why no alarm was raised immediately as to the suspicious nature of events unfolding under this roof. It would also probably prove to be a wise assumption that these poor, unfortunate wretches' fate was sealed all at once by what they discovered here on that night," he concluded solemnly.

Alanis Blackmore answered her father's grim conclusion as though the terrible events that she described had just unfolded before her remarkably perceptive eyes in that very second.

"Indeed, Father, their lives ended abruptly here in a most violent fashion when in an instant they became unwitting participants, and ultimately victims, in this vile chain of events. The remnants of the corpses that were discovered upstream are undoubtedly theirs, dispatched as would the day's refuse be cast down into the shaft mentioned by Detective Sergeant Jackson in his earlier report, and into the river below. This shaft too was our elusive pair's route of escape. At this point my vision becomes somewhat clouded as would clear sight be hampered by a thick city smog. I can tell you no more."

"So, our pair of miscreants have progressed beyond their usual parameters of grave robbing onto the heinous capital crime of murder in order to procure fresh raw materials for their vile practices," added Phineas Jefferson.

"Florence, my love, is the box of souls likely to be forthcoming with additional information that might assist us further with our investigation?" he asked of his wife.

"Indeed it is, Phineas" was her immediate response.

"As Alanis stated earlier the residual psychic energy that remains here which emanated from both Clavel and Von Waldheim is still present all around us and quite simple to decipher and interpret using the box. As well as offering a full mental profile of each subject, which I shall include in great detail within my final written report for this case, we are able to utilise another function of this remarkable device that we have named the psychic compass. This will enable us to track our quarry to their intended location. Alanis and I need but a few more minutes to interpret the data that we are receiving as we speak."

"A remarkable invention to be sure, Florence," began Blackmore.

"Does anyone know the whereabouts of James since our arrival?" he questioned as it occurred to him that his old brother at arms was not present within the group.

"I believe that upon our arrival he immediately tasked to locate the stone steps down into the tunnels below our feet as described in great detail by Marcus, as though he knew instinctively where they would be," said Phineas.

"He was well aware of their location, as he was sure of the labyrinth that lies beneath us," answered Blackmore knowingly but uncharacteristically betraying the concern he showed in his voice for his companions to sense with ease. Almost seeking to redress the balance of his statement instantly he continued...

"We are both well aware of the many secrets that this place attempts to conceal beneath its grey gothic façade and its cold flagstone floors. A decade ago James and I became all too familiar with this edifice as we pursued the Whitechapel Ripper to these very portals where we stand. I ask you, nay beg of you, to ask of me no further questions concerning this matter for I will not, more to the point cannot for the present, answer them."

Blackmore's last sentence was ended abruptly with the sound of two loud cracks echoing around the room made by the pistol belonging to James Bass who had re-appeared among the group with ghost-like stealth, as if transported among his colleagues by some kind of strange, ethereal magic spell. His speech was abrupt and cut his companions to the quick...

"Tiberius! I must warn you once again, by all that is holy and hopefully for the final time, my brother, let no more be spoken of those events ten years past and we might be able to continue, for the present anyhow, to shield innocent ears and protect the lives of our loved ones and colleagues from the corrupt and deadly agents that we know to exist throughout the very highest echelons of power and privilege.

"The proper time will manifest itself soon to divulge the whole sordid story in full and precise detail when the day of reckoning for those owed the ultimate retribution for their threats and crimes will be at hand, but that time is not yet arrived and the day of judgement for those in waiting is yet to be decided."

Turning his attention directly to Florence Jefferson, Bass continued...

"Florence. Pray tell does the box of souls offer any indication as to the direction that our marks took when they left this place?"

"It most certainly does, James," Florence began.

"The residue of psychic energy was suitably strong enough for the psychic compass to inform us that they intended to travel north, their destination being a small mill village named Cromford that is located in the Midland county of Derbyshire.

"The village is bisected by a working canal system on which is located, about a mile upstream along the towpath in a south/south easterly direction towards the town of Ambergate, a pumping station that matches the type of architecture and equipment type of this station where we presently stand almost exactly, thus making it a prime location for our two deviants to continue their work.

"There exists, however, a second possible location nearby which they might have chosen to utilise also. It is a winding house that hauled heavy goods and equipment up a very steep gradient from the canal and the Black Rocks lead mine further on up the tracks to meet the Trans-Pennine railway link that shunts cargo between Derbyshire, South Yorkshire, Cheshire and the other northern industrial counties.

"The building is situated approximately two miles in a westerly direction from Cromford station, just about one mile from the Black Rocks lead mine and stands alone at the very peak of a place known as Middleton Top."

His question answered in full, Bass continued...

"Excellent, flawless work, Florence and Alanis both. Your remarkable skills might very well have offered us a prime opportunity to conclude this case a good deal swifter than any of us might have anticipated."

Bass turned and addressed the whole group as he made his final speech...

"If the box of souls and Lady Alanis' psychic insight both have given us all of the information that we can hope for we must with all haste return to meet with the League and prepare for a final confrontation."

As they proceeded to exit the building, Blackmore beckoned his comrade back inside and began to speak...

"James, a brief word with you if I may. On our moment of arrival, you left the group to access the tunnels beneath our feet that we both know so well from a decade ago. I stand here before you justly rebuked by yourself for a second time on this day concerning speaking out of a past case history best left buried deep within Nadir's pit where in all probability it should remain for the rest of eternity, but please, brother, answer this one question: What motivated you to act alone, as did you on the night of your injury when you were all but lost to us. Why, James, did you seek out that labyrinth that may well lead us one day to the very gates of hell itself with no obvious regard for your own well-being? Why, James? What motivates you to act alone and without counsel?"

Bass eyed his companion from behind the dark lenses of his spectacles. As he began to speak he removed his spectacles to reveal his eyes to Blackmore. They were as black as pitch.

"Tiberius, my brother, please try to understand that if from this day I decide that I must spontaneously act alone then I do so not out of any egotistical folly on my part but out of a truly genuine need to protect the many, even though my seemingly erratic and selfish actions might one day facilitate the demise of the one, the one never meant to be any other than myself.

"My purpose, my function and indeed my pledge is as it always was, my old and trusted friend: to serve and to protect the greater good with yourself and the League by my side, as I will always stand by yours. That pledge of allegiance to you all remains as resolute and true as it always was and ever will be, but this 'gift, or curse' that I find bestowed upon me, for want of a better pair of phrases to describe it, continues to offer my sharpened senses opportunities that I could scarcely before have dared dream of to aid us in ways that I never could before.

"Every new day is a voyage of self-discovery and I need both yourself and the League to trust in my judgement, erratic, introspective and out of character as it might seem to be at times, as I continue to understand and develop my new found 'skills'."

"Of course, James, take all of the time that you require in order to understand completely this thing that wrestles for control of your spirit, possibly even your very soul," Blackmore began.

"If, nay when, you master the probing tentacles of the wolf spectre that torments you so remember that you do not face this ordeal alone. Connie, myself, and the other members of the League are much more than your companions, much more than your friends. We remain all for the one and one for the many as would any family, no matter what the cost."

Bass clasped his companion's hand and repeated the heartfelt sentiment of his trusted friend…

"All for the one and one for the many, no matter what the cost."

"In the tunnels, James, what did you discover?" asked Blackmore inquisitively.

"Two things primarily more about myself but that nonetheless might have significant bearing on this and future cases," Bass began.

"Firstly, it seems that my eyesight has improved to the keenest level imaginable. I can see very well in the dark."

"Could be a useful tool, and secondly?" enquired Blackmore slightly impatiently.

"Secondly, Tiberius, and probably most important of all, I can detect their scent. They leave a trail of pheromones before me as blatant and clear as the psychic energy that was interpreted by the box of souls.

"I caught hold of their putrid stench the moment that we arrived and it led me directly to the stone steps that were described in such minute detail by Marcus and downwards into the labyrinth below. They made good their escape into one of the many tunnels that stretch far beyond under the city, the maze-like network of tunnels that we both know very well," answered Bass.

He paused for a few seconds, and the response that was forthcoming from his lips answered the thoughts of his colleague precisely, negating any need for the obvious question waiting to be asked by Blackmore...

"I propose that our number be divided into two groups for the impending hunt, Tiberius. A first group led by Pontius comprising Phineas, Florence, Leopold, Beatrice, Connie, Pandora, The Undertaker and Marcus follow the psychic trail mapped out for us in such great detail by the box of souls. We shall meet at the burned out remains of the Arkwright cotton mill situated on the Cromford canal where the next portion of our plan might be perused and decided upon."

"So, I would surmise that we two follow your keen nose into the labyrinth then, my brother?" enquired Blackmore.

"Just so, Tiberius. We shall follow the strong and obvious scent which will reveal their exact path through the maze and if my suspicions are correct will confirm a distant anomaly that has troubled my subconscious mind incessantly for years concerning our case from a decade ago."

Just as Blackmore began to ponder asking the multitude of questions that burned within him Bass continued...

"Let us without further delay put our plans into operation, Tiberius. The longer we tarry the weaker their scent becomes, thus all the more difficult they become to track. I promise you that as we travail the facts that I hope are relevant to our trials and tribulations long ago will manifest themselves and our shared desire to finally administer justice and retribution to the guilty will be satisfied once and for all."

Chapter 18

'All for One and One for The Many'

The remains of the Arkwright cotton mill located at the heart of the Derbyshire village of Cromford rose up out of its foundations like the remains of a desolate, long deserted edifice of charred timber and stone. Built by Sir Richard Arkwright in 1771 when the potential water power of both Bonsall brook and the old lead mine drain of Cromford sough were utilised as the prime energy source to drive the water frame cotton spinning machines that became an early and important innovation during the continued and rapid development of the early industrial revolution.

The mill was extended, firstly in 1776 then again in 1791, reaching its full potential as a commercial venture when the inauguration of the Cromford canal in 1793 provided a cheap and easy method of transporting cargo from the area by riverboat barge. By the mid-nineteenth century, however, the mill had been rendered all but obsolete in the advent of steam powered turbines that ran newer, more modern and efficient machinery and in 1890 a large portion of the extended mill was destroyed by fire leaving what remained an abandoned, derelict shell of a building.

Here, within this once proud and prosperous palace of modern progressive industry and wealth now reduced to a desolate forgotten place fit only for the spirits of its long dead employees to wander its charred empty corridors, the key protagonists belonging to The League of Ghosts had convened as they were requested to do so by their two detective colleagues whose imminent arrival they awaited. Phineas Jefferson drew his pocket watch, flipped open its silver cover, held its satisfyingly tactile shape in his right hand and eyed its face impatiently before speaking...

"I would hope that our two esteemed colleagues' motivation for travelling separately to this group merit sound reason and explanation" was his slightly exasperated opening sentence as he snapped shut the watch and swung it theatrically in a double circle back into his left waistcoat pocket.

"Whatever their agenda for travelling a different path to our own, rest assured, Phineas that their reasoning for such action will be sound and in the best interests of us all" was the reassuring response from Aston.

The precise moment that he finished speaking a loud crack of thunder directly overhead heralded the start of an almighty storm. The rain began to fall heavily and vertically like some sub-tropical hail of glass shards into the ground outside. As the first spectacular bolts of forked lightning punctuated the intermittent blasts of thunder in the darkening skies above, Tiberius Blackmore and James Bass entered the building with this demonstration of heaven's full fury at their backs, almost as though the whole scenario had been theatrically stage managed in order to dramatise their entrance to maximum effect.

"Quite a spectacular entrance for a pair of ageing old Whitechapel warhorses," began Aston. "Though if our intelligence as to the whereabouts of our two miscreants proves to be correct, the weather conditions as they are now could bear some major significance on events that, if unchecked presently, might unfold beyond the remit of our control in very little time at all. May we ask, gentlemen, what will be our next course of action?"

Bass was the first of the detectives to speak...

"Indeed, Pontius, we must act swiftly and with the utmost stealth if we are to apprehend both Clavel and Von Waldheim here on this night. We shall proceed by long boat on the canal as one group from Wheatcroft and sons coal merchants' wharf in a south/south easterly direction towards Ambergate village for approximately one mile until we reach a swing bridge across the waterway where Connie and Pandora will commandeer the High Peak Junction station house in the name of the Crown and the League of Ghosts as a forward command centre. Here they will assemble a reserve force of six constables should they be required, and also set up a medical facility in the event that it be needed. Here I propose that we divide our remaining forces thusly: Tiberius and I will be accompanied by Pontius, Phineas and Leopold as we take the towpath half mile 117 degrees south/south east towards the Leawood pumping station in order to commence our search there. A second party led by Beatrice comprising Florence, The Undertaker, Marcus and half a dozen of Derbyshire's finest constables will ride the pulley train 282 degrees in a westerly direction from Cromford station beyond the Black Rocks lead mine and up to the engine house on the summit of Middleton top where a second search will take place.

"We know for certain that within one of these locations both Clavel and Von Waldheim will be found. If any questions are to be asked now is the time..." was Bass' closing sentence.

Blackmore reacted almost immediately with a single question... "Why these specific personnel to be deployed at the two locations, James?"

"Both Beatrice and myself have certain, ahem, qualities at our disposal that might prove an advantage to each group when attempting to apprehend our villains, especially upon encountering the thing inside which festers what remains of the life force, mind and hopefully a remnant of the conscience and reasoning of Henry Clavel."

"Point taken and understood, James," answered Blackmore. "Might I suggest then that without further hindrance we proceed with all possible haste about our business," he continued in almost the same breath.

"Indeed, my brother, we deploy at once and may whatever spirit guides and strengthens our resolve, in the name of The League of Ghosts, justice shall be the ultimate victor on this night."

As the group began their short journey along the canal an eerie silence fell over them, except for the sack cloth-muffled hooves of the two great shire horses that drew their long boat forward via their long, steady, measured gait along the towpath. A cloying, putrid mist was rising from the water making any sort of meaningful visibility, backwards or forwards, increasingly difficult as it thickened with what seemed like every passing second. Blackmore and Bass were huddled in whispered conference in the long boat stern...

"This pea soup of a fog might prove to be somewhat of an advantage to us as we close in on our prey, James," hissed Blackmore. "It's as thick a cloak of fog as ever I've witnessed, even on our own perpetually cloudy streets of Whitechapel."

"And we are now in the eye of the storm, Tiberius," answered Bass. "Observe as we approach our first stop at the swing bridge how the storm seems to rage above what I would assume to be the Leawood pumping station a mere few hundred yards beyond."

Bass stood and beckoned for the attention of his colleagues by tapping the silver wolf's head of his cane on the starboard mooring cleat of their boat...

"Our time is at hand, fellow Ghosts," he began.

"We deploy immediately on disembarking as planned. Lock and load your weapons, sharpen your steel and God speed with hope for a safe and successful campaign to all here present."

Chapter 19

'In the Name of Justice, and The League of Ghosts'

As the boat came to a steady stop two constables alighted first in order to unhook and operate the counter weights that allowed the bridge to swing on a central pivot in order to allow their boat to pass through and continue on its journey. Just as the boat began to move on steadily through the now opened channel, Beatrice Aston led her group consisting of Florence, The Undertaker, Jackson and six constables to a waiting rail carriage at the foot of a harsh incline and immediately began the long, steep ascent to the Middleton Top engine house.

Constance, Pandora, and six more constables entered the High Peak Junction station house and began to organise a frontline command base and medical post.

The remainder of the group continued on the water for approximately half of a mile to within sight of the Leawood pumping station, out of the storm's eye and back into its almost cataclysmic maelstrom of natural chaos, until Bass hissed out a command to the boat pilot who was leading the two great shires along the towpath.

"Stop here! We complete our journey on foot."

The boat came to a stop for a second time a mere thirty yards from its final destination, directly opposite an old engine house on the far bank of the canal, just before a bend in the waterway that naturally concealed the boat from possible detection from the pumping station situated a little further along the towpath. Bass, Blackmore, Pontius, Leopold and Phineas swiftly alighted to the tow path and followed the silent signal given by Bass with trained military precision: two fingers raised, one to each eye, calling for each man to be completely focussed on the task and watch intently for instructions, five spread fingers signifying the five comrades, a half raised fist ordering a momentary pause for a few seconds while Bass checked that the five comrades' weapons were locked, loaded and ready, then a flat palm levelled vertically, fingers pointing in the direction of the nearest tree line that would offer them immediate concealment from the Leawood pumping station ahead. After descending a shallow embankment, the group continued along a rough single-track path through the trees, bypassing a series of foul-smelling slurry pits, and onwards towards the pumping station, the tall chimney of which stood out as a clear beacon in the misty blackness as regular shards of forked lightning constantly struck the lightning conductor at its peak. As the comrades approached what they assumed to be the rear of the building Bass raised his right fist, the clear sign which all present were aware was the signal to halt. Phineas Jefferson was the first to speak...

"See how the lightning is harnessed by the conductor and slithers down the contact attached to the side of the chimney like some crackling electrical serpent."

"Yes, Phineas, as I surmised and indeed had hoped in my private thoughts, both Clavel and Von Waldheim are present at this location," answered Bass.

"I was able to track their evil scent with ease along the very same route that we have just taken a mere few minutes earlier. I sent the others to the engine house at Middleton Top knowing that but for the possibility of a few acolytes loyal to our two marks that might need apprehending, they would be well out of harm's way. Each one present here with us possesses the weapons, the military skills or the somewhat 'less conventional' qualities that might be needed in order to bring this case to a satisfactory conclusion."

"Will you now share more of your 'private thoughts' with us, James?" asked an inquisitive Aston.

"Please enlighten us as to how we proceed once more into the gaping abyss of the unknown."

Bass answered his colleague immediately...

"Both Phineas and Tiberius are without question the best two marksmen among our group, possibly ever to have come from within the ranks of the whole British army. This obvious attribute, plus their combined extensive military skills and keen guile will prove a distinct advantage to our cause. I have recently been made aware of a weapon designed and built by your son Leopold that has the ability to manipulate the sound waves that surround us into a form of sonic stunning device.

"I believe that the sonic blunder blaster will be the only weapon that we possess in our arsenal that will give us the opportunity to render the virtually indestructible, super humanly strong, undead shell of Clavel weak enough for us to apprehend. The constables who follow us carry with them extra strong cast iron chains and manacles that we might utilise in order to restrain the beast whilst under the stupefying influence of a prolonged sonic attack."

Turning directly towards Leopold, Bass continued...

"Professor Aston. Yours is the key action with regards to this portion of our mission. The very moment that you encounter Clavel at a range that suits your purpose, deploy your weapon in his direction with all the accuracy and power it can muster. We simply must not allow him the opportunity of being able to protect or aid the escape of Von Waldheim in any way.

"Think only of engaging Clavel with the sonic device, Leopold. Both your father and Phineas are here to protect you from any random elements that might be present so your concentration on the task at hand must be paramount and unhindered. Tiberius and I will concentrate our efforts solely on the apprehension of Von Waldheim."

With Bass' last sentence evaporating into the mist the group fell silent of word. Amidst the random loud cracks of thunder overhead and the sound of heavy vertical rain that now peppered the trees above their heads and the muddy ground beneath their boots, Bass gave the stark command:

"GHOSTS, WE GO NOW! LEOPOLD, PONTIUS, PHINEAS; ACCESS THE FRONT ENTRANCE BY WHATEVER MEANS LIES AT YOUR DISPOSAL, TIBERIUS AND I SHALL ACCESS THROUGH THE SIDE ENTRANCE; CONSTABLES, CLOSE QUARTERS TO SUPPORT THE FRONT ENTRANCE TEAM AND READY THOSE CHAINS FOR USE. DEPLOY ALL FORCES AND GOD'S SPEED AND GOOD FORTUNE TO ALL."

As the group splintered into its pre-arranged squads each faction descended down a second slightly steeper embankment and across an open area of scrub grassland and shrubbery made slightly more difficult to traverse at speed due to the persistent heavy rain that had created somewhat marshy conditions under foot, and on to the pumping station. Both teams gained access to their designated entrances with surprising ease.

Once inside they made their way as silently as possible towards what they believed to be the outer gallery of the main pumping station using the cast iron pillars that rose up out of the stone floor like iron trees to the vaunted ceiling above and the machinery that lay throughout the room and around its perimeter as fortuitous and welcome cover from immediate detection.

As they surveyed the scene before them it became immediately obvious to both groups that Von Waldheim and Clavel were engaged in the final stages of galvanising life into their latest creation using equipment that was almost identical to that which they had discovered back at the Greenwich pumping station. They were also close enough to hear Von Waldheim speak to Clavel above the crackle of thousands of volts of electricity as it was directed from the conductor above their heads along primitive, deadly live terminals and into the lifeless body of their creation that lay before them on a long, hinged copper table.

With an almost insane levity present in his voice they overheard Von Waldheim say...

"This is our time, Heinrich. All of the personal and professional sacrifice on my part, all of the horrendous physical pain and suffering on yours, my great and one true friend. Every last morsel of the underqualified and uneducated ridicule that I've had to endure from my so-called peers and colleagues. All of the scorn and bile from my many detractors will be swept aside and forgotten in an instant after the glorious triumph of the actions that unfold on this most wondrous of nights are made public. Now without further delay open the roof portals, my loyal retainer and prepare the batteries to accept the ultimate power of the gods."

Upon hearing Von Waldheim's request Heinrich took a heavy chain that hung from a pulley high above their heads in both of his huge, calloused hands and began to pull. As two great roof panels began to swing inwards on huge iron hinges, the copper table on which lay the still lifeless creation of Von Waldheim began to rise up towards the now exposed angry night sky, lifted by four huge pulleys on each corner. Just as this action began Pontius Aston turned to his son Leopold and began to speak...

"The great physical strength of the Heinrich creature in order to perform such a feat is immeasurable. We dare not risk any form of single combat with such a monster in any proposed attempt to secure an arrest, nor should we expect a round from any conventional weapon that we carry to be any more effective in bringing it down. Our course of action is clear: Leopold, deploy the sonic device immediately in the direction of the beast for the instant we break cover our presence will be detected. Phineas and I shall cover your flanks in case of random incursion."

Within the few scant seconds the three companions left the safety of their concealment and put their plan into operation Heinrich had raised the alarm.

"WE ARE COMPROMISED!" he exclaimed in the direction of his companion von Waldheim.

"Victor, The League of Ghosts is upon us. Make good your escape as I severely test their courage, their handsome reputations and their legendary stoic resolve" was his ominous boast in the direction of his rapidly advancing assailants.

Heinrich proceeded to let go of the mighty roof chain and rounded on his bold confronters with a surprising turn of speed. Equal to this swift action by his would-be assailant, Leopold Aston levelled his sonic blunder blaster directly towards the swiftly advancing Heinrich creature and opened fire. What transpired next was a chain of events that none present had ever witnessed before.

A low-level hum began to emanate from the weapon the moment it was engaged. Then what seemed like an ethereal ripple of expanding rings, quite probably the controlled directional field of soundwaves emanating from the weapon, reached out from one of the devices twin barrels and enveloped Heinrich in its paralysing sonic hug. In an instant the monster clasped his great hands over obviously troubled ears and began to scream as if in severe, tortured agony. Upon witnessing this compelling yet obviously brutal scene unfold before them, Aston exclaimed...

"Quite a remarkable weapon, son. Possibly requiring a few refinements in order to make it a viable, effective tool for use by our law enforcement agencies but on this day it would seem that for our purposes your prototype will more than suffice."

Aston's appraisal of his son's remarkable invention was short lived, however, as Phineas Jefferson called their immediate attention to more pressing matters at hand...

"Look to your flanks, Pontius. We have multiple hostiles bearing down on our position from all points."

"Just so, Phineas. Make each shot count for we must protect Leopold and give him adequate time to complete his task."

With a pistol in each hand and flanking Leopold Aston on each side as he continued to hold Heinrich helplessly captive within the paralysing sonic field, both Jefferson and Aston unleashed a torrent of searing lead projectiles upon the hordes of acolytes that seemed to be appearing from everywhere around them.

'CRACK, CRACK, CRACK... "RELOADING!" 'CRACK, CRACK, CRACK, CRACK... "RELOADING!" 'CRACK, CRACK, CRACK...

The process repeated itself time and time again as the two experienced old soldiers fought a valiant rear-guard action to protect the prime directive. Jefferson began to speak over the increasing cacophony of noise with more than a little concern present in his voice...

"Hell's teeth there's too many of them," he began. My ammunition pouch is almost spent."

Aston continued...

"Leopold, how fare we with regards to incapacitating our large friend?" he questioned in between precisely aimed volleys.

"Heinrich is proving to be a remarkably difficult and extremely tenacious subject to subdue, make no mistake," began Leopold. "I would surmise that his great physical strength and unnaturally stout constitution is equal to that of a good few normal men in tandem but holding him within the sonic cone at maximum intensity will render his resistance ineffective very soon now."

"Sooner rather than later, son, if you please. Our ammunition cache is almost spent and..."

The words of Aston were curtailed short mid-sentence by an almost unbearably high-pitched squealing and the overbearing sound of what seemed like the flapping of thousands of tiny winged creatures as they battered the air all around them. Just five words were necessary to be uttered by Aston in order to immediately placate his two besieged colleagues and put their minds totally at ease...

"Beatrice... God help them all!"

Chapter 20

'Beatrice'

An undulating, screeching black cloud entered through the front entrance of the pumping station. A huge murmuration of vampire bats with the barely visible black form of Beatrice Aston carried along at its core flocked over and enveloped the now terrified and randomly scattering attackers.

They were subsequently lifted, two, three even four at a time high into the air by this black cloud of doom and their lifeless bodies dropped unceremoniously to the ground like discarded, loose limbed, limp rag dolls, lifeless and drained of all their blood. Within what seemed like an instant of the purge beginning it was over and the familiar human form of Beatrice Aston was gently set down in front of her grateful and relieved colleagues by her fluttering shroud of shrieking acolytes.

"I trust that you are all unharmed" was her opening sentence as she took out a delicate lace trimmed handkerchief from a pocket in her tunic and without showing the slightest hint of self-consciousness or remorse for the lives she had just taken dabbed away drips of human blood from both corners of her mouth.

"Dining out these days can prove to be such a messy business," she quipped dryly.

"Leopold, I imagine that the cowering, gibbering rather large pile of rags that you still hold within your sonic cone is now subdued enough for your constables to apply their substantial restraints without being unduly challenged," she concluded as she gave her son a loving and slightly relieved peck on each cheek.

"Oh yes, of course, Mother. I was momentarily distracted from the task at hand," he answered. "That entrance of yours was indeed quite a spectacle to behold."

"I concur, Beatrice," agreed Pontius as he took his wife in a loving embrace and kissed her lightly on both cheeks.

"Quite the most spectacular and effective of entrances to any stage on Earth I would imagine. But please divulge how you became aware of our predicament, Beatrice. How could you have known that we faced such mortal peril?"

"Even before we arrived at the summit of Middleton Top, Florence had engaged the psychic compass function of her box of souls and the residual psychic energy that it detected was so weak as to suggest that both Clavel and Von Waldheim were not present at our designated rendezvous, merely a few disparate, hapless accomplices who were using the engine house and its outbuildings as a storage facility and were possibly embroiled in the earliest stages of developing a brand new location for a laboratory.

"Knowing that Florence, Marcus and The Undertaker, with the support of their squad of constables, were more than capable of making the necessary arrests by themselves, I concentrated all of my energy and focus on making for your location as quickly as my surrogate brood of night wings could carry me. We must maintain the forward momentum our actions have pressed forward at great pace here and seek to support James and Tiberius as they attempt to apprehend the fleeing Von Waldheim" was Beatrice's direct reply.

"Even now he seeks to use this melee we have instigated in this place as an effective cover to make good his escape."

Indeed, as events unfolded before them Bass and Blackmore remained completely focussed on their prime task of apprehending Von Waldheim. Even the ensuing firefight between Von Waldheim's minions and their fellow Ghosts, coupled with the subsequent dramatic arrival of Beatrice Aston carried by her undulating black wave of vampiric mayhem, could not distract them from their designated mission, save for a few irresistible and well-aimed shots in the direction of the enemy, purely medicinal, slightly self-indulgent but always with the best interests of the successful outcome of the case firmly in mind of course!

"See, James, to our left flank. Our comrades have the Clavel Golem in chains," observed an almost jubilant Blackmore.

"And look there, ahead of us on the mezzanine floor above, Von Waldheim attempts to take his leave of such lively proceedings without asking for permission to do so it would seem," he continued and without pausing for breath effected a loud, shrill whistle through his teeth before bellowing out the chilling warning that had struck terror into the core of the two great detectives' enemies' souls throughout the years...

"Von Waldheim... Baron Victor Joseph Von Waldheim... Halt and yield in the name of the Queen, the law and The League of Ghosts or prepare to accept the ultimate justice that we are deemed and lawfully sanctioned to administer."

Turning to acknowledge Blackmore's warning, Von Waldheim began to speak in his typically arrogant, almost mockingly aristocratic manner...

"Detective inspectors Tiberius Blackmore and James Bass, late of the Prince Regent's own ninety fifth rifle Brigade and the Prince Regent's Hussars, ex-army covert special forces operatives and currently employed by the City of London as official 'street sweepers' and sewer dredgers in that rat-infested cauldron of filth that is Whitechapel.

"What a privilege it is for me to finally make the acquaintance of two of the Queen's most respected and decorated establishment lap-dogs, even in these less than auspicious of circumstances. Oh, and I thank you, Blackmore, for at least being aware of your lowly station and addressing one by one's correct Royal title."

"Recently promoted detective chief inspectors Bass and Blackmore, if you please, your worshipfulness" was Blackmore's mocking reply.

"Are we to assume that you will not yield to common sense and continue with your charade of god-like pretence?"

"Yield!" exclaimed Von Waldheim.

"Prometheus does not consider yielding to mere mortals. My power is now absolute and unassailable to all those who would oppose and refuse to bow down to the nineteenth century Prometheus here on Earth."

"Alas you would prove to be just one more potential waste of otherwise useful cell space at Bedlam asylum to us. A chronic waste of human life to be simply moved aside and cast down like the useless refuse you undoubtedly are" was the withering response from Blackmore as he reached underneath his overcoat and drew out his trusted old Le Mat revolver, aiming it squarely at Von Waldheim.

"Let us observe how the great Titan Prometheus, nought but a proven common murderer here among mortals, might bleed like a mortal," he mocked with one last damning sentence before expertly discharging a single, potentially paralysing round into the left shoulder of the Baron.

'CRACK!'

The lethal lead projectile tore into its helpless mark shattering tendon and bone as it forced a rough-hewn path clean straight through and out the other side of its feeble flesh target. Reeling backwards from the heavy punch of Blackmore's bullet into a panel of large wooden handled contact switches and unearthed electricity cables von Waldheim screamed out in agony as searing pain ripped through every nerve in his body.

"Do you see, James, Prometheus bleeds out admirably and displays all of the physical frailties and susceptibilities to pain as we mere humans do," mocked Blackmore mercilessly.

"Let us together now consign this delusional pretender to the 'case closed' files for the rest of eternity."

Needing no further bidding from his colleague, Bass raised his revolver in unison with that of his brother in arms, cocked the hammer and prepared to fire on the hapless and seemingly helpless Baron.

In the same fleeting instant, Von Waldheim reached over his good right shoulder and instinctively pulled down one of the heavy wooden handled contact switches on the panel at his back. As he did so he uttered one last teasingly defiant sentence in the direction of the two detectives…

"But is not an eternity too long a sabbatical from further gamesmanship between nemeses of our undoubted calibre, my dear Tiberius, to ensue and provide us with more rakish and entertaining folly. Until the next time we meet, and rest assured my tenacious friends there will be a next time, I take my leave of these rapidly deteriorating proceedings in the name of self-preservation and rejuvenation for said future escapades."

All at once the entire panel of switches and wire conduit behind the Baron exploded into a blazing cacophony of electrical and pyrotechnic chaos. The batteries and galvanising equipment too that lay all around the room erupted in unison with the initial blast thus creating a wall of cascading fire and sparks between the two detectives and von Waldheim.

"He destroys his own creation utilising previously laid charges so as to cause deception and confusion towards our resolve in his bid to evade our attentions," exclaimed Bass as he shielded his eyes and face from the melee of fire and destruction that was erupting all around them. Gathering his composure after a brief few seconds, during which his senses were momentarily stunned into numbness by the Baron's clever ploy, Bass continued with no shortage of both anxiety and concern in his voice...

"See there, Tiberius, through the flames that rage around us. The Baron makes for the far side of the iron mezzanine floor upon which he stands, to a staircase that may well lead to a pre-arranged route of escape through the levels below. We mustn't lose sight of him now or I fear the flames that lap both around our ears and feet may well mask his scent even from my keen senses and his trail will be directly lost to us."

Heavy, almost molten girders, charred and still burning wooden joists and great chunks of dislodged masonry fell randomly about the two detectives hampering their proposed direct pursuit of Von Waldheim, thus making their progress in any direction almost impossible. As the weakened structure of the building began to buckle and crumble around them, Bass felt the need to shout at the top of his voice so his colleague might barely even hear his words over the catastrophic maelstrom that was raging all around them. Looking around frantically in an attempt to discover an escape route, he alerted his colleague to an opening that had manifested itself into the wall beside them.

"Tiberius, look to our immediate right. The wall is breached wide open and offers us an opportunity to exit this rapidly crumbling edifice."

"I see it, James. I suggest we waste no time and vacate this place immediately" was the short affirmative reply given by Blackmore.

With barely a few seconds to spare before the ceiling collapsed completely into the building raining down a deadly debris of molten iron, dislodged stone blocks and lethally sharp wooden shards upon those who might remain inside, Bass and Blackmore exited the pumping station through their fortuitous exit in the wall and made for a set of stone steps that led them upwards and to the relative safety of the canal towpath. Looking back along the path Blackmore observed that their companions had reached safety themselves and informed his colleague of this fact with some measure of relief in his voice.

Chapter 21

'Rise of the Wolfman'

"**O**ur colleagues have reached safe haven, too, James and what's more they have Clavel in chains. Their mission is successfully accomplished in fine style," he stated.

"Yet ours is just unfolding to its conclusion, Tiberius," was the immediate riposte from Bass.

"See there, not one hundred yards in front of us and just about to cross a footbridge to the opposite bank of the canal. The Baron attempts to make good his escape into the Cromford mire that lies festering and deadly beyond the aqueduct. If he succeeds in his endeavour to reach the marshland beyond we might well lose him for good."

"Should we then not allow him to try his luck, James?" questioned Blackmore. "If it transpires that the marsh takes his soul to purgatory then all the better for it I say. Saves us a few rounds of ordnance too," he concluded wryly.

"BUT I WANT HIM, TIBERIUS, KNEELING BEFORE US IN IRONS, BODY AND SOUL!" was the terse response from Bass. "I am convinced now more than ever that Joseph Von Waldheim holds the key information that we seek in order for us to conclude once and for all our unsolved case file from a decade ago."

"Very well then, James, we give chase and may providence and a good tail wind converge and charge our ageing limbs with the speed that we require," answered Blackmore.

The two detectives sprinted along the towpath towards the footbridge only to observe von Waldheim vault a low stone wall that was the boundary between the canal towpath and the infamous Cromford mire.

At the moment they crossed the bridge and looked out over the wall in search of their fleeing quarry, a series of unprecedented events unfolded in the space of a mere few fleeting seconds that neither Bass nor Blackmore could possibly have perceived, nor possess the ability to alter.

A single pistol shot spat out of the misty night air, not from any weapon discharged by either of the two detectives' revolvers but rather from von Waldheim. The expertly aimed projectile found its mark with a deadly unerring accuracy and struck Bass squarely in the centre of his forehead.

From this moment forth, however, from the perspective of Blackmore at least, the scenario now began to unfold in an altogether more surreal and quite unnerving manner.

His colleague had just received a wound that would surely take the life of any normal, mortal man in an instant. James Bass had, however, transcended the fragile mortality of a human being. His human spirit was now shared with that of a Lycanthrope, and upon receiving the potentially fatal wound he did not fall back mortally wounded as one might expect that he should have done. In actual fact he was barely rocked back on his heels by the force of the powerful bullet as it entered his skull with a sickening pop.

As his hat and dark spectacles fell to the ground behind him his head at first was knocked sharply backwards by the impact of the bullet then lolled forward, almost in slow motion with his chin coming gently to rest on the top of his chest. Instinctively Blackmore had drawn his pistol with lightning speed and proceeded to scan the misty area before him in order to identify a viable target to rain down his own personal form of instant retribution upon.

The fact that his stricken comrade did not instantly fall to the ground beside him might well have been enough to register in his peripheral vision for a second, but to be distracted enough into being forced to deviate completely from his instinctive action as a highly trained soldier by the occurrences of the next few seconds was a completely new experience for the battle hardened detective that left the blood in his veins running as cold as an icy stream. Bass raised his head and tilted it back slightly while inhaling deeply.

Blackmore noticed as he looked on incredulously at events unfolding before him that his partner's eyes had turned totally black within their sockets, whites and all. He also observed that Bass' whole body had tensed as if he were experiencing some kind of excruciating pain or discomfort, understandable in the circumstances, he supposed.

He observed that the entry wound on Bass' forehead was emanating some kind of vapour and as he looked on. Now scarcely daring to contemplate what might happen next, the remnants of the projectile that had entered his colleague's head but a few moments previously exited from the wound that it had caused and fell harmlessly to the ground.

"That was quite possibly the single most excruciatingly painful experience of my life" was Bass' deadpan, almost comedic opening sentence.

"Please, my brother, for your own safety I ask you to stand aside."

"TIBERIUS, PLEASE DO AS HE BIDS AT ONCE AND ACCEPT ALL THAT TRANSPIRES DURING THE NEXT FEW MINUTES AS IF IT WERE THE GENESIS OF A NEW ERA OF EVOLUTION FOR JAMES BASS, AND LIKEWISE FOR THE LEAGUE OF GHOSTS."

Pontius Aston had joined Blackmore and laid a strong, steadying hand on the transfixed detective's right shoulder as he spoke.

"Lower your pistol, Tiberius. Look on with impunity and compassion as you accept that in James' mind what seemingly random actions may transpire from this moment forth were a total last resort on his part, and could not be avoided."

Just as Blackmore was about to reply he heard and observed a sight that he'd never expected, or indeed hoped to experience again. The sound of bone and sinew cracking and re-setting to suit larger, more pronounced and muscled limbs. The long, razor sharp claws that emanated from elongated fingers. The snout that protruded from the familiar and beloved human face of his brother, before his very eyes, that housed an array of gnashing, drooling teeth and the blood curdling, heart stopping howl that sent a cold shiver down his spine. The unmistakeable howl of a wolf.

"Holy Mother of God!" exclaimed Blackmore, now rocked back on his heels at the sight of the eight-foot-tall white beast that stood but a few feet away from him.

"If I had not witnessed such an occurrence once before I'd never have thought this was possible," he continued with a few tears making their way down his craggy, battle scarred features.

Aston began to speak as the great white werewolf readied itself to pursue its intended 'prey', as the fleeing Baron had now unwittingly become.

"See how he noses the air in anticipation as if to catch the scent of his mark. Speak to him fondly, Tiberius; wish him God speed and a safe return for he remains our James Bass."

Blackmore addressed the wolf with just two short emotionally charged and heartfelt sentences…

"JAMES. JAMES BASS, for you are undoubtedly him. Go now with God on your side and come back safe to us, you old stogie chomper."

The great white werewolf turned around sharply from facing outwards over the Cromford mire upon recognising the voice of a long and trusted friend.

The moment its black, seemingly soulless eyes fixed upon the familiar forms of both Tiberius Blackmore and Pontius Aston, a monumentally loud roar emanated from deep within the body of the beast as if this were the only method it possessed of communicating an affirmative or possibly even grateful response to the glad tidings Blackmore had just a brief moment ago offered.

Then turning once more towards the mire the wolf took one mighty standing leap of ten feet or more forwards and upwards in one simultaneous motion onto the top of the low stone boundary wall between the canal towpath and the marsh. For a few seconds more Bass perched there as he nosed the crisp, clean night air for a scent that would lead him back onto the Baron's blood trail.

A proud, muscular, possibly even handsome specimen, Blackmore thought.

As the cold evening rain rested its droplets of water on the wolf's pure white fur like a diamond encrusted shroud that glistened brightly in the full moonlight, Blackmore was well aware, however, that what stood before them was a feral, untameable wild beast that, though assurances had been made to the contrary by several knowledgeable parties many times of late, was still nonetheless almost certainly capable of the most random acts of savagery and murder if the stoic resolve of James Bass loosened control over the wolf spirit within him for the briefest of moments.

Both Blackmore and Aston looked out over the wall as Bass let out a howl to chill the blood of any person and took a mighty leap into the branches of a knurled old tree that grew twenty or thirty feet tall about seven or eight feet into the mire. As the two colleagues looked on, at first entrenched within the stunned silence of their own thoughts as

124

these curious events unfolded before them, the wolf used a network of trees whose roots had forced their way out of the grip of the mire and gave the impression themselves of disembodied, walking spirits held aloft by the night mist, as its aerial pathway to leap effortlessly between them in order to avoid falling into the cold and deadly grip of the cloying mud trap below.

While this most surreal of scenes played out on the stage set before them, the familiar sound of high-pitched screeching heralded the arrival of a dense murmuration of vampyre bats, bearing at its centre the dark barely visible form of Beatrice Aston into the fray. Pontius Aston was the first of the two companions to speak...

"Behold, Tiberius. Beatrice joins the hunt. Look on in wonderment and anticipation of the limitless possibilities for the future as we witness the evolution of our species acting out its part to perfection before our very eyes."

Blackmore's reply was immediate and equally as relevant in its truthful assessment of the situation as that of Aston's.

"But we see before us two highly disciplined and trained minds, proven to be extremely strong-willed individuals both and capable of holding their respective demon spirits in check, and so we all expect and hope that they shall be able to continue to do so.

"We have recently, however, experienced the negative effect the unfettered, rampant, uncontrolled spirit has forced upon a hapless soul. Remember that pitiful creature Yuri Tokalev whose light we were compelled to extinguish in the Whitechapel 'maze' had not the mental capacity or stubborn resolve of a James Bass or a Beatrice Aston to keep his demon in check.

"For every James Bass or every Beatrice Aston whose identity we might be able to discover, then take the time to nurture and educate accordingly in the discipline of controlling their affliction, for it must ultimately be regarded as being such, there might exist a thousand, ten thousand, a million or more blood demons or Tokalevs that will require instantly retiring with extreme and merciless prejudice."

"Indeed, Tiberius. Your counter logic offered as an alternative method of resolution to a conflict of perspectives between colleagues on a debated theme of great importance as usual is flawless and offers the sound argument that common sense once more should prevail over fanciful notions and whimsical folly," Aston began.

"One might even assume that such controlled discipline of the mind that we now bear witness to wresting within our beloved Beatrice and James respectively may well be a trait of mental strength unique only to them alone or perhaps to a selectively small group of individuals that might yet still exist. At any rate we must approach any new such anomaly as being first and foremost hostile and therefore liable to instant termination unless proven otherwise."

"Agreed, Pontius, but proven very quickly!" exclaimed Blackmore with a knowing wink cast in the direction of his companion as he patted the left breast of his overcoat under which his Le Mat revolver was holstered.

"It is a simple mantra that has served both James and myself very well for many years and shall continue to do so by the continued application of stoic resolve, streetwise awareness, human courage, the good grace of God and a steady, true pistol hand."

"Much of what you say is true, gentlemen, on both counts."

Blackmore and Aston turned swiftly on their heels, pistols instinctively un-holstered, cocked and ready to open fire on their random intruder.

Beatrice Aston had touched down silently as would a feather borne by the lightest breeze behind her totally unaware husband and his colleague, and continued to speak in a calm, controlled manner...

"Please curb your still most impressive warrior instincts, my fine fellow Ghosts. They are not at this precise moment needed and, I'm sorry to say, would serve you little purpose if they were."

"Beatrice, my love," began Aston as he approached his wife, took her in a welcoming, relieved embrace and kissed her tenderly on each cheek. "What news of the search?"

"As you see before you James continues his 'rather enthusiastic' but nonetheless extremely effective combing of the Cromford mire but alas it will be to no avail. Baron von Waldheim has somehow made good his escape, even accounting for the fact he is wounded and to our minds had little chance of absconding from justice – his meticulous plans have obviously included a remarkably effective escape strategy. He will not on this day be found."

Just as Aston was about to answer his wife, Beatrice raised her right hand as if to halt his words and continued...

"Grant me a moment longer if you please, my husband. As I said earlier, to some extent you are both correct with regards to the so-called evolution of our race.

I feel that we must approach any contact with anomalies such as myself, James, the Clavel creature or whatever else might manifest itself before us in the future with the caution that Tiberius suggests, otherwise we must be prepared to suffer the catastrophic consequences that will undoubtedly follow if we leave them unchecked.

"Look upon that magnificent creature beyond the wall as he leaps effortlessly from bough to bough in a seemingly random manner as would any untamed, wild beast. Except his movements and his actions are not random at all. Nor are they the spontaneous actions of a confused, unordered or murderously brutal mind. James is somehow able to channel all of his intense training, all of his experiences shared with yourself, Tiberius and Phineas during your distinguished military careers and all of his formidable physical and mental strength into harnessing the power of the lycanthrope's spirit that wrests for control over his human soul and when called upon using that power as a force for good, able to offer the seemingly hopeless scenario advantage and hope where there was previously little or none and to ultimately remain true to the human spirit of James Bartholomew Bass; a true guardian of The League Of Ghosts.

"Now might I suggest we rendezvous with our colleagues back at the High Peak Junction station house to recount our reports of what has transpired this evening, for I fear that there is little more to be achieved by any of us here in this place."

"I must reluctantly concur, Beatrice," agreed Blackmore displaying the resolute manner of acceptance that their situation needed fresh direction and perspective. "But what of James? Does he continue his search still convinced that a successful outcome will ensue or is he resigned to the fact that on this particular occasion justice will not be served on the guilty as it should have been" was his question to Beatrice. Pontius Aston answered almost immediately...

"The lycanthrope's search will run its course as would any meticulous search that might be carried out by his human counterpart James Bass," he began. "The initial adrenaline rush of the chase and the anticipation of success, then the stark realisation that failure to apprehend the mark is more than a distinct possibility, are the very real emotions shared by both the human and lycan spirits within him. His frustrations will be as real as yours or mine would be, Tiberius, when confronted by what any one of us would view as total failure to complete what was deemed to be such an important mission."

Aston's words were met with nothing more than a silent knowing look, a wry grin and a raised eyebrow of acknowledgement from Blackmore that told the Captain his logic had been processed and understood perfectly by the old detective. Never a man to utter a word in excess unless absolutely necessary, Blackmore's answer was as short and conclusive as he deemed necessary in the circumstances...

"Please allow me a moment to gather James' belongings that were not torn into ribbons and discarded during his metamorphosis and we shall tarry not a moment longer in this desolate place."

Turning back in the direction of the High Peak Junction station house the three comrades began their short half mile or so walk back along the canal towpath. In the ensuing melee that had erupted not fifteen short minutes previously all around them a pitch black darkness whose enveloping cloak was unhindered by the subtle glow of any nearby town's light pollution nor any star or bright moonlit night had fallen, but nevertheless their pathway was un-naturally illuminated more than adequately by the still intensely burning wreckage of the Leawood pumping station that raged on and remained still as yet unchallenged by any bold firefighting team on the opposite bank of the canal.

Pausing for a moment to face the fire, its incredible heat almost scorching their faces so close were they to its intense radiance, Aston and Blackmore stared directly into the fire's dancing wraiths as if attempting to draw some meaningful conclusion to the evening's curious events. Aston was the first to speak, glib humour being the only significant nuance he could muster from within his mind that was of any use at this particular moment in time.

"Would one be correct in observing that this trail of mayhem and devastation is a regular occurrence with regards to the outcome of yours and James' cases, Tiberius?" he questioned dryly.

"Oh no, Pontius, not at all. Absolutely not," Blackmore lied unconvincingly.

"No. No, my very dear friend, never, well perhaps very, very rarely. Perchance on just the one, possibly two, but on no more than three or four previous occasions when our enthusiasm has got the better of us.

Purely in the best interests of reaching a favourable and just conclusion to our case, you understand."

Aston raised a knowing eyebrow in Blackmore's direction and gave a wistful smile conveying to the detective that the wily old Captain was well aware of the distinct possibility that the conclusion of a great many of their cases followed a similarly destructive pattern. He was just about to answer Blackmore's attempted explanation of events when his wife cut him completely to the chase.

"Gentlemen, I believe that I have discovered the present whereabouts of our werewolf colleague."

Blackmore and Aston turned from the warming fire and joined Beatrice at the wall opposite what remained of the Leawood pumping station. As they looked down to the near river bank, some fifteen feet below the wall, crouched on a rocky outcrop that jutted out into the dark water of a river into which he seemed to be staring intently was the completely naked, extremely grubby and yet totally familiar human form of James Bass.

"A lovely evening for a moonlight dip, James," quipped Blackmore.

"You rather seem to have misplaced your bathing suit though I notice."

"Tiberius, Pontius and Beatrice," offered a clearly exhausted Bass. "Please excuse my state of undress as I seem to have misplaced both my everyday garments and lately my fur coat and I do this moment feel the cold night air around my nether regions somewhat."

"I am at the very least able to assist with one of your discarded garments, James" was Blackmore's reply as he rolled up and tossed Bass' heavy overcoat downwards and into the grateful arms of his colleague.

"Your brandy, smokes and dry matches are still inside the usual coat pocket. I surmised that you would require both as soon as possible," he concluded reassuringly.

"You are not incorrect on that score, Tiberius, my very good friend. A thousand grateful thanks. I shall imbibe a copious amount of brandy, smoke a stogie to warm my chilled bones and join you all in a moment."

Within five minutes of his final words tapering off into the night air, Bass joined his companions on the short walk back along the canal towpath to the Cromford station house whereupon they rendezvoused with the remainder of their group. Greetings were immediately exchanged between the assembled 'Ghosts' and as Bass and Constance broke from a fond, and somewhat relieved embrace on the part of Constance, it was Bass who was the first one of the group to speak.

"Connie, fellow Ghosts. It warms my heart to be here with you all once more. Connie, my dearest love, I was forced to call upon the lycan spirit that dwells within my soul to aid in our endeavours to ensnare the Baron.

"Alas even though Beatrice summoned forth her vampiric hordes in an attempt to assist the wolf in its hunt our endeavours proved fruitless. Somehow the Baron factored a cunning escape route into his plans that could not be thwarted even by the keen attentions of both vampire and werewolf. I would like to be excused for a moment and attempt to wash the stink of failure away and access the valise of fresh apparel that you have brought along in order to re-establish my modesty."

Beatrice Aston continued to deliver their portion of the report as Bass left the room.

"There is little more to divulge concerning our failed efforts other than to draw stark conclusion that a man, a quite badly wounded man no less, whom one might have assumed had been weakened to the point of exhaustion by his wound and the copious blood loss that he undoubtedly sustained, should therefore and to all intents and purposes have been a simple arrest proves to us in the definitive moment that his is an intellect and a constitution of superior quality.

"A remarkable individual who possesses reserves of great physical strength and is able to remain resolutely calm and rational when forced to make key decisions in the face of seemingly impossible odds stacked against him suggesting a highly trained and disciplined mind.

"A man too capable, in some fantastic way known for the present only to himself, of totally nullifying what should have been both an exceptionally clear blood trail for the vampire to follow and an equally strong scent that the wolf was able to track. The Baron is an exceptional individual whom we dare not underestimate for a second time."

"Indeed we shall not allow him to escape justice again Beatrice."

Bass had re-joined his colleagues, his modesty fully restored by donning a fresh suit of clothes from the carpet bag valise his wife had brought along with her, the mud and disappointment of his recent exploits washed away in the cold, clear water of the Cromford canal. Puffing out grey rings of smoke that seemed to hang in the cold and now very still evening air for an age before melting into the mist as he took long pulls of the finest Indian tobacco from the stogie he was smoking, Bass continued...

"We should be grateful at least to Pontius, Phineas, Leopold and Beatrice for the apprehension of the Heinrich creature. I look forward to hearing a full account of how the most successful part of our mission was undertaken and concluded as we make our way back to London."

"London, James?" questioned Tiberius. "Would it not serve us better to continue our pursuit in these parts while we might still align ourselves to some remnant of a trail that might still exist? Perhaps the psychic compass might be of use to us..."

Blackmore's sentence was curtailed somewhat abruptly by Bass' instant reply...

"Forgive me, Tiberius but the psychic compass would in all probability reveal to us, in some small part anyhow, what I already now believe to be solid fact. Baron von Waldheim will make with all haste to the one place where he would feel truly safe. A place he will consider a sanctuary, hidden even from our own agents' resourceful detections, a place that has eluded our major attentions this ten years past until this very moment when the clarity of all things becomes so obvious to me. He will make for eighty-nine Manning Place in the centre of Whitechapel, which lies but a short traverse through Millers Court."

"Of course," interjected Blackmore. "The very court in Whitechapel where the horribly mutilated remains of Mary Kelly were discovered, publicised nationwide to be the ripper's final victim by an establishment desperate to bury a case that had already become something of an almost overwhelming embarrassment to it...

"But alas not by we two, Tiberius," Bass continued as he turned to address The League of Ghosts.

"I truly believe that beyond all reasonable doubt and assessing the evidence that myself and Tiberius gathered on our journey to this place that we can finally bring the case of the Whitechapel ripper to its final and just conclusion."

Chapter 22

'Autumn 1898 II...
A Moment's Digression Revisited'

~ **Present Day** ~

"**A** nd now, my love it is time to pay my due owed for the other half of your penny, for I do believe you will consider it a penny well spent. If you might recall the case of the Whitechapel ripper ten years past, the infamous case that Tiberius and I were commissioned to the Metropolitan Police force and specifically tasked by her Majesty's government to solve after months of fruitless labour and toil by the existing, seemingly incompetent, hierarchy."

"A case the conclusion of which eluded even yours and Tiberius' meticulous attentions, James" was Constance's reply.

"Alas not so, Connie" was Bass' surprising retort. "Our initial investigations proved most fruitful in that they yielded to us both the identity of the Whitechapel ripper, his accomplice and the motive for their heinous crimes, largely with thanks to the meticulous report that was submitted by your good self, if you have good cause to remember, my love."

"Yes, James, I remember very well the meeting between yourself and I, Tiberius, Francis and doctors Phillips and Clark during which was ascertained that Baron Josef von Waldheim was the 'Ripper's' accomplice," exclaimed Constance.

"Even then he was using the harvested fruits of the 'Ripper's' carnage as components for his galvanised corpses."

"Indeed, Connie," continued Bass, "we are now certain that von Waldheim was, or what is more to the point, remains the loyal accomplice to Lord Augustus De-Fanque Arbogast, also known as 'Jack the Ripper'!"

Obviously mentally perturbed for a few seconds, Constance allowed herself a moment to steady herself and take full control of her thoughts and emotions before she offered any tangible response to her husband's chilling reminiscence.

"Augustus Arbogast!" she exclaimed. "He remains to this day the epitome of old London aristocracy. A respected pillar of City society. Surgeon in Chief at the Royal College of Medicine and the Guild of Surgeons, personal physician to the most elite of society and to the Royal Family and Master Mason of the United Grand Lodge of England Freemasons.

"I was proud when he became mine, and my colleagues' mentor during my tenure at the Royal College of Surgeons in London. Possessor of one of the most brilliant minds that I've ever encountered and a pioneer in many of the modern medical techniques that we take for granted today. A true innovator within his chosen field of expertise, a true nineteenth century genius. It makes no sense that one so gifted, so exalted in rank and one so well respected by his students, colleagues and peers alike could become such a psychopathic monster."

"Actually, it makes perfect sense, Connie," countered Bass immediately.

"Consider this if you will. Tiberius and I were first introduced to the questionable ethics and frequent malpractices of 'Sir Augustus the butcher' during the Russo-Turkish war of 1877-88 and please be under no illusion as to the credibility of the sobriquet that was bestowed unto him by many of all rank and station, for it was well placed.

"The man, nay, the 'abominable thing' was then, and I see no reason for his despicable demeanour to have changed to this day, that of a depraved psychopath who utilised the chaotic cover of major conflict, and his privilege of rank and title, in order to satiate an ingrained depravity from deep within and proceed to butcher and murder his way across several continents over a period of twenty or more years.

"Move forward a decade to 1888. The 'Sir' had been elevated to Lord in recognition of services rendered for Queen and country by the very establishment that was to ignore his murderous tendencies, thus enabling him to satiate his grotesque and rapidly developing perversion for murdering the unwanted and unloved street people of his next chosen hunting ground, the streets of Whitechapel. Unforgiving, isolated streets that are ripe for the picking of lost souls which few of any standing in society, or even normal life, would miss."

"So where in this fabric of depravity is von Waldheim's patch first woven, James?" questioned Constance.

"Every army field surgeon requires a trusted orderly, or in this particular case a fully qualified registrar already educated to the highest level of medical etiquette and in the most modern surgery techniques at the University of Leipzig..." Before Bass could offer the remainder of his answer Connie interjected...

"Baron Josef Von Waldheim! He was the registrar. Oh James, for decades the evil has walked freely amongst us. Down every corridor, during every lecture, dining at the highest tables of society and even enjoying the unsuspecting patronage of Royalty."

"Alas yes, Connie," answered Bass. "Two brilliant but catastrophically flawed intellects somehow segued together as one in order to fulfil each of the other's separate warped visions of their own, twisted utopias. One to satiate his own basic perversions by using his considerable surgical knowledge and skills to butcher the hapless and lost souls of whatever God forsaken place on earth his depravity led him to next, and the other to slavishly aid his mentor whilst opportunistically harvesting organs from the corpses created in order to fulfil his own twisted ambitions of furthering and developing the cult of galvanism that he had so readily and enthusiastically championed and endorsed."

"And all of this evil perpetrated whilst the bloated and largely corrupt aristocracy, from which both of this privileged pair of inbred sociopaths was spawned, observed from a distance whilst ensconced safely in their ivory towers and did nothing to eradicate its putrid stench," added Constance.

"But were not the exhaustive efforts of the law enforcement authorities in serious remission up to the moment of yours and Tiberius' introduction to proceedings?" was Connie's question to her husband.

"The Metropolitan Police force's ability to provide the solid base of investigation necessary in order for this case to be properly conducted to a satisfactory and just conclusion had been compromised and terminally undermined by the highest level of government intervention.

"This much was wholly apparent to us from the very outset of our deployment. Our commander and trusted comrade of countless incursions abroad long past, Detective Chief Superintendent Frank Abilene, formerly Colonel Francis William Abilene of the Prince Regent's Own 95th Rifle brigade, was well aware of our numerous accrued credentials and special skills acquired whilst earning the Queen's shilling and, taking a massive personal gamble as to our integrity remaining untainted by any unsavoury external source, recruited our services to the Metropolitan Police force personally, and at great risk to both himself and to his family I might add.

"To Francis William Abilene, Tiberius and I owe a great debt of gratitude, the tariff for which can only be paid for in full with either undying loyalty or blood.

"To him, we offer our utmost respect and service wholeheartedly without prejudice as we continue onwards with our ultimate quest for the real truth to be revealed and ultimate justice to prevail upon those most deserving."

All at once, Bass' demeanour changed dramatically from that of the rational and controlled individual his wife recognised as he continued on with a more agitated and quite frustrated tirade of words...

"WE HAD THEM, CONNIE! Tiberius and I. We had both of these vile, evil and twisted excuses for humanity stood directly before us, in the drawing room of 89, Manning Place. Our pistols were primed and we had the bastards at point blank range only to be stood down hard by the very government that brought us back to 'the abyss' in order to sweep the streets of these terrible atrocities.

"Orders rescinded immediately by high government office and warned that completion of the mission by means of extreme prejudice on our part would result in ourselves, our families, friends, colleagues, all we had ever worked for, all those closely associated to our actions or privy to any files concerning the case and all those we had ever loved being systematically erased from existence.

"We had little choice but to agree terms. Tiberius and I both stood down on the premise that our families, colleagues and friends would go unmolested indefinitely, depending on our total discretion remaining absolute concerning all knowledge of matters appertaining to 'the Ripper'.

"When satisfied that an agreement of sorts had been reached by both parties, we were forced to look on with dual feelings of astonishment and disgust as those two stinking pieces of fish bait continued on with their conversation as though what had just transpired moments ago was merely a frustrating and somewhat rude interruption by elements of the lower caste to their goose, port and cigar soiree."

Constance countered her husband's words with wisdom of her own immediately...

"James, my love, have you not yet perceived the obvious truth in this betrayal of sorts? Yours and Tiberius' valiant efforts were never meant, nor expected, to be rewarded with a spectacularly successful outcome. Consider this for a moment: two highly decorated, ex-army special forces operatives called upon by their respected old commander, Francis William Abilene, at the behest of Her Majesty's government are immediately set to task hunting 'Jack the Ripper'.

"After a relatively short period of time, by utilising a combination of both the massively improved forensic techniques now at their disposal and some rather quite unorthodox policing methods known only to themselves, their success in locating not merely one, but two guilty perpetrators proved a total surprise to all but themselves and their few trusted allies."

"Our bold, perfectly realised and executed campaign was doomed to failure from its very inception," added a rather dejected Bass.

"But how could it not be, James?" continued Constance.

"The highest, most exalted echelons of government and the aristocracy have always taken, and will always continue to take, very good care of themselves, whatever the economic cost, or the collateral human damage incurred as a result."

Bass fell silent for a few seconds before speaking again...

"Even taking all of what has transpired into careful consideration, both mine and Tiberius' ultimate decision would always parallel one another's. The guilty must always be held accountable for their crimes. I swear to you that we will discover a way to make these two bastards pay for what they have done, and for all that they most surely intend to do.

"So now my dear, sweet Connie, I am compelled to speak words that you would not ever want to hear emanate from my lips. The extreme actions Tiberius and I are henceforth compelled to take in the cause of true justice will bear us outside of authority's far-reaching umbrella of protection, beyond even the closed, impenetrable iron curtains of our own League of Ghosts and far away from the caress and care of our family's tender love.

"We must go forth alone, completely stripped of all emotional ties and totally unguarded deep within the belly of the beast, back to the unforgiving streets and hovels of Whitechapel, where we will seek to finally lay this festering evil bare and exposed for all to see, vanquished and broken for good.

"We will be shunned by almost all parties, hunted as would be a rabid dog by our own colleagues, ostracised from the very society that first shaped our characters and nurtured our youth, and even typecast as villains by the same media that has previously lauded our many successfully concluded exploits past.

"Arrangements will be made post-haste with Pontius and the League of Ghosts for yours, Pandora's and Alanis' safety to be made a priority; Don Blackmore will remain one of our small band of trusted allies on the street privy to our true plans, as will the Jeffersons and presently, when our scheme is set into irreversible motion, Markus Jackson."

After a brief moment of silent contemplation Constance spoke, with the faintest hint of emotion tinged with frustration audible in her usual calm and measured delivery...

"You are certain that this is the only course of action left open to you both?"

Another brief silence ensued before she continued...

"Of course it is! Who could you possibly hope to approach in authority that had not been infected by the creeping disease of corruption? As always, a meticulously reasoned strategy that will take both yourself and Tiberius to the very edge of the place where depravity and wanton brutality are very familiar bedfellows."

"On this occasion, Connie, we step over that precipice willingly and face a dark maelstrom the like of which we have never done so before. Pray for us, for I cannot promise that the outcome this time will be of a favourable nature for all concerned."

Driven on by her disciplined mind, Constance answered briefly and concisely in the only manner she felt appropriate to the moment...

"I shall pray for both of you, James and I shall also remain, albeit covertly at your request, one of your chosen band of agents as, I'm sure, will Pandora and Alanis. Now please disclose to me before we part, my dear, how you plan to proceed."

Bass took a sharp intake of breath and exhaled through pursed lips in a blowing motion, not dissimilar to that of a fatigued horse exhaling, before answering his wife's question...

"Our first action is simple, my love. We need to discredit ourselves from all levels of decent and lawful society. To ostracise ourselves completely from all we know, love and trust. To become outside of the law that we have endeavoured to serve with such courage and loyalty for so long."

He paused for a moment before disclosing the shard of information that sent an icy chill to the core of Constance Bass' bones...

"And we shall begin by killing Frank Abilene!"

Chapter 23

'A Despicable Act'

Marcus Jackson was with some reluctance attending to several of what he considered to be the more mundane tasks relating to police work. 'Better this door-to-door footwork be suited to ambitious young constables, or so it was always in my upcoming days,' he grumbled silently to himself as he crossed the threshold of the front entrance to the Leman Street police building situated in the heart of Whitechapel.

'Delegate, Marcus, learn to delegate tasks and not be such a good friend to the lower ranks. They will learn to respect authority of outstanding quality and leadership that is hallmarked by the consistent good examples set by a senior officer' was the advice he remembered from a distant conversation with one of his mentors and closest friends, namely Detective Chief Inspector Tiberius Blackmore.

'That's all well and good, Tiberius, my good friend but it eases my burning feet and aching limbs not one iota,' he continued quietly lamenting to himself as he checked around randomly for the sanctuary of an empty office, 'any free office would suffice' he mused on. "Any place in this bedlam on earth where a poor, weary, over-taxed soul might get a moment's peace and quiet!" he exclaimed out loud into the startled face of a young constable.

"No, sir, all the offices are at present occupied" was the young constable's reply. "Lots of interviews and the like going on, I shouldn't wonder, police type business I'd wager, sir," was the constable's almost sarcastic response.

Jackson eyed the constable with a serious and steely glare as he began to deliver his withering retort...

"Constable..." Jackson held on for a surname.

"Harper, sir, Jack Jonathan Harper of Bethnal Green" was the response.

"Well, constable Jack Jonathan Harper of Bethnal Green, consider yourself on report for two counts, firstly for insubordination delivered with not inconsiderable attitude to a weary senior officer whilst searching for an office to sleep in, and second, for being from Bethnal Green! Now hop it and rustle up a pot of tea please, lad, and a desk somewhere so I may at least attempt to finish my unforgivingly large backlog of paperwork," said Jackson, offering a knowing wink in the direction of the much-relieved young constable.

"Oh, one more thing, constable Harper," added Jackson as Harper turned nervously to face his superior officer.

"Keep your wagers for the bookies and not the front office, there's a good la... What is that unholy commotion coming from the chief super's office!" he exclaimed loudly to no-one in particular.

The angry raised voices of three men could be heard clearly above all the general cacophony of the station house as they cut through the ambience with the ease of a sharpened cleaver. Such was the ferocity of the verbal interplay between the three, punctuated with a profanity of language raised several levels above what might be considered 'street normal', that all business within the station, regardless of its importance, ceased immediately and all the souls within, both felon and police officer alike, were stunned into silence as they hung on to every utterance emanating from within the confines of Frank Abilene's office.

Jackson raised himself from the precious desk space he had just a minute ago procured for himself and with all the haste he could muster made for Abilene's office, which was situated at the end of a short corridor towards the rear of the station house. The words that he heard as he approached the frosted glass door of the office cut him deeply to the bone as he realised that this was about to escalate far beyond the confines of a 'heated discussion' between colleagues.

The first voice he heard clearly was that of James Bass, caught in mid-sentence. He decided to pause and listen before entering the office and offering some lame excuse for doing so, thus defusing this situation by steering raised tempers into calmer waters...or so he had supposed...

"...By God, what has happened to you, Frank? You've become a prancing, subservient puppet of the chronically corrupt establishment, the very same establishment whose bloated paymasters employ us to sprinkle a fine, sweet sugar frosting of credibility over their questionable and alarmingly frequent malpractices."

Frank Abilene was then heard to answer Bass' tirade with a levelling verbal broadside of his own...

"You arrogant, self-important, egotistical pair of mongrels. A mangy, rabid street cur would show more loyalty and respect to its abusive master than that you have latterly shown to me. Was it not I who raised you both up from the rank and file in the ninety-fifth and gave a steady course and true meaning to your then miserable lives?

"Was it not I who mentored you both through those damned pits of hell we trod, bound together as brothers to become what I perceived could ultimately be the union to end the very corruption that I fear has blinded you to the ultimate and righteous truth? I loved you both as I would my own sons and this is how you repay me.

"I curse the day that I sent for you to return in the now all too blindingly obvious forlorn hope that you'd aid me in my quest to make some kind of difference. Now go on, turn tail and get out. I would never wish to lay eyes on either of your miserable, ungrateful, tainted faces again. Consider yourselves dead to me from this moment on and fugitives from the law that you once swore to uphold."

Jackson remained rooted to the spot, paralysed by the ferocity of the exchange ensuing behind the very office door where he stood. 'I've heard altercations between the guvnors before, even borne witness to more than one heated, roof-raising barney or two settled amicably always tho over a stogie, a pipe full of finest Hindu shag baccy and a few wets of brandy but this time it was different. This was bad. This was very, very bad indeed.'

It was about to get a lot worse.

From within came an almost indecipherable dialogue between the three as their words crossed and merged together. A confusing raft of loud, intelligible and seemingly random gibberish, each man vying to be heard above the other, neither one succeeding in achieving very little towards any kind of amicable solution to this titanic rift but merely aiding between the three of them to raise the temperature and anger levels so obviously within the office to a dangerously higher plateau. This lasted a mere few seconds before the voice of Tiberius Blackmore rose up above the ranting of the other two. Jackson clearly heard Blackmore's words, emotion clearly cracking his voice as he spoke...

"Damn you, Frank. You were the guiding light we both loyally followed. A bold beacon in the darkness, the strength that we constantly craved to heave us back from the abyss. After all that we've suffered together, all of the filth we waded through together, the brotherhood we forged in order to vanquish the odds always seemingly piled high against us, always challenged to the limits of our physical endurance yet, somehow, always rising above the shit piled high above our heads to achieve ultimate and glorious victory. All, it seems, for naught."

Jackson, now beginning to tremble and experience his own emotions welling up inside him uncontrollably upon hearing this emotional tirade from Blackmore, tightened his left hand around the tactile and well-worn brass office door knob and prepared to enter, his right hand reaching across his chest for the butt of his Webley pistol that was side holstered under his left arm pit. He realised full well that in the event of any kind of gun play or if any form of martial art utilising a weapon or otherwise ensued between himself, Blackmore and Bass that he was more than a good bet for being hopelessly outmatched.

He steeled himself to enter, hoping that the element of surprise might be the edge he required to surprise the raving pair when all at once he realised in that very instant that he had been joined by a group of heavily armed constables and duty desk sergeant William Smith. Buoyed by this welcome cohort of support he immediately began to issue orders...

"The moment we enter, sergeant Smith, constables Gould and Hendricks flank left, constables Lightfoot and Perkins flank right. Shoot only on my command and remember well what we propose to do; to take down the best two there is of us in existence. Eyes open, wits sharp. On my mark, 3, 2, 1 and... GO!"

Even whilst in mid-final sentence, his hand tightening around the brass door knob, weight fully pressed against the door frame to facilitate his forceful entrance, Jackson's momentum was halted by the voice of Bass issuing a stark, concise warning to Frank Abilene, closely followed by five loud yet distinctively differently sounding cracks that could only belong to a trio of discharged heavy calibre sidearms.

"Don't you dare to reach for that stock, Frank," began the chilling warning from Bass.

"This is not the conclusion to this maelstrom of deceit, lies, conjecture and misunderstanding either you, nor Tiberius and myself would seek. We are swifter than you, trained in part by you to put down any and all threats to our personal safety and well-being with extreme prejudice, no exceptions to the rule. Don't skin that iron, Frank, or there'll be no hesitation in our next course of action, painful as it will surely be for us to carry out."

"You leave me no discernible choice to make, James. This old soldier's heart is glad that his early passing is to be brought about by your actions and not some errant, nameless stranger. May your aims be true. Farewell, my brave boys and try all ways to find a pathway back into the light and to somehow make amends. Now fire away and fall back" were Abilene's final words as his right hand lunged forward to grasp the stock of his old Webley service revolver that lay before him on the green leather topped desk separating him from Blackmore and Bass.

Needing no further prompting, nor hesitating for a second more than was necessary, both Blackmore and Bass drew a revolver from their customarily concealed side holsters and each discharged two lethally aimed lead projectiles directly into Abilene's chest, the impact from which threw his body backwards as if kicked by a rampant horse and forced the token round loosed from Abilene's revolver to harmlessly thud into the plaster ceiling above his now prone body... 'CRACK... 'CRACK' 'CRACK... 'CRACK' 'CRACK'

The office door proceeded to burst open inwardly revealing to the entering group of officers the scene of unexpected and unprecedented carnage that had unfolded a mere few seconds before. Upon witnessing the seemingly lifeless corpse of their chief superintendent, a man they had come to regard as being a respected father figure and mentor to them all, gunned down by two of the most revered and many times decorated officers both the Metropolitan police force and the British army had ever known.

The brief sliver of stunned silence and confusion within the ranks of the deploying officers that ensued was all the time Blackmore and Bass required in order to take the only logical course of action left open to them both. Not to surrender and face the ultimate penalty for murder, rather to survive. Always to survive, and live on to fight another time; to live and perhaps to die another day.

Rounding on the stunned group, four pistols were now initially raised aloft, a round from each discharged into the crumbling plaster ceiling and were then levelled expertly and swiftly, covering completely each deployed flank of the now visibly shaken young men.

"Easy, boys" came the first calming words from Blackmore. "Lower those irons if you please or St. Peter's Gate is going to be a very busy terminus on this evening. This little fracas will be explained at a time and place of our own choosing so for yours and your families' sakes stand yourselves down. Frank Abilene made his choice and the ferryman now demands his pennies. Please make the wiser choice for yourselves."

Jackson was the first one to answer Blackmore...

"Oh Tiberius, James. Was this truly the price required to be paid for any argument that could not be settled amicably, as was usually the case between brothers? This 'little fracas' to which you so glibly refer, Tiberius, has resulted in the fatal wounding of our father. How could you both be a party to this abomination? How and by what twisted reasoning on God's earth could this debacle ever be conceived to happen? WHY!" he concluded, the emotion clearly altering the timbre of his voice, tears streaming down each of his cheeks, not only for his fallen captain, but also because he realised that he must now endeavour to bring the entire resources of the Metropolitan police force together in order to hunt down two of the men he had come to respect over any other in the whole world, if he was to survive the next few moments, of course.

"Stand easy, Marcus," began Bass as he levelled one of his pistols to aim directly between Jackson's eyes. "Tiberius and I will now take our leave. I would ask you all to stand aside and allow us good, unhindered passage well beyond this building's outer boundary marker before you consider any notion of pursuit."

Just as Bass began to move towards Jackson, he continued addressing the younger detective inspector whom, he sensed, was beginning to gather his wits after the chaos that had just ensued. 'An experienced senior officer, in full control of his considerable capability to command could prove a tricky proposition presently,' Bass reasoned to himself.

"Please forgive me for what I am about to do, Marcus, but confusion and lack of command within your ranks must remain of paramount importance for the next few minutes."

When Bass had Jackson well within the confines of his own personal space he raised his right arm high across his chest and with the sweeping motion and power of a master swordsman utilising a cross-cutting, sweeping stroke brought the full weight of his pistol down onto the detective inspector's unprotected clavicle.

An instant, searing pain electrified what felt like every nerve ending in Jackson's body as he quite clearly heard the right side of his clavicle bone snap under the weight of Bass' brutal, hefty blow. Falling immediately to the ground, he was momentarily aware of Bass stooping to within whispering earshot of his prone body. As consciousness conspired to leave him helpless, he heard Bass clearly address him...

"I am so very sorry, Marcus. Listen to and understand my words very carefully before unconsciousness envelopes you; we need you to take care of Frank's body personally, no exceptions. Trust no-one but the people closest to you who are specifically known by yourself to possess guaranteed integrity and take great care to vet meticulously the provenance of their credentials thoroughly before engaging any assistance. All details appertaining to this conundrum will be revealed in detail at the League of Ghosts' headquarters in four days' time. Now off to sleep and heal well, my very good friend."

Jackson was conscious just long enough to overhear Bass addressing Blackmore as they proceeded to move beyond the confines of Abilene's office...

"A brief stop to liberate my old 'yellow boy Winchester', the shotgun too I think for your personal use, my brother, and we'll be set to flee this coop of clucking chickens. Cover to the rear, Tiberius if you please..."

"CLEAR!" came the reply from Blackmore.

"Cover to the front and flanks, James," barked Blackmore as the two experienced soldiers began utilising an exit strategy plan that they had used time and time again during many incursions together behind hostile enemy lines.

"CLEAR!" was the instant echo from Bass...

All the while, as they moved with the grace of classical dancers across the surface area of the station house, covering each other's escape with the graceful movement and counter-movement of the well drilled special forces operatives they were, the two detectives discharged rounds from their pistols in order to confuse the more experienced duty officers and to terrify the civilians present, but curiously not, or so it seemed, with any intention to injure anyone.

Confused thoughts drifting around inside his aching head akin to the pieces of a jigsaw whose correct places within the puzzle remain frustratingly unfathomable, Jackson focussed on what he considered to be the key sentence in the words Bass had but this last few seconds past imparted to him... 'trust no-one'. Time and again, over and over again he repeated these words to himself and wondered, 'why trust no-one, why? trust...no-one..."

Then all at once, as the searing pain emanating from his broken bones finally enveloped his clouded senses, darkness...

Chapter 24

'Welcome Home, Boys' 'Autumn 1888'

~ 10 years Prior ~

In the late autumn of 1888 the Tower Hamlets borough of Whitechapel and its neighbours Spitalfields and Bethnal Green up to the point where Middlesex Street marked the boundary line between the East and West End of London were still enveloped, and being systematically terrorised to its very foundations by the continuing reign of terror being perpetrated by a multiple 'serial' murderer, given the macabre pseudonym by an ever-excitable media of 'Jack the Ripper'.

Crossing the threshold of Leman Street police station for the first time, or more to the point for the very first time as duly appointed officers of the law and not as the wayward pair of habitual miscreants responsible for perpetrating any number of unsavoury deeds in and around the district of Whitechapel many years previously, held little in the way of trepidation nor prompted any feelings of anxiety or nervousness in the demeanours of either Major James Bartholomew Bass or his colleague of long standing for many years, Commander Alan Tiberius Blackmore.

As they crossed the oak, parquet-patterned floor of the station house and made directly for the front desk the two colleagues allowed themselves a few seconds to reminisce...

"Do you recall the last time we were invited under this most auspicious roof, James?" Blackmore enquired.

"If memory serves an old soldier well enough, we were cordially invited to partake of free board and lodgings, at Her Majesty's gracious pleasure, in order to assist the fine and true officers of law enforcement herein with their ongoing enquiries into several of our, shall we say, questionable, many and varied extracurricular activities in and around 'the abyss' I believe, Tiberius." Bass answered with a clear recount of a grim and distant memory that surprised even him.

'The abyss' was the name given to an infamous group of streets in the Whitechapel area, namely Dorset Street, Thawl Street, Flower Street and Dean Street. The extremely deprived and overcrowded slums where Jack the Ripper began his murderous, and mercifully short, spree of what were at first believed to be random killings.

Striding up to the front desk with the confident gait of a disciplined soldier, Blackmore made direct eye contact with the young desk sergeant on duty and began to speak...

"My name is Commander Alan Tiberius Blackmore; this scruffy, furtive looking reprobate answers to the title of Major James Bartholomew Bass. Formerly both of the Prince Consort's own 95th Rifles and orphans late of these stinking streets that surround us as would a cheap Petticoat Lane suit; and what name are you generally known by?"

"Sergeant Marcus Jackson, Commander, sir. Very pleased to make both of your acquaintances. We've been briefed that your arrival was imminent. How may I assist you both?"

"Set us fair in the direction of Frank Abilene, a copious cache of Hindu shag baccy and a large decanter of quality Italian brandy, if you please, Sergeant Marcus Jackson" came the instant request from the scruffy, furtive looking reprobate.

Beckoning to his right and down a corridor that bisected the rear section of the station house, Jackson continued...

"Traverse this corridor to its end and you'll find the chief billeted in the last office along to the left."

"Much obliged, Sergeant, agreeable to make your acquaintance," said Blackmore as he offered a large, knarled hand for Jackson to shake. Bass nodded his own greeting silently but still offered his right hand to Jackson's right hand in a clasp of friendship. As the pair began their short journey to the office of Detective Chief Superintendent Frank Abilene, Jackson's crucial first impressions of Leman Street's two new detective inspectors were very favourable indeed.

Francis William Abilene welcomed Bass and Blackmore's arrival with the strong clasped handshake and hearty bear hug reserved for long-standing, trusted brothers in arms.

"James, Tiberius, it gladdens this old soldier's heart to have you beside me on the battlefield once more. I thank you for rallying to my call, though I fear that as your new commission to this division develops and unfolds presently you may both have cause to offer me little by way of thanks in return.

"Sit you both down, sup a brandy or two and smoke a stogie with your old commander whilst he divulges the reason for your recall back into the eye of this shithole of despair and depravity."

"Nought of significant importance has altered on the home front, then, Frank," alluded Blackmore as he waved away the offer of a fine imported Indian stogie in favour of filling himself a pipe full of the finest Hindu Shag tobacco from the leather pouch he always carried about his person and helped himself to a generous tumbler of Italian brandy.

"Alas, Tiberius, nought has altered but for matters appertaining directly to the gradual and systematic decline of my powers with regards to maintaining and delivering fair and swift justice for the decent people of our borough. I'm assuming that you are both familiar with the ongoing case of the Whitechapel ripper that grips our community within its iron fist of terror and has done so for a good many weeks now.

"What you are probably not aware of is the burgeoning media campaign designed in order to raise public feeling to a general level of unrest and dissatisfaction with both the Metropolitan and City police forces' methods in regards to the management of the case.

"So well informed and regularly reported to the public is the lack of progress on our part that a level of what can best be described as working-class anarchy is being nurtured on our streets by organised stewards who seem to be well schooled in the dark arts of cobblestone politics and street corner, soap box oration. Very influential and dangerous tools if used in a certain manner."

Bass took a long pull on his stogie and proceeded to expertly fashion undulating rings of grey smoke into the air as he reached for another tumbler of Italian brandy. He sat in quiet contemplation for a few seconds before he began to speak...

"Working class anarchy, street corner politics, soap box oration; nothing new of note to ponder here, Frank. The imminent rise of trade unions within the workplace is offering common people a voice of hope for their protection and rights of decency that can now be clearly heard above the clatter of factory machines and the inane chatter and braying of privileged wealth within the ivory towers of management, aristocracy and government chambers alike.

"Whether or not the flatulent, greedy hordes bloated by their wealth and prosperity choose to listen to that voice is subject matter for another feisty debate, on another more appropriate occasion.

"The anarchy of which you speak is a product of the oppression and poverty from which it gestates, as would a rampant Japanese knotweed that, if left unattended, would spread and strangle anything of common use or beauty.

"Your 'Jack the Ripper' is nothing more than a catalyst, depending on how you would perceive to view this theory I propose of course. A convenient anomaly used to fan a flame that burned already, albeit as little more than an ember at the start.

"His presence serves a specific purpose in that if it is managed in a skilful way by a very sharply educated mind, and I also add to this the manipulation of the media being used in order to discredit those of us who would know the truth of this sordid affair, then, Frank, your cycle of anarchy and unrest is complete and the working class are mercilessly put down and made docile, ripened so as to be manipulated and fed whatever mis-information a government, or even possibly a hitherto unforeseen outside third-party influence, would see fit to use in order to hide the corruption that festers within its contaminated corridors of power."

Abilene drained the tumbler of brandy he held in his right hand, sat back in his green leather wing-backed Chesterfield chair and let out a huge sigh, possibly because he had finally discovered a pair of allies both wily, experienced and fool-hardy enough to aid him in his quest for the ultimate truth but most probably because the truth he sought was very likely to be of a nature that he had always privately feared.

"Ah, my boys. My brave, brave boys. I kept an eye on your progress up through the ranks, hoping you'd both survive the horrors I knew you'd have to face in the wide, unforgiving world, looking forward, possibly in some perverse way, to seeing you back here in 'the abyss' with old Frank Abilene, attempting once more to 'make a difference'!

"I called you both back here because my hands are tightly bound, by both toxic, petty bureaucratic meddling and most probably by the very government that employs us to protect its citizens. All the avenues of enquiry that my experience and confidence oblige me to explore are either systematically closed down or yield little or no tangible evidence that can be utilised in order to build a credible case file of any note. Thus, the media is compelled, or more to the point in actual fact cleverly manipulated, into feeding information to the hitherto largely unsuspecting public that instigates the counter-productive atmosphere that festers at present on our streets."

"And what precisely would you expect of us, Frank?" questioned Blackmore as he puffed away sagely on his old clay pipe.

"Our methods of investigation are crude, some might say barbaric even when examined in the context of what is required to be the correct protocol adhered to by police officers employed in the service of the crown during this last quarter of a rapidly evolving century where commerce, industry, government and how even basic morals are perceived within the public domain. A code of 'political correctness' is developing to which, one day very soon, we all must surely embrace and adhere to.

"James and I were raised up hard on these streets, Frank, as you well know. We are able to go deep inside 'the abyss' and melt away into its darkest recesses , as would a spectre skulk unseen in the shadows until the moment of its own choosing, in order to expose your 'Jack the Ripper' but be under no illusion to the contrary, the evidence that will be gathered as we strive to uncover the final truth of this matter may not be to either the media's, the government's, the aristocracy's or even to your taste.

"Remember this well as you prepare to let loose these two seasoned 'dogs of war' onto the streets, my friend, that it was you who called us back and it is you, along with we two of course, who will ultimately answer for the consequences of our actions."

Abilene was quick to answer...

"Yes, indeed, Tiberius. My motivation when making the final decision to ask for your return was well considered and sound within its reasoning. I required you to operate impartially and without the merest hint of prejudice, as two individuals unaffected by the possibility of any outside agencies influence upon your integrity, to utilise your knowledge of Whitechapel that remains ingrained deep within you both and to employ the raft of special skills I am well aware that you've acquired whilst posted abroad earning the Queen's shilling. Remarkable, dark skills my boys herein do not possess.

"I have two officially sanctioned commissions for the rank of Detective Inspector here in writing and signed by our chief commissioner himself, Sir Charles Warren, to be activated with immediate effect from the moment of your arrival. Needless to say, you will have my full support and in addition you will be able to call on all of the resources that you require, or mores to the point that you feel you can trust, belonging to both the Metropolitan Police and city police forces combined to aid you in your efforts to solve this case."

The two newly appointed Detective Inspectors raised themselves up from their respective seats. Bass wasted no time in making his first official demand.

"We'll require full case files detailing every scrap of information collated for each murder thus far attributed to 'The Ripper' and separate files with regards to any incidents that you might have considered connected to the case in any way."

"Anything else?" questioned Abilene.

"We'd appreciate no mention of our black ops background be made, if you please, Frank. Conventional military involvement perhaps by way of an introduction to your staff but after our decommissioning from the Prince Regent's own Hussars when we were systematically selected to serve in Queen Victoria's newly commissioned special black operations unit, named Covert Special Forces, any file appertaining to our posting or rank thereafter ceased to be. To all intents and purposes, we became ghosts in order to be able to accomplish some of the more, how shall we say, questionable tasks that the military were expected to perform on occasion" was the answer given by Blackmore.

"Good, then let us away immediately to our first port of call, Tiberius," began Bass.

"A strategy forming so soon in that keen tactical mind of yours, James?" came the direct response from Blackmore.

"Not so much a strategy, Tiberius. More of a notion that we should first pay a call on the one person who might be expected to yield some valuable information with regards to aiding our enquiries, after administering a little unorthodox persuasion from two very old friends, of course" was the response from Bass.

Blackmore eyed his colleague with almost an air of resigned acceptance present in his facial expression from under the brim of his weather-beaten old bowler hat as he groaned...

"No, James, please God no, not Billy Verlaine. A more indignant, malignant, offensive, base, waste of human space I've yet to encounter on my extensive travails, and my travails as you well know, James, have taken me far and wide. An encounter with the self-appointed baron of 'the abyss' so soon is destined to end in only one way considering the outcome of events the last time our paths crossed. This will most definitely not end well!"

Bass was swift to answer...

"Ah, but I'd wager on the bad blood that exists between the two of you working to our advantage, Tiberius. Many years ago, you already possessed the street acumen and whatever basic skills that you had accrued whilst living hand to mouth as we two did for many years outdoors on those unforgiving cobbles.

"You now possess more than enough of the skills necessary to best Verlaine with ease in whatever type of combat he might see fit to choose and, if you can resist the temptation that will surely manifest itself for you to end his miserable existence once and for all, force him to owe us a substantial favour in exchange for that very same miserable existence to continue on for a little longer."

"Persuade Billy Verlaine to turn police informant!" Blackmore uttered incredulously whilst shaking his head.

"Part of me wishes for him to decide that he'd rather die than turncoat towards the law. However, I do see the logic in your suggested plan, James. I'm pretty certain that he'd have known some, indeed if not all, 'the Ripper's' poor, hapless victims and want an end to this ongoing reign of terror himself. For a worthless pimp the like of Verlaine, the longer this situation continues, the worse his whore peddling business suffers through the lack of casual footfall it requires to flourish."

"Excellent, then let us tarry not a moment longer, my friend," said Bass as he opened the office door and beckoned for his still grumbling colleague to exit first.

As the two newly appointed detectives turned to leave the office, they were halted briefly by Abilene's parting words to them both...

"Remember, boys, you are now officially regarded as commissioned law enforcement officers, answerable in action to the chief of this office, namely myself! Go steady, boys, take great care and God's speed to you both."

Both Blackmore and Bass turned back to face Abilene briefly before Blackmore offered his parting sentence...

"And you mark this well, if it pleases you to do so, Frank. I reiterate once more that it was you that called upon us to return, in order to assume the responsibility of becoming the covert harbingers of your wrath. We shall ultimately prevail but you must give to us, without hindrance from any official channels hereafter, the run of the street."

Abilene eyed them both knowingly and as they left uttered incoherently under his breath...

'And God help anyone or anything that offers the will to hamper their progress. What on earth have I been forced to unleash upon an unprepared city...'

Just as Abilene began to shift his focus in order to deal with the thousand and one other matters on file that demanded his attention, Bass appeared at his office door...

"One more thing, Frank. We'll require the use of an office, privacy being of paramount importance, if you please."

Without looking up from the plethora of notes and case files that he had laid out before him, or even bothering to speak, Abilene raised his right thumb and in a backwards motion over his right shoulder gesticulated to his rear.

As Blackmore and Bass strode towards the exit that led out into Leman Street, Bass was the first to air his immediate thoughts...

"We'll make Miller's Court our first port of call. I'd wager that even after all these years Verlaine would still be arrogant enough to hold court and govern his loyal acolytes from somewhere within the underbelly of his own little shit pot of a kingdom. He shouldn't be too difficult to locate.

"Oh, just to clarify a point, Tiberius, do you still carry about your person that rather well-used pair of brass..."

Bass was halted in mid-sentence by a disturbance that was systematically unfolding within the station house. A pair of desperate looking individuals had broken free from the restraining arm locks put on them by their stunned young constable escorts and were proceeding to wreak all sorts of havoc in their attempt to vacate the premises.

Without requiring or indeed wasting precious seconds waiting for any instruction as to how one should proceed in order to defuse such an incident, Bass and Blackmore, each man reacting to the situation instinctively with highly trained synchronised movement whilst displaying all the swiftness and grace of a hummingbird in flight, removed a Webley service revolver, turned in hand so as to use the gun butt as a cudgel, and a pair of well-worn brass knuckle dusters respectively from concealment beneath their heavy tweed overcoats, and using a combination of dextrous, almost graceful movement in order to place themselves in a prime position to do so, and utilising the skills they had each honed to perfection whilst serving in the military, proceeded to administer several harsh and unanswerable blows with pinpoint accuracy upon chosen key areas of the two miscreants' bodies, rendering them both incapacitated almost immediately.

Blackmore emitted a loud, shrill whistle through gritted teeth that cut through the atmosphere of chaos as would a sharpened knife through a side of raw beef and captured any straying attention left within the station house not yet already totally transfixed by the whirlwind of activity that had just occurred. His orders, barked out with the authority of the experienced commander that he undoubtedly was and displaying the irked tone of a superior officer who sought to make an instant impression upon the seemingly lacklustre staff he and his colleague would henceforth command, were meant specifically for all present to hear clearly...

"In future, any and all suspects, be they man or woman, regardless of rank, station or title, is to be brought before this desk with hands clasped tightly behind their backs in irons. My colleague and I would expect children to pose no such threat to this station's security."

Turning his attention to the two arresting officers who were standing before him mute, agape and embarrassed, from whom the pair of miscreants had escaped, Blackmore's orders appeared to be meant as a calming lesson in professional deportment and disciplinary procedure, rather than the brutal rebuke that they might have expected from a superior officer...

"Easy lads, no harm done. Now put these two pieces of damaged rubbish in irons and quick about it, mind, they're taking to bleeding all over this rather fine parquet floor."

The two constables looked around as if to catch the eye of a superior officer for confirmation that these orders from a hitherto unknown personage should be adhered to. The eye they caught was that of Frank Abilene, who stood impassively by the front admissions desk and answered the two constables' enquiring looks with a simple resigned nod of his head. Abilene then addressed the whole station house...

"I see that you've all become acquainted with Leman Street's latest commissions, Detective Inspectors Bass and Blackmore. Every courtesy of rank to be shown by all personnel, all standard protocols observed to the letter. Carry on."

As the two detectives turned to leave the station house, Blackmore exclaimed...

"Knuckle-dusters!"

Bass eyed his partner with an inquisitive stare before he remembered the content of their original conversation a few minutes ago...

"The answer to your question previously asked of me is yes, most assuredly I do still carry this well-worn pair of brass knuckle-dusters," he continued, raising both of his fists into plain view upon which he still sported the now quite bloodied pair of heavy cast brass dusters.

"Remarkable, quite remarkable," chuckled Bass as he shook his head and gave his old comrade a hearty pat on the back.

Chapter 25

'Saint George of the East Dock'

Dorset Street, formerly Datchet Street, was once a vibrant and prosperous area within the heart of London's East End that was home to several high-quality garment makers, silk weavers and the first commercial outlet for the pottery of Thomas Wedgewood. In stark contrast to this prosperity, however, the Dorset Street of late 1888 had become notorious as the series of low-rent, decaying boarding houses that flanked either side of its somewhat short length attracted all manner of the most unsavoury and dangerous characters associated with London's dark underworld. Situated at either end of the street and at its centre were three public houses, The Britannia, The Horn of Plenty and The Blue Coat Boy, the latter of which James Bass and Tiberius Blackmore found themselves about to enter as they commenced their search for one such individual, Billy Verlaine.

As they entered through the front door of The Blue Coat Boy, even though they were both local boys and familiar with its less than salubrious surroundings and the area in general, enquiring eyes glanced furtively in their general direction, steely and observant to the arrival of unfamiliar persons entering into their sacred inner-sanctum. A rather scruffy looking individual seated at a table facing the door beckoned a young boy over to him, whispered instructions into his ear and bade him on his errand.

"You see there, James. That messenger is being dispatched directly to Verlaine," whispered Blackmore...

"Indeed, he most probably is" answered Bass.

"I surmise that discovering the whereabouts of Billy Verlaine will pose no problem to us. Our hardships will commence once we have gained entrance beyond the threshold of his manor. I suggest, therefore, that we begin our enquiries at the table hence from where the message emanated," he continued, as he pointed towards the table directly in front of them.

Blackmore nodded his approval and the pair made directly for the scruffy individual in question. As they were about to seat themselves in two chairs opposite their mark, Blackmore emitted a piercing whistle through gritted teeth towards the messenger boy who was just about to leave the building...

"YOU, BOY! Tarry a while and wait over there for me if you please." He beckoned towards a chair and table in an opposite corner of the bar.

The boy replied simply and with a street-wise confidence that Blackmore empathised with immediately... "What's in it for me, guv?"

Reaching into the left pocket of his waistcoat, Blackmore retrieved three copper coins and without uttering another word raised them high above his right shoulder and rubbed them together so as to make that familiar chinking copper on copper sound, so the lad could clearly see what his reward would be.

Turning their attention directly to the scruffy individual seated before them, Bass and Blackmore at first eyed their contact silently, as if reading his unkempt, heavily bearded, filthy features and overall body language for any trace of uncertainty, nervousness or any potential weakness that they could systematically exploit and use to their advantage. It turned out to be an easier read than either of the two

Detectives could have hoped for as the scruffy individual, probably unnerved by both the confidence exuded by these two new faces and the initial silence that faced him, decided that he would break the deadlock and be the first one to speak...

"A very good evening to you, gentlemen. I can't remember seeing you round these parts afore. If you're lookin' for a warm 'n' willin' 'bessie' to give you a good old polish you come to the right place. My girls's cheap an' I got plenty o' stock to tempt any an' all exotic tastes, if you knows' wot I mean, sirs."

Bass eyed the grotty specimen sat across the table impassively, revealing no indication as to his own thoughts or emotions, for a few more seconds before delivering his withering response that was succinct and directly to the point...

"Stop talking and listen very carefully. I don't care who you perceive yourself to be or at this present moment in time what form your business takes. I merely require one thing from you on this night. One tiny piece of information divulged over this table, in the strictest confidence between we three here seated, and you can go and ply your sordid little trade to your black heart's content. Just one tasty morsel offered to us as a sign of friendship in exchange for your continued liberty. How does that sound?"

Obviously taken aback by what he perceived to be the arrogance of Bass' introductory speech, the scruffy individual reacted in the only fashion his untrained and totally unprepared mind allowed him to...

"Well, I never did!" he exclaimed. "Big, bold words from a new face in these parts. You 'n' your friend must be either very 'fakkin' brave, or very 'fakkin' stupid, to come in 'ere lookin' for anything but a good time. Now I strongly advises you both to turn your toff tales about face an' go back west as fast as your still functionin' legs can carry you or..."

The rest of his response to Bass' stark proposal melted away into nothingness as the actions that unfolded during the next few seconds moved the discussion forward at pace and on to its next brutal phase. As the scruffy individual spoke, Bass' highly trained senses became aware that his right hand had disappeared from view below the table's edge. His attention was focussed solely on that hand as it emerged brandishing a pistol, cocked and ready to discharge.

In the blink of an eye Bass reached over, selecting a familiar key pressure point on his assailant's right wrist and without the need to exert a great deal of pressure twisted the wrist inwards, instantly disarming the helpless hand and snapping that wrist as if it were a dry, dead twig.

Even before the sound made by the sickening crack of bone had dissipated in his and the surrounding clientele's ears, Bass retained his grip on the now limp limb and stretched out the hand that it was attached to so it lay open and helpless on the table in front of him. Without wasting a second, and showing neither compassion nor a flicker of remorse as to the potential consequences of his actions, Bass brandished a bone-handled, eight-inch blade from a concealed leather scabbard and proceeded to pin the helpless outstretched palm to the wooden table top; THUNK!

As the blade's sharp tip penetrated skin, sinew and bone with consummate ease, its progress was halted somewhat by the hardness of the heavy oak table top beneath the hand. Such was the force of Bass' initial thrust, however, that the blade still managed to embed itself a good inch and a half into the wood after it had cleared through the back of the hand.

The scruffy individual emitted a pitiful howl and displayed a demeanour that suggested intense pain, anguish and surprise at the speed of his assailant's assault coupled with an abject fear of what might occur additionally within the next few seconds.

"You 'fakkin' vicious bastard!" he exclaimed, tears streaming from each eye into the bush of his unkempt beard. "I'll 'fakkin'… Arghhhh!"

Another loud exclamation of intense agony as Bass twisted the blade ever so slightly, pinning the scruffy individual's hand to the table...

"You'll shut the 'fuck' up whining and listen very carefully to what I have to say," continued Bass, who remained to all intents and purposes during the whole altercation, calmness personified and offering the impression to those few patrons of the pub observing proceedings as they unfolded that this was not the first time such extreme tactics of interrogation had been used by this particular individual...

"Now, sir, you will recall perhaps. I put the question to you a mere few moments ago, in a most respectful and polite manner I might add, that I required the tiniest sliver of information from you, in return for which I would allow your dubious business dealings to continue unhindered for now, yes? No? Just nod your head in the affirmative if you understand me please" was Bass's next question to the gibbering mess of humanity that was now sat stooped over and pathetic in the chair opposite.

It nodded silently and eyed first Bass, then the blade that pinned its broken hand to the table, then towards Bass once more, hoping to gauge some glimmer of compassion that might be present within the expression of his torturer's face. Sadly, for him no indication of the latter was forthcoming and whilst maintaining with ease his seemingly emotionless façade, Bass continued on with his interrogation...

"Excellent, we finally seem to be making some real progress, my fine, filthy friend," he continued.

"You see, common ground was the denominator required in order to aid our cause as we went about building the bridge of trust and respect that we both needed to cross in order for you to furnish me with the information that I require. Where is Billy Verlaine?"

"No, no I can't. Anything but that," whimpered the even scruffier and now quite pathetic individual. "He'll kill me stone dead if 'e finds out I gave 'im up."

Another slight twist of the blade by Bass, provoking the required agonized squeal and wince of pain from his hapless interviewee, was the only action Bass required in order to finally glean the piece of information that he sought.

"I would ask you to ponder for a brief moment what wonderful, cruel and exotic agonies I might well be capable of visiting upon your person from my position of relative comfort whilst sat upon this very chair, in this precise moment if my curiosity is left unsatisfied. A thousand glorious torments, not one of which you could imagine in your wildest dreams, to which I could acquaint you with intimately this evening. Now, sir, I shall only ask you politely but once more: where is Billy Verlaine?"

The answer was immediate, an answer the validity of which under the circumstances Bass saw no cause to doubt ...

"Miller's Court. He's down Miller's Court. He uses McCarthy's shop and the Shed this end of the court to conduct business, but he's in the store room at the other end, beyond the lamp next to the privy."

"Singing with the dulcet tone of a sweet nightingale," deadpanned Bass. "Much obliged to you for your candour and openness, sir."

As Bass continued to speak, he yanked his bloodied blade from the man's broken hand and made a point of addressing those who had remained and bore witness to proceedings as they unfolded...

"Our names, for all of your future references, are Detective Inspector James Bartholomew Bass, here beside me sits Detective Inspector Alan Tiberius Blackmore. We know all of you. We know where you live, with whom you choose to consort and we know of your business, and should your business ever become a matter for our concern we will locate you because we ARE you, every last one of you..."

Turning to face the dishevelled lump opposite him nursing his broken, skewered hand, Bass continued...

"...and we knew of you, St. George of the East Dock, from the very beginning."

St. George, as he was from this moment forth to be known, spoke through gritted teeth...

"Well, well, well. Jimmy Bass and Tiberius Blackmore! You two were proper minted and bona-fide bastards years ago. Four score and ten times worse than Verlaine could ever hope to be, potentially worse than anyone on the east side, 'praps even the 'ole city. We'w're all of a mind you'd 'bin transported out to the colonies, and good riddance to the pair of you it would've 'bin too."

"We were offered and gladly accepted the Queen's shilling instead, George. For thirty years we traded one kind of filth for another only to return full circle back into 'the abyss' where we started out from."

"So, now you both returns to us as fully paid up lapdogs of 'er glorious Majesty's Leman Street 'cozzers'," sneered St. George.

"We'll all enjoy sweet golden slumbers and pleasant fackin' dreams every night from now on in our cots 'an 'angin on our dosser's ropes 'dhan Paternoster Row knowin' you is 'ere lookin' out for us all, Jimmy Bass, and make no 'fackin' mistake about it."

Bass fixed St. George with a stare so cold and piercing that he could have sworn his blood was turning to ice. As Bass began to speak there remained little doubt as to the intentions of the two Detectives with regards to how their own particular type of justice would be administered, their own interpretation of the law upheld...

"Our mandate is clear and precise, St. George. We have pledged to serve and protect the innocent to the absolute best of our ability and if we are tested by your resolve to hinder our progress in any manner you might see fit, you and your kind will discover very swiftly that our abilities are of a type and quality far beyond anything you could possibly conceive or ever hope to deal with.

So, with the greatest respect to your title 'king of the privy' I offer you fair warning. What has transpired between us on this night was nothing of consequence. A mere trifle of spontaneous happenstance. A necessary occurrence borne out of the frustration of the one whilst seeking the merest trifle of information from the other."

Turning to face Blackmore, Bass continued...

"Well, Tiberius, I believe our work here on this fine autumnal evening is complete."

As Bass and Blackmore raised themselves from the chairs they were occupying, Bass turned to face St. George once more...

"Oh, one more thing of note I should make you aware of, St. George. If the need ever arises for my very good friend Tiberius and I to visit you again bearing anything other than the most cordial of greetings, I shall have no hesitation in erasing your worthless soul from existence. Now we bid you a very good evening, sir."

With that both Bass and Blackmore flicked the brims of their respective hats in a show of mock respect towards the sore, bewildered and bleeding St. George and turned to leave the pub. Just as Blackmore approached the table at which the young lad had sat transfixed by all that had just occurred, Blackmore beckoned him over to where he and Bass stood by the exit door...

"What's your name, boy?" Blackmore asked.

"Jackie Taylor, sir," he replied with the kind of streetwise confidence both Blackmore and Bass were very familiar with...

"Listen carefully to what I have to say, Jackie Taylor."

Removing the three coins from his waistcoat pocket that he had shown to the young lad earlier, Blackmore continued...

"These three penny pieces belong to you, Jackie Taylor, provided you agree to complete a simple task for my colleague and I."

Eyeing the precious coins with a needy hunger, Jackie's answer was nevertheless both measured and cautious...

"Three whole pennies, all for me. What simple task, guvnor sir, could be worth the princely sum of three whole pennies?"

"Do you know Billy Verlaine, Jackie?" asked Blackmore.

"Yes, guvnor" was Jackie's immediate response.

"And if I were to recite verbally unto you a message meant for the ears of Billy Verlaine, and mark my words well, Jackie Taylor, only for the ears of Billy Verlaine, could you deliver that message swiftly and word for word as I tell it to you now?"

"Yes, guv, I can do that for three pennies, 'fakkin' right I can."

Upon receiving his payment Jackie placed his new riches discreetly inside a small pouch that was secured to a rope belt tied tightly around his waist, thanked the detective, and just as he turned to leave on his errand, Blackmore continued briefly...

"When your message is safely delivered to Verlaine, I want you to turn tail and hot foot with all haste to Leman Street police station. Upon arrival you should ask for Sergeant Marcus Jackson. Inform him on my behalf to escort you personally to the markets at Spitalfields where you will seek out the fruit and vegetable pitch of Mr Charlie Johnstone. Mr Johnstone is an old acquaintance of long standing whom you will inform politely that I, Tiberius Blackmore, would consider the great debt that he owes me paid in full should he offer you steady employment and safe lodgings away from this festering menagerie of filth."

Jackie Taylor studied every word intently, transfixed on every single syllable of the proposal offered by Blackmore and once more answered with the wise acumen of a seasoned and disciplined mind that was far in advance of its obvious youth, a keen and observant mind that seemed to have been waiting patiently for a gilt-edged opportunity such as the one presenting itself here, served right in front of him on a silver platter and with all the trimmings on top to boot...

"Well, 'guvnor, I got nothing or no one 'ere abouts to call family, real family that is. All I got to look forward to is bein' 'ungry, robbin' watches an' wallets for Verlaine from plump toffs in return for rotten vittles' an' a grotty old cot darn Millers court, doin' 'ard time in Newgate nick or bein' either conscripted or transported to them far off colonies so I reckons what 'ave I got to lose if I takes you up on your very generous proposal? Nought as far as I can see. Nah, wots this message that you require I drops in Billy Verlaine's shell-like, Mr Blackmore, sir?"

"Good lad," began Blackmore.

"The message is quite simple and will be very easy to memorise and deliver, Jackie Taylor, every word conveyed directly to Verlaine as its told."

"For sure, 'guvnor' Blackmore, sir, every word as clear in 'is shell-like as the sweetest sung gospel verse" came the answer from Jackie Taylor.

"You will please ask Billy Verlaine, at the special request of James Bass and Tiberius Blackmore, to prepare himself in whatever manner he sees fit because Hell is coming, today!"

Chapter 26

'Mary'

Blackmore and Bass stepped out of The Blue Coat Boy public house into the early evening smog of Dorset Street. The lamp lighters were going about their nightly routine of igniting the gas lamps that were set at seemingly random intervals on either side of the street. Each lamp drew towards it moths in flight instinctively seeking out the comforting glow of bright light and Bass could not help but wonder openly upon spontaneously observing this most common occurrence that the actions both himself and Blackmore were about to instigate would liken them both in some manner to the habitual tendencies of an insect...

"Moths to the flame," Bass mused aloud.

"What's that you say, James?" asked Blackmore of his wistful companion in a slightly frustrated manner on account of his mind already becoming engaged in formulating their next plan of action.

"Should not our being constantly drawn towards encounters with insurmountable dangers and seemingly impossible odds be likened in some way to the instinctive actions of the moth as it is drawn towards the light?" questioned Bass...

By way of a swift, spontaneous but nonetheless polite response to his friend's somewhat whimsical aside, Blackmore grudgingly offered his own logical answer...

"Perhaps we might turn the proverb around a little to suit a more tangible truth in that we, the flame of justice, are drawn towards the insect, which in this particular instance would manifest itself as Verlaine, in order to expose the pest for whatever malignant business it represents and possibly to extinguish its lifeforce, should there be cause to do so, beyond all reasonable doubt."

"An interesting and logical point raised, my friend, and one we shall no doubt continue to peruse and cogitate over at a later date over a decanter of fine brandy and a smoke, but I would now ask you, with all respect due of course, to concentrate fully on the matter at hand as we approach the portal that will lead us to our destination."

Blackmore shook his head slightly and eyed his colleague incredulously for a few seconds from beneath the brim of his old and weather-worn bowler hat as they stood under the narrow brick archway that was the dark and wholly uninviting entrance to Millers Court. Here they paused for a moment whilst discussing how best to proceed...

"I fear that a possible tactical nightmare awaits within, Tiberius," began Bass, the concern apparent in his voice.

"Beyond this arch the light is limited to one gas lamp and what little emanates from the rooms above. The walls rise three storeys high up on either side a good thirty feet, with windows offering vantage points aplenty. Quite similar in configuration to any defensive barbican and just as effective if utilised in the context of a well-laid ambush."

"Blackmore pondered for a few seconds before offering his tactical suggestion as to how he thought they should proceed...

"I propose that we concentrate our collective attentions on a side of the street apiece, yourself to cover the left flank, whilst I will proceed to cover the right, proposing to meet, hopefully without initial engagement or hindrance, outside of the store room and privy located where the Millers Court cul-de-sac ends. I surmise by this time that Verlaine will be aware of our presence and we shall either have been readily engaged in harsh banter with members of his loyal group of acolytes, or perhaps some form of physical altercation might manifest itself, before being non-cordially invited to an audience with the one that we seek."

Bass nodded once in silent agreement and proceeded to check that both of the pistols that he carried were primed and ready for immediate use, should the need arise. As Blackmore made sure that his own pistol was loaded and close to hand, he continued...

"I would ask of you one specific thing, James, that when the moment of contact with Verlaine himself takes place, to please allow the initial engagement between Verlaine and I to unfold directly and unhindered on your part unless absolutely necessary, and at my discretion."

Bass nodded once more in silent agreement to the request of his friend, but answered whilst emitting a knowing, wry smile...

"And I would ask of you one specific thing in return, my brother. I implore you not to inflict too much damage upon Verlaine's person, at any rate before we have the opportunity to extract the information that we require from him, Verlaine himself being our key perspective prime source of useful street banter is too fine an opportunity for we two to ignore."

As Blackmore replied to his partner's request he unsheathed the formidable six-inch hunting blade that he always carried concealed about his person and began to juggle it from one hand, and then the other, with both the controlled, expert skill of the highly trained martial arts master he was and the cold, calculated acumen of a trained killer...

"I propose to hurt him, James, to visit upon his unprepared, untrained and vulnerable body and consciousness quite a substantial amount of pain and discomfort I shouldn't wonder," he alluded coldly.

"I'm going to make him suffer supreme agony and humiliation times over for every one of the hapless souls he has exploited and systematically destroyed whilst plying his despicable wares, ultimately selling those innocent souls to the devil in exchange for his wages of filthy lucre. I will bring him to his wretched knees before his loyal covenant of thieves and force him to be our confidante supreme. Willingly or unwillingly, Billy Verlaine will divulge his inner most secrets unto us on this very night."

Blackmore and Bass paired off to their respective sides of the passageway and, pistols drawn and primed in readiness for immediate use, moved with the stealth and silence of a pair of ghostly shadows towards the store room at the opposite end of Millers Court.

As the two detectives approached an open area of the court that was lit by a solitary gas lamp, they both became aware simultaneously that this light might well compromise their presence prematurely. In that same moment Blackmore turned directly about, pistol raised in anticipation of an imminent assault, at the sound of footfall clacking on the damp cobbles behind him.

"James. Hold fast! Our position is compromised" came the hissed command from Blackmore.

"Hold fast and declare your intentions!" was Blackmore's insistent order hissed directly towards their unexpected visitor.

Blackmore was taken aback slightly to hear the voice of a young woman answer him...

"I declare, sir, a hard-working girl wanting to get to her vittles' and rest her pins and all else after a hard day's toil doesn't expect to be accosted at gunpoint outside of her own front door of an evening!'" she exclaimed somewhat brazenly.

"Sure, if you'll be wanting some private company from a lady all you need do is ask my lovely and we can get down to the business directly. I live just here, so I do, look, at number thirteen...

"I, er, I'm... no, I really don't want to... er, no, madam, pardon me," Blackmore stuttered almost apologetically as he lowered his pistol from the face at which it was aimed...

As the light from a single gas lamp mounted on the wall behind Bass – who had both of his pistols raised and trained on their surprise visitor – illuminated the face of the young woman to whom he was speaking, his analytical mind began logging details of her appearance for possible future reference.

She was of a fair to almost blonde complexion, not exactly svelte of body shape, nor full enough of figure to be regarded as being in any way obese, and exceptionally neat and well presented for a 'working' lady of the street. Blackmore also noticed that although her speech was peppered with typical East End brogue and the odd obligatory profanity, these typical traits of normal 'street speak' almost completely concealed the fact that her true accent was almost definitely of a mid-western Irish origin. She also had the most strikingly attractive and unmarked face. As she took a key from the black beaded purse she was carrying and proceeded to unlock the door in front of her, she continued...

"Well, sir, are you proposing to stand there like a fekkin' dozy 'eejut all night long or will you close your gaping trap and let a tired Oirish lassy from Limerick get indoors to her fekkin' bed?" she deadpanned back at the slightly stunned Blackmore.

Blackmore closed his 'gaping trap' immediately and attempted to locate and restore what meagre remnants of his composure he could find, though a clumsy stammer was all he could seem to muster...

"Er, of course, madam, quite so. Please, retire to your, er, lodgings and, erm, have yourself a pleasant evening."

Just as Blackmore began to re-focus on his primary task at hand the young woman spoke to him once more...

"Might I be asking, sir, just to settle my own curiosity, you understand, who might be a creeping down the old court all secretive like and tooled up to do mischief to whoever?"

"Blackmore. Detective Inspector Tiberius Blackmore at your service, madam," Blackmore answered...

"Ah, I should've twigged. A cozzer!" exclaimed the young woman.

"So, I'm a guessing that you and your brooding friend over yonder there be after finding that Billy Verlaine."

Impressed by the young woman's perceptiveness and the consistently intelligent questions that she asked, and satisfied that she posed no threat to either himself nor to the successful outcome of the mission, Blackmore decided to divulge their intentions in the hope that a valuable new ally had been discovered...

"You know of his whereabouts?" he began. "It is imperative that we locate Verlaine this very night, in order for him to aid us with our ongoing enquiries."

"Well mister Tiberius Blackmore sir, Billy Verlaine is a vicious, filthy deviant and a user of helpless and vulnerable humanity and I would gladly see him turn up missing from around these parts, to be sure I would," answered the young woman.

"He's been around the corner in 'The Ringers' tonight conducting all manner of devious business and I'd know this for certain on account of I've been in there myself most of this evening too. He moved on from there to his lock-up down at the end of this very court, and, Tiberius Blackmore, please be wary. He was accompanied by several devious malcontents, all in possession of the lowest moral standards imaginable."

"Thank you for your concern and for your open candour, madam," answered Blackmore.

"Please rest assured that our conversation, and the information voluntarily divulged by yourself, will be regarded and acted upon with the strictest confidence by myself and my partially anonymous colleague, whose character and integrity I vouch for implicitly. Now please, for your own safety, I ask you to go inside your abode, lock the door up securely behind you and dwell not on matters as they unfold outside of these walls until dawn breaks upon a new day of hope and fresh opportunity."

As the young woman turned to enter the open door of number thirteen Millers Court, Blackmore asked one last question of her...

"Madam, without seeming to appear presumptuous beyond civil cordiality, in that you now hold me at a disadvantage with regards to acquaintance by title, might one enquire please, what is your name?"

The young woman turned to face Blackmore once more and said...

"My name, good Tiberius Blackmore, for the sake of future cordial liaison, is Mary Jane Kelly and I bid you a very fond, and hopefully safe, evening, sir."

Chapter 27

'Verlaine'

"**A**re you quite finished with regards to implementing your revolutionary new community policing programme, Tiberius?" offered Bass with an exasperated, almost sarcastically witty aside...

"A time and a place, my friend. Might this grizzled, cantankerous, ageing soldier suggest that a more opportune time and place for such a relevant and necessary process to be implemented will surely present itself at a more convenient moment?"

"Indeed, it will, James, but that young lady has just this minute proceeded to offer cordially, and without the necessity of resorting to the use of, ahem, harsher interviewing techniques, the precise location of Verlaine. I would conclude that result in itself as being a positive endorsement for the future implementation of such tactics."

"Positive only if the information so divulged is proven to be sound, Tiberius," offered Bass cautiously.

"Well, if it transpires that we two have been delivered into the hands of the devil by a fair and somewhat beguiling agent provocateur and taking into account that we survive the impending encounter, of course, at the very least I know where she resides!" reasoned Blackmore...

Re-united on the same side of the court, the pair moved on cautiously from under the wall lamp that illuminated their presence for all who might see and on towards the store room situated just a few more yards on and to their left. When they reached the high fronted, heavy double doors of the dour old warehouse they halted. In a hushed, guarded manner Blackmore spoke first…

"This entrance seems open and unguarded, as though our imminent patronage were expected. I will proceed through here alone. James, if I might ask your countenance in the manner of seeking entrance with stealth via another alternative portal in order for you to be able to oversee and to cover my actions, such as they may unfold within."

Bass raised both of his pistols, a .44 calibre Smith and Wesson Schofield special and his faithful old Webley service revolver, barrels raised above shoulder height and both of their taught hammers cocked in readiness for whatever firefight might ensue. He nodded a silent affirmative to his partner's request and disappeared down a narrow passageway between the store room and a vile smelling, filthy privy.

Buoyed by the knowledge that his every movement within would be observed and supported by possibly the finest and most effective exponent of covert operations and stealth tactics ever to serve in Her Majesty's special forces, Blackmore lifted the rusty iron latch that lay across both of the heavy wooden doors of the store house and pushed one of them ajar just enough for him to enter.

He gave himself a few seconds before venturing further into the cavernous black space for his eyes to adjust their focus and become accustomed to the semi-darkness within. Satisfied that he could navigate comfortably through what he now observed were barrels of beer and packing crates, stacked over ten feet high, probably containing bottles of spirits, tobacco and all manner of other contraband that had been processed and readied to be moved on, possibly directly into the cellars of the many licensed, and unlicensed, premises that lined Dorset Street and the surrounding area.

'Quite a lucrative little business empire you have built up here, 'Billy boy',' Blackmore thought to himself as he made his way to the back wall of the seemingly deserted warehouse, where he had spotted a single open doorway.

Upon reaching the doorway, left tantalisingly ajar as if on purpose, Blackmore instinctively turned about in order to check his rear guard remained clear, then entered through the door into a narrow passageway that seemed to run for a good thirty or forty feet to his right before opening out into a wider square court yard, 'possibly part of an intricate network of similar smugglers' passageways that service the public houses on Dorset Street and all hereabouts no doubt', so Blackmore supposed to himself.

Pausing for a moment to peruse over which tactical option might be best utilised in order to improve his position, none of which presented much immediate comfort to him, Blackmore decided to gamble his personal wellbeing on revealing his presence by moving to the centre of the square and thus openly exposing himself to all manner of possible harm.

'Well, Tiberius, this'll either draw out the curious rat from his bolt-hole or attract a silent, lethal assault from any number of would-be anonymous assailants,' he thought to himself...

Pistol holstered, both hands raised with open palms outstretched in order to show a dozen inquisitive pairs of eyes a willingness to instigate peaceful negotiation over violence, Blackmore stepped from the comforting concealment of the shadows out into the exposed centre of New Court, located almost directly behind the Blue Coat Boy public house.

"Well, well, well. Tiberius 'fakkin' Blackmore," came the initial abrasively sarcastic greeting from a voice that Blackmore recognised only too well. It was the voice of Billy Verlaine.

"Was it the fair lady of providence, sheer 'bladdy' good fortune or the good lord 'imself 'oo delivered your miserable carcass into my back yard? You've got some real front commin' dahn 'ere all on your lonesome, Tiberius, that or your balls's bigger than your common sense."

Before Blackmore had the opportunity to answer, Verlaine emitted a shrill, piercing whistle through pursed, dry lips and what little remained of his rotten teeth. Blackmore became instantly aware of subtle movements in the shadows all around his perimeter, as if the four high walls of New Court had come to life and were beginning to close in all around him.

It soon became abundantly clear to Blackmore that he was now completely surrounded by at least a dozen of what he presumed were acolytes loyal to Verlaine, both men and women, some of whose faces he recognised from his own time spent surviving day to day, living hand to mouth in the same neighbourhood many years previously, none of whom owed him any favours.

"Hello Billy Boy. Still relying on your tiny piss ant army to hold your little hand and wipe your arse for you," he began sarcastically whilst all the while weighing up his somewhat limited tactical options, none of which seemed for the moment to present him with too much comfort.

"My boys 'n' girls, Tiberius," began Verlaine. "You knows some of 'em from back in the day; Johnny McCarthy 'ere, 'ee knows you, Tiberius. An' old Lenny Fraser, the 'geezer' 'oos left ear 'ole 'an 'arf of 'is 'scnoz' you 'ad off darn Gun Street, Befnal Green all them years ago. They 'ain't forgot you, Tiberius, an' they wants to say 'ello an' all."

"Yeah, you skanky, long fingered bastard," piped up Fraser, buoyed on a wave of bravado courtesy of Verlaine's introduction. "I owes you plenty of 'art ache' an' misery for messin' up my 'boat race' for the ladies, you 'fakkin' bastard cozzer."

"Well, I could put your face back to how it was, Lenny," offered Blackmore glibly, "and let all friends here gathered around be under no illusion that any action on my part, with regards to your potential facial re-construction surgery, would offer a marked improvement on the features that you currently sport."

A ripple of tittering and muted amused banter from the assembled menagerie in response to Blackmore's barb of comedic dry wit provoked the exact reaction from the hapless Fraser that Blackmore had hoped for...

"Them's big, bold words spillin' out the mouth of a 'fakkin' dead man standin' alone in no man's land, you long streak of donkey pi..."

Blackmore didn't allow Fraser the courtesy of finishing his tirade...

"Alone? My dear, sweet, demented Lenny. Whoever in their wildest fantasies, except for yourself of course, would imagine that I might take a walk down into this crap house alone and unguarded," Blackmore answered, almost gloatingly, as he spotted the timely arrival of a friend at the outer perimeter of this most bizarre conclave, an arrival that he greeted with single nod of his head in the direction of his mysterious, yet very familiar, supporter...

Sensing his moment to act was at hand, Fraser lunged towards Blackmore, a stout iron pry bar raised menacingly above his head, catching the startled Detective slightly off guard. Blackmore needn't have worried, however, as Fraser was instantly felled by the forceful impact of a large and heavy bone handled hunting knife thrusting deep into his right shoulder that had been expertly thrown from a good distance away by Bass.

Moving silently and utilising his extensive skills in the art of cover and concealment, thus being completely unhampered by any random third parties who might provide a troublesome hindrance to his cause, Bass had positioned himself in a defensible corner of New Court that had high, solid walls on each side that protected his back and each flank.

Inching steadily forward in order to willingly break his concealment and so his words could be heard clearly by all ears assembled, each step a controlled action, every movement calculated and precise, he was able to tactically assess the situation and act accordingly. Composing himself after his impressive display of knife skills and with both his pistols now raised and cocked for immediate discharge, Bass announced his arrival to the momentarily startled group...

"A fond evening's greeting to you, Tiberius. Please accept my most humble apologies for the lateness of my arrival on account of a rather enthusiastic altercation that occurred momentarily between myself and a pair of unruly and downright disagreeable gentlemen who, for whatever reason known only to themselves, and perhaps one other individual who I see stands here among us, had it ensconced within their somewhat twisted mindset that my progress to this reunion of old comrades should not be allowed to continue.

"I regret humbly and with deepest sympathy and heartfelt condolence offered to any family members present, to inform our illustrious hosts that their friends will not be joining us... ever!"

Without warning from his left flank, a tall, heavy-set man of around forty years old flung himself with singular purpose and gusto towards Bass. A large meat cleaver raised high above his head, he began a tirade of threats spurred on, so Bass supposed from the content and voracity of his words, by the instant emotions brought about by grief for a lost loved one or family member...

"Arrrgh, you rotten, stinkin' 'fakker'... You've done for my brothers, you 'fakkin' murderin' bastard cozzer... I'll..." 'CRACK!'

"You'll join them on this day in hell" was the simple answer given by Bass as he discharged a single round from his Smith and Wesson

Schofield pistol directly and precisely right into the centre of the advancing and rather large forehead of his would-be assailant.

Stepping over the corpse that he had just created, Bass continued on with his dialogue almost totally untroubled by what had just occurred, except perhaps for displaying an expression of mild irritation on account of his introduction to the group being so rudely interrupted...

"I really must apologise for our rude friend's rather enthusiastic greeting. I would warn all of you, however, with the exception of my esteemed colleague who stands among you, of course, that any further spontaneous and uninvited attempts to enter my personal area of space will be met by the very same lethal force that befell your fallen comrade. I hold in my two hands a hungry round of lead for each of you, and you may all rest assured, I am capable and willing, without betraying hesitation or remorse, of ending each of your miserable, wasted lives in an instant."

"Well stone me, Jimmy 'fakkin' Bass" was Verlaine's opening sentence...

"I should 'ave 'fakkin' twigged. Wherever goes one, the other 'fakkin' bastard is sure to come creepin' behind an' wiv' a nasty 'fakker' of an attitude to match."

Bass simply nodded once in the direction of Verlaine and as their eyes met in an all too familiar steely, ice-cold and emotionless glare, they realised simultaneously that, considering the circumstances of past and quite vicious altercations between the two of them, no further dialogue between the two men at this point in the proceedings was necessary.

Others in Verlaine's gang, however, obviously were not aware of any dubious reputations that either Bass or Blackmore might have earned, or whatever respect they may once have commanded from the hard-core criminal fraternity of Whitechapel many years ago.

Several East End accents crossed over as the bravado of a group of hardened street thugs who outnumbered their cornered prey six to one emboldened them to consider taking immediate action against the two detectives.

"Let's 'ave 'em, Bill." "Winners odds all 'fakkin' day at eleven to two." "Fakkin' bastard cozzers. 'Oo does they think they is, comin' swannin' down our manor an' puttin' it about like 'fakkin' street royalty comin' 'ome." "Well cozzers, we're goin' to carve our names into your still warm corpses before we 'feeds' what's left of 'em to old Tommy Ryan's 'ogs." "COME ON, LADS, LET'S 'AVE THIS PAIR O' COZZER BASTARDS AWAY!"

Before Verlaine had the opportunity to warn them off, five members of the remainder of his rapidly diminishing group split away from the rest, two made for Blackmore with sledge hammer and sharp cotton bale hooks raised respectively in anger, three targeted Bass brandishing the discarded cleaver that belonged to the corpse, a blacksmith's six-pound ball peen hammer and an old army bayonet, all of the incensed individuals intent on doing both Bass and Blackmore serious harm.

Both men being highly trained and very experienced Army special forces veterans gave them an overwhelming advantage regarding the use of unarmed combat techniques.

Blackmore and Bass engaged their assailants simultaneously. Able to assess a situation of extreme danger and act accordingly to within a fraction of a second, the two old warriors went directly and efficiently to work on their hopelessly outclassed attackers.

Bass chose not to waste precious ammunition on decommissioning his assailants. He turned his two pistols around so as to utilise their stocks as stout cudgels and proceeding to employ all manner of perfectly placed boots to knee, groin and calf, not to mention extremely brutal blows to chest and clavicle, thus shattering undefended bones instantly, was able to conclude his work within a matter of seconds, leaving three broken, bloodied and whining excuses for humanity writhing in agony on the cold, damp cobbles at his feet.

Blackmore's assault was even more brutal than the one just undertaken by his efficient partner. Again, arriving upon his personal strategy in a second, Blackmore decided that he would offer a fatal example to the rest of the now transfixed group, as to the deadly capabilities of the two Detectives and their intent to use lethal force without compassion or regret, should the moment necessitate itself.

As the sledge hammer of one assailant was raised to offer its potentially skull crushing downward blow, Blackmore, now sporting a pair of brass knuckle-dusters that were previously concealed within each of his coat pockets, instinctively moved to one side and taking a lower stance whilst focussing on the now vulnerable rib cage before him, offered a classic one-two combination punch into the exposed torso, fracturing several of the brittle bones beneath as each powerful blow met its mark.

Doubling over in agony, Blackmore's opponent had little time to regain any sort of meaningful composure as the initial heavy, brass enhanced body blows were followed immediately by Blackmore's head raising up sharply under an unwary chin to stun his already flagging assailant even more. Finishing this particular portion of his work with a flurry of punches to the face, nose and jaw that made certain the man's features would be altered drastically forevermore, and satisfied that he was no longer a viable threat, Blackmore turned his sole attention to the second attacker, all the while being confident in the knowledge that Bass, his part of the operation completed successfully, was once more locked, loaded and covering his flanks.

Concentrating first upon disarming his opponent of a pair of lethally sharp cotton bale hooks with relative ease, Blackmore began to formulate his initial plan of offering his ultimately example of their intent to the group, who were by this time beginning to openly quake with fear.

Aiming all manner of kicks, punches and boots to key impact points of the body, a bizarre form of ballet ensued, almost graceful in its exquisite choreography but ultimately brutal in its precise and potentially deadly execution, whereby Blackmore proceeded to sap every last ounce of physical strength, mental fortitude and will to resist from his now defenceless assailant.

Satisfied that he could continue engaging the final phase of his plan unchallenged, Blackmore proceeded to raise up the almost lifeless bundle of rags knelt pitifully before him, engage it in a formidable choke hold and turn it about to face the incredulously transfixed features of Billy Verlaine.

Whispering close to the right ear of his helpless captive, wishing for his dialogue to remain private between the two of them, Blackmore hissed the chilling home truths of which he was well aware and of his imminent intentions with regards to the continued existence of his prisoner...

"I know you, Lucas Wainwright. I know who you are and I know what you are, you debaser, exploiter and murderer of lost and lonely souls, you purveyor of flesh and illegal contraband to the highest bidder, you vile rapist of women, you despicable molester of innocent children. I remember you very well, Lucas, but do you remember in turn the words that I spoke unto you all those years ago."

A feeble groan and a splutter of blood emanating through an expertly choked oesophagus was the only response of which Wainwright was capable, so, his question answered to his satisfaction, Blackmore continued his dialogue ...

"I want you to remember that I swore if our paths should ever cross but once more, I would end your worthless waste of a life in an instant. Now that time has finally arrived so I ask you to make your peace swiftly with whatever spiritual institution you might hope would accept your damned soul as it departs this earth and go forth to your maker safe in the knowledge that the fashion of your demise sends a stark message to all those gathered around us who now observe, by word of mouth to the rest of 'under-London' and in particular to that piece of filth stood in front of you. Goodbye Lucas…"

With merely the slightest visible combination of movements from his arms and hands, first a twist to the left and immediately to the right, then pushing forward precisely whilst administering exactly the amount of pressure required, Blackmore proceeded to snap Wainwright's neck as if it were no more than a tinder-dry, brittle twig. 'CRACK!'

As Wainwright's lifeless corpse flopped to his feet, Blackmore stepped over it as if it were merely a discarded sack of refuse and purposefully entered the personal space of Billy Verlaine.

"Very 'fakkin' impressive, boys, very 'fakkin' tidy indeed. I 'sees' that you've not been idle while you've been away from 'ome'…" began Verlaine as his words were curtailed by the insistent orders of a calm and extremely focussed Blackmore…

"Shut your mouth and listen very carefully! I care not for the bloated and often greatly exaggerated reputations of others, be they earned formulating and pursuing a dubious career in crime or otherwise bestowed upon the altogether more deserving individual in return for legitimate services rendered for the continued security of the Empire. Neither in this moment, nor at any time in the past were your actions and counsel of any use to myself personally, nor did your tyrannical and brutal leadership of the East End street people offer any notion to me other than on a glorious day such as this I might return and settle accounts outstanding between the two of us once and for all.

"I am prepared, however, to allow past indifference between us to go unanswered for the present in exchange for your counsel regarding matters relating to our ongoing investigations concerning the whereabouts of...

Now it was Verlaine's turn to interrupt Blackmore in mid-sentence...

"Stone me, you're lookin' for Jack the 'fakkin' Ripper!" he exclaimed...

"Well, Tiberius Blackmore, and Jimmy Bass, I got the knowledge to tickle those taste buds o' yours right enough, up 'ere in this noggin," he taunted as he firmly tapped his right temple with the index finger of his right hand.

"But you 'knows' for sure that this ain't no easy noggin to crack open, Mr Blackmore, sir," he continued sarcastically as he brandished a tarnished but nevertheless very sharp six-inch fish gutting knife from a concealed leather scabbard under his jacket.

Blackmore, slightly taken aback by Verlaine's show of bravura, took a couple of steps backwards, using the corpse he had created a few minutes earlier as a barrier between them, in order to allow himself the space and time to react in the face of this obvious provocation.

"Don't be silly, Billy boy, please. What's all this ruckus for?" questioned Blackmore, arms outstretched with both empty palms visible.

"All we ever wanted to achieve here was to send out the word that Bass and Blackmore had returned home and laid down a clear marker as to our quite legitimate and peaceful intentions. Now, perhaps our slight over-exuberance in dealing with the, erm, shall we say more enthusiastic personal attentions of your boys was perhaps in hindsight a tad extreme but, in all honesty and I'm sure you will agree, they've had it coming to them in this way for a good few years now.

"But then, all of a sudden, you get yourself upset and draw a shank on an old friend, and well, that's just plain rude. Bad form, Billy boy, bad form. You don't really want to be pulling knives out and waving them about in a threatening manner, not when I've got one as well!" and with that Blackmore unsheathed his own blade from secret concealment, an act that momentarily rocked a startled Verlaine back on his heels. Blackmore continued, the rising menace apparent in his voice as he spoke...

"I'm proposing to hurt you, Billy boy. I'm going to bleed you a little, humiliate you in front of your pathetic band of human detritus and I'm going to enjoy myself doing it. I'm aiming to pay you back tenfold in several forms of agony that your feeble mind could not possibly conceive for all the innocent souls you've either exploited or murdered and just at the precise moment I consider you might be in a position when begging for your worthless life may well be the only viable option left open to you, and depending very much on where my mood rests at this point during the proceedings, you understand, I might see fit to offer you an ultimatum in exchange for my allowing you the privilege of continuing to draw your stinking breath.

Now, if this all sounds reasonable and my terms are to your satisfaction, I see no further cause for delay... Let the dance commence!"

Needing no further invitation Verlaine was the first to attack, expecting to catch Blackmore off guard with a swift slash of his blade but the wily Detective dodged the clumsy and ill-timed challenge with ease. As he moved backwards slightly and then sideways under the scything backhand thrust of his opponent, Blackmore, gripping his own blade so as the blade pointed outwards, made three swift and shallow stabs into Verlaine's unprotected abdomen.

Wincing with pain and clutching his bloodied right-side, Verlaine rounded on his heels and staggered backwards so as to make a wider space between Blackmore and himself.

"Very 'fakkin' clever, Tiberius. Very neatly done, you bastard turncoat cozzer. Nah', let's see what else you got in that bag 'o' tricks you 'as brought 'cos you 'is' 'gonna' 'ave' to dig deep into it, boy, very 'fakkin' deep to best ole' Billy Verlaine."

Again, Verlaine attempted to strike with a random and wild slash of his blade but was impaired by his lack of both refined finesse and speed, plus the injury he carried had been designed by Blackmore so as to cripple his opponent and slow down any progress that he might have made.

Blackmore was able to navigate this latest ill-timed attack with ease and chose on this occasion to place a well-aimed boot to the inside of Verlaine's right knee cap.

Buckling as his broken knee gave way, thus becoming unable to support his own body weight, Verlaine attempted in vain to block Blackmore's blade as it swiftly stabbed three times into his left shoulder and slashed upwards in an arc across the side of his throat all the way up to his left ear.

"Yield, Billy boy, you've had more than enough," Blackmore said, almost betraying a sympathetic tone in his voice as he spoke...

"I'll be tellin' you when I've 'ad enough, you 'fakkin' bastard cozzer. Nah', 'ave some 'o' this..."

Using the last remaining vestiges of his physical strength Verlaine somehow raised himself up onto his two feet and began wildly slashing his blade, first to the right, and then to the left, in a vain attempt to lay some form of meaningful contact somewhere, anywhere, upon Blackmore's person.

Avoiding each speculative swipe of the blade with consummate ease, Blackmore first disarmed Verlaine by aiming his faithful and accurate right boot at the knife hand of his assailant, sending the offending weapon spinning and arcing well beyond Verlaine's reach.

Now realising full well that Verlaine was all but a spent force and totally at his mercy, Blackmore first brought a reinforced elbow to bear across the unprotected bridge of Verlaine's nose, shattering it in an instant. As Verlaine arched to topple backwards, Blackmore grabbed a tight hold of his shirt collar, thus preventing his fall, and yanked his broken body forwards whilst during the same fluid movement and sliced open the Achilles tendon of his right ankle with one swipe of his consistently accurate blade.

Resting the sole of his right boot on the prone and helpless body of Verlaine, now propped up on all fours and suffering the many agonies that he had been promised but a few moments ago, Blackmore gently pressed sideways so as to roll Verlaine onto his back. Crouching down beside his agonised victim, Blackmore began to speak...

"I warned you of what I proposed to do, 'Billy boy' and now look at the state you're in. All of this silliness and carnage because you and your boys went and made the wrong choices. Now, though, is the time for you to take stock of your life and make another choice, a wiser choice. You can never hope to make amends for what you are, Billy, not that you'd ever choose to follow a righteous path I'd wager. Nor can there be offered official pardon for the many atrocities that you have committed, or the countless others that you should be held accountable for by your own personal sanction.

"What I am able to offer you, here at this precise moment, is a simple choice. Quite possibly the single most important choice that you will ever have to make during the remainder of your entire, miserable existence, however much longer that existence might continue, of course, depending solely upon the answer you decide to give at this juncture in the proceedings. The choice I offer to you is this: information and continued, unbiased fealty to mine and James' ongoing quest for justice, or..."

As he spoke, Blackmore proceeded to toss his blade into the air, arcing and spinning as it travelled from one hand to the other in a scintillating display of dextrous and quite spectacular juggling the like of which the mesmerised Verlaine had never witnessed before.

"Or, my dear and badly broken old nemesis, all I can promise you is that the alternative will be swift."

"Awright, awright enough! I've 'ad enough, you vicious bastard cozzer. You've got me bested right enough, Tiberius, an' that's a fact. Ask yer' 'fakkin' questions for all you think they might be worth," spluttered Verlaine.

Blackmore wasted no more time with what he considered to be idle words...

"The perceptiveness you hinted at earlier was correct, Billy boy. James and I do indeed intend to seek out and impound the anomaly who has become known as 'Jack the Ripper.' Please, if you'll take a moment, reflect upon these names: Emma Smith, Mary Ann Nichols, Annie Chapman, Martha Tabram and Elizabeth Stride. All of these poor, unfortunate creatures who more than likely fell prey to the one individual that we hunt, and every one of them used, abused, exploited and fleeced for a few coppers of their meagre whore's earnings by one Billy Verlaine. Their employer of sorts and self-styled guardian. A trusted and capable protector from the many rancid and twisted evils that course freely and swiftly through the veins of this city as would a terminal disease.

"But alas, you did not earn the percentage of hard coin upon which you insisted be paid by these women in return for your protection."

"I COULD NOT 'FAKKIN' PROTECT THEM!" Verlaine sobbed, his emotion spilling beyond the parameters of the physical agony from which he suffered...

"They were my 'fakkin' life blood, the bread 'an' cheese on my table. They 'was' family to me an' I loved 'em' all, every last one of 'em', but tell me 'ow, Mr Blackmore, sir, even 'wiv' all your la-di-da, soldier tricks 'an' fancies an' the like, 'ow can even you, Tiberius 'fakkin' Blackmore an' James 'fakkin' Bass, begin to protect anybody from a ghost, 'cos even Billy Verlaine came up short!"

Blackmore thought for a moment before giving his answer...

"Well, 'Billy boy', perhaps we should look upon this moment as being the opening chapter of a new beginning. Our business encompasses many complex facets, most of which will concern no-one but we two, but in the context of our new business concerns, here in Whitechapel, let us assume that part of our mandate is to offer protection to those who might require it the most."

"You calls 'wot' you just 'dun' to me protection, you brutal bastard! When I'm able I'll..."

Verlaine spat back through his broken teeth before he was silenced by Blackmore's cold riposte...

"You will, I fear, never 'be able', 'Billy boy' and as for the minor altercation that transpired between us this evening, well, if I were you, I'd regard your pain and suffering as payment in part for an outstanding debt owed to me by yourself from long ago. I've just called to collect my percentage, Billy boy! You had better hope that I do not decide to make a collection call often.

"Now, listen well to what I have to say for we two have a further use for you. We propose to cast a net over Whitechapel, Spitalfields, Bethnal Green and all of the surrounding boroughs so tight that not even a rat could pass between its tightly woven covering. What we require, with the gracious and willing participation of your many and varied underworld accomplices with whom you will negotiate on our behalf, is to spread our network from the Truman brewery, Spitalfields market and 'Itchy Park' in the North right down to Swallow Gardens and the East Dock in the south, from Mitre Square in the east right the way across to the station platform and the London hospital at Buck's Row.

"I want every public house, every alleyway and 'rookery', every square, court and privy in-between observed so keenly that even your so-called 'ghost' could not pass through unnoticed, and I want every microcosm of information, no matter how insignificant it might appear to be with regards to its importance within the scheme of things, reported directly to Leman Street police station where, rest assured, it will be processed with due diligence and acted on accordingly and with the swiftness that its importance demands. Do you understand, Billy boy?" questioned Blackmore...

Verlaine grunted in the affirmative and nodded his head slightly as he did so.

"Good. Very good indeed. I'm elated that the opportunity arose for us to re-acquaint ourselves after however many years that have passed between us. Old friends should never lose contact with one another entirely, do you not agree? Perhaps either myself or James will see fit to call on you again in, shall we say, four days' time in order to finalise the finer details appertaining to our proposed little scheme."

Taking out his watch from the right-hand pocket of his waistcoat, Blackmore flipped open its silver cover and checked the time...

"Good gracious me, time has become our enemy and we really must depart so we two may attend to more pressing concerns, so, with the deepest regret at breaking up this extremely necessary, if not altogether cordial or pleasant re-union between old friends and accomplices, both James and myself offer our fondest farewells and felicitations to one and all, for the time being," continued Blackmore with an ominous overtone present in his voice as he wiped blood from the blade of his knife on Verlaine's jacket sleeve.

"Make no mistake, you always 'was' an unpredictable an' dangerous 'fakker', Tiberius but how in the name of sweet baby Jesus did you manage to become such a 'fakkin' cold hearted bastard?" asked Verlaine...

Blackmore pondered Verlaine's question for a while before answering matter-of-factly...

"I never professed to being anything other than an unpredictable, dangerous or even perhaps a fucking cold-hearted bastard, Billy boy, went away to war as such, but came back home from war a cold-blooded monster!

"We are leaving now and would strongly advise against any form of surveillance, nor would we tolerate any form of misplaced or random repercussion in retaliation for events that have transpired between us here this evening. Any such action undertaken on your part will be met with the swiftest and most extreme force imaginable. These words I speak to you now should be deemed to serve not merely as a warning, but as a solemn oath taken on the blessed graves of fallen comrades. Now all that remains is for James and I to bid you all a very good evening."

Bass continued to survey the area with trained and focussed precision for any possible threat that might still be posed by any of the group that had not been rendered physically incapable of doing so. Satisfied that his colleague's retreat was more than adequately covered, he called out a simple, two-word direction...

"CLEAR, TIBERIUS!"

Safe in the knowledge that his retreat was more than adequately covered, Blackmore rose and backed steadily away from the prone body of Verlaine and, drawing his own pistol so as to reciprocate exactly his partner's actions, barked out the same two-word direction...

"CLEAR, JAMES!"

Holstering his pair of pistols, Bass took a few steps forward to where Lenny Fraser still lay on the cobbles where the sheer force from the impact of his blade had left him.

Crouching down to his haunches he reached over and grasped tightly hold of the carved antler handled knife protruding from Fraser's right shoulder. As he did so Fraser winced in agony and spat a tirade of abuse directly at the detective, who remained impassive throughout...

"You 'fakkin' rotten cozzer, you could've 'dun' for me right enough. One inch south an' your blade would've sent me directly to 'ighgate boneyard, you 'fakkin'..."

"When you are finally laid down to rest, Len, it will more than likely be in a shallow dug pauper's lime pit somewhere down the Mile End Road or more than likely after dancing the 'Tyburn jig' within the boundary wall of Newgate jail, but now is not your time to accept the Lord's judgement. Now is the time to return the blade that you borrowed to its rightful owner."

Utilising a quite unnecessary side to side motion, meant to cause maximum discomfort, Bass yanked his deeply embedded blade clear of Fraser's shoulder.

"Ooh, that's a nasty one and make no mistake about it, Len. I'd strongly recommend getting that wound cauterised with a white-hot iron and bound tight with a mustard and mandrake root hot poultice at once or you'll bleed out and, well, you would quite probably die. Goodbye for now and I really do hope to see you again very soon."

With that final farewell delivered, betraying just the merest hint of mock sarcasm from Bass, the two Detectives disappeared swiftly from view and melded with consummate ease into the surrounding maze of labyrinthine alleys and 'rookeries' that networked the area, a neighbourhood of abject destitution and extreme danger to which both Bass and Blackmore were very well acquainted.

Arriving back once more under the brick archway that was the entrance to Millers Court, both Blackmore and Bass shared a couple or three welcome drams of medicinal brandy from Blackmore's silver hip flask and smoked a pipe full of Hindu shag tobacco and a 'Rajah' stogie respectively.

As they stepped out into Dorset Street, a brand-new, mid-autumn October morning was breaking over Whitechapel. The lamp lighters of the previous evening had become the lamp extinguishers of this new dawn and went about their usual work routine oblivious to the violent proceedings that had but a few minutes earlier unfolded covertly under the secretive veil of darkness, behind the very street on which they stood.

Blackmore, taking a long pull from his comforting clay pipe, was the first of the pair to air his views on how the evenings proceedings had unfolded...

"I would conclude, taking into account the four score and ten random anomalies that always seem to manifest themselves during this type of operation, our spontaneous duel strategy seemed to unfold on schedule and we were able to reap its bountiful rewards admirably well, would you not concur, James?"

"I would indeed, Tiberius. A very agreeable and, might one be so bold as to say, even satisfying night's work to some degree," agreed Bass as he expertly blew thick, grey rings of smoke into the cold, early morning air while he allowed a wry grin to crack across his bristled, angular and age-gnarled face.

"A most rewarding conclusion to yet another successfully managed campaign. On this particular occasion the 'fear and hope to honour, respect and obey the iron hand of justice' seed was well and truly sewn and will, one would hope in a very short period of time, bear us the most succulent and ripe fruit aplenty for harvesting."

"An interesting analogy you make, James, but if I might be allowed to digress for a moment, with regards to your timely entrance during proceedings as they began to unfold in New Square. The knife throwing skill you exhibited was quite possibly one of the finest displays of the art that I have ever witnessed," exclaimed Blackmore, his admiration for the unquestionable knife punting skills shown by his partner fully apparent.

Having just taken a mouthful of brandy, Bass spat the precious, smooth, warming spirit directly out again, as if displaying total consternation at his colleague's remark of praise in recognition of his exemplary knife-throwing technique...

"SKILL, YOU SAY, TIBERIUS! ONE OF THE FINEST DISPLAYS OF THE ART THAT YOU'VE EVER WITNESSED WAS IT INDEED! I WOULD CLARIFY FOR YOUR INFORMATION THAT WITHOUT DOUBT IT WAS QUITE PROBABLY THE SINGLE WORST PRECISION PUNT OF A BLADE OVER A SUBSTANTIAL DISTANCE THAT THIS OLD SOLDIER HAS EVER MADE IN HIS ENTIRE LIFE!"

"How so, my brother?" questioned an incredulous and quite surprised Blackmore...

Bass answered immediately...

"The simple point of fact, my dear old friend, is that my errant shard impacted the shoulder area of your assailant, resulting in dealing merely a crippling blow, when in actual fact my intention was for my blade to pierce the throat area and thus result in an instant kill!"

"Remarkable!" exclaimed Blackmore. "Even by your usual standards of presenting what appears at first to resemble a totally spontaneous and somewhat chaotic strategy, that then somehow seems to deliver the positive results that we originally envisaged, I say again for want of a more adequate turn of phrase one might use... really quite remarkable!"

Whilst debating the success of their latest mission, Blackmore and Bass continued along Dorset Street in the direction of The Britannia public house where they knew a hansom cab that would take them back to Leman Street would be easy to hail.

"Remarkable in what manner, Tiberius? Remarkable skills with blade in hand? With pistols, fists, boot or cudgel? Remarkable in the use of stealth, cover and concealment tactics? Remarkable in what way?"

"Just...quite...JUST BLOODY REMARKABLE YOU INTOLERABLY IRRITATING BUFFOON!"

Chapter 28

'Stoker'

"**I** do believe that perusing, cogitating and agonising over the minute detail ensconced deeply within countless hundreds of pages of case files may well become the single most tedious task associated with police work," alluded Bass whilst emitting a huge, disenchanted sigh of discontentment as both he and Blackmore set about painstakingly dissecting the copious amounts of documented evidence folders that had thus far been accrued during the course of investigations which bore direct relation to the recent so-named 'Jack the Ripper' murders.

Blackmore peered over the rim of his wire framed reading spectacles at Bass across the large oak desk that the two detectives shared in their Leman Street office and began to speak…

"After due consideration and taking into account all of the tangible evidence that substantiates the theory that the four murders that have taken place since that of Emma Elizabeth Smith on April 3rd, the so-named 'canonical four' murders attributed thus far to the 'Ripper', I still remain unconvinced that the murder of Emma Elizabeth Smith should be disregarded altogether from our investigations, James."

"I agree completely, Tiberius," answered Bass…

"Our killer, or killers perhaps, for I believe there is sound enough reason for assuming that there is every possibility in the existence of an accomplice, and that they have systematically developed the butchery or indeed and is intrinsically more likely the medical skills necessary in order to perform the horrific, and yet precise and seemingly well-practised and expert mutilations of the 'canonical four' victims.

"An accomplice would also offer the security necessary in guaranteeing the copious amount of time required in order to carry out these seemingly well executed assaults.

"The murder of Emma Smith was in all probability carried out by our pair as their first attack and judging by the fact that Miss Smith initially survived the assault before eventually succumbing to her horrific injuries, they were either disturbed whilst perpetrating the act and thus were unable to complete their foul deed or were merely less precise because of their inexperience. Either way, unless evidence is forthcoming to substantiate this particular theory, we'll probably never uncover the truth of this particular thread."

The two Detectives were distracted from their work by a knock on their office door. Sergeant Marcus Jackson entered...

"Beggin' your pardon, sirs, a Billy Verlaine to see you both. Says it's a matter of the utmost urgency an' requires your immediate attention."

"Show him in, Sergeant, if you'll be so kind," said Blackmore as both himself and Bass turned their chairs to face the office door.

Verlaine hobbled in using the support of a stout cane and stood before the two Detectives, hoping they would offer him a seat sooner rather than later. Bass rose first and placed a chair at the centre of the office...

"Hello 'Billy boy'. How decent of you to drop by a full day in lieu of our agreed rendezvous. Very impressive manners, to be sure. A most cordial and gentlemanly gesture indeed. I can't imagine for one brief moment that this would be a mere social call so one would therefore assume that you have information pending that might have bold relevance to our ongoing enquiries. Now… sit you down, make yourself comfortable and sing, sweet nightingale, sing…"

As he spoke Bass moved behind Verlaine, put a hand firmly on each shoulder and exerting a great downward force slammed him into a seated position on the chair. He then backed away as Blackmore rose from his chair and approached the seated and very uncomfortable Verlaine as he spluttered…

"ARGH, no need for any of that 'fakkin' rough-'ouse' stuff, Jimmy Bass, I 'comes' 'ere' as a friend, 'bringin' important words 'an' the like for your two's ears only."

Blackmore stood directly in front of Verlaine and began to speak…

"Your 'important words' had better be worth at least the stinking breath on which they travel, Billy boy, because the consequences that befall you should those 'important words' prove to be lacking in either value or credibility will be so much more, how should I best convey to you my innermost dark intentions towards your personal well-being, final than a nasty limp!

"Now, as you are sitting comfortably, I suggest that you proceed as my colleague has so requested and… SING OUT LOUD, BILLY BOY!"

Verlaine squirmed uncomfortably in his seat and addressed Blackmore directly, all the while aware that the ominous presence of Bass lurked silently behind him, lying in wait like some unseen, life-threatening leviathan, ready to unleash its dormant savagery upon a near-defenceless foe.

"Tiberius…" he began, only for his first speech to be curtailed by Blackmore's instant riposte…

"Mr Blackmore sir. Today you shall offer the courtesy of referring to myself as Mr Blackmore sir, and to the gentleman who was gracious enough to grant you a seat in order to alleviate your obvious discomfort you will use the title Mr Bass sir. Now, do please continue…"

"Well Mr 'fakkin' Blackmore... SIR," spat Verlaine sarcastically, "I'm 'ere' of my own volition, an' at great discomfort to myself I might add, to bring 'youse' both choice information regardin' your case, an' all's you can muster as a greetin' is more 'arshness and 'ard treatment on my poor an' abused body, but..."

Bass rose up from his seat behind Verlaine and brought both of his hands down firmly on each of Verlaine's shoulders as he began to speak...

"No 'ifs' or 'buts', Billy. Neither will be tolerated any whys, wherefores or attempts by yourself to pit your keen street-wise wits against those of our own, nor any sort of procrastination on your part whatsoever. Now is your time, Billy. Now is your moment to shine most brightly and reveal unto us that you can offer some worthwhile service to the people of Whitechapel, if that notion might perchance make you more comfortable than perhaps believing that you might be of some use to both Tiberius and myself directly."

Verlaine's muscles tensed as he attempted to conceal the discomfort that he was feeling behind a nervous and very feeble grin that momentarily became an obvious grimace of pain.

"Awright, Mr Bass sir, 'awright. No more, I begs of you, no more grief.

"My associates on the cobbles 'ave been aware of certain suspicious comings an' goings on my manor for a couple of months or so now."

Sensing a rising level of both tension and fear in the demeanour of their guest, Blackmore poured a large measure of brandy and offered the generously sized tumbler to the increasingly restless Verlaine.

"Drink this, 'Billy boy' and feel free to smoke if you've a mind to."

Accepting the brandy gratefully, Verlaine sank the warming spirit in one gulp and proceeded to remove a battered Hindu shag tobacco tin from an inside pocket of his threadbare jacket. Upon removing the tin's lid he took out a tightly rolled cigarette and placed it in the right-hand corner of his mouth, lighting it by expertly flicking the head of a match to ignition with his right thumbnail.

Blackmore poured him another generously sized brandy and continued...

"Still you choose to addle what remains of your mind with those mean, tightly-rolled 'special herbal-type' ciggies, 'Billy boy'. No matter, so long as your dialogue remains sound and your reason is true.

So, you were about to elaborate on the 'awareness of certain suspicious comings and goings on your manor'."

Verlaine, his discomfort now eased somewhat by the combined effect of imbibing his second large brandy and toking deeply on his 'special herbal-type' cigarette vapour, continued his report as Blackmore and Bass listened intently to every uttered syllable, punctuating Verlaine's speech with well-researched questions as they meticulously went about the business of constructing a solid foundational platform for their case to rest upon.

"Suspicious comings and goings is 'fakkin' right, Mr Blackmore. Men not belongin' to our streets, clearin' out courts an' squares of folk goin' about their business for gawd knows what ends."

"Tell us more about the men, Billy boy. I am under the assumption that these men were not perceived by your agents to be canvassing for the usual plethora of 'working' female companionship indigenous to the area, nor were they seeking the more non-salubrious indulgences that 'the abyss' has to offer the gentleman seeking such toxic diversion?" asked Blackmore...

"Dark men, Mr Blackmore. Dark, menacin' men an' throwin' down a right an' proper beatin' to any poor pilgrim 'ood be either too 'fakkin' slow or too 'fakkin' stupid to move their arses out the way sharpish like. An' they was organised, you could even say they was working to a plan like 'cozzers' or army types is likely to..."

"Army types, you say!" interjected Bass as he rose up from the seat he had taken behind Verlaine, his attention grasped instantaneously and stimulated by Verlaine's last revelation.

"Can you describe any one of these 'army types' to us in greater detail, Billy boy? Ponder a short while if you feel the need to sieve through that drug addled, spirit-soaked rats' maze of a mind of yours, but offer us some tangible evidence that we can utilise to our mutual advantage.

"Perhaps a certain gait or disability belonging to one, a distinctive scar or discerning feature on another. Any instantly recognisable mannerisms or methods by which any orders might have been issued by one man or indeed received by another. Now SPEAK, you filthy, festering piece of privy dung, and hope that your revelations are worth a good deal more than the stinking breath on which they travel."

"Awright Mr Bass sir, Awright. No needs to be comin' over all 'ostile an' unfriendly like on account of the fact that I have laid my own 'mince pies' on the very persons of which I speak, Mr Bass sir.

"There was four of 'em altogether but one in particular was givin' out orders to the other three, all officer-like in 'is mannerisms. 'Ee' was tall, straight an' I caught a good 'butchers' at 'is face an' all, for no more than a second or two, mind, under that gas lamp outside number twenty-nine, 'anbury street."

"TWENTY-NINE HANBURY STREET. SPITALFIELDS! WHAT DAY WAS THIS, VERLAINE, WHAT DAY AND MOST SPECIFICALLY, WHAT TIME!" exclaimed Bass as he rounded sharply to face Verlaine, as if setting himself in position to knock his startled interviewee from the chair upon which he sat.

Verlaine raised both of his hands in order to cover his face from what he believed to be the imminent assault about to be administered by Bass and spoke immediately, needing no time to recall the information for which Bass had asked to mind...

"SATURDAY, SEVENTH OF SEPTEMBER, ABOUT HALF-FIVE, SIX O'CLOCK OF AN EVENIN'. PLESE DON'T 'IT' ME NO MORE, MR BASS.

"I was up the Black Swan on 'anbury Street, about six o'clock 'wiv' 'Arry the 'Awker. We 'ad' business matters to discuss 'an' was in there for half an hour or so. When we comes out we turns left onto 'anbury Street 'an' sets off to 'the spike' down Brick Lane to find a 'geezer' we needs to 'tap up'. That's when I sees these four 'dark 'an' dangerous lookin' 'geezers' clearin' out the street all the way along but especially in front of the row of 'ouses next to the old 'rub a dub'.

Me 'an' 'Arry didn't think nothin' of it, Mr Bass, 'till one of the bastards kicked my stick away, puts me down on the cobbles and tells me an' 'Arry 'an every 'fakker' else in the vicinity to 'fack off an' don't come back 'ere tonight or else."

"I won't strike you again, Billy boy, leastways not until such deserving a misdemeanour on your part manifests itself and gives me just cause to do so. Now, rest easy and continue on with your report" came the surprisingly reassuring words from Bass.

Verlaine settled as best he could and continued...

"As I was sayin', Mr Bass sir, 'is' face, the one givin' the orders. 'E' 'ad a thick 'tache an' a long battle scar that ran from 'is' left eye right the way down 'is' cheek 'an' under 'is' chin. 'E' didn't appear to 'ave much of a face at all really, not like yours an' mine any 'ow. 'Is nose tho', or that much as was left of it. Almost flat to 'is face it was. Broken quite badly once upon a time I shouldn't wonder."

"Ben Stoker!" exclaimed Blackmore. "Commander Benjamin Roderick Stoker. The last time our paths crossed he was still serving his commission in the Coldstream Guards. If you remember, James, during our initial secondment protocol after our recruitment to the newly commissioned Covert Special Forces Unit, Stoker was one of the senior staff training officers."

Bass frowned as he gave his reply...

"Oh, I remember Stoker well enough, Tiberius. A soldier's soldier. A highly respected and decorated veteran of multiple campaigns and a more proper, top line, pure evil bastard of the sub-human species it would prove difficult to find anywhere on earth, or indeed beyond its wider universal boundaries, I'd wager."

Turning once again to face Verlaine, Bass addressed him directly...

"Heed these words well, Billy boy, as you would deem fit to do so as if those words were spoken from a true and trusted friend. Under no account should any attempt be made to approach or hinder these men, especially Stoker. The consequence of direct contact by any of your agents, accomplices, associates or friends will result in the instant termination with extreme prejudice of your people. Heinous, vicious and immediate crimes that will go unreported to and unpunished by the authorities, perpetrated by who I now perceive to be officially sanctioned men, and so protected by the impenetrable judicial shield of the government, who show not one small iota of conscience when they are so engaged to perform such a task.

"We would ask of you to remain vigilant at all times and to continue your thus far exceptionally well executed mission with your surveillance of these men and their movements throughout 'the abyss' and to maintain a regular dialogue with us here at Leman Street. Now, Billy boy, if you would be so kind as to close the door on your way out, Tiberius and I have much to discuss."

Verlaine nodded his head once, alighted his chair and without uttering another word left the office, closing the door behind him as Bass had asked.

"You have a theory to share appertaining to our case, I presume, James?" inquired Blackmore upon recognising the now all too familiar facial expressions and mannerisms his colleague exhibited whilst mentally cogitating intently with a view to imminently revealing his thoughts.

"Benjamin Roderick Stoker! I remember him well from our very first encounter. Just a few weeks following my raising from the ranks of the Ninety-Fifth as a temporary standing second lieutenant and placed in charge of my first small command, Stoker arrived at barracks as the replacement full pips Lieutenant and proceeded immediately to personify the troubling stories that preceded his arrival with regards in particular to his brutal method of command.

Floggings were administered for the slightest indiscipline, both during and off parade. What might be considered as minor kit indiscretions by most non-commissioned officers and dealt with in a strict but ultimately fair manner were rewarded with severe, brutal beatings courtesy of Stoker himself or members of his trusted senior staff, and any sign of mental or physical weakness was punished with prolonged incarceration in the battalion jail where, behind the privacy of high walls, locked gates and grey iron bars, all manner of degrading tortures were meted out to the hapless squaddies unfortunate enough to have been deemed deserving of Stoker's personal base and depraved attentions."

Blackmore listened intently to his colleague as the full horrors of Stoker's barbaric method of command were divulged. After a brief moment of silence, he spoke.

"Might one ask, James, how did your own fortunes fare upon the arrival of such a beast?"

"From the outset, chance intervened to ensure that my initial fortune proved most favourable. Fortunately, in recognition of my recent exemplary service as acting lieutenant, that it seemed had not gone unnoticed by higher command, I was raised to full lieutenant and given command of my own small unit of green jacketed chosen men, the best and proudest sharpshooters in the British army, within a few days of his arrival. Thus was I able to avoid any form of subordinate contact with the man initially, save for the mandatory briefings both pre and post ops and during training exercises, when our respective units tended to merge and joint command would be shared between the two lieutenants.

"As time and several campaign deployments went by, my men would return from 'ops' in a demoralised and visibly broken state of mind. Not only by the acceptable stresses and rigours of warfare, as an attentive commanding officer would surely notice immediately and deal with accordingly, but rather by their unwarranted and unnaturally brutal treatment at the hands of Stoker and his command staff.

"As I recall, we had just returned from our expedition designed to outflank the Russians at Kerch, just east of Sevastopol, sometime in mid-1855 if my fading memory serves well enough. Our dual commands were once more divided, my sharpshooters being requisitioned in order to carry out special operations under the already proven to be dubious auspices of Stoker. When they were finally returned to my command, the surviving twenty five of the fifty men deployed were in a sorry state, both physically and mentally. Their green tunics, which set them apart as a much-respected, highly-trained special forces unit and gave each man chosen to wear them immense pride, had been replaced by the standard red coats of the infantry and their own personalised sharpshooters' rifles confiscated, to be replaced by standard issue army muskets.

"After listening to the harrowing de-brief report submitted by my seriously wounded corporal it became clear to me that the original orders designated to the green jackets by high command, comprising of expert covert covering fire from high ground designed to protect a key section of the battalion as it proceeded to advance on its flanking mission around the Russian Army, were spontaneously vetoed by Stoker who in turn ordered the sharpshooters to spearhead the assault as little more than a forlorn hope.

"Stripped of their green jackets and their superior quality weapons, each man mustered the legendary courage of the ninety-fifth, courage that had made the green jackets' battlefield exploits revered throughout the world, they advanced forward into the waiting cauldron of hell.

"Sickened to my very core by the graphic report delivered to me by my corporal, who incidentally died shortly afterwards as a result of his terrible wounds, the desperate condition of those poor souls who survived, and completely convinced that Stoker had abused his command of the green jackets in this heinous manner purely as little more than a method of retribution towards myself, I vowed that from that moment forth I would await the opportune moment to manifest itself in order to even the score with Stoker once and for all."

"I believe that after all of these years passed as both your colleague, and more importantly, your trusted friend and brother at arms, that I know you well enough, James. Well enough to know that you're proposing to kill Stoker, are you not?" questioned Blackmore.

Bass' answer was simple and straight to the point...

"Have I become so predictable, so very open a book for you to read with consummate ease, my dear old friend?

"As a final payment in full of sorts. Not just for the callous manner in which he decimated the ranks of the brave ninety-fifth whilst displaying not one iota of pity or remorse, but also for the many innocent souls that he has systematically destroyed during his worthless career, and the souls that he continues to abuse and destroy still to this day.

"My answer to your question is a simple, unequivocal and emphatic yes, Tiberius. When the guilt-edged opportunity arises, which I'm positive it most certainly will do very soon indeed, I shall aim to put a bullet between the dark eyes of Ben Stoker and show nor feel one hint of regret or remorse for doing so."

"Might I then be so bold as to ask one more question with regards to our potentially soon to be departed Mr Stoker, James, if you will allow me the privilege."

"Of course, Tiberius. Ask of me anything you wish freely and I shall endeavour to answer with honest truth and veracity always."

"With regards to the current seemingly random configuration of Stoker's facial characteristics, particularly in the nasal area, as so described in great detail by our mutual friend Billy Verlaine. Would you, by any chance...?"

Before Blackmore was able to complete his question, Bass began his answer...

"Indeed, I would, Tiberius. It is I who am responsible for giving Stoker his, ahem, shall we say somewhat distinctive facial profile.

"When my men returned, with both their green jackets and rifles confiscated by Stoker, I decided to pay an immediate visit on the man whom I considered to be little more than a common thief of personal property, purely in order to retrieve the stolen items, you understand."

Blackmore rolled his eyes and shook his head slightly whilst emitting a wry grin as he anticipated Bass' next few words almost to perfection. He continued to listen intently as Bass continued...

"Stoker was encamped but a few tents away from my own billet so locating him proved to be no hardship. As good fortune would have it, I found him to be alone, curiously so as it seemed to me at the time, possibly even awaiting my imminent arrival. His words, therefore, came as no surprise to me as those of a rampant, arrogant egotist, displaying openly all the traits of unfettered megalomania.

"In short, he craved power through rapid advancement in rank and cared not what human cost would be incurred in order to achieve his ends. His initial greeting was cordial, polite even as one would normally expect between officers in conference, but my mood was sombre and I sought instant closure, in hindsight possibly even revenge, for the wasted lives of my men and all the many other souls he had tainted and destroyed merely to enhance his own ambitions towards rapid personal gain. This is how I remember events unfolding at the time."

With that, Bass began to recount his memory of the fateful confrontation that ensued between himself and Ben Stoker…

"Ah, Lieutenant Bass. I'm so pleased you could find the time to call by. Please, would you…

"Shut your fucking mouth and listen, Stoker, you extraordinarily generous lump of festering faecal matter! I care not at this moment for the pleasantries or cordial manners normally exhibited by officers towards each other. Nor do I fear any malicious repercussions towards myself that might be rendered by your aristocratic subordinates.

"I care even less about your greatly exaggerated and unquietly trumpeted reputation for hard soldiering and for the oh-so-many tall tales regarding your so-called 'special skills' accrued whilst engaged in all manner of derring-do on the field of battle. I too have accrued a good many 'special skills', as a result of a genuinely hard-won reputation, so any perceived advantage on your part in the advent of a physical match that you might anticipate occurring between we two at this precise moment in time might well be ill advised on your part.

"Based upon my own private enquiries within the regiment, with regards to your seemingly formidable reputation, I say these words to you, Benny Stoker.

"You are a poor, sad excuse for a human being. Your crimes are beyond reproach and fully deserve to be vilified, indicted and dealt with accordingly by administering the severest of punitive measures by the highest military authorities."

"Are you quite finished, Bass?" asked Stoker.

"No, I most certainly am not fucking finished. Not by a good long stretch," countered Bass immediately.

"You will answer for your crimes, Stoker, and you will pay the ultimate price in return for murdering my men, but not today. Today, I call on you and demand the return of the fifty green jackets and the fifty sharp shooter rifles of the ninety-fifth rifle brigade that you stole from my men before you forced them into unfamiliar red jackets, armed them with unfamiliar muskets and sent them on a suicide mission to lead the forlorn hope at Kerch, the mission that you didn't possess the courage to lead yourself, the mission that you and your shit command were originally ordered to carry out."

"Ah gentlemen, so good of you to join us. Please, come in and partake in the fray, anytime please, gentlemen, when it suits," said Stoker gloatingly as a burly, sweaty corporal and equally sweaty and seemingly twice as wide Colour Sergeant Major belonging to Stoker's command entered the tent in which they stood.

Bass eyed the new arrivals intently for a few seconds and, remaining calmness personified, began to speak, an air of authority and menace growing in his voice with each passing second ...

"Please add cowardice to your growing list of shame, 'Benny boy'. You should learn never to make other ignorant parties, especially hitherto innocent other ignorant parties, privy to your sordid little schemes."

Even before his final sentence faded away into the tense atmosphere, Bass twisted to his right and forced the hard heel of his right hand upwards and underneath the burly, sweaty Corporal's stubbly jaw, breaking the lower jaw bone in several places with one movement and dislocating what was left from the sockets on either side of the Corporal's broken face.

In the chaos that ensued, as the sweaty Corporal went to ground screaming in fits of agony as best he could, utilising what little sinew of that portion of his face that remained intact, Bass faded to his left and diverted his attention to the equally sweaty and twice as wide Colour

215

Sergeant. Concentrating first on both of the Sergeant's knees, in what seemed like one gracefully simultaneous movement, Bass proceeded to use each of his heavily booted feet as if performing some obscure far-Eastern dance routine.

Firstly, his right boot came into devastating contact with and shattered the Sergeant's right knee cap. Then, avoiding with ease the wildly flailing swathes of a bayonet that had been brandished by the Sergeant, Bass set himself in a low position to the hapless officer's left side and kicked out so that the sole of his left boot came firmly into contact with the cartilage of the sergeant's left knee.

Finally, Bass turned his body once more and, displaying perfect balance similar to that of the majestic crane whilst in its one-legged repose, raised his right knee to meet the falling face of the crippled Sergeant and, as his broken and unconscious body slumped to the floor, Bass righted himself immediately and, his composure fully restored in an instant and his mind prepared to accept any attempted assault that might occur from his one remaining aggressor, turned to face Stoker head on, who had taken the albeit extremely short opportunity whilst Bass dispatched his men to arm himself with a large, bone-handled knife.

Arm outstretched, levelling his blade directly at Bass, Stoker began to speak...

"Very impressive work, James Bass, very impressive indeed. Skilled, brutal and oh, so very decisive for one boasting such tender years. Cold, clinical, precise and quite an exquisite act in its overall execution. You, sir, are a very dangerous individual indeed. A man with whom one should most definitely not trifle with on any account. A veritable 'green devil'. A man who..."

"A man who recognises immediately when the arrogant, over-confident, pompous ass confronting him has chosen the incorrect weapon in order to complete his sanction," Bass interjected almost nonchalantly as he simultaneously and whilst utilising great speed in doing so entered Stoker's personal space and, crossing both his hands over in a scissor-like motion, proceeded to slap the lethal blade away from Stoker's grasp with consummate ease.

Noticing a rifle that lay on the floor between himself and Stoker, Bass stooped to pick it up. Stoker was alert to this minute lapse in Bass' concentration and lunged forward with purpose directly at Bass, hoping to catch him off guard.

Bass, however, remained alert to any potential threat and upon retrieving the rifle successfully stepped backwards three generous paces in order to give himself space and ample time in which to act. Gripping the heavy weapon tightly with both hands, he proceeded to raise the rifle high above his right shoulder and brought the full weight of its brass edged stock down and hard into Stoker's advancing face; THUD!

Reeling backwards and going to ground immediately as a result of the sickeningly solid blow, Stoker lay dazed, prone and helpless on the ground. Fully aware that his nose had been very badly broken and that he was now totally at the mercy of a man whom he now realised would feel no remorse for taking his life, should he choose to do so, he prepared himself as best he could to speak.

At the precise moment that he began to plead for his life, Bass interjected with a tirade of words so designed as to strike terror into the heart of anyone at whom they were directed, all the while continuing to pummel the rapidly disintegrating features of Stoker into an unrecognisable pulp whilst continuing to speak...

"SILENCE, YOU PUTRID FILTH! Listen to my words as if they were the last ones you might ever hear in your miserable life you mangy, whipped cur; THUD!

"I would like to take this opportunity to introduce you, in intimate fashion, to the weapon of a chosen man; THUD!

"A brave man, THUD, an honourable man, THUD, and now a dead man as a result of your warped aristocratic ambition and your craven cowardice; THUD!

"Twenty-five souls sent to meet their maker too soon, sent out as the forlorn hope that they should never have been; THUD!"

"Twenty-five good souls and true wasted on the whim of an egocentric, public school-pampered, pompous, preening piece of stinking aristocratic flotsam that is not fit to wear the proud colours of his regiment, nor fit even to lace the boots of my murdered green jackets, THUD, THUD... THUD!"

Halting for a moment from his brutal assault, Bass surveyed what few recognisable features remained of the face that he had been mercilessly and systematically erasing with the aid of his now very bloodied rifle butt.

Shaking his head whilst gesturing in turn towards Stoker's fallen accomplices Bass continued...

"As a result of your actions that man now has only half a face, and that man more than likely will only be able to walk again by utilising a cane, if indeed he is ever able to walk again; and what of you, Stoker?

"You now sport a face that your wife, your siblings, your colleagues, your friends, even you yourself would not immediately recognise. Every time you look into a mirror this moment will remind you of what has transpired between us here today.

"I would hope also that your every waking hour be tormented, if not by feelings of remorse and guilt for the lives that you have tainted and taken, then more so with the thought that on another more appropriate occasion, engineered precisely to suit my own purpose, tomorrow perhaps, or a year on from now, two years on, or three years on, possibly even on this very night, I will seek you out from whichever concealed bolt-hole or privy you choose to cower within and end your tormented, pathetic existence for good.

"Now, don't you die on me, Benny Stoker. Rest easy, or at least as easily as a dead man walking is able to do so; THUD, THUD... THUD!"

As Bass completed his tale Blackmore remained silent for a few seconds before giving his deadpan answer...

"Finally, James. Finally, it becomes perfectly clear to me after all of this time. The reason for your curiously fearsome sobriquet within the regiment. So obvious, and so very apt in view of your current revelations."

Bass eyed his comrade incredulously and asked in return...

"I'm intrigued, Tiberius. I sport a sobriquet within the regiment. Might one ask what that sobriquet might be?"

Blackmore answered immediately, a wide grin appearing on his chiselled features as he did so...

"Those few of us who garner respect from the regiment by offering fair command and give leadership by exhibiting bold personal example, of which you are one such highly respected individual within the regiment, James; and might one add, a fully deserving individual of your affectionate title too.

"You, my dear old friend, for your fearsome reputation alone, were dubbed very early on in your career 'the Green Devil'!"

Chapter 29

'The Report'

Within the confines of the Leman Street office of Bass and Blackmore a meeting between the two detectives was taking place in order to determine what their next course of action would be. Bass was the first to speak...

"I would prefer if Connie were to speak with the police surgeon of H Division personally, here at Leman street, Tiberius. A meeting between two of the leading and most respected authorities in Europe, with regards to offering an insight into advanced surgery techniques and theory, might provide keen insight into the case and also help to validate, possibly even substantiate indubitably a theory that I am in the process of formulating."

Blackmore's answer was immediate.

"I believe that the venerable Doctor George Bagster Phillips is in house on this very day. I will send word immediately to the Royal College of Surgeons where Connie is presently engaged as chief lecturer in the subject of advanced surgical procedures, and the development of new techniques in relation to the advancement of police forensic science. Assuming both hers, and the good doctor Phillip's busy schedules allow us the time, a mid-afternoon conference this afternoon shouldn't be out of the question."

... ...

Constance Bass arrived at the Leman Street police station at fourteen hundred hours precisely as requested to do so by Blackmore on that very same afternoon. She entered the office of Frank Abilene to be greeted, first by her husband, James, then Tiberius Blackmore, Frank Abilene himself, her good friend and colleague Doctor George Bagster Phillips, whom she had met and befriended whilst studying for her doctorate and professorships in surgical techniques and forensic science at the London Royal College of Surgeons, and his assistant doctor Percy John Clark.

"Good afternoon, husband, and gentlemen. It is most agreeable to see you all on this rather fine autumnal afternoon. However, much as though I would dearly love to tarry a good while, take a late afternoon tea and idly exchange long overdue pleasantries, especially with you, Francis, and of course your esteemed self, George, my dear old friend and colleague, whose agreeable acquaintance time has seen fit to grant no favours towards these last few years; and of course, Percy, a true pleasure to see you as always.

"Speaking of time as my momentary nemesis a lecture theatre populated handsomely with eager students ravenous to partake of a veritable smorgasbord of knowledge, awaits with all of the dubious youthful anticipation that they are able to muster my late-afternoon oratory concerning the finer points of exploratory heart, lung, intestinal and renal surgery!

"If one might be allowed to digress momentarily, dear Francis, might I take up the kind offer of afternoon tea as was previously mentioned if you please? The arid dryness of the Whitechapel air, coupled with the unintentional inhalation of dust particles risen from the cobbles as my cab hastened to your presence has brought about a slight recurrence of my allergies."

Abilene smiled politely and dispatched a young constable who was attending the group to bring them tea. He continued his address, firstly directly to Constance Bass, then to the group as a whole...

"My dear Connie. As always, it is a pleasure to welcome you to this office, even though it languishes in these less than salubrious surroundings of H division here at Leman Street, which I apologise profusely for asking you to attend at such short notice. However, our need for your professional insight in order to corroborate key medical theories appertaining to the Whitechapel murders and perhaps possibly to offer a fresh, or even an alternative perspective to our case study at this juncture of our investigations necessitates your presence here at this meeting.

"Our venerable Dr Phillips, with whom I believe you are well acquainted, leads our medical investigation and the possibly not-so-venerable but none the less, and by implementation of their own dubious methods, singularly effective pair of reprobates to whom you are well acquainted seated to your left retain command of H division's ongoing field investigations.

"Dr Phillips. If you would be so good as to offer us a brief synopsis of the medical investigations thus far."

Phillips cleared his throat and after briefly swapping cordial pleasantries with his old friend and colleague Constance Bass, began his report...

"Based on the medical evidence that has been accrued from each of the canonical 'Ripper' victims, and the pair of earlier assaults that are loosely associated with the case, I believe that there is a distinct possibility that our perpetrator is a man, or indeed a woman, in possession of some not inconsiderable skill set, possibly a medical person or a butcher.

"Our initial observations led us to the assumption, however, that in order for a skilled hand to have perpetrated these crimes a fair portion of time would have been required. As the mutilations became more precise with the advent of each new murder the suggestion of a trained hand became more plausible, as did the distinct possibility arise that the perpetrator might well choose to operate with the aid of an accomplice."

Constance thought for a moment, took a sip of tea and began to speak...

"I have been able to peruse your extensive and quite remarkably well-ordered reports at great length, George. I commend you for their complexity and their attention to the most minute details appertaining to each murder and I concur with your findings, up to a point.

I have to make plain from the outset that I do not deal in the likelihood that assumptions of any kind lead to a satisfactory conclusion, even those based on exemplary case work such as yours obviously is, George. However, I do concur with much of the content within your reports and based upon the results of my own extensive forensic research after several painstaking examinations of the victims' remains, I would like to take this opportunity to contribute my own personal report to this investigation, if I may, gentlemen."

After noting nods of approval from all those assembled, Constance continued...

"Your assumption, for want of a more appropriate phrase, that the murderer could possibly be of the medical profession is correct, George. Though I would have preferred to have attended each murder site and examined in greater detail all of the victims as they were discovered, in their respective undisturbed conditions, I can nevertheless conclude with certainty that after examining the wounds present on each victim, with particular reference being paid to those distinct lacerations made in the oesophagus and torso regions, that our murderer is a surgeon who is in possession of a very impressive skill set indeed. I would suggest that the list of suspects who could boast of presenting such impressive credentials in the whole world will be quite a short one.

"Also, your observation that a second party might have been involved in carrying out at least some of the murders is a sound one that should merit due consideration and further investigation."

Upon hearing this sentence, particularly the part relating to a second party being involved with 'some' of the murders, Dr Phillips questioned simply...

"You add to my initial observation 'a second party might have been involved in carrying out at least 'some' of the murders', Connie, emphasis directly on the word 'some'. How so 'some' of the murders, if I might be so bold as to enquire?"

Constance continued...

"Of course, George. The first two killings that were at first thought to have been the work of 'Jack the Ripper' but never proven to have been so, those of Emma Smith and Martha Tabram, were obviously carried out very quickly, on account of the seemingly frenzied and multiple stab wounds that were present on each of the bodies.

"However, striking similarities between the horrific wounds of these two victims and those found on the bodies of the later poor souls gave cause for serious credence to be given whilst considering these remarkable comparisons, comparisons as yet extraordinarily overlooked as evidence up until this moment. Vital new evidence also recently came to light that a similar blade was used to carry out the first two mutilations, as was used in the murders of the following four women."

"The same blade used throughout. Of course. Elements within your report would greatly explain why the murderer's technique became more refined over a period of time."

"Indeed, George. He was, more than likely still is, developing his art momentarily, refining the quality of his artistic craft as he most likely views his murderous proclivities as being and all the while satiating a simple and compelling obsession to kill. Preying on a quarry he feels will not be mourned nor missed as a result of any conspicuous absence, in this case ladies of unfortunate circumstances who are made vulnerable by choosing to ply their trade in areas of 'the abyss' made dangerous by their isolation.

"Our man, for I now believe the 'Ripper' to be a man, is the worst kind of sociopath imaginable for he probably has the ability to move within the highest tiers of society and avoid arousing any sort of suspicion. He has become an experienced master of hiding in plain sight.

"I too am of the opinion that the suggestion made previously that the addition of a third party to participate in proceedings, initially employed as a lookout for sure, possibly even an equally skilled apprentice if you will, whose presence offers 'Jack' more precious time to spend at each new scene in order to enhance his creativity to the next level, is a sound one."

"Thus does the great artist present his next 'masterpiece' to his captive audience. An audience terrified by this ongoing spate of 'serial killings', as so dubbed by the ever-sensationalist revelations printed on a daily basis by several broadsheets of dubious source and quality.

"An audience disconcerted and disgusted to the point of anarchy by street-corner soap-box preachers who seek nothing more for themselves than to canvass the fragile and suggestible lower-class mentality and to exploit the civil unrest that ultimately occurs as a result but ironically achieves little more than to enhance and to further their own political ambitions.

"A captive, frightened audience whose perception of the lack of progress being made by the seemingly inept police investigation relating to the crimes remains an alarming concern and yet, even though terror grips the public psyche in a manner that it probably never has done before, we sense an attentive, perhaps even expectant audience almost salivating in anticipation as to what fresh horrors are yet to come.

"The apprentice more than likely has his own twisted agenda and is merely using this gilt-edged opportunity that has manifested itself before him somewhat fortuitously to suit his own ends."

"If we are in agreement that Connie's report will from this moment onwards provide the core incentive for our investigation, we must therefore concentrate our undivided attentions upon key medical personnel belonging to the absolute hierarchy of the surgical profession currently engaged in this city," began Abilene.

Addressing first the two Detectives directly, Abilene continued…

"James, Tiberius, this will be your personal remit. I shall endeavour to assist as much as I am able with regards to gaining access into the higher echelons of society in order for you both to secure your necessary interviews, but please be under no illusion that your task will not be an easy one.

"Once an investigation by H division is detected by the special operations unit, as it is most definitely sure to be, bureaucratic doors will close and lock in our faces, files that we might wish to peruse in order to garner information vital to the success of our mission will mysteriously vanish and even personal sanctions might be made covertly on key personnel attached to our investigation. With this last point particularly in mind I can bring to mind no better or more qualified pairing currently seconded to H division with more than a half-chance of concluding this part of the plan favourably."

Turning his attention to Doctors Phillips and Clark, Abilene continued…

"Doctors Phillips and Clark. I ask if you would return to your laboratory with haste and continue with your examinations of the prima-facie evidence for each murder. Draw your final conclusions as to whether each one of our cases will have both the strength and legality to be successfully prosecuted should they come to trial, under the assumption that successful arrests be made and the suspects are charged, of course.

"Now gentlemen, I thank you both for your invaluable contribution to this meeting and for all of your painstakingly hard work completed thus far to assist in bringing this sad business to a satisfactory conclusion, but now I must bid you both a good afternoon as I have other pressing matters of unrelated Police business to discuss with my colleagues."

The two doctors alighted their chairs, left Abilene's office and closed the door behind them. Waiting a brief moment until he was certain of absolute privacy, Bass was the first of the four to speak...

"Connie, I sense that you have more information to divulge, relevant facts appertaining to our case that you believed could not be shared with our two good doctors just this moment excused."

"Yes, James, my love. As always, you are wise to my foibles. Your senses in this instance do not lie.

"You will recall, gentlemen, as my report was delivered I remarked upon the possibility of there being a second suspect involved in the perpetration of these crimes. I am convinced that based upon the evidence I have submitted this is indeed a fact and what is even more relevant to our cause, I believe I am able to offer with full confidence a credible suggestion as to the identities of two chief suspects."

Chapter 30

'Thirteen Millers Court'

"**C**onnie, am I to understand that you truly believe that you are finally able to name our elusive 'Jack the Ripper' himself, or rather themselves!" exclaimed Frank Abilene.

"I do certainly believe so, Francis, yes. I believe that I am able to give names to your prime suspects with the utmost confidence," said Constance assertively.

"Have a care, Connie, for this is indeed a bold revelation, especially from one so venerable and respected within her chosen field. Should your theory prove groundless many, if not all, of your colleagues will ostracise you from their professional echelons as well as from the privileged corridors of their society. You will be vilified by the general public, primed and goaded to a fit of frenzy by the baying jackals of the gutter press and you will be castigated mercilessly by your peers and detractors to the point of your venerable career becoming irreparably damaged. I could not bear for any of this to happen so, I beg of you, if not merely for yourself then for James' and my sake, please do not reveal your thoughts to the public arena."

Constance interjected immediately, attempting to belay the genuine concern showed towards her well-being by her dear friend...

"Dear Francis. Might I be permitted to digress for a brief moment and refer you back to a point that I alluded to earlier, in that I do not countenance assumption with specific reference to the interpretation of case evidence and its validity on any account.

"The information that I am about to divulge here in this room can never be made public knowledge. The repercussions that would undoubtedly be experienced throughout the very highest echelons of society would without doubt cause major consternation and open revolt within the most senior tiers of our government and possibly even the name of the Royal household might be tarnished, simply by professional or even personal association with these names, should they be openly revealed.

"A few years ago, whilst I was abroad on a working placement at the world-renowned University of Leipzig in Germany, I became most impressed by the work of a brilliant scientist by the name of Baron Josef von Waldheim the third.

"Already, for one of such a relatively young age, boasting the enviable reputation of a remarkably gifted surgeon, he specialised in all areas of advanced surgical procedures relating to exploratory anatomical studies, experimental neurological, heart and brain surgery, plus the introduction of revolutionary new practices devised by himself for the development of multiple organ transplant techniques.

"He was also a keen advocate and publicly endorsed a form of organ re-animation known as galvanism. The morally questionable process involved utilising specially commissioned equipment to pass extremely strong electrical charges throughout the anatomy of an ailing or lifeless body, thus, and to all intents and purposes, re-energising the corpse. In short, producing life from death.

"This continued obsession with the cult of galvanism and the moral implications that such a practice suggested, coupled with him displaying openly his total disdain towards colleagues, mentors and peers, led to his expulsion from the faculty and to a lifetime disbarment from practising medicine in any of its many forms.

"As for presenting a brief character reference of the man himself; I found him to be arrogant and self-assured, displaying outwardly all the traits of a rampant egotist who believed that all people and all things were an encumbrance to his own progress, mere insects to be used and then cast aside as he saw fit.

"I also noticed, too, that he had begun to display obvious signs of acute sociopathic behaviour, quite a common condition for one so self-obsessed and driven to realise their immoral ambitions at any cost.

"I conclude therefore that this man is the assistant. A man whose obsessive compulsion compels him to harvest the human organs he requires in order to further develop what have now become his quite obsessive experiments concerning the concept of galvanism. Fresh, untainted organs made readily and so abundantly available by the convenient and quite regular handiwork of the 'Ripper'."

Abilene, Blackmore and Bass listened intently and as Constance continued with her compelling briefing a similar stark understanding of the murders and their perpetrators' motives for committing their atrocious crimes occurred to each of them simultaneously. The horrific realisation that a pair of dangerously psychotic personalities who were each proceeding to fulfil two totally separate agendas were in the process of murdering their way through the dark streets of Whitechapel.

Abilene was the first to break the silence...

"I congratulate you on your exemplary work, Connie. Not only a brilliant forensic case report but also firstly to acquire the evidence, and then to produce such detailed psychological profiles of each suspect. Quite astounding, truly, a remarkable achievement and I fear there is yet more of a major revelation to be heard."

"Indeed, Francis. A major revelation that, if made public directly, has the potential to cause a scandal throughout both the government and the aristocracy of potentially cataclysmic proportions, if not sensitively handled by calm and prepared minds," added Constance.

"Ten years ago, I was offered an opportunity by the Royal College of Surgeons in London to take on the responsibility of continuing research into the advancement of surgical and forensic techniques that were to be made available for specific use by the Metropolitan and city police forces. During the initial extensive restructuring process that the antiquated research department required in order to function in the particular manner that suited the needs of both myself, and my hand-picked staff, we were supported and mentored by the dean of the college, surgeon-in-chief and surgeon to the Queen and the Royal household, Lord Augustus De-Fanque Arbogast.

"Outwardly a benevolent, courteous though at times arrogant and somewhat belligerent man, should the mood arise within him, thus befitting his station in society as wealthy, old aristocracy. He was, however, always generous with his time when granting audience to his subordinates and gave the distinct impression that he was content with the expectation that as his great knowledge spoke, so the wisdom of others should be to listen, to learn and so to ultimately benefit from this great gift that he saw fit to bestow upon them."

"The arrogance borne of high breeding and privilege knows no bounds, Connie," mused Bass thoughtfully.

"Lord Augustus De-Fanque Arbogast. Recognised by many in another far distant time and place by his more familiar sobriquet of 'Sir Augustus the butcher'. Known now in this place and time by the four of us as 'Jack the Ripper'."

"Now it becomes patently obvious as to how the evidence submitted by our friend Billy Verlaine serves to clarify the reason for the involvement of Ben Stoker and his special forces colleagues in our little melodrama," alluded Blackmore...

"Engaged by the highest authority, Stoker's prime directive is to swiftly and mercilessly sweep the next carefully selected 'Ripper' site of any and all stray personages by utilising any dubious means that lay at their disposal. Your previous suggestion of 'the aristocracy taking care of its own' personified, James."

Bass nodded once, signifying his acknowledgement of Blackmore's observation but it was Constance who continued on with the thread...

"What is more, gentlemen, I believe that I know of a place where one might seek to locate our pair of errant miscreants. Located deep within the 'abyss', I have heard talk amongst the hierarchy of my profession, concerning a club of sorts that outwardly respectable gentlemen frequent as a precursor to perusing their nocturnal philandering in the bars and brothels of Whitechapel. The address of this place is eighty-nine, Manning Place.

"As you would probably not be surprised to learn, Connie, eighty-nine Manning Place is not unknown to us, from a purely professional standpoint, you understand," Blackmore spluttered, as if momentarily embarrassed by letting slip a guilty secret.

"Oh Tiberius. I am indebted to you for at least attempting to appear chivalrous but please understand that in my profession, I too am privy to much hearsay, and startling revelations aplenty concerning all manner of indiscreet disclosures concerning the questionable proclivities of so-called gentlemen who really should know better how to manage more discreetly their unsavoury nocturnal expeditions into the bars and bordellos of the 'abyss.'

"In short, not only would it probably be quite remiss of me to do so, but I would find extreme difficulty in putting the professional conduct or the etiquette of either yourself, my sweet James, or dear old Francis under any kind of profound scrutiny whatsoever. Results, you sweet old thing. The favourable results of one's hard won endeavours speak loudly enough for themselves!"

"Ahem, yes, quite, Connie. I thank you for your honesty and... your candour with your regards to your explanation of... err... the obvious indiscretions of the... err..."

"TIBERIUS, CEASE YOUR INANE AND POINTLESS GIBBERING!

"For your information, dearest Tiberius, among my raft of qualifications I hold a degree certificate, first class with honours, that qualifies me to practise as a psychiatrist and I am under no doubt whatsoever that taking either yourself, James or even Francis on as patients would afford one a lifetime's worth of profitable work and several valuable paragraphs of ground-breaking text concerning the general psychosis and mental derangement of an ex-army special operative Police Inspector that would be lauded by the highest of the high within the Psychiatrists' Guild! Now please, take a moment to compose yourself and... proceed."

Blackmore shuffled uncomfortably in his seat. He was a highly decorated veteran of several military campaigns abroad, had survived countless potentially suicidal incursions behind hostile enemy lines and in this brief moment became fully aware that the aura of invincibility perceived by many to surround both himself and James Bass had been clinically breached by the expertise of a psychiatrist, albeit an exceptional one.

"Yes, of course, Connie. So, with regards to eighty-nine Manning Place. A respectable gentlemen's club situated close to Crossinghams lodging house on Little Paternoster Row and a prime location for the 'Ripper' and his accomplice to exploit as a base from which to go forth into the 'abyss' and perpetrate their atrocities, suspected by no-one therein and therefore completely unmolested."

Composure regained in full, as Blackmore continued on with his brief, the privacy of their meeting was interrupted somewhat rudely as

Marcus Jackson unceremoniously burst into the office unannounced, displaying an obvious demeanour of high anxiety as he gave his report.

"Pardon the intrusion, ma'am, sirs, but there's been another murder. Thirteen, Millers Court, just off Dorset Street. 'Indian Harry' went down the court to collect rent for McCarthy at about half ten this morning and discovered..."

His words tapered away as an uncontrollable wave of emotion overcame him and it became instantly clear to the assembled group that Jackson had been extremely traumatised by the graphic contents of the report he had just received concerning the murder. Composing himself momentarily he finished by disclosing simply...

"The worst one yet, by all accounts."

Abilene was the first to respond, displaying immediately his formidable ability to issue succinct and rational instructions whilst under the most extreme emotional pressure...

"Connie, muster any assistance and resources that you see fit to utilise and accompany Dr Phillips directly to attend the murder scene, if you please. I need incontrovertible, hard evidence meticulously gleaned from this site bonding these two malignant, obscene bastards tightly to our case, leaving absolutely no doubt as to their culpability and guilt. Only then can we move decisively and with swift purpose to end this carnage once and for all."

Focussing his attention on the two Detectives, Abilene continued...

"James, Tiberius; accompany the forensics team and attend to the necessary security protocols required so as to provide as uncontaminated a site as can be guaranteed under the circumstances."

Finally, addressing the whole group, Abilene concluded...

"As you go forth from this place, rest assured the actions that you are a party to on this day will define our great purpose and prove to be our moment of absolute triumph over the malignant, inherent evil whose poisoned roots continue to permeate throughout our vulnerable society."

Upon leaving the front entrance of the station house the assembled group began boarding the fleet of hansom cabs that had been hurriedly commissioned to transport them all the relatively short distance between Leman Street and the murder site at Millers Court.

As they neared their destination it became clear to both Bass and Blackmore, as they surveyed from the relative security of their cab the undulating wave of obviously troubled humanity that accompanied them on their short journey, word had quickly spread amongst the general public of another 'Ripper' murder that had taken place.

"A high level of anxiety is rife on the streets this day, my brother," alluded Bass as the sense of unrest amongst the public became wholly apparent to him.

Blackmore nodded his head once and remained silent as he surveyed the scene of public unease that greeted them as they approached the narrow-arched entrance to Millers Court.

Upon alighting their cab, the two Detectives forced their way through the gauntlet of baying people that had overpopulated the narrow court. With taunts of 'oos next, you useless 'fakkin' 'cozzers', 'where's the 'fakkin' protection for us' and 'Jack's runnin' you ragged, you useless bastard cozzers' ringing in their ears, Bass and Blackmore approached the slightly ajar door of number thirteen.

Before he entered the badly dilapidated, one room slum, Bass sought out the sergeant in charge of the scene and after severely reprimanding him for the distinct lack of discipline and protocol the Detective had expected to be in place, both inside and around the crime scene, proceeded to take command of the situation himself.

"Sergeant?"

"Daniels, sir," the young sergeant answered sheepishly.

"Detective Inspector Bass, H division. Sergeant Daniels, I see that this crime scene is now severely compromised. Considering that previous to our arrival you were the commanding officer of the watch and thus made responsible by your superiors for adequately cordoning off the area from public contamination, let us hope for your sake not irrevocably so to the detriment of losing vital forensic evidence that could prove an important asset to our ongoing investigation.

"I require that this baying mob be dispersed at once by any means you see fit to employ in order to get the task completed swiftly, forced back through the passageway and out into Dorset Street where it can be best managed. See to it that no one enters the court through the arch from Dorset Street or by any other possible access points unless given specific permission to do so by either myself, Detective Inspector Blackmore, Chief Superintendent Abilene, Inspector Reid or doctors Bass and Phillips.

"In addition, begin interviewing all of the residents within this court and all of those here present, paying close attention to those who offered their opinions so vociferously upon our arrival, those residents of the surrounding streets, all of the public houses, the bordellos, the clubs, every shop, every livery, every rookery, passageway and privy. Do I make myself perfectly clear, Sergeant Daniels?"

"Y... yes, sir... p... perfectly clear, sir... At once, sir... r... right away, sir," spluttered the physically shaken Sergeant Daniels.

Just as he turned away to enter thirteen Millers Court, Bass rounded upon the hapless Sergeant Daniels once more...

"Oh Daniels, one more thing. Eighty-nine, Manning Place; are you familiar with this property, moreover its location and of its significance within the area?"

"Y... yes sir. A gentleman's club just off Little Paternoster. Nothing more than a toff's 'knocking shop', sir" was Daniel's nervous response to Bass' question.

Bass' response was terse and immediate...

"LEAVE IT ALONE! Under no circumstances whatsoever during your enquiries are yourself or any of your officers to consider this location one of those to be 'fine-sifted' for information. I want those ensconced within to remain blissfully unaware of any uncharacteristic Police activity outside of its seemingly secure portals. Do you understand, Sergeant, LEAVE... IT... ALONE!"

With that Bass entered the room to be confronted by one of the most horrific examples of human butchery that he had ever encountered.

The room itself was approximately twelve or thirteen-feet square at most, damp, tawdry and sparsely furnished. An aged oak table and chair pairing stood by one of the two windows that both looked out into Millers Court, the smallest of them sporting two broken panes of glass and the only sign of any sort of attempted decoration was an old, nondescript print that hung forlornly over the fireplace, in which the embers of last night's fire offered an almost welcoming glow. A bedside table stood close by the door and next to that a bed that was pushed against the far wall. On that bed lay the horribly mutilated body of a woman.

Constance Bass looked up for a moment from her grim forensic duties, tears streaming down her face, in order to attend her husband's arrival and to make the first report of her initial findings...

"She was partially undressed, perhaps in the process of entertaining the one who would turn out to be her murderer, or alternatively merely preparing herself for sleep. The carotid artery was severed deeply, all the way across the throat and right down to the bone, and, according to Dr Phillips' initial crime scene report, was most probably the eventual cause of death. Her face is completely unrecognisable as her nose, lips, eyebrows and ears have all been removed, as too have both of her breasts.

"As you can plainly see her abdomen has been opened outwards and the internal organs that remain have been removed and meticulously arranged as you see them at certain intervals around the body and upon the bedside table, with the exception of her heart. That is conspicuous by its absence. Both of her arms and thighs have been stripped of skin. I believe that the murderer has attempted to erase this poor woman's identity from ever having existed at all."

Having completed her report, Constance turned silently away from her husband and persevered with her harrowing work alongside doctors George Bagster Phillips and Thomas Bond. Frank Abilene and Inspector Edmund Reid of H Division were engaged in private conference by the door, their solemn, obviously troubled faces eerily illuminated by a single candle that still burned brightly inside of an old fruit jar that had been placed on the table to approximate a lamp.

Blackmore stood in silent contemplation by the fireplace as he surveyed the atrocity before his almost disbelieving eyes and as Bass approached him Blackmore spoke, his voice cracking with emotion...

"What kind of man could be capable, even within the confines of his own demented mind, of visiting such atrocious violence upon another human being, James? She must have suffered horrible torture and humiliating indignity at the mercy of this murdering bastard before the eventual relief of her death became a welcomed release."

Bass put a consoling left hand upon the right shoulder of his troubled companion as he began to speak, his own words remained strong and suggested the well of stoic resolve and courage from within that they must once more draw from in order to successfully complete their mission.

"Rest assured, my friend; these barbaric crimes shall not go unpunished. All we await is the discovery of one miniscule fibre, perhaps the familiarity of a discarded trinket or distinctive print left carelessly by either hand or finger. Any small indication here present that would associate Arbogast and von Waldheim with both this unfortunate woman and this dour little room, and thus provide the incontrovertible shred of proof that we require in order for us to deliver the swift and absolute justice that they both deserve."

Bass fell silent for a few moments as if offering Blackmore the opportunity to speak. When satisfied that there would be no immediate reply he continued on himself...

"You remain deeply troubled, Tiberius. As horrifying a scene as this one most certainly is that lies here before us, possibly one of the most dehumanising acts of barbarity that we two have ever borne witness to on our extensive travels, I refuse to believe that this alone would offer cause for Tiberius Blackmore to brood so deeply."

The warm air emanating upwards and outwards from the dying embers that lay smouldering in the hearth of the fireplace did little to comfort Blackmore on this chilly autumn afternoon. After a few more seconds of silent contemplation he gave Bass an answer...

"Do you remember, James, a few days ago as we two returned towards Dorset Street via Millers Court from our impromptu reunion of sorts with Billy Verlaine? I saw fit to tarry awhile at this very doorway and speak with the pretty little Irish 'tom' who lives here of matters specifically concerning Verlaine and aspects of his business."

Bass countered...

"I recall that you appeared somewhat taken by her demeanour... and also possibly by her not inconsiderable other 'worldlier' charms, Tiberius. More so, if memory serves, you identified her sharp intelligence and her potential worth to us as an integral member of our group of 'street agents'."

"Indeed, James. A rare and remarkably keen-minded beauty. Perhaps in another lifetime..."

Blackmore's wistful words melted away into nothingness as he continued to gaze into the prancing wraiths dancing for their lives within the fast fading firelight. Pausing briefly, he prepared himself to reveal the source of his true sadness to Bass...

"My God, James. I believe that dehumanised thing lying there is most likely all that remains of sweet Mary Jane Kelly."

As if attempting to offer both words of consolation and possibly even a forlorn hope to his dispirited comrade, Bass continued...

"And it may also prove not to be her, Tiberius. This poor soul's face has all but been erased. The mutilations performed on the entire surface area of her body were administered by such savage means as to suggest that a positive identification of the body might never be established. Have a hope, my friend, that the pitiful remnants of a human being lying over there may yet prove not be those belonging to Mary Kelly."

"Gentlemen, could I have your attention please if I may." Constance gathered Blackmore, Bass, Abilene and Reid around the corpse and began to speak...

"I apologise for subjecting you directly to this most gruesome of examinations first hand but my colleagues and I are under no doubt that the evidence we have just this moment discovered is damning and will prove beyond all reasonable doubt the guilt of your two prime suspects.

"Consider this for a moment, gentlemen. Just as every writer utilises certain distinctive prose that familiarise the reader with their unique work so too the greatest surgeon displays an instantly recognisable style that, to the trained eye, not only shows the work of a gifted artisan but also often betrays the idiosyncrasies and flawed character traits that lie inherent within that same person.

"If you will notice how each of the organs removed from the body has been meticulously placed with great care and precision, as if habitually so. Her uterus and both kidneys are set by the head, the spleen is on her right side, the intestinal tract on her left side and both kidneys are down by her feet.

"Notice also how distinct a line the incisions of his blade trace; here, where the skin has been removed from her thighs and arms, and here, where the neck has been severed down to the bone. This explicit attention to detail, the precision and peculiarity of such work, sets this man a world apart from his peers as the most brilliant of artisans, a genius of the Surgeons' Guild. He has, whether inadvertently or not, left us his signature. This is without doubt the mark of Lord Augustus De-Fanque Arbogast."

His spirits instantly rejuvenated upon receiving this latest intelligence from Constance, Blackmore spoke with a renewed vitality present in his voice, all the while unconsciously turning the loaded chamber of his LeMat revolver slowly with his left thumb and forefinger; click, click, click...

"And so, it follows that along the path one malignant mongrel chooses to tread so the other faithful lap dog will almost certainly follow. We have them, James, the 'Whitechapel Ripper' and his accomplice. At long last we have them within our grasp."

Overhearing the buoyant tone in Blackmore's voice as he spoke to Bass and anticipating the pair's raging intent to administer sanction with extreme prejudice as instant payment for the murders, Abilene barked out his orders with both experienced military authority and great moral purpose, forcing the two Detectives to take notice...

"Leather that weapon immediately, Commander Blackmore, and the both of you mark my words! I require that Arbogast and Von Waldheim be taken alive; do you understand me well enough; I REQUIRE THAT THEY BE TAKEN ALIVE! Justice must have a hand in punishing this terrible evil by administering the full judicial might of her moral equity upon it."

Lightening the stern timbre of his initial delivery somewhat, Abilene continued...

"My brave, brave boys. Have a care and take one small moment to heed the words of this old campaigner. Concerning this particular matter, the hangman must not be cheated his payment in favour of the form of justice that you both propose. Please, gentlemen, abide by my wishes for if you choose unwisely to follow your perceived course of action to its predictable conclusion the possible ramifications of those deeds undertaken might result in a slew of catastrophic consequences that will ultimately affect us all.

"I respectfully appeal to your better judgements and for all of our sakes, select the next pathway that you both intend to tread very wisely."

Blackmore proceeded to holster his revolver. As he did so, the forthright answer that he gave to his commander left no doubt in Frank Abilene's mind as to the level of both trust and faith in their abilities as Police officers that Blackmore and Bass perceived should be granted in fulfilling their designated mandate.

"Frank, I speak to you first as your friend and offer the due respect and love to that dear friend and colleague of long standing. Simply place your trust in us to accomplish our task in a manner that suits the circumstances of initial engagement."

Abilene readied himself to answer immediately but Blackmore raised his right hand sharply, as if to halt his commander's proposed words, and continued on himself...

"And now, Frank, I speak to you as one soldier to another; if James so endorses my words as being spoken for both of us..."

Blackmore looked across to his colleague for the merest hint of a reaction to his request. Satisfied with the single slight nod of Bass' head to signify his agreement, Blackmore continued...

"As you are very well aware, Frank, in our shared collective experiences as soldiers the rules of engagement are explicit and really quite simple to understand; assess the tactical situation immediately and react accordingly, depending on the level of action deemed necessary.

"Be under no illusion whatsoever, sir, that if the decision to use force with extreme prejudice in order to achieve the optimum outcome for this case is deemed necessary, then that choice will be made by us with the full understanding that the entire burden of potential consequence as a result of such a deed will be ours to bear alone.

"Now please, let us make all possible haste to eighty-nine Manning Place and seek to bring this serial of murderous activity to its timely and final conclusion on this very night."

Chapter 31

'89, Manning Place'

Manning Place, Whitechapel. An unremarkable, anonymous street that was located in the centre of one of the less than salubrious areas of the district. The street's anonymity was well suited to its purpose as being a convenient haven of mock-respectability from where so-called gentlemen would begin their evening's pursuit of the more clandestine pastimes of which they chose to indulge themselves within the vice emporiums and opium dens of the notorious Whitechapel 'abyss'.

Eighty-nine Manning Place was commissioned as an office premises by the East India trading company in 1803, primarily chosen for its central location to the vibrant and profitable markets that were in abundance at the time. Eventually, the long-established region of lucrative commerce and trade shifted its locale to a more convenient and secure site within the city as the number of vice, gin and opium emporiums that were managed by the rising and increasingly powerful East End criminal fraternity grew, and in turn their business empires began to expand and take unofficial control of the whole region.

The property itself was purchased by the Freemasons' Guild in 1858 and, aside from its legitimate use as a lodge by the grand order of freemasons in the city also became a gentlemen's club of some notoriety.

Outward appearance suggested an austere, innocuous Regency façade that was, fortuitously, conveniently situated and therefore regarded as the ideal base from where all the dubious delights of the 'abyss' could be readily and covertly accessed.

"Might one suggest a strategy, Frank?" enquired Bass pensively as the group of officers, comprising Bass himself, Blackmore, Abilene, Detective Inspector Edmund Reid and a dozen police constables approached the front door of number eighty-nine Manning Place.

"All suggestions duly noted and considered, James" came Abilene's immediate reply...

"I propose that both yourself and Edmund, plus six of the dozen constables approach and enter through the front door, sifting the place fine for any presence of those that we seek.

"Meanwhile, Tiberius and I, accompanied by the remainder of our force, shall gain access by another means and proceed with similar intent. Allow my squad five minutes to get inside and then proceed to make your own entrance."

"Agreed" came back the immediate response from Abilene. Beckoning Reid and six constables towards his position Abilene continued...

"Edmund, yourself plus six constables, to me; the rest of you, to Chief Inspector Bass' command."

As Bass and his group mustered and prepared to leave, Abilene imparted, almost betraying a forlorn hope in the timbre of his voice as he spoke...

"Remember, James, I want them alive."

Bass aimed a single sharp nod of his head in affirmation of the order issued by his Commander and turned to address his own group...

"On my mark, boys. Our immediate task is to discover an alternative entrance. Around the back, I think, might be a good place to begin our search." And with that Bass' group set off at double-time pace southwards along Markham Place to find the rear of the building.

Abilene's group entered through the front door of the building to be greeted immediately by several men of dour appearance whom Abilene recognised instantly as belonging to Her Majesty's Covert Special Forces unit. Beyond this human shield, their faces eerily illuminated by the light of dancing firelight, standing in conversation were three gentlemen of some considerable substance.

Two of them he identified instantly as Arbogast and Von Waldheim. He was not familiar, however, with the third man's features. He observed a neatly attired man sporting a tall, lean gait and a full set of well-groomed facial whiskers, possibly those belonging to a naval officer of high rank.

Without waiting for verbal contact from any of the men, Abilene proceeded to deliver his orders, succinctly, confidently and with some authority...

"ALL OF YOU. STAND TO AND YIELD IN THE NAME OF THE LAW!"

The dark line of men drew a formidable array of revolvers and shotguns from concealment beneath their long, dark great coats and proceeded to aim their deadly, primed barrels directly at each one of Abilene's startled group.

Reciprocating their aggressive stance, Abilene's colleagues instinctively proceeded to draw their own revolvers and found themselves locked, loaded and directly facing their aggressors, caught hopelessly within the grip of a bizarre and potentially catastrophic stalemate.

The bearded man whom Abilene did not recognise was the first one to speak...

"Gentlemen, though this is a private club, the exclusive membership of which is granted by special invitation only, you are nonetheless most welcome within these sacred halls as our esteemed guests, Detective Chief Superintendent Abilene, Detective Inspector Reid and your finely uniformed constables with whose names, I am most embarrassed to admit, I am not familiar. Now please, if we are able to retain at least some semblance of civility between our somewhat agitated groups, I feel sure that this impasse that we now face will be resolved presently, and thus avoiding any unnecessary violence inflicted upon your group of devilishly handsome young men."

'You sir, are a conceited, arrogant, inbred bastard and, even though we are not yet formally acquainted, I would gladly welcome an opportunity, in another more convenient moment in time, to shoot you right between the eyes!' Abilene thought inwardly to himself.

When he composed himself and began to speak, however, he retained the dignity and authority befitting a respected officer of his rank...

"You take me at a disadvantage, sir. You know my name, and the name of my colleague, but we do not know who you are. Please, enlighten us as to the title you favour, if you would be so kind."

The bearded man stepped away from the fireplace and into an area of the room where Abilene was able to make out his features more clearly. On his head he wore a tall stovepipe hat, an obvious sign of wealth and high breeding and from both of his double-breasted waistcoat pockets dangled an expensive looking solid gold Albert chain sporting a large diamond fob. He was also wearing a long, thick, double-breasted naval officer's greatcoat that hung nearly all the way to his ankles.

"Why, gentlemen, how remiss of me. Please, excuse my quite appalling lapse in the most basic of social etiquette. Allow me to formally introduce myself. I am 'The Architect'."

Chapter 32

'The Architect'

An unnerving silence descended upon the room that seemed to last for a very long time indeed, which was eventually broken by the voice of Abilene...

"Might one assume that your title does not refer to an artisan of design and construction skills?"

'The Architect' answered Abilene's question immediately...

"Your assumption would prove to be correct, sir and on this one occasion I will excuse the glib and really quite naïve undertone of mockery present in your voice."

Consciously aware that he was displaying an outward expression of incredulity openly on his face Abilene proceeded to listen as 'The Architect' continued to speak...

"I, sir, am 'The Architect' of all that was, all that transpires now, and all things yet to pass."

His incredulity turning into blind rage, Abilene retorted with a rising and unnervingly menacing vehemence present in his voice...

"Whatever, or whomsoever, you might choose to believe that you are, sir, is far and away removed from the actual fact that in simple terms of understanding, you are just a man. What you most certainly are not, even though your blasphemous attempt to describe yourself as being so was blatantly and shamefully arrogant in the extreme, is God!"

Almost sneering his reply, 'The Architect' continued...

"Your rankled demeanour denotes a misunderstanding of my words sir and I apologise profusely if your initial perception of their intended meaning caused offence. What I should have made abundantly clear from the outset is that any being, be they perceived as perhaps a comforting spiritual totem or otherwise, that was able to harness one ten-thousandth of the power that I am able to summon would naturally be worshipped as a living God by any vulnerable society in need of a strong, benevolent leadership and the readily available comfort of reliable spiritual support."

Just as Abilene readied himself to answer 'The Architect' with what he considered to be a well-conceived and, under the current circumstances, wholly appropriate retort, the distinct sound of gun shots from another part of the building reverberated around the room; CRACK, CRACK, CRACK, CRACK... CRACK, CRACK, CRACK, CRACK... CRACK... CRACK!

"How many men were stationed elsewhere in the vicinity, covertly or otherwise?" asked Abilene with an air of resignation, and just perhaps the merest hint of pity present in his voice, as if he was already well aware of what had just transpired.

"Six bold men belonging to her glorious Majesty's Covert Special Forces unit, answering to my personal command, deployed herein as protection for my esteemed companions here standing," stated 'The Architect' as he beckoned nonchalantly towards Arbogast and Von Waldheim, who seemed to display outwardly a behaviour and appearance that suggested amusement as to how proceedings were unfolding before their eyes, as if this were some form of vaudeville entertainment that had been staged for their own benefit.

Abilene answered 'The Architect' with an obvious tone of resignation present in his words...

"Alas, I regret to inform you that they are all deceased."

Before any more dialogue between the two was able to continue, two spinning blades arced out of the darkness and with lethal accuracy thudded home into the chests of their intended targets... 'THUD, THUD'!

Three pistol shots followed by in close succession and five of the six remaining Covert Special Forces operatives fell dead to the floor... 'CRACK, CRACK, CRACK!'

"NOT THAT ONE, TIBERIUS. LET THAT ONE WITHOUT A FACE FESTER WITHIN HIS SOILED BRITCHES FOR A MOMENT LONGER," barked the unmistakable voice of James Bass.

"Well, well, James Bass; and Tiberius Blackmore. Impressive. Swift, precise, economical of excessive movement. A textbook example of exemplary skill culminating with devastating, deadly accuracy. Very, very nice work indeed, gentlemen. I notice that you have both learned a great deal more of the eastern martial arts since our last encounter all those years ago."

"Ben Stoker," countered Bass.

"But of course. The minutely detailed description, as received from a very reliable source. That of a tall, dark personage displaying an obvious military gait and sporting distinctively rearranged facial features that could only belong to one man, that man being the piece of stinking human refuse standing before us in a puddle of his own piss, Commander Benjamin Roderick Stoker, still of her Majesty's Covert Special Forces one would assume?" enquired Bass.

"But of course, James. Only the very best of us so engaged to shadow and secure the nocturnal proclivities of our high-born, noblest elite, however questionable or inhumanly debase those proclivities might prove to be. No pertinent questions asked, no answers given.

The absolute polar opposite of 'noblesse oblige' with regards to every conceivable understanding of the phrase, wouldn't you agree, James?" asked Stoker inquisitively...

"Indeed, 'Benny boy'. As complete and shameful a perversion of the noblest obligation, honourable intent and generous integrity of the gentleman's code of righteous conduct I have yet to encounter. All four of you who remain standing are not fit to be called men, let alone regarded by your so-called peers as prime examples of the noblest and most highly regarded of gentlemen.

"Now take what little time remains of the last few seconds that you draw breath to contemplate on all of the atrocities for which you are responsible that have led you to this moment of destiny."

As Bass' speech came to an end both he and Blackmore nodded at each other simultaneously, instinctively raised their pistols in synchronised unity and took aim at the foreheads of Stoker, Arbogast, Von Waldheim and 'The Architect', clicked back the hammers on each of their weapons and prepared to fire.

"Goodbye and may whatever God chooses to notice and listen to your worthless final confessions have mercy on your black hearts" was Bass' final, chilling aside.

All at once, without a hint of warning, the ambience within the room exploded into a cacophony of chaos and noise as the two doorways that led into the room in which they all stood burst open. Through the breached entrances poured several red coats of the Duke of Wellington's regiment who chaperoned in the Home Secretary, the Right Honourable Henry Matthews.

"STAND DOWN ALL WEAPONS! STAND DOWN IN THE NAME OF HER MAJESTY QUEEN VICTORIA OR PREPARE TO ACCEPT THE FATAL CONSEQUENCES OF YOUR ACTIONS! Call off your rabid dogs, Abilene" came the very explicit command issued directly by the Home Secretary himself.

Abilene addressed his men collectively and then directed his comments solely at the two Detectives, who stood before him primed and ready to resume their onslaught imminently.

"Easy men, easy now. James, Tiberius; floor those weapons, boys. There is no profit to be had by us if this brave action culminates with your meaningless deaths here today. Tomorrow is a brand-new day which will present to us opportunities anew. Of this, I promise you, you can rest assured."

Both Bass and Blackmore, heeding the common sense of Abilene's wise words and realising immediately by themselves that they were hopelessly outmanned, outgunned, cleverly outmanoeuvred and that, albeit with a grudging reluctance, making the decision to capitulate in this moment was the only remaining sensible option left to them at this time, let their still smouldering pistols fall to the ground and surrendered their hands.

"A wise decision, gentlemen. I thank you for your assistance in avoiding more senseless bloodshed," began Mr Matthews. Motioning towards Arbogast and Von Waldheim, he continued...

"Both Lord Arbogast and Baron von Waldheim are under specially sanctioned protection from Her Majesty's government. Any physical molestation of their persons, or any such similar conduct considered to be an infringement of their rights as respected citizens of the Crown shall be deemed by a court of law as a treasonable act perpetrated against the Crown, punishable by either a substantial custodial or terminal sentence. Do I make myself perfectly clear, Mr Abilene?"

"Abundantly clear, Mr Home Secretary," answered Abilene.

"If I may be so bold, sir, might one ask what part 'The Architect' plays in this charade?"

Matthews, incensed by what he considered to be Abilene's attempt at brash sarcasm, answered tersely...

"This 'charade' to which you so glibly refer was brought to my personal attention by sources whose identities are of no concern to either yourself, Abilene, or to any H division personnel.

"Understand this: the only reason that you and your men are not this moment sent directly from here to fester in Newgate prison awaiting trial for both high treason and the wilful murder of lawfully sanctioned government officials is the fact that respected persons of high rank and privilege who exert some obvious influence within the higher corridors of government power have taken into account the exemplary military service each one of you has given to his Queen and country for many years, and has vouched for each one of you personally. You all certainly boast friends in very high office.

"I want no official report of this sorry affair filing, nor is there to be an after mission de-briefing of any description upon your return to Leman Street. This incident never took place, do you understand, none of this ever transpired. Consider yourselves very fortunate indeed, gentlemen that your liberty has been granted and your lives as you know them allowed to continue.

"Now I bid you all a very good evening."

"And what of 'The Architect'?" asked Abilene, the rising feelings of frustration and incredulity building up inside him becoming openly obvious to all…

His question was answered with silent, blank and inquisitive stares from all in attendance, all except Edmund Reid, who looked Abilene directly in the eye and, ever so slightly, shook his head once in each direction, as if hoping to prevent his commanding officer from experiencing any further embarrassment. Both Bass and Blackmore's expressions remained impassive as ever, outwardly displaying nothing of the thoughts within each man's mind.

"THE ARCHITECT, THE OTHER MAN. HE STANDS GLOATING BY HIS ACCOMPLICES OVER TH…"

As Abilene gestured over towards the fireplace where Arbogast and von Waldheim now stood alone and obviously gloating over Abilene's awkwardness, his expression altered to one of disbelief and mystification as to how 'The Architect' had managed to remain shielded from the plain sight of almost everyone present and then proceed to abscond the room undetected.

Henry Matthews eyed Abilene with a look of disbelief, combined perhaps with a hint of sympathy for the ageing Police Commander.

"Go home, Abilene. Expect an official summons for you to attend a special meeting at the Home Office presently with regards to discussing this matter further."

As the room cleared, with both Arbogast and von Waldheim following nonchalantly in the protective wake of the Home Secretary and his soldiers, Bass stood in front of Ben Stoker to halt his progress.

"We will meet again very soon, Benny boy, when 'old Nosey's finest' aren't present to wipe your arse, and rest assured, next time I will clean your clock, permanently."

Stoker gave a nervous grin and sneered...

"I look forward to our next meeting with relish, James. It will be... glorious."

Abilene stood alone for a moment in the aftermath and was totally oblivious to the fact that he was muttering out loud.

"'I saw him, spoke to him. I know he was there. 'The Architect', he called himself 'The Architect'. Edmund, you saw him too."

"Yes, Frank, I saw him too; and then, he was gone."

Abilene turned towards Bass and Blackmore, hoping for some corroborative statement from either detective that would confirm both his and Reid's affirmation.

Already in the process of retrieving and re-loading their discarded weapons, Bass and Blackmore nodded their heads towards Abilene in unison. Spinning the chamber of his Schofield pistol and clicking it shut as he spoke, Bass answered in the affirmative, just as Abilene had hoped that he would…

"Yes Frank, we saw your 'Architect'."

Chapter 33

'Introducing... The Grand Meister'

A sombre mood permeated the usually buoyant atmosphere within Frank Abilene's office that was akin to a cloying, stifling marshland fog. Abilene himself, Bass and Blackmore remained ensconced in deep discussion, where they had been for the past two hours, as they attempted to understand what exactly had transpired on the previous night inside eighty-nine Manning Place.

"So, as we now know for certain to our cost, Arbogast and von Waldheim are, for whatever reason, protected jealously by an as yet unknown faction belonging to high government office. The Home Secretary's presence on last night's intrusion upon our proposed arrest procedure would corroborate that fact," stated Bass.

"Agreed," began Blackmore. "I would add, with some concern, that this 'unknown faction' to which you allude, James, were made well aware in advance of our intended plans to make an arrest last night. The location where we intended to confront our marks and exact time to the second when our arrest would take place were somehow put into the hands of our usurpers."

"A traitor from within our own ranks?" questioned Bass.

"Unlikely," continued Blackmore.

"Our operation was conceived and deployed almost immediately, purposefully so and with the express intention of avoiding any possibility of treacherously meddlesome intent from within. I would offer a suggestion at this juncture that I believe 'The Architect' is able to cast some kind of hypnotic influence at will over certain, or indeed all, members of our hierarchy. Whatever form that influence adopts, how far abroad it stretches out its treacherous tentacles, or whoever in high office is affected by its manipulative effect is open for question."

"Perhaps I might be able to offer an explanation as to both the identity and purpose of your 'Architect'."

Startled somewhat by the unannounced and sudden arrival of this extremely tall, well-groomed, extravagantly attired uninvited guest, who had mysteriously materialised silently and ghost-like into their private conclave, Blackmore was the first to speak...

"GOOD HEAVENS ABOVE, PONTIUS ASTON. How long has it been, ten, twelve years or so since James, Frank, Phineas Jefferson, your good self and I served together in the second Anglo-Afghan war?"

"Ten years, Tiberius. Ten long years, passed by second by second, hour by hour, day by day, month by month, year by year, or so it might seem to those of you who perceive the passage of time in the normal sense."

"Still waffling on in nonsensical rhymes and riddles, Pontius, you old stove pipe- wearing peacock," interjected James Bass as the two old comrades hands clasped tightly together in friendship.

"And you, James my old friend; it pleases me that you still somehow succeed in cheating the ferryman of his meagre pair of farthings toll in exchange for your long overdue crossing of the Styx."

"But for the timely interjections of Tiberius on several occasions that toll would have been paid long ago and the final ferry ride to the isle of the dead taken," quipped Bass in return.

Reacquaintances with trusted allies of old settled over more than a few brandies imbibed, and with all those present satisfied Aston's seemingly spontaneous presence was both legitimate and would no doubt yield information vital to their cause, the meeting continued...

"Gentlemen, please forgive the rudeness of my interruption but the extraordinary tale that I am about to impart, implausible though it may seem to your accepted processes of logical thought and understanding, justifies my presence here in this moment."

Each of the three Detectives were kept from posing their myriad questions to Aston by the sharp raising of his right hand.

"Please, my fine old comrades. I ask, nay implore you to hear my words. Whether or not you deem their content plausible enough to merit your serious consideration is for you alone to decide. Only then shall I willingly endeavour to answer your questions, of which I am certain you will have a great many to pose.

If you will remember, gentlemen, the year of eighteen eighty-five. It was three years ago when James, Tiberius and I received official notice of honourable discharge with full honours from our respective military commissions, Her Majesty's Covert Special Forces unit and the 95th Rifle Brigade respectively.

"Upon receiving word of your discharge from the Army, our dear friend and colleague Francis proceeded to recruit both of you, James and Tiberius, into the ranks of the Metropolitan Police force."

"You were the one who informed Frank of our 'availability', Pontius?" questioned Bass.

"It was I, my friend, for reasons that I shall now attempt to clarify," continued Aston.

"Agencies and institutions, formed a millennia ago, with the primary objective of enforcing law and true justice in order to serve and protect the well-being and best interests of ordinary people, specifically require unimpeachable, incorruptible and remarkably exceptional personnel within their ranks in order to function without issue.

"Your personal profiles, whose distinctive and quite unique characteristics were at first honed during many years of inconceivable hardship suffered whilst surviving on the harsh streets of London, matched the criteria that we sought perfectly. These randomly accrued, basic attributes, coupled with the intense military training later received and the experiences dually shared during countless campaigns and covert missions abroad, were perfectly developed and ready to be utilised as part of the grand plan, of which I shall reveal more momentarily."

"And what of yourself, Pontius?" quizzed Blackmore. What of the agency to which you so obviously offer your loyal service?"

Addressing all three of the Detectives at once, Aston continued...

"Imagine if you will, Tiberius, James and Francis, the passage of time as it exists within the normal parameters of conscious thought, as three dimensions. Forwards and backwards motion would constitute the first dimension, upward and downward motion the second dimension and side to side motion the third dimension. Consider for a moment, then, the existence of a fourth dimension. A corridor of sorts, if you will, that enables the individual gifted with both the fantastic knowledge and great power to do so, to not merely gain access inside this corridor, but also to engage wilful transience backwards and forwards in time, and thus visit any fixed point in history past, or indeed, future to come."

A moment of silence fell upon the room as the three Detectives cogitated over the fantastic revelations presented by Aston. Bass was the first to speak...

"Time travel, the existence of a fourth dimension. You, Pontius, are yourself a time traveller?"

"Precisely, James. I am able to traverse backwards and forwards to fixed points in time within the fourth dimension. I am, therefore, to all intents and purposes, a time traveller."

Bass eyed his old friend thoughtfully from behind his dark lensed, horn-rimmed, tortoiseshell spectacles and continued posing his questions, displaying the calm logic of a disciplined mind, a mind prepared to recognise the possibility that a hitherto thought of as improbable concept, however implausible the existence of that concept might at first appear, must ultimately be considered as a distinct and very real possibility, especially when presented with tangible evidence that corroborates such a concept as being reality.

"Pontius. Based upon what you have told us thus far, let us then accept that the fourth dimension is in fact a reality, and that traversing this corridor to fixed points in time, either forwards to the future or back to the past, is indeed possible.

"Would it therefore be correct of one to assume that an entity of such universal importance, not merely for its access as a portal to be utilised by scientists and historians alike with regards to aiding the research and development of their respective areas of study, might also to be shamelessly exploited by organised criminals who could either seek to profit greatly from its misuse or even perhaps alter the true course of history as it should unfold to suit a potentially twisted private agenda.

"I would therefore suggest that a special Police organisation would need to be commissioned in order to maintain the equilibrium of lawful traffic within this corridor."

"I commend your impressive powers of deduction, yes, James, yes indeed. A covert agency was duly formed by the various governments of the world, with the full approval and patronage of her Majesty Queen Victoria herself, and tasked with the express mandate of policing movement and all business conducted within the fourth dimension.

I am commissioned as a special agent to an organisation named the 'Time Enforcement Agency' and the very grave matter which I have visited you here today in order to discuss is one that, if left unchecked, could cause irreparable damage to the future of our very existence."

The three Detectives listened on intently as Aston continued to divulge more of his fantastic tale, each new hitherto inconceivable revelation becoming unquestionably believable as key facts concerning their current case began at first to coincidentally appear, then weave seamlessly within the fabric of Aston's words, making perfect sense of the puzzle as it unfolded before them...

"So, gentlemen, we come to the anomaly who has introduced himself to you as 'The Architect'.

"In order to first be considered a suitable recruitment candidate for the 'T.E.A.' the professional manifests of each perspective agent must display exceptional standards in their tireless, unselfish work ethic, exhibit a flawless, incorruptible character and display exemplary qualities in both leadership and command protocols.

All of the 'raw units' are then subjected to a series of rigorous tasks designed precisely to determine the level of their resolve and commitment, and to force the boundaries of both their physical and mental stamina up to and beyond the absolute maximum level of human endurance. Only at a time when this ordeal is completed to the satisfaction of the high council of thirteen 'Grand Meisters', and each of the exacting criteria necessary for recruitment met, is a 'raw unit' then deemed as suitable, and therefore has earned the privilege of being invited to serve the agency, for the rest of their lives."

"Might one then assume that you are yourself a 'Grand Meister' of the 'T.E.A.', Pontius?" asked Blackmore.

"And, would I be correct in the assumption that 'The Architect' is a rogue agent, who has seen fit to break from the stringent protocols adhered to by your organisation, in order to pursue the course of his own lofty, misguided personal ambition?"

"Your assumptions are accurate on both counts, Tiberius. I was selected to inherit the honorific title of 'Grand Meister' two thousand years ago.

"For the individual, upon accepting this great honour, a coveted seat on the high council of thirteen 'Grand Meisters' is assured, each of whom is entrusted with the 'overseeing' of all that was, all that is, and all that is yet to come, every member of the collective responsible for maintaining balance, harmony and order throughout the timelines, thus ensuring the essential and unaltered equilibrium within the fourth dimension remains undisturbed and intact.

"'The Architect' is indeed a rogue 'Meister', his position on the council revoked two thousand years ago when he became seduced by a dark, malevolent influence to the infinite possibilities of utilising his great knowledge and power in order to facilitate his own sociopathic ambitions.

"Part of my personal mandate became to pursue this immoral aberration through time in an attempt to counter the potentially catastrophic ripples that he was, and still is so it would seem, wilfully causing within the timelines, and to serve justice upon the most dangerous criminal any one of us could ever have imagined."

"Might one ask, Pontius? The position left vacant on the council of thirteen, at the time 'The Architect' absconded. One assumes that this prestigious seat was offered to yourself..." asked Bass...

"Yes, James, two thousand years ago."

"Two... thousand... years... ago... Pontius. Your age, you appear to be..."

"I appear exactly as I should to your eyes, my dear old friend, just as a naturally ageing human male should. At my next birthday I shall reach what is considered by many to be the somewhat celebratory age of sixty years.

"You see, James, time itself is the unforgiving enemy to us all. It tarries for no-one and offers precious few second opportunities for recompense or redemption. It is the eternal flame in which we all burn, the wheel within a wheel inside which each one of us has a pre-destined, significant part to play."

Aston fell silent for a moment. He raised his right hand sharply a second time as a sign for his captivated audience to remain silent as he gathered his thoughts and continued to speak.

"At this stage of proceedings time dictates that I digress awhile to matters of great importance concerning your current case, my friends.

"The T.E.A. involves itself in either government or world affairs only if the probability of a major paradox within the fourth dimension is detected, one that could potentially alter or irreparably damage the timeline, and therefore needs to be addressed and corrected immediately.

"The specific murders committed by 'Jack the Ripper', inhumanly grotesque though his crimes have proven to be, provide little of any interest to the T.E.A. Our gravest concern lies specifically with the involvement of one Baron Victor Josef von Waldheim, who we are now aware of as the accomplice.

"For many years he has used his quite exceptional knowledge in the fields of both engineering and advanced surgical techniques to nurture and develop his fanatical obsession with the manipulation of electrical energy, in order to re-animate a corpse constructed from body parts and organs, most recently those harvested from the victims of 'Jack the Ripper'. The science of utilising extremely powerful sources of electrical energy specifically for this purpose is, as you are all now well aware, known as galvanism.

"You see, gentlemen, 'The Ripper' is nothing more than a sick, deranged psychopath, whose extreme sociopathic tendencies have festered within and tortured his tormented mind for years.

"Finally, compelled to commit his murderous spree by an overwhelmingly damaging psychological flaw that was originally buried deep within his inner psyche, possibly a violent hatred of all women that saw its genesis sometime during his adolescent years in the form of the sustained violent physical and mental abuse so administered by an overwhelmingly dominant matriarchal type figure, Arbogast now regards himself as a lone crusader of sorts.

"A cleanser of dark souls blessed with a divine right to purge the tainted streets of all the evil peddlers of cheap, available flesh, in this case the helpless, unfortunate whores he has recently selected as his victims.

"It is, however, von Waldheim who is the stage manager of these proceedings. He manipulates the activities of 'the Ripper' to suit his own ends and his intention to raise the dead must be thwarted, at all costs."

"Should the Baron's sole ambition be regarded as merely to 'galvanise' a corpse to life, or must we assume that his personal agenda is further reaching still?" questioned Blackmore...

"To answer your question, Tiberius, I must revisit a previous aside in order to discuss further the involvement of 'The Architect'. His is the role of the master schemer. He senses here a gilt-edged opportunity, in that by giving both his substantial patronage and protection to the unhindered advancement of Von Waldheim's work, an unassailable army of the dead shall rise and, under his manipulative influence, proceed to wreak havoc within the fourth dimension. Need I explain that such an unprecedented shift of authority and power within the timelines would cause a catastrophic ripple that would affect the very fabric of all things inside, and possibly even beyond the boundaries of our universe?"

"WE HAD THEM, PONTIUS! We had both von Waldheim and Arbogast within our grasp, only to be humiliatingly stood down by the very government that we have sworn to serve. When will another opportune instance such as the one just passed arise for us to end this waking nightmare for good?" exclaimed a somewhat exasperated Abilene...

"I cannot say 'when' your next opportunity will manifest itself, Frank – the risk of causing multiple and irreparable chaos within the time vortex is too great – but I am able to reveal that, in time, one more perfect and unhindered circumstance will manifest itself during which true justice and righteous good shall finally prevail over evil, administered by the hands of James Bass and Tiberius Blackmore."

Chapter 34

'Genesis of The League of Ghosts'

The Black Bear public house was situated within short walking distance of Leman Street police station. Ensconced in their preferred back room, this small area of defensible sanity and calm was the private place where Blackmore and Bass chose to privately discuss impending business matters, or merely to enjoy each other's company as old friends often do, and partake of a not ungenerous decanter of good quality brandy and a smoke of the finest imported tobacco, free from the unwarranted attentions and immediate pressures of their work.

Joining them at their table on this occasion was Pontius Aston and another ex-army colleague and trusted friend, Doctor Phineas Theodore Jefferson. Beginning their 'old soldiers' reunion by reminiscing about times long past, and of foreign campaigns hard fought, the four colleagues soon found their conversation naturally guided towards the inevitable subject of business.

"Our purpose now is as clear to us as it has always been, my friends," began Blackmore...

"We are both, James and I, commissioned to serve our city as we served our Queen and country for many years; with honour, with pride and with a compulsion to deliver all those many helpless souls in desperate need of our assistance from inherent evil. This is the pledge that we made to ourselves long ago, this is our destiny.

"We believe, however, that a new danger to the security of our very existence is now, in the advent of recent previously inconceivable occurrences, very much more than merely a possibility. The dawning of a new, potentially world-altering era of supernaturally enhanced crime is now obviously imminent, thus the need for the formation of a unique organisation, its prime directive being to seek out and combat this oncoming threat, has never before been so immediate and so necessary.

"The operatives considered to be a part of this most extraordinary league would be selected based upon the special skill-sets each one possesses, the exemplary records of each candidate from previous engagements and an overwhelming desire to administer and serve justice in its purest, truest form. The league would operate covertly, attracting little or no unwarranted attention from established authorities by its actions, with a base of operations that is covertly secreted away and totally undetectable by any normal means. This would be a league of justice, a league of dark shadows, a league of extraordinary, unimpeachable, exemplary, individuals... 'THE LEAGUE OF GHOSTS'."

Bass continued...

"Such an exceptional league would require a formidable roster of outstanding excellence. We would firstly propose the League have no set commander or figurehead, all enter as equals to debate, detect, decide and to enforce the law, sworn to administer true justice and stand together as one before the impending wave of extraordinary uncertainty fast approaching us.

"We propose Captain Pontius Maximillian Aston and his wife Beatrice Juliette Aston as our liaison between the League and the Time Enforcement Agency, to which they are both commissioned as agents. Beatrice Aston's reputation as being a leading and highly respected authority on world history and geography will also serve great use and purpose to the cause.

"We propose Doctor Phineas Theodore Jefferson, ex-surgeon in chief of the Prince Consort's 95th rifle brigade and inventor of special weapons and ammunition, and his wife Professor Florence Elizabeth Jefferson, professor in charge of The Institute of Paranormal Activity and Psychic Phenomena.

"I propose my wife, Doctor Constance Matilda Bass, whose expertise as a renowned physician and surgeon, and her pioneering research into the development of forensic techniques used to aid the work of the Police force will prove vitally important to the League."

Tiberius Blackmore interjected...

"I propose my wife, Dame Pandora Scarlett Blackmore, world renowned musician, once a Covert Special Forces operative. Using her legitimate cover of high-profile celebrity, she will be able to infiltrate with ease the higher echelons of aristocracy and privilege where few others would either be accepted, or allowed to do so.

"And finally, I propose James and myself as chief Detectives and enforcers in the service of the League. Our extensive experience gained whilst serving in the military, coupled with intense special forces conditioning in recognising a potentially challenging situation utilising our succinct acumen, plus our ability to wilfully eradicate a pre-determined mark with extreme prejudice, showing no fear, doubt or remorse for such an action, qualifies us both perfectly for this role.

"This initial collection of remarkably gifted individuals will form the nucleus of an organisation responsible for the administration of untainted law and maintaining the equilibrium of balance and order throughout the world, each one a sworn keeper of the eternal flame of true justice...

"...guardians of 'The League of Ghosts'."

Bass took up the thread...

"It naturally follows that such an organisation would require a covert base of operations, preferably somewhere accessible and within the city limits."

Aston replied immediately... "I believe that I know of the perfect place."

Chapter 35

'Fugitives... Autumn 1898'

~ Present Day ~

Blackmore and Bass were not unaccustomed to wilfully and cleverly avoiding contact with the law. With an encyclopaedic knowledge of both the complex industrial and burgeoning multi-cultural infrastructure of the area, coupled with the crime-orientated boroughs of the Eastern side of the city embedded deeply within each of their minds, dissolving into the festering and very hazardous underworld of 'the abyss' presented no immediate problem for the two Detectives.

During the early morning of their fourth day as fugitives, Blackmore and Bass sat together in a secluded, dimly lit corner of 'The Three Hooks' tavern, located just off the East Smithfield Road on the Eastern dock side. Joining them at their table was the proprietor of 'The Three Hooks', long-time associate and true friend 'Emerald Eye' Rosie Gallagher. Bass was in mid-sentence...

"This will be our last morning here, with our 'Emerald Eye' Rosie. We can no longer expose you to the risk of being implicated in our business, such as it is, but know this: The well of our gratitude remains overflowing, for both your hospitality and for your discretion over these past few days, and as always for your loyal friendship that knows no bounds. Should you ever require assistance, all you need do is put out the word and one, or both of us, will rally to your call."

'Emerald Eye' Rosie studied both Bass and Blackmore intently through her one good remaining eye, then reached across the table at which they sat and took a hand of each of them into her own two hands. Her emerald green left eye seemed to glisten like a precious stone as it caught the light from a solitary candle that was placed on the table. Cascades of well-kempt ringlets of very long red hair fell across her shoulders and over the right side of her face, under which was purposefully concealed a terrible scar that ran from her forehead, through her right eye and down below her right jaw bone, and marked her otherwise flawless, and quite beautifully fair Irish features.

"Now you know you've always been my boys, to be sure you have. Your business is your own, so it has always been and no questions asked, but I'm 'hearin' all these tales of two Detectives' gone rogue, and stories of murder. Horrible, senseless murder of one of their own. All sorts of bad things that my sweet boys have supposedly done."

She paused for a moment, a solitary, crystalline tear forming in the corner of her good eye that eventually ran down her porcelain white cheek. She continued...

"Please, tell me that it's not so. Enlighten this breaking Irish heart by convincing me that what transpired up on Leman Street three nights ago was an action that benefits a greater good."

Blackmore continued...

"Know this, sweet Rosie. All that we do is well considered and for good reason. To offer a more succinct explanation of our recent activities and to reveal any aspect as to our intended course of action at this juncture would endanger your life and that is too precious a jewel to place in jeopardy. Rest assured that we are now, as always we ever were, your boys and that we shall always remain."

"See how this old Irish gypsy lass still weeps for you pair of 'street rogues!' You make certain that these tears are not shed in vain."

As Bass and Blackmore rose from their seats and began walking towards the tavern's rear exit, Rosie called Bass back...

"Jamie, boy, spare a moment more of your time for an Irish tinker lass, if you please."

Blackmore continued on his way as Bass returned to the table and re-seated himself opposite Rosie.

He sat in silence as Rosie continued to speak...

"There are a good many of us true-blood Romany gypsies blessed with a special gift. We are able to see things that no one else can see, sense a moment in time before it occurs and in some rare instances, read a person's innermost thoughts.

"I myself cannot read, nor indeed am I able to sense but I see things very clearly, and I see a great change deep within you, Jamie. I see two strong spirits wresting for overall dominance of a tormented soul, one the human Jamie Bass, the other a wild animal. I see a great, white wolf. You are Lycan?"

After a pause that seemed to last an age Bass answered...

"I am, but how..."

Rosie interrupted Bass before he had time to continue...

"As I said before, I have the sight of my ancestors and, so as with an experienced Detective such as yourself, my own powers of observation are somewhat enhanced; the mark of the pentagram, covered discreetly by the leather strap worn upon your right wrist, and your eyes. Underneath those dark lensed spectacles, your eyes are as black as pitch, are they not?"

"Err, not always... but... probably at this moment perhaps..." Bass stammered as he shifted uncomfortably on his seat.

As if to prove Rosie's suggestion had merit, and in part to appease both the concerns and the curiosity of a trusted friend, Bass removed his spectacles to reveal his eyes that had indeed turned as black as night, whites and all.

"Brought about by a discomforting situation, and possibly rage I'll warrant; oh, Jamie. The torment and the pain you must endure. Is the struggle constant, does the wolf tear at you from within to be free?"

Bass' answer was short and to the point...

"Every cursed second of every damned day!"

Chapter 36

'Visiting an Old Friend'

Bass joined his companion outside the ageing tavern on the rotten, decaying wooden boards of a 'rookery' that joined 'The Three Hooks' onto an adjacent building; a decrepit, stinking leather tannery named 'The East London Docks Leather Company Ltd'.

"And so, my friend. One final port of call prior to our promised rendezvous with Marcus Jackson and the League this evening, I think," began Bass.

"Oh lord, please... surely not... Billy fucking Verlaine! Really James?" questioned Blackmore, whose openly resigned expression betrayed just a little more than a man accepting of the fact that some form of confrontation between himself and Verlaine was inevitable.

Bass merely gave his old comrade a wide, knowing grin that broke into a hearty, smoke and brandy ravaged cackle and the pair set off in a northerly direction towards Millers Court.

Reduced to navigating a much longer, and therefore more indirect and altogether more hazardous route out of necessity, in order to avoid detection, time had once more unkindly conspired against the two Detectives, so much so that the late afternoon haze had melded into a typically foggy, extremely chilly, early autumn Whitechapel evening.

Upon entering the narrow, brick-arched passageway that led into Millers Court, Blackmore stopped for a moment at the door of house number thirteen, the location of the last recorded 'Ripper' murder.

"Old memories stirring within that rats' maze of a mind, my brother?" quizzed Bass…

"Old, troubling memories, James. Vivid recollections of how low into the maelstrom of depraved and warped depths the human soul is capable of sinking and reminders of scores to be settled, promises made long ago to be honoured. Debts long outstanding due to be paid, and on this occasion, paid off in full by shedding the tainted blood of the guilty!"

Picking their way through an intricate network of dark, uninviting passageways that lay behind the buildings that lined the north side of Dorset Street, the two Detectives soon found themselves arrived at New Square and in the immediate presence of an old acquaintance.

"A very good evening to you, Billy boy. Are you still prone to filching the pennies from the eyes of the dear departed lying in state at Saint Mary's All-Saints chapel of rest down Great Paternoster Row? I see from the look of you that neither your circumstances of abode, nor indeed the quality of your wardrobe, have improved even marginally during these ten years past since our last meaningful encounter," said Blackmore as a group of Billy Verlaine's loyal acolytes began to appear from various points of concealment within New Square and proceeded to adopt a menacing perimeter, completely surrounding the two Detectives.

"Stand-off 'em', lads, well off. Nah', these two gentlemen 'ere', an' I uses the term 'gentlemen' very loosely 'ere, 'oo've' wandered uninvited and all brazen-like into our manor, is the most devious, 'ard-nosed, 'unforgivin' pair of 'fakkin bastard, and nah', it seems, murderin' cozzers' you'll ever clap your 'mince pies' on in your miserable lives, an' if you gives 'em' 'arf' a chance, they'll 'ave' your flayed, dead carcasses 'angin' on meat 'ooks an' drippin' claret 'dhan' the ice 'ouses in the old Smithfield meat market before you even knew wot was 'appenin'."

Billy Verlaine's stark words of warning were heeded by all but one of his band, a scruffy looking, younger man who proceeded to brandish a long-bladed fish gutting knife and, though displaying little in the way of trained combat etiquette or even any noticeable finesse of movement, launched himself vigorously, yet with no shortage of forceful intent, directly at Bass, whose reaction was both decisive, swift and brutal.

As his aggressor came within his close personal area of space Bass planted his left foot forward and, enhanced by the deceptively powerful momentum a simple left sided twist of his body generated, skilfully utilised both of his huge, raised swinging palms to literally slap away to safety the wildly scything blade. Using the natural force generated by his body as it twisted back to the right, Bass raised his right elbow to meet the oncoming face of his bewildered attacker; THUD!

Standing over his easily vanquished assailant, Bass began to speak, firstly to Verlaine, and then to the bloody heap of rags left sprawling at his feet...

"Hello, Billy boy. How not entirely agreeable it is to see you looking in such average fettle on this raw autumnal evening. Tiberius has business with you, which no doubt he will be very keen to attend to presently."

Bass lowered himself down into a crouching position before his prone attacker and continued...

"And to whom might I be speaking, my foolish, bloody friend?"

"I 'ain't your friend, you 'fakkin' murderin' 'cozzer', an' I 'ain't no fool neither; I'm Albert Kray, from Bethnal Green, an' I eats 'cozzer' for breakfast, elevenses, lunch, tea, dinner an' supper every 'fakkin' day of the week; an' I owes you for a smashed nose an' a barrow load of tarnished pride an' all, you 'fakkin' slick-handed, clever bastard!"

Bass flashed a wide grin in Kray's direction and continued...

"You've got keen spirit and a raging fire burning in those eyes of yours, young Albert Kray from Bethnal Green, I'll give you that, but now is not your time to rise. I'd wager that yours, or probably mores to the point your relatives' and associates' time of ascension is almost certain to come eventually, but rest assured, we will now be watching you Krays from Bethnal Green with great interest.

"Now, Tiberius, if you would please..."

Blackmore shot a swift 'if you've quite finished, may I please continue?' look in Bass' direction. Satisfied that his colleague's impromptu display of albeit necessary force was concluded as Bass nodded in the affirmative, Blackmore began to proceed with his own business matters...

"I'll cut straight to the chase, Billy boy. Ten years ago, dark, military types clearing out the 'rookeries', streets, courts and squares so perpetrators of heinous, terrible murders could work unseen and unmolested. DO YOU REMEMBER, BILLY BOY!"

Verlaine answered immediately, surprising Blackmore with the succinctness, the informal delivery of his answer, and the seemingly genuine fear that was still present in the tone of his voice...

"I remembers it clear as day, like it 'appened just yesterday, Tiberius. Like it was branded permanent on my soul for eternity with some white 'ot' farriers iron.

"After that 'orrible business on Millers Court ten years ago, when we lost our precious Mary to 'Jack the Ripper's' murderous blade, well, we all thought you'd done for old 'crafty Jack' good an' proper on account of the killings coming to a halt, all of a sudden, like. 'Appy days back on the manor 'till about six months ago, when those dark military types, an' that big, faceless bastard barkin' out the orders, came back to doin' their clearin' out for..."

Verlaine hesitated for a moment, as if frozen in mid-sentence by instant recollections of what kind of horrendously depraved mind could conceive of, let alone have the temerity to perform, the horrific murders that he had recently witnessed.

"Might one suggest your sentence was to conclude... 'Clearing out for 'The Ripper', Billy?" asked Blackmore as he handed Verlaine his silver hip-flask filled with his favoured Italian Del-Vecchio brandy.

"Take this, Billy boy. Calm yourself and pray continue on with your tale..."

Verlaine took a long, grateful swig from the flask, waited a few seconds for his frayed nerves to settle and took a second even longer glug of the warming brandy from the flask. Handing the drained flask back to Blackmore whilst nodding his gratitude, Verlaine continued...

"We believes so, Tiberius, clearin' out for old 'Crafty Jack' to do 'is worst once again but..." he paused briefly...

"...but these corpses... were... are left in so much worse a state than before."

"How on earth could the corpses be left in a poorer state than before, Billy?" interjected Bass incredulously...

"Oh, they is much worse, James, much, much worse. 'Eartless an' lungless most of 'em, all manner of organs taken from some just like last time; but this time legs, arms, torsos, even 'eads taken away from others. 'Orrible, it's been, an' still it continues on bein'... 'ORRIBLE!"

Bass and Blackmore listened intently to the remainder of the horrors being divulged by the obviously terrified Verlaine and each drew to the similar conclusion that the terror of a decade past that ran so prevalently and rife throughout the people and the very streets of Whitechapel had indeed returned.

Addressing the whole group, Blackmore said...

"Know this. That the final end-game to these atrocities is about to be played out, this we swear to you as two who were once raised within the heart of 'the abyss', this cess-pit you call home, for believe us when we say that home is this moment where all of us stand.

"Now we ask, nay implore you, to go to ground, one and all. Deliver yourselves, your loved ones, any desperate, homeless soul in need of immediate shelter from the streets to safe haven and especially keep yourselves absent from the East and West dockland wharf side on this night lest mayhem and chaos be what you seek."

As Bass and Blackmore turned to leave New Square, Verlaine said...

"James, Tiberius; please, excuse Albert's youthful exuberance. 'E's got a lot to learn about the possible catastrophic consequences of wrongly judging a man's character but 'e's..."

"He is dangerously unstable and should be made very aware that the consequences of his actions on this night were made far more lenient than he deserved them to be," interjected Bass as his now un-covered, blackened eyes stared soullessly into the eyes of the still prone Albert Kray.

As Kray shuffled backwards on the damp cobble stones in an attempt to put some distance between himself and the chilling sight of Bass' soulless, black stare, Bass continued...

"And you pray to whatever deity you may hold dear that I never have good cause to seek you out in anger again, young Albert Kray from Bethnal Green."

With those parting words Bass replaced his dark lensed spectacles, bid a fond and polite good evening to the now bewildered assembly around them on both himself and Blackmore's behalf and left New Square swiftly via the complex network of passageways through which they entered.

Chapter 37

'Into the Vaults of Trajan'

A vast network of labyrinthine tunnels secreted beneath the Tower of London was conceived as part of a secret underground system that ran its course for large areas under the centre of the old city.

Commissioned and built by the Roman emperor Trajan in the year 100 AD as a network of complex subterranean channels, in order to facilitate the swift movement of provisions and army personnel underneath the congested roads of the rapidly expanding metropolis above, the long ago abandoned and totally forgotten Trajan's vaults became the optimal location for 'The League of Ghosts' to commandeer for themselves, and to utilise this prime location as their covert base of operations.

Bass and Blackmore each knew the Eastern part of the city very well indeed. Every street name, every dilapidated building, alleyway, court, strand and rookery were places the two Detectives once knew as their home many years ago and that now served as a haven of safe retreat for a pair of desperate fugitives absconding from the law that they had both once sworn to uphold and to serve with honour and pride.

Their course remained perfectly clear. They realised that to successfully reach the sanctuary of Trajan's vaults unmolested would make their detection by any standard means virtually impossible, treacherous as the maze of tunnels would prove to be for anyone who attempted to navigate them without prior knowledge of their geography.

Upon leaving Millers Court with some considerable haste Blackmore and Bass wasted little time, maintaining as south-westerly a course that was possible through the city, bisecting the most uninviting and unpredictably perilous areas of 'the abyss' imaginable, making their way ever cautiously towards the west dockland area, known locally and for good reason as 'the maze', where they were perfectly assured of avoiding any mustered group, officially sanctioned or otherwise, that chose still to pursue them.

Across Manse Street, Cross Wall and then turning due south down Cooper's Row, behind Trinity Square and into Tower Hill, the pair of wily Detectives utilised their remarkable ability to move swiftly within the darkest shadows, as would an ethereal spectre, and made for the relative safety of the Western docks. Looking out in a Westerly direction towards the dimly lit, mist-enshrouded Tower of London from their hidden vantage point beneath the rotting wooden trestles of a crumbling wharf-side warehouse building, Bass whispered...

"If we are able to traverse this new and as yet un-used Tower Bridge approach road unseen, in order to reach the front of the Tower, the concealed entrance into Trajan's vaults that we seek lies just a few steps beyond, underneath the Traitor's Gate."

"Hold on to that thought for a moment, James!" hissed Blackmore as he noticed several dark shapes moving at random intervals, seemingly as if searching for something, or perhaps someone, directly in front of them.

"A squad of London's finest seek to enhance their promotion prospects at the expense of our liberty. However, traversing this stretch of road before us is of paramount importance, James. A diversionary measure of some considerable spectacle is required in order to occupy our pursuer's keen attentions, if only to afford us the vital few seconds that we require in order to negotiate a swift and undetected crossing."

Bass looked around their storage area hiding place for anything that might be of use to them. He noticed that they were crouched between several rows of tall wooden packing cases, each one of which was stencilled in red paint with undecipherable Far-Eastern characters. Upon closer inspection, an English translation of what he presumed to be the characters' meaning was clearly stencilled underneath in bold black letters which read simply 'CHINESE FIREWORKS/KEEP DRY/ ABSOLUTELY NO NAKED FLAMES!'.

"I believe that I may well have discovered the means by which our diversionary tactic might unfold, Tiberius," said Bass, a wry grin forming across his craggy, stubbled features.

"If, perhaps, a carelessly discarded spent match stalk or two, still smouldering from a momentary ignition, were to be idly discarded within an unsealed box or two of these Chinese fireworks, then would not the ensuing cacophony of erupting chaos occupy the unwarranted attentions of our seekers and offer us the perfect opportunity to traverse the street unnoticed?"

Blackmore returned his colleague's grin with interest, nodded his head once and the two Detectives each struck a single match simultaneously. Without bothering to extinguish the tiny, flickering flames they each expertly flicked their respective matches directly into two of the largest boxes of fireworks and proceeded to wait for the inevitable chaos to ensue.

Within seconds, it seemed as though all hell had suddenly erupted in the customarily eerie silence of the misty Whitechapel night. These relatively innocuous things that were originally designed with controlled displays of colour, wonderment and beauty in mind had suddenly transformed into projectiles of deadly ordnance that resembled a lethal barrage from enemy cannon fire, albeit completely random in its trajectory.

Rockets shot skyward exploding into falling cascades of brilliant, overlapping colours, Catherine wheels spun randomly out of control and in all directions, untethered Roman candles shot sparks sideways, upwards and outwards, igniting the tinder-dry wooden structure where they were stored and thus creating a raging inferno that was very soon on the verge of becoming completely out of control.

Amidst this tableau of unfolding destruction Bass and Blackmore were able to break their cover and slip silently across the Tower Bridge Road as they had planned, avoiding any contact with their now otherwise occupied pursuers. As they were about to dissolve once more into the welcoming and all-encompassing shadows of the night they even took the time to stop for a brief moment and turn to survey the quite spectacular result of their handiwork.

"Quite a spectacle, if a tad excessive to suit our purpose, wouldn't you agree, Tiberius?" questioned Bass.

"Oh, most assuredly so, James. The results of our impromptu, erm, pyrotechnic display might suggest possibly a little over-exuberance on our part. However, those Western dockland store houses were detached from other wharf side properties, suggesting a danger of the fire reaching out into the city was of minimal concern."

"And those dilapidated old storage houses were in dire need of cleansing and refurbishment," added Bass matter-of-factly, as if attempting to somehow justify their act of wilful destruction...

"They were indeed, James, and behold the cascading spectacle unfolding before us. A free, exciting show of spectacular proportions for the East End public to savour amidst the mundane normality of their everyday existences."

"The conscientious arsonists are we then, Tiberius?" quipped Bass dryly...

"That we are, James, that we are indeed."

Turning back towards Tower Hill, Bass and Blackmore were soon enveloped once more by the all-encompassing night-time cloak of dark shadows, on this occasion cast over them by the high outer walls of the Tower of London. As they dropped lower onto a path that ran alongside of the moat surrounding the Tower, the ominous, heavily fortified façade of Traitors Gate soon loomed up high above them out of the dark water of the Thames.

Their narrow pathway seemed to end abruptly, directly in front of the huge iron gate. On the other side of the once grim portal could clearly be seen the infamous stone steps that led up towards the central 'bloody' tower and the old executioner's block, still sitting exuding silent menace on Tower Hill green, as if for many centuries merely lying in wait for its next hapless victim.

Approaching the gate, Bass and Blackmore moved slightly to their right, where part of an ancient, heavy stone wall rose high up out of the depths of the river. Upon locating a concealed entrance behind this wall, they proceeded on down a flight of well-worn steps and into a short passageway, at the end of which stood a great iron door.

The heavy door swung inwards with little effort after the correct sequence of turns and twists was administered to the two massive brass handles on either side, revealing as it creaked steadily ajar a vast open space sporting intricate mosaic patterns embedded into its walls and floors, and huge marble columns rising high up to the grand, exquisitely frescoed ceiling above.

Equal in area and size to the great Sistine Chapel in the Vatican City, at the far end of this remarkably well-preserved monument to Roman art and architecture could be seen the extraordinary sight of Trajan's Arch, believed lost many centuries ago under the rising tide of the Thames, built as a lasting monument to honour the achievements of the Roman emperor Trajan who had done so much to develop and improve the modern city of London, now nothing more than a partially ruined artefact from a once great era leading into the labyrinthine vaults below, and the first unofficial marker on the perilous pathways that led to The League of Ghosts.

After successfully navigating several precarious twists and turns throughout the dimly lit, arch topped passageways, Bass and Blackmore entered into yet another impressive vast open space that was brightly illuminated by an ingenious series of huge crystal glass chandeliers, each one powered by solar batteries that were re-charged at regular intervals utilising natural daylight harnessed from above.

The room itself was circular in design, reminiscent of the great Pantheon in Rome, and from its centre, emanating outwards in all directions of the compass and as far as the eye was able to see, were shelves upon shelves consisting of rare books, priceless documents and the rarest of both religious and historical artefacts, all relating to decisive points in the entire chronicled history of the world.

At the very central core of this grandest, most opulent of libraries was situated a large, round oak-topped table, around which were set sixteen heavy, high-backed oak chairs, one seat on the high council for each member of the League of Ghosts.

Already seated at their places around the table, awaiting the pre-arranged arrival of the two Detectives, were Constance Bass, Pandora Blackmore, Commander 'Don' Blackmore, Alanis Blackmore, Pontius Aston, Beatrice Aston and their son Professor Leopold Aston, Doctor Phineas Jefferson and his wife Professor Florence Jefferson, Sergeant Marcus Jackson and someone the hearts of both Bass and Blackmore were gladdened, and somewhat relieved, to see.

"So, our little rouse designed to feign your death proved successful, Frank," were the first words uttered by Blackmore upon taking his seat at the table.

"Only Phineas, Frank and Connie were made privy to the existence of a special ether and red dye filled tranquilizer round, brilliantly conceived and designed by both Phineas and Connie, that when discharged from a conventional weapon into its intended target gives to all who bear witness to the act the distinct impression of a kill shot."

"Very effective work, boys," said Frank Abilene proudly.

"Four very nicely grouped chest taps that even had young Marcus here initially duped good and proper into believing that you'd both gone rogue on us all. Left some very nasty bruising on my chest that my May will be keen to take the both of you to task over, though..."

"Our fall from grace needed to be swift, absolute and made public instantaneously, thus affording us both the opportunity to work for the past few days unfettered by the intrusive, stifling constraints of lawful protocol and correct etiquette. We became pariahs on both sides of the law intentionally, the number one priority on the hunted fugitives' roster, in order to purposefully court the maximum attention of the authorities towards us and so hopefully in turn to draw out into the open arena our triple nemesis, emboldened by the apparent lack of interest shown by the establishment in their business, confidence sufficiently replenished to resume their obsessive, murderous proclivities."

"Quadruple nemesis, Tiberius. 'Arbogast 'the butcher', Von Waldheim the galvanist, 'The Architect'... and Ben Stoker," added Bass as he drew both of his pistols and placed one of them on the table in front of him.

"On this occasion, however, there will be no embarrassment of a stand down, as was the case many years before."

As he spoke, Bass continued to drop cartridges into the empty chambers of his Schofield revolver. Upon completion of the task he slammed the heavy pistol down hard onto the table, as if to forcefully drive his point home...

"This time, there will be... nay... cannot afford to be, any mercy shown, any quarter given. For the sake of all those poor, defenceless souls already lost, and to prevent all of the damage and chaos that might yet ensue should their barbaric and obsessive ambitions be allowed to flourish, all four of them must be permanently retired."

The assembled group remained silent for a few seconds that seemed to last an eternity, until that silence was eventually broken by the words of Pontius Aston...

"I concur wholeheartedly, James. The perpetrators of these indecent acts must be dispatched with extreme prejudice, erased from existence, of that fact there should remain no reasonable doubt. As for the fate of 'The Architect', though the formidable influence he currently exerts throughout the corridors of power will weaken and quickly evaporate the moment that he senses his plans are successfully compromised, his powerful life flame will prove somewhat more challenging to extinguish."

"But is he not as human as you or I, Pontius, thus as susceptible to human frailties?" enquired Blackmore, more in hope than positive expectation...

"He is undoubtedly human, Tiberius, most assuredly so. His human frailties remain intact and as vulnerable to compromise by a keen and prepared mind as do yours or mine. However, and remember these words well, my friend; his remains the superior intellect overall. He possesses a mind of great genius, a temperament of extraordinary guile and cunning.

"He is, too, the archetypal trickster. An expert manipulator of normal perception and circumstance towards and beyond the very slender precipice of international disarray and universal catastrophe, merely in order to serve his own obsessive need for power. He is, and I cannot reiterate this statement enough, the most dangerous being alive."

As Bass proceeded to re-holster his loaded pistols the words that he chose to use were succinct, precise and left no doubt in everyone's minds how he perceived both himself and Blackmore should proceed...

"Should the suggested directive entailing the use of deadly force be unanimously agreed upon amongst ourselves, I propose that both myself and Tiberius, operating within the parameters of our agreed role as officially sanctioned enforcers on behalf of The League of Ghosts, be dispatched immediately in order to bring this waking nightmare to a conclusive end, once and for all."

Frank Abilene interjected, only to be halted mid-sentence by Bass...

"I shall at once summon a group of officers, loyal and true, who will proceed to..."

"No, Frank! Absolutely no-one but myself and Tiberius shall be in any way implicated with even the slightest suspicion of involvement whatsoever, with either the planning or participation, in the actions that are about to ensue. I would hope that in the moment Arbogast and von Waldheim are dispatched, the influence exerted by 'The Architect' will immediately evaporate, and thus restore clear perspective and common sense to those who were for so long misled by his great deception."

"But what of the inconceivable alternative, James?" asked an obviously concerned Abilene.

"If a satisfactory conclusion rests merely on an element of chance unfolding in your favour, what of the inconceivable, yet ironically obvious alternative that awaits the pair of you?"

Bass sat back in his chair and answered simply and succinctly, with both arms outstretched as if attempting to convey that this was indeed their only viable option...

"Then, my old comrade, the existence of 'Jack the Ripper', along with those of his opportunistic ally, and also possibly 'The Architect', who we are now aware of as being an enemy of the whole universe, are all erased for good. Unfortunately, both myself and Tiberius would remain vigorously pursued fugitives, a situation to which, as you very well know, Francis, we are both quite accustomed.

"However, the potential rewards to be gained as a result of our proposed actions necessitate that we seize upon this gilt-edged opportunity to right great injustice."

"Might one enquire as to precisely how James and I might hope to gain an advantage of any description over our nemesis, considering the 'all-seeing eyes' of the Time Enforcement Agency remain open and accessible for use by 'The Architect'?" asked Blackmore, a hint of nervous trepidation apparent in his voice...

Aston, as ever, was swift to give his answer. As he did so, even though he acknowledged Blackmore, he proceeded to look diametrically into the covered eyes of Bass and gave a single nod as he finished...

"Even the 'all-seeing eyes' of the T.E.A. are not totally infallible, Tiberius. We too may occasionally be susceptible to the element of random chance."

Chapter 38

'The Element of Random Chance'

Upon re-entering the artificially generated half-light of the dimly-lit vaults, Bass and Blackmore were nonetheless familiar enough with the intricate maze of pathways so as to be able to navigate the route towards their intended destination of eighty-nine Manning Place.

"Both Arbogast and von Waldheim must have utilised the privacy these vaults afforded to them for decades, in order to move around freely and undetected, thus enabling the pair of them to access with ease and with deathly silence their pre-prepared murder sites above," began Blackmore.

"It's of little wonder that they themselves were never formally identified by any reliable witnesses and the urban legend was born and nurtured over time of a murderous spectre roaming the streets of Whitechapel."

Bass remained silent.

"Oh, and might one ask whilst the conversation flows freely between us, what pressing subject, apart from wishing each other your fond farewells of course, could yourself and Connie have been discussing at such great length that would hinder our departure so, James?" continued Blackmore, his mood now turned to exasperation by being blatantly ignored by his colleague twice...

Bass stopped walking and turned to face his disgruntled, grumbling companion.

"Please excuse me, Tiberius. A brief, stolen moment of tenderness between a husband and his beloved wife, nothing more. Rest assured, however, my mind engages with thoughts similar to those of which you allude; of these ancient vaults being less private than we might have imagined with regards to them being used by Arbogast and his allies.

"And yes of course, thoughts of my Connie, always. At the dawn of every battle, during each incursion into the perpetual maelstrom of hell or on this time as we set forth, together once more, to face evil incarnate.

"We prepare as best we may to engage yet another formidable enemy with the full realisation that a favourable outcome to our endeavours on this particular occasion might not be achievable; so, yes, Tiberius, always thoughts of Connie, as I'm certain Pandora and the children would inhabit your thoughts in a similar fashion."

"Of course, of course, my dear old friend... I merely..."

"SHHH!" hissed Bass, as he instantly curtailed Blackmore's attempted apology...

"Another time, Tiberius, over an excellent brandy and a quality tobacco perhaps; I sense movement ahead of us. Footfall suggests five, no, six pairs of heavy soled boots, possibly military issue, each now peeling away from a central group."

"Covert Special Forces operatives. Undoubtedly deploying into different tunnels, covering every conceivable entrance into the cellar of eighty-nine Manning Place. The wily bastards are aware that we are coming!" exclaimed Blackmore...

"But how can you be so certain of their identity, James?" asked Blackmore...

"I can hear them, Tiberius, and I can taste their distinctive scent, all of them!"

Continuing forward for a short distance Bass once more brought them both to a halt as the two Detectives approached a wider, circular intersection in their path, at which their route divided into six different directions. Using the arch-topped passageway in which they stood for concealment, Bass began to speak in hushed tones as he studied the brass mariners' compass that he had removed from a pocket in his long overcoat...

"From this bearing the North/North-Eastern passage would prove to be our obvious choice, giving us the swiftest route to our intended destination."

"Agreed" was the simple answer given by Blackmore...

"And might one suggest that the use of deadly force in dealing with our spellbound soldier friends be differed, until such a time as it becomes absolutely necessary to apply such measures, of course."

Bass nodded his approval and the pair set off with some urgency in their chosen direction.

It wasn't long before Bass and Blackmore encountered a group of four C.S.F. operatives who had re-grouped in the passageway ahead of them. Using the long shadows cast on either side of the arched tunnel by the flickering flames of oil lamps which were hung at random intervals on the walls the Detectives silently edged along each side wall of the tunnel until they were near enough to observe their marks at close quarters.

Noticing immediately that none of the men held any kind of weapon in hand, both Bass and Blackmore moved with great swiftness, as if simultaneously receiving a telepathically transmitted message to do so.

Utilising great speed and dexterity of movement to ensure that none of the C.S.F. operatives were afforded an opportunity to arm themselves, and in what seemed like no time at all, the four men lay incapacitated and unconscious at the two Detectives' feet.

Pressing onwards for what Blackmore estimated to be at least another mile in the North-Easterly direction of the tunnel they eventually found themselves approaching a steep set of wooden steps that rose sharply upwards towards what appeared to be a solid stone wall.

After climbing the steps, upon closer inspection Bass located a concealed locking mechanism which, when engaged correctly, enabled the heavy stone panel to swing inwards on its great iron hinges, revealing what the two Detectives recognised immediately as being the cellar of eighty-nine Manning Place.

Making their way quietly towards a second flight of wooden steps they instantly recognised as those leading up to the entrance hall of the house, and remembering to close and lock the stone panel behind them, Bass and Blackmore paused for a few seconds in order to take stock of their situation and review the next crucial phase of their strategy.

"If memory serves, the room in which we last confronted our adversaries lies atop this staircase and but a step or two across the hall."

"I believe that you are correct, Tiberius, what's more..."

Bass raised his left index finger to his lips sharply, silencing himself and bidding Blackmore to remain so.

Upon hearing a door handle turn, Bass gestured towards the steps as the remaining two C.S.F. men began to descend into the semi-darkness of the cellar.

Realising immediately that their vision would require a few seconds to acclimatise in the dim light, Bass and Blackmore were able to break cover unchallenged and instantly incapacitate the two unprepared men with relative ease.

"And two more equals six," quipped Blackmore as the man he had chosen to engage fell in an unconscious heap to the ground.

"I sense the presence of four more, one of whom wears similar military footwear to the pair of hapless souls lying prone here in this basement, and the four who lie sleeping soundly in the labyrinth below."

Making their way up the wooden staircase and through the cellar door, Blackmore and Bass crossed the narrow hallway of eighty-nine Manning Place and entered into a room they both remembered very well.

All of a sudden, a strange feeling of déjà vu overcame them both as they were greeted by the unnervingly familiar sight of Arbogast, von Waldheim, 'The Architect', Commander Benjamin Stoker and the current Home Secretary; the Right Honourable Sir Matthew White Ridley, who was flanked by several red coats belonging to the Duke of Wellington's Regiment.

Distracted from their post-dinner conversation as if in the first instance they had been rudely interrupted by some inferior personage, 'The Architect' nonetheless remained gracious as he acknowledged the arrival of the two Detectives and greeted them with the cordiality generally reserved for expected guests of quality...

"Gentlemen, please come and join our après-dejeuner port and cigar soiree. To suggest that you were not expected would be a falsehood. I notice, however, that our reception committee, sent post-haste to chaperone your safe passage to our attendance here, is conspicuous by its absence. No matter, here you both are and you are most welcome."

"We regret to inform you that your most enthusiastic, and really quite rude 'reception committee,' regrettably, as was the case on the last occasion we conversed many moons ago, will not be joining us for coffee, cigars and idle banter this evening," retorted Blackmore sharply as he drew his Le-Mat revolver and aimed directly towards the gloating visages of Arbogast and von Waldheim.

Bass immediately followed his partner's lead, provoking an immediate offensive reaction from the group of assembled redcoats.

"I ORDER YOU TO STAND DOWN, IN THE NAME OF HER MAJESTY QUEEN VICT..."

The Home Secretary's words were instantly curtailed by the briefest of retorts from Blackmore before both himself and Bass proceeded to fire a volley of three shots apiece, each one precise and deadly in its accuracy; two taps to the chest, and one single tap to the forehead of their chosen targets.

"Alas, on this particular occasion, we choose to stand fast, and in so doing accept the full consequence that our actions might provoke, sir. Be under no illusion to the contrary, however, that on this night the horror of 'Jack the Ripper' and the potential rise of an army of the undead ends here in this place, once and for all."

'CRACK', 'CRACK'... 'CRACK.' 'CRACK', 'CRACK'... 'CRACK!'

The unerring accuracy of the expert marksmen's aim meant that every one of the searing, deadly projectiles found its intended mark with ease. As expected, upon the lifeless corpses of Arbogast and Von Waldheim falling to the floor at their feet, the Redcoats raised their primed rifles, took aim and awaited the inevitable order to fire upon the two Detectives.

"REDCOATS, OPEN F..."

The Home Secretary's command was instantly stifled when his and the attention of everyone in the room became totally focused upon James Bass as he dramatically threw off his heavy overcoat, as if some overwhelming madness had befallen him.

Turning his head towards Blackmore, who stood at his left side, he uttered a brief, but nonetheless stark warning...

"Tiberius. For your own safety and wellbeing, I implore you, please stand aside. At my behest, the spirit of the wolf is rising and... oh... my... God protect you all..."

Bass threw off what clothing he was able to before the swift, agonising metamorphosis from man into werewolf began.

All who bore witness to the terrifying phenomena that was unfolding before their unbelieving eyes, with the exception of Blackmore who was quite familiar with the whole process and remained totally calm throughout, recoiled in abject horror as the sound of bones cracking and re-setting themselves, limbs contorting and unnaturally elongating beyond all human proportion, claws forcing themselves from bloodied finger ends, snarling fangs replacing teeth, snow-white fur growing from hardened grey skin and finally, the long, tortured howl of an eight-foot tall wolf, caused many of the battle-hardened troops to literally lose control of their most basic bodily functions.

Nor did any of them in their blind terror even consider firing a single shot from their poised rifles, each one of which was instantly flung to the ground in unison as though surrender was the only option left to them in order to preserve their survival.

Blackmore stepped forward, carefully avoiding crossing into the great wolf's considerable wake, and began to speak as he almost nonchalantly proceeded to re-load his revolver...

"A very wise thing for you to do, my friends. Very wise indeed.

"Oh gentlemen. Oh, dear me. My most heartfelt sympathies to you all. Not since my very good friend James here" ; beckoning towards the snarling beast by his side; "and myself were a part of the forlorn hope at Sevastopol have I witnessed such an overwhelming, and quite understandable I hasten to add, loss of basic bodily function control amongst grown men.

"Now, the immediate situation to which we find ourselves bound at present is one of an extremely delicate nature, do you all not agree?"

Gesturing towards the lifeless corpses of Arbogast and von Waldheim, Blackmore continued...

"Not one person of sound mind, nor those who purport to be of clear and untainted conscience, who have studied the content of detailed reports concerning their unnatural nocturnal proclivities or borne witness to recent past atrocities attributed to the spectre commonly known as 'Jack the Ripper' could disagree that these two pieces of recently deceased sub-human refuse lying at your feet did not deserve the fate that has befallen them on this night."

Altering his focus towards 'The Architect' who stood impassively alongside the Home Secretary and whose face, somewhat surprisingly it seemed to Blackmore, displayed the smile of someone who actually appeared to be revelling in how proceedings were unfolding before him, as would a player participating in some bizarre game of wits, almost appreciating the fact that his plans had been irreparably thwarted by the unforeseen element of random chance.

"This man who stands here amongst you is the archetypal grand master of deceit. It has remained this past three months his sole purpose to manipulate the events, commonly referred to by the media as 'the Ripper murders' as they unfolded, in a manner that would suit his own obsessive ambition to raise an army of the dead, galvanised into life utilising the scientific genius of Baron von Waldheim, created from remains harvested from the poor, unfortunate victims of 'Arbogast the Butcher'; better known to you all as 'Jack the Ripper'.

"The effectiveness of his influence over yourself, Mr Home Secretary, sir, and other key personnel within the halls of government, and possibly even over our exalted Royals themselves, has been so spectacularly effective as to render you all utterly and completely unaware of the fanatical determination that motivated the Whitechapel murderers to carry out their despicable crimes, and to force your hands in so much as to shield them from the undue attention of any curious authority, in order for his grand scheme to develop and come to fruition.

"This man who stands brazenly in our midst, known only to us by his rather apt sobriquet of 'The Architect' might well be the single most dangerous nemesis that all of humanity has ever encountered and must be taken into secure custody without further delay..."

As he raised his pistol and took aim in the direction of 'The Architect', Blackmore's words seemed to dissolve away into a spontaneous haze as, just for a few seconds, an overwhelming sense of disorientation and confusion overcame everyone in the room, including the wolf.

A loud roar of frustration and anger emitted by the wolf brought everyone immediately to their senses.

"Yes, so I see, James. 'The Architect' has utilised his vexatious gift for trickery and subterfuge, and somehow once more succeeded in eluding our immediate attentions," observed Blackmore, just at the precise moment that Pontius, Beatrice and Leopold Aston, Frank Abilene, Phineas and Florence Jefferson, Pandora and Alanis Blackmore, Commander 'Don' Blackmore, Marcus Jackson, Lord Thor Ragnar and Lady Anna Freya Olaffsson, and finally but by no means least Constance Bass entered the room and took up positions of support alongside Blackmore and the snarling white werewolf, the sight of whom whilst occupying his full, magnificent form they were now each well acquainted and comfortable with.

Blackmore greeted his fellow 'League of Ghost' compatriots with a simple nod of his head and, turning to face the Home Secretary and the cowering Redcoats, continued to speak with the fortitude and conviction of the great leader he had become...

"The ones who stand here before you now are without question a truly exceptional collective of humanity. Each one carefully selected for their superior intellectual and physical capabilities, one and all pledged to serve the cause of true honour and justice with their lives.

"We move silently amongst you, hidden in plain sight until the precise moment of our choosing, spectres drawn forth from within the darkest, forbidding shadows of the sub-conscious mind.

"We are the champions of those in desperate need, the nemesis of those who propose to peddle despair, darkness and corruption.

"We stand together as sworn defenders of the precious jewel that is humanity, protectors of the realm and guardians of the fourth dimension of time."

Stretching his arms wide as if to formally introduce the arrival of his colleagues into the gallery of public awareness, Blackmore continued...

"We are the antithesis of all evil. Here stands before you 'The League of Ghosts'."

Sir Matthew White Ridley listened intently to Blackmore as he spoke, his initial visage of fear turning first to one of wonderment, and then the quizzical expression of a man with several hundred questions that demanded an answer.

"Commander Blackmore and, erm, Major Bass, I presume. Your exemplary military records precede you, gentlemen, your reputations amongst both your peers and throughout the higher echelons of society and government are known of and greatly admired. Your many daring missions, selflessly undertaken in the name of Queen and Country, are greatly discussed and respected by all but I am compelled first and foremost to enquire, what malady afflicts the Major so to be the cause of such an horrific abomination of mother nature's folly? How can this be so?"

As the Home Secretary spoke, Bass began the agonising metamorphosis back into his human form before Sir Matthew's startled eyes, and, as his wife Constance proceeded to cover his perspiring naked body with his old, heavy overcoat, regained his composure and proceeded to answer the question in part himself...

"With the greatest respect, Sir Matthew, as to how the lycanthrope's spirit came to find a home within me is a tale to be told on some other more appropriate occasion. Suffice to add at this juncture that this 'horrific abomination of mother nature's folly', as you so rudely referred to my spirit animal personified, is as loyal a servant to the Crown and its subjects as any one person affiliated to the cause, be they in this room standing, or otherwise situated."

"I consider myself soundly and correctly rebuked, Major Bass," began Sir Matthew rather sheepishly...

"Please, accept my most humble and heartfelt apologies and excuse my complete lack of understanding appertaining to your condition. I meant no disrespect. If anything at all, abject fear was the key motivator that governed my rash and totally inappropriate rhetoric. I am ashamed and truly sorry."

Bass took a long, welcome swig from the hip flask Connie had supplied him with containing his favourite Italian brandy, lit up and took several, generous puffs from a large cigar and said...

"Were I in your position, Sir Matthew, rhetoric would no doubt be considered third only to the reassurance afforded by the comfort of a sound, sharp blade or a trusted firearm. I thank you for your honesty, and for your candour with regards to your own perceived short-comings, sir.

"As for 'Jack the Ripper', there he, or rather, there they lie and so too should the completed case file be allowed to lie from this moment onwards, entrusted into the secure custody of 'The League of Ghosts' who will ensure that the document remains inaccessible to the general public until such a time as we see fit to release its content."

As Bass turned towards his wife and began to dress himself in a suit of clothing from the large carpet bag that Constance had brought with her, without turning his head in the direction of Sir Matthew White Ridley, Bass continued to speak...

"There would be one more extremely relevant official item of note to rectify, Sir Matthew, that being mine and Tiberius' total absolution for the murder of Frank Abilene. As you can plainly see, here he stands before you, very much alive and well.

"The manner in which we decided our investigation should be conducted necessitated our discommendation be perceived by all as being authentic and made public domain very quickly, and that our ostracism from lawful society be so convincing and absolute as to leave us outlawed in the perception of both law-abiding, and criminal fraternities alike, thus focusing the considerable resources of the justice system solely upon Tiberius and myself in the hope of emboldening our recently deceased friends here to resume their unnaturally brutal nocturnal proclivities. All things taken into consideration, the culmination of a spectacularly successful strategy, wouldn't you agree, Sir Matthew?"

Having finally settled back into his customary demeanour of experienced parliamentarian and world statesman, his composure now fully restored after his extremely traumatic experience and the revelations that followed, Sir Matthew answered quickly, and with the authority that was expected from one holding such high government office...

"Most assuredly, Major Bass. The culmination of a spectacularly successful mission. Extremely hazardous to both yourself, and to Commander Blackmore, and possibly as ill-conceived a strategy as to which one has ever borne witness to, wouldn't you agree, sir!"

Bass merely smiled and nodded his head in approval of the now fully restored Home Secretary's obvious logic...

"But somehow, Major, the phrases 'extremely risky' and 'ill-conceived strategy' and yourselves might well be perceived as being common bedfellows, are they not?"

"And of course, not forgetting the all-important phrase 'spectacularly successful' too, sir," quipped Blackmore dryly, much to the delight of both his League of Ghosts colleagues and the now much more at ease, but still slightly soiled Redcoats...

"Quite so, Commander Blackmore, quite so. One fundamental fact remains glaringly obvious, however, in that two of your number did mercilessly, and without displaying the slightest notion of warning, nor offering the lawful option of arrest, proceed to gun down in cold blood a pair of well-respected members of the old European high-born aristocracy!"

"THE VERY ARISTOCRACY, TO WHICH YOU SO GLIBLY REFER, MR HOME SECRETARY, THAT SEES FIT TO OFFER SAFE HAVEN FOR THE CULPRITS OF CORRUPTION FROM WITHIN ITS RANKS, WHO HIDE CRAVENLY BEHIND ITS SHEEN OF MOCK RESPECTIBILITY. THEY TOO MUST BE SEEN BY ORDINARY PEOPLE TO BE HELD ACCOUNTABLE FOR THEIR ALL TOO FREQUENTLY OVERLOOKED CRIMINAL ACTIVITIES!" exclaimed Pontius Aston fervently...

"Occasionally, is not the spontaneous action the catalyst that satisfies the moment admirably?

"It is true to state that these two men acted ultimately on impulse alone, but did not their impulsiveness provide the favourable conclusion that we all sought as it should have done ten years ago, were it not for the meddlesome attentions of 'The Architect'?"

"Ah yes, of course, Captain Aston, 'The Architect', the elusive 'master of deceit' whose involvement in proceedings you alluded to so fervently at an earlier juncture," said Sir Matthew, displaying a rather sarcastic manner...

"DO NOT FOR ONE SECOND UNDERESTIMATE HIS ABILITY TO DECEIVE, SIR!" exclaimed Aston, instantly angered by the Home Secretary's rather casual, almost disrespectful aside...

"Even though his aspirations on this particular occasion were thwarted, by the timely interventions of these two brave men I might add," (gesturing towards Bass and Blackmore) "his mandate is to relentlessly persevere on task regardless of the humanitarian cost and his resolve to do so remains unequivocally strong. Be under no illusion whatsoever, sir, 'The Architect' will undoubtedly return."

"A most dangerous individual indeed then, this 'Architect' fellow, Captain Aston," began Sir Matthew...

Shifting his focus once more towards the two Detectives, he continued...

"So then, what to do about the involvement of Commander Blackmore and Major Bass?"

This time, infuriated by the apparent lack of understanding displayed by the Home Secretary, Aston spat forth...

"WHAT TO DO ABOUT...

"NOTHING, YOU IGNORANT, BLIND FOOL! YOU WILL DO ABSOLUTELY NOTHING TO JEOPARDISE EITHER THE LIBERTY OR THE LIVES OF THESE MEN, THEIR FAMILIES AND FRIENDS. NOR SHALL YOU SEEK RETRIBUTION UPON ANY ONE OF THEIR COLLEAGUES OR STREET AGENTS. DO I MAKE MYSELF PERFECTLY CLEAR, MR HOME SECRETARY, SIR?"

Somewhat stunned by the ferocity of Aston's verbal assault, Sir Matthew's reply was merely restricted to a simple muted nod of his head.

"They acted upon a mandate agreed upon many years ago by both the 'Grand Meisters' council of the Time Enforcement Agency and 'The League of Ghosts' council as they should have been allowed to ten years ago, thus averting a potential world-altering cataclysm from developing further.

"They will also in turn be admonished of all guilt appertaining to the murder of Detective Chief Superintendent Francis Abilene, their considerable reputations restored in full and untarnished, and under no circumstances will either man be implicated, nor mentioned as being in any way involved with carrying out the long overdue termination of this filth lying here before us."

Visibly stunned, Sir Matthew paused for a few seconds as he cogitated Aston's words very carefully before regaining his composure once more to answer...

"Eloquently put, sir. Flawlessly logical reasoning, succinct in every fine detail. Very nicely orated indeed.

"Were it not for the remarkable occurrences that I myself have this past few minutes witnessed here, within these very walls, both Major Bass and Commander Blackmore would have been placed under close arrest and no doubt charged with the murders of not only two respected members of high-born aristocracy, but also that of a respected public servant. However, as I said, that was before..."

Following another brief pause, Sir Matthew continued...

"Rest assured, both Commander Blackmore and Major Bass will be completely admonished of all guilt appertaining to the murder of Francis Abilene.

"With regards to the other, erm, shall we henceforth refer to them as 'retirements', explanations will surely be required, detailed reports being submitted to a higher authority, regarding events that have transpired here this evening."

Addressing Aston, Blackmore and Bass directly, Sir Matthew continued on to his conclusion...

"At some point in the near future, Captain Aston, Commander Blackmore and Major Bass, you will most certainly be summoned to attend a higher office in order to offer your reports personally. I would strongly suggest that regardless of your business concerns and personal commitments, either pending or otherwise, that you make allowance to attend. Now gentlemen, ladies, I believe that our business here is concluded, for the time being."

Seemingly satisfied with Sir Matthew's conclusion, Bass and his colleagues turned towards the door with a view to leaving the room. All at once, as if alerted by some subliminal message informing him of one more vital task to address, Bass turned sharply, drew out his Schofield revolver and took aim…

"How remiss of me. A trifling matter that almost slipped my mind in all of this excitement," began Bass as he cocked back the hammer of his pistol and picked out his target.

"Ben Stoker. I believe that the time is finally upon you to pay the ferryman his due. Goodbye 'Benny boy', and may you rot in hell for the rest of eternity." 'CRACK', 'CRACK'… 'CRACK.'

Bass fired three precise taps. Two directly to the chest and one dead centre to the forehead, that sent Stoker's lifeless corpse falling to the floor right next to the visibly shaken Home Secretary.

Bass holstered his still smouldering pistol and, showing not a hint of emotion or remorse in his voice, simply imparted towards the incredulous Sir Matthew…

"Please excuse the seemingly random spontaneity of my actions, Sir Matthew. Now, I believe that our business here is properly concluded. On behalf of myself and my colleagues may I take the opportunity to wish yourself and your rather splendidly attired, if not now somewhat soiled, soldiers a very pleasant evening."

Chapter 39

'God Save the Queen'

The sudden and unannounced arrival of several darkly attired men of sombre disposition provided the surprising event of an otherwise normal and really quite mundane day of routine at the Leman Street Police station.

Disregarding any sort of formal waiting process, the group of six men proceeded directly towards the front desk, where the young Captain in charge of the men confronted the somewhat startled desk sergeant on duty.

"Yes, sir, how can I..." the sergeant stuttered before he was rudely interrupted by the young captain...

"Commander Alan Tiberius Blackmore, Major James Bartholomew Bass; WHERE ARE THEY?!"

"Chief Superintendent Abilene's office, down the corridor, first door on the left" came the reply.

Not bothering to wait for an escort, or any kind of formal presentations to be made, the men barged through Abilene's office door without knocking and confronted Bass, Blackmore and Abilene himself with the most basic and downright rudest of introductions...

"Major James Bartholomew Bass, Commander Alan Tiberius Blackmore; by order of her Majesty Queen Victoria you are hereby instructed to accompany us immediately."

Showing not a hint outwardly of either the frustration nor the burning anger he was actually feeling on account of their private meeting being so rudely interrupted by a group of strangers, Bass enquired of the one who had spoken, the one he assumed was in charge and, in his opinion, deserved a lot less than the cordial, and not unreasonable, request that he was about to make...

"And where exactly, might one ask, are we to be taken?"

"NO QUESTIONS!" came the terse, ill-mannered response from the young Captain...

"Should you both choose not to comply with our request, we are authorised to employ other less than cordial means to ensure your compliance in this matter is made absolute."

Carefully surveying the faces belonging to their potential escorts for any revealing signs of doubt or weakness, Blackmore was immediately able to gauge a certain unease in each of their young, and what he considered to be inexperienced faces. He decided that the impact of his words should leave each one of them under no illusion as to the consequences any forceful confrontation would entail.

"Your demeanour, your dour choice of wardrobe coupled with your appalling lack of respect denotes C.S.F. operatives' manners, gentlemen. Your obvious lack of experience betrays you as 'raw meat' perhaps?"

Turning to address both Bass and Abilene, Blackmore continued displaying an almost mocking sarcasm in his voice...

"Observe, gentlemen. They've sent 'raw meat' to bring us in!"

Turning once more to face the encroaching group, Blackmore continued delivering his withering tirade whilst steadily moving towards the now extremely nervous face of the young Captain until they were literally eye to eye...

"Your initial introduction betrayed both a lack of experience and basic civility, gentlemen, which is forgivable. However, the absence of respect shown towards not only myself and Major Bass, but also in dealing with the Commanding officer and operatives of this station to whom common courtesy at the very least is due, on another day might have resulted in all of your deaths."

Feeling uncomfortable beads of cold perspiration forming on his brow, and slivers of sweat beginning to seep down to the small of his back, the young Captain, realising the fundamental error he had displayed whilst delivering his introductory speech, quickly attempted to make amends...

"My apologies, sir, I merely..."

"YOU'VE SAID ALL THAT YOU NEED TO FOR THE MOMENT, SOLDIER!" snapped Blackmore tersely directly into the soundly rebuked face of the young Captain...

Stepping back a few paces, Blackmore continued...

"Now, I suggest that you escort both myself and Major Bass to the designated location so as to satisfy your superiors that the mission parameters have been successfully carried out, do I make myself perfectly clear... Captain?"

"C... Captain L... Lucas Fortnum, sir" was the rather nervous answer given...

"Y.. Yes, sir, of course, sir. If you wouldn't mind at all... accompanying us, sir... sirs... if you please... sirs!"

Blackmore and Bass were duly escorted from Leman Street Police station and politely asked to board a large, black carriage bearing a royal coat of arms on each of its two doors. Once settled inside the opulent décor of the carriage interior, coupled with the blacked-out windows making identification of their route impossible, immediately informed the Detectives that they had indeed been summoned to attend the very highest authority.

"Covered windows," noted Bass.

"Captain Fortnum. Would there be any profit in asking as to the destination to which this most salubrious of carriages traverses?" Bass enquired of one of their two travelling companions...

"No profit at all, sir, I'm afraid. Please, if you would remain calm, sir, our destination is close by," replied Captain Fortnum flatly, but still nonetheless betraying a very apparent nervousness in his voice, as if he were very well aware that his charges were capable of overpowering his men and taking their leave at will.

Sensing the young Captain's growing unease, Bass' answer was designed more as a calming influence than a threat...

"Please, Captain, be at your ease. There would be no profit gained on our part if we chose to abscond. Either for myself, or for Commander Blackmore, nor for your men who, rest assured, Captain, would profit least of all if such a circumstance were to unfold. So be at your ease and complete your 'fetch and carry' mission, Captain Fortnum, such as it is."

The carriage finally came to a sudden halt.

"Remain seated, if you please, gentlemen," asked Captain Fortnum of his sceptical passengers, now himself displaying an altogether politer demeanour.

Blackmore, who had chosen to remain silent for the duration of their journey, waited until Fortnum and his colleague had alighted the carriage before checking his pocket-watch and breaking his silence...

"An hour-long journey, James. Judging by first our westerly direction, then accounting for a course adjustment to a more northerly route. Recognition of several familiar street profiles as our carriage navigated its passage throughout them, the sounds outside as we halted are concurrent with those of a major metropolitan train station. King's Cross in the north-westerly quarter of the city, I'd wager."

Upon alighting the carriage Bass was surprised to discover that Blackmore's deductions as to their whereabouts were correct.

"I must commend you once more on your impeccable sense of direction, Tiberius, King's Cross it is," stated Bass, matter-of-factly...

"Gentlemen, if you would be so good as to accompany us into the station?" asked Captain Fortnum who, along with the rest of his men, had joined the two Detectives who now stood on the busy concourse directly in front of King's Cross railway station.

"Please, lead on, Captain," instructed Blackmore as, flanked on either side by two C.S.F. operatives, one more to their tail and Captain Fortnum taking the point, Bass and Blackmore were escorted through the front entrance of the station. Having moved just a short distance inside, Fortnum halted the group...

"This way if you please, gentlemen."

They proceeded on through a stone archway to their left and descended a deserted and very steep set of steps into what seemed to be some kind of arched, man-made tunnel. After negotiating several changes of direction through a complex network of ceramic tiled tunnels they came upon a second steep stairway that was duly descended, which led them out onto an underground station platform that was being patrolled along its considerable length and at each of the three arched exits that could be seen at various intervals along the wall of the tunnel by several armed C.S.F. operatives and soldiers belonging to the Duke of Wellington's regiment.

As Bass and Blackmore were led out onto the platform it became plainly obvious to both men just as to why the high level of security designated to this particular part of the station was required.

"I do believe that is the Royal carriage, James," observed Blackmore.

"Indeed, it is, my old friend; and one might assume that we have not been summoned to this most secluded of locations to be in any way honoured in recognition of our recent exploits!"

"More than likely discommended dishonourably and disappeared post-haste I shouldn't wonder," assumed Blackmore warily.

"I would suggest that the wolf within you be readied, my brother, for we may have use of his presence and the need to move swiftly and decisively should the need arise."

Bass and Blackmore were duly escorted towards the door belonging to a grandly decorated train carriage bearing on its side what they instantly recognised as Queen Victoria's personal coat of arms. Approaching a small table set just to one side of the carriage door, the two wary colleagues were halted by the sound of a formidable, booming voice; a voice from their past which they both instantly recognised...

"James, Tiberius; check your weapons here if you please, gentlemen." As they both proceeded to lay their numerous tranklements onto the table, Blackmore remarked...

"Good lord, Barney Whitehouse. Strike me sideways; it gladdens our hearts to see one of our old boys of the ninety-fifth still alive and, by all accounts, doing very well for himself. I..."

"And the pair of brass 'dusters', Tiberius," interrupted Whitehouse knowingly whilst tapping the table-top with a stout, well-used heavy wooden cudgel.

"One inside each of those bottomless coat pockets of yours, you sly old devil."

Once satisfied that the extent of their formidable cache was accounted for, Whitehouse proceeded to address the young lieutenant stood to his right with a view to ensuring that each item was meticulously committed to inventory before next issuing precise instructions of protocol to the waiting Detectives.

"Commander Tiberius Blackmore; one modified forty-five calibre LeMat 9 round chamber revolver: three spare chambers: fully loaded, one sheathed, seven-inch Sheffield cast steel blade, brass pommelled hunting knife, well used; a pair of custom cast brass knuckle dusters, also well used," remarked Whitehouse as he eyed Blackmore with a knowing wink and a wry grin...

"Major James Bass; one six round chamber army issue Webley service revolver, one six round chamber forty-five calibre Smith and Wesson Schofield revolver, American made," uttered Whitehouse, an air of disdain apparent in his voice.

"One leather sheathed eight-inch blade, bone handled, brass pommelled Bowie knife, also American made! I would strongly advise that the wolf inside of you stays inside of you for at least the duration of your visit, if you get my meaning, sir."

Tapping the left breast of his heavy greatcoat and gesturing all around to make certain that Bass was made well aware of the strategic positions adopted all around them by heavily armed C.S.F. agents...

"Rest assured, James, we have the means and the knowhow to put you down, permanently and may God almighty strike me down dead if the need arises," imparted Whitehouse, somewhat apologetically.

As Bass gave his own wry grin and nodded his head once signifying that all was well, Whitehouse continued to speak...

"Thank you, gentlemen. All personal items will be returned to you upon your disembarkation. Finally, a brief word on protocol and etiquette; upon Her Majesty entering the carriage you will stand to attention and, as your rank requires, offer a formal military salute to your sovereign. You will not speak unless invited by her Majesty to do so. You will not stand easy unless invited by Her Majesty to do so. Any questions, gentlemen?"

A simple sideways movement of each detective's head denoting that no questions would be forthcoming was enough of a sign for Whitehouse to continue issuing his precise raft of instructions...

"Good. Please enter and exit the carriage through this door. Her Majesty will join you presently."

Doing as they were asked; Bass and Blackmore entered the carriage. The thing that occurred to both of them first and foremost was the sheer opulence of their surroundings. Four crystal light shades, two of which were set into the quilted ceiling at each end of the carriage, illuminated the sumptuous blue upholstered, intricately carved bird's eye maple furniture and the silk panelled walls. Ivory carved light stands adorned the table tops and Royal blue velvet curtains hung from all of the windows.

A leather-topped desk that stretched almost the whole width of the coach, 'not a usual feature of this most opulent of places, looks completely out of character with the decor' Blackmore supposed to himself, took precedence at the far end of the carriage, the entire floor space being completely covered by the finest Persian carpet.

After waiting for fifteen minutes, that seemed to the two Detectives as if it lasted a lifetime, the door directly behind the desk opened, through which stepped a Colonel belonging to the Duke of Wellington's regiment. Standing to attention immediately upon assuming his position to the far-right hand side of the desk he barked out the distinct order: "A... Ten... Shun"

– to which both Bass and Blackmore responded immediately by snapping to attention.

Following the colonel through the door came the Home Secretary, Sir Matthew White Ridley, The Prime Minister, the most honourable Robert Gascoyne Cecil, Captain Pontius Aston, and finally her Majesty Queen Victoria, who was formally introduced to the Detectives by the Prime Minister as they remained stood at full attention.

"Her Majesty Queen Victoria; Queen of Great Britain and Ireland, Empress of India."

Seating herself behind the desk the Queen took a few moments to peruse the papers that had been prepared in order for her to read; 'a clever ruse, no doubt, designed to allow herself time for self-composure prior to her speech' wondered Blackmore to himself again...

"Welcome, Commander Blackmore, Major Bass. Your attendance at this meeting is most appreciated," began the Queen, rather informally.

"Yes, Ma'am, thank you, Ma'am," blurted out the two Detectives as they each gave the tidiest salute of their careers.

"Please stand at ease, gentlemen. Your exploits have become something quite akin to the stuff of legend amongst your peers, Commander, Major. Indeed, even at Court we have been regaled regularly with tales of your bold exploits and your exemplary service rendered selflessly in the defence of your Queen and country.

"For these things alone, our country owes you both a great debt of gratitude, which we offer to pay in part today. Commander Alan Tiberius Blackmore, James Bartholomew Bass, on behalf of oneself, and a very grateful nation, we thank you."

"Thank you, Ma'am" was the correct official reply demanded by protocol, duly delivered by the two Detectives.

"Additionally, in recognition of your many remarkable achievements, we are very happy to offer you both promotion to the rank of Colonel, commissions to be made active immediately. Very nicely done, gentlemen."

Whilst somehow managing to maintain their exterior visage of unemotional stoicism, both men were in fact bursting inside with unbridled pride. Their sparing verbal response to the Queen for bestowing on them this great honour remained one of professionally controlled calmness personified...

"Thank you very much indeed, Ma'am."

The Queen wasted no time procrastinating and immediately proceeded onwards to the next item on her agenda...

"Official duties concluded, we must therefore concern ourselves with more mundane business orientated matters, gentlemen; matters of great importance that will undoubtedly require the input and utilisation of your remarkable raft of talents.

"We understand that the conclusion of the recent Whitechapel murders case was brought about, in part, as a result of your rather 'unorthodox' method of policing. A final resolution to a particularly nasty episode which was, in the main, welcomed by the majority of the government.

"However, the proven involvement of two members raised from influential English and Eastern European aristocracy could in turn prove to be something of a major embarrassment, not only to the government of Britain, but also to both the European government and family involved, should they be implicated in any media exposé of the true events.

"We therefore conclude that after speaking with Captain Aston at great length regarding a proposal previously suggested by Major Bass, the identities of the Whitechapel murderers be withheld from the public domain indefinitely, or until such a time as is deemed that this most sensitive of subject matter might be more prudently explained and the full case file be made available. In short, gentlemen, as far as the general public are concerned the murderer merely vanished; case closed."

After a brief pause, during which the Prime Minister, The Home Secretary and Captain Aston each spoke in turn with the Queen, about what both Blackmore and Bass could only suppose, the Queen continued...

"Gentlemen, the dawn of a new century is almost upon us. We look forward to an age of great prosperity and eventual peace as our great nation opens her welcoming arms to embrace our friends and allies across Europe, and the whole world.

"As you are both very well aware, crime in its many forms continues to develop and flourish on a parallel with the infrastructure it infests at an almost inconceivably alarming rate.

"The advent of supernatural anomalies also, of which you are both very familiar with in their various guises, raised the question of the necessity for a special kind of enforcement agency to be raised in order to police these so-called anomalies effectively, whilst maintaining total anonymity from public attention.

"The Time Enforcement Agency was conceived for such high purpose, as was your League of Ghosts organisation, a remarkable and uninformed piece of foresight and perception by yourselves as to the future greater needs of our small, fragile world."

Suddenly, the Queen rose to her feet, immediately snapping Bass, Blackmore, Aston and the Redcoat Colonel back to attention. Eyeing Bass and Blackmore intently, she spoke to the Detectives once more before turning to leave the room...

"Colonel Blackmore, Colonel Bass; we shall continue to oversee your careers as they unfold with keen interest, and rest assured, gentlemen, we will continue to have a use for you."

In an instant, as quickly as she had arrived, Queen Victoria was gone, followed by the Prime Minister, the Secretary for State and the Redcoat Colonel. Aston remained and proceeded to offer the ever so slightly disorientated pair of newly commissioned Colonels each a generous tumbler of brandy from one of the three cut glass crystal decanters belonging to an ornate oak and silver tantalus that rested prominently upon the Queen's desk.

"That all culminated in a more favourable outcome than expected, Colonel Bass, wouldn't you agree?" deadpanned Blackmore as he drained his tumbler with one almighty gulp.

"That it did, Colonel Blackmore, and that I most surely would," answered Bass as he reciprocated Blackmore's action by tipping the contents of his own tumbler directly down his dry throat.

"Colonel Blackmore, Colonel Bass; may one be amongst the first to offer congratulations to you both on receiving your promotions. Your military authority was enhanced as a necessity in light of the fact that your higher rank will prove to be something of an advantage to us during our future, and indeed our past endeavours to come."

Aston beckoned towards the carriage's exit as he continued to speak...

"Firstly, reclaim your considerable cache of ordnance, gentlemen; then walk with me, if you please."

Chapter 40

'Look to the Future'

As the three colleagues alighted the Queen's carriage back onto the platform, Bass and Blackmore halted at the table where their formidable array of weapons had remained, untouched, under the ever-attentive eyes of Major Barney Whitehouse.

"Colonel Blackmore, sir, Colonel Bass, sir, might I offer my personal congratulations on receiving your promotions, sirs," he barked somewhat formally as he snapped to attention and gave the pair of fledgling Colonels a full salute.

Returning the towering Major's salute, Bass displayed a rather uncharacteristically jovial presence as he spoke…

"Ease up, Barney. We entered that carriage so named by our mothers as James and Tiberius and to a select few family, friends, acquaintances and colleagues we alighted as James and Tiberius. Now, hand over my irons and steel, you old war dog, for I have felt naked without them for a good long while enough!"

Bristling with the pride of someone realising that the attitudes of two 'raw meat' colonels towards the lower order would not be sullied or altered in any way by the privilege of rank, Whitehouse bristled simply…

"Yes, sir, right where you left 'em, sir."

After reclaiming, re-holstering, re-sheathing and re-pocketing their formidable array of weapons, Blackmore and Bass joined Pontius Aston as he walked along the station platform towards the first of three tiled archways cut into the wall, equidistant from each other at thirty-foot intervals along the platform.

Passing under the arch, they began navigating what seemed like an endless myriad of newly tiled tunnels, 'similar in their complexity to a more modern realisation of the labyrinthine maze of Trajan's Vaults' observed Bass to himself in a moment of silent contemplation. Aston began to speak as they walked further into the maze of tunnels...

"The tunnels which we traverse are part of the vast underground expansion that when completed will link the inner city to its outlying boroughs and wards. A massive, labour intensive undertaking and one of the most ambitious engineering projects ever undertaken, the section that we now enter was conceived over three decades ago as part of the original Great Metropolitan Underground Railway system."

"This briefing of yours concerning the improvements being made to the Great Metropolitan Underground Railway is quite enlightening, Pontius, but might one ask the significance this rather informative vignette of engineering prowess and achievement offers to our immediate business aspirations?" asked a rather frustrated Blackmore.

"The importance of my words, and their significance upon our 'business aspirations' as you call them, will become wholly apparent to both of you presently, my impatient friend" came Aston's reassuring words to an increasingly irksome Blackmore.

As the three colleagues alighted a second steep staircase they found themselves passing under the same high stone archway as they had done less than an hour previously, and immediately recognised the familiar sights and sounds of the busy King's Cross railway concourse.

Aston turned towards his companions and began to speak...

"Gentlemen, before we proceed, I would draw your attention to one of the key points raised within Her Majesty's briefing concerning primarily the policing of supernatural anomalies that we know exist, both on our plane of existence, and within the corridor of the fourth dimension.

"In short, James, Tiberius; I wish for you both to be trained with a view to act as special agents seconded to the service of the Time Enforcement Agency."

Blackmore and Bass eyed Aston with their customary blank expressions intact, well-practised expressions that in this case concealed the fact that they each had a hundred or more questions burning inside them that demanded answers. It was Blackmore who took the opportunity to speak first, asking just one simple thing...

"Might one enquire, Pontius, why it has taken so long for you to ask?"

Aston's impeccably coiffured beard twitched as his face cracked uncharacteristically into the widest of smiles.

"We, the council of thirteen 'Grand Meisters' of the T.E.A., needed to be certain beyond all doubt that you both matched the criteria we seek when canvassing perspective new agents. The selection process is long, meticulous in its requirements and the tests arduous in the extreme for each candidate to endure.

"During the course of the past decade, considering your many successes whilst engaging various supernatural entities, plus James' obvious qualification that guaranteed him instant selection, you both earned the right for a 'Grand Meister', for it is a 'Grand Meister' of the T.E.A. solely who has the authority to offer a perspective agent the opportunity to pledge service to the agency, to nominate the pair of you as viable candidates for selection"

There was a brief lull in Aston's speech before he continued solemnly...

"Think on this very carefully indeed, gentlemen. This opportunity is offered to the individual but once in a lifetime. If you should choose to forego selection, no second chance will be forthcoming. No feeling of animosity towards yourselves will be harboured by the 'Grand Meisters', your new military rank would be honoured and your lives here in the nineteenth century would run their natural courses but the opportunity to alter your perceptions of life and its very many and wider parameters, to become explorers within the realms of the fourth dimension of time, would be lost forever."

Bass and Blackmore eyed each other thoughtfully with not a word passing between them. All at once, as if prompted to respond by some subliminal message, each man turned to face Aston and uttered simultaneously, without the slightest hesitation...

"When, pray tell, do we begin?"

"Excellent," replied Aston.

"We begin immediately, gentlemen, by first taking a few steps outside of this building."

As the three companions picked their way through the usual throng of late afternoon crowds of commuters leaving and entering the station, Aston proceeded to reach inside a pocket of his long black velvet overcoat and produced a pair of rather familiar looking brass instruments.

Upon handing one of the tactile pieces of beautifully crafted metal to each of the Colonels, grateful though they were to receive their fine gifts, Bass mirrored Blackmore's own slight mystification as to how such an innocuous object, common enough equipment issued to all military personnel, could be regarded as being so important...

"Thank you, Pontius. A mariners' compass? A beautifully crafted instrument, make no mistake, but not in appearance at any rate to dissimilar to my own."

Aston emitted a wide grin as he made his immediate reply...

"Exactly, James, similar only in appearance alone, for this is a dimensional compass. This remarkable piece of equipment will enable you to access the corridor along which we T.E.A. agents travail as we police the timelines within the fourth dimension.

"Each device is personalised for its owner's exclusive use, their thought patterns ingrained into its complex machine matrix from the first moment that it touches its guardian's hand."

"Guardians?" alluded Blackmore quizzically...

"Is this trinket then not merely an inherited bauble, an heirloom of sorts?"

"In this instance, the gift of fourth dimensional travel is the true inheritance, my friend," answered Aston...

"The instrument itself is but a port-key which from this moment forth is totally at one with both your biometric physiology and your spiritual psyche. In short, gentlemen, with just a simple adjustment to the compass, and a thought given to either future or past locations, emanating from a fixed point in time, the fourth dimension will open up its portals so as your explorations may commence."

Bass and Blackmore each eyed their compass for a few seconds, opening the face of each one to reveal the finely crafted, yet still unremarkable characteristics of a standard mariners' compass, before Aston continued...

"Please observe, gentlemen. If you will, set co-ordinates Azimuth 280* North-by-Northwest on the face of your device and form a picture vividly in your minds the street in front of this station. Also, retain a mental image of the numbers eleven and twenty-one, then follow me."

The two mystified colleagues did exactly as they were instructed. As they followed Aston through the crowded terminus towards the exit a familiar feeling of sublime disorientation, as though reality were fading all around them, enveloped their senses, but on this occasion, unlike any of the similar previous instances, a comforting notion of lucidity and calmness was also very apparent.

As they stepped out onto the station forecourt, both Bass and Blackmore were left momentarily speechless by the wondrous sights that greeted their disbelieving eyes. Horseless carriages moving at great speed, seemingly under their own power; People speaking into devices clasped tightly to their ears and using the same device in such a manner as would a photographer capture an image, but without using flash powder as an artificial light source and buildings so tall, the architecture so unfamiliar and yet somehow completely familiar to both men as being a place they knew very well.

Realising full well that his charges required a few minutes in order to process the wondrous environment into which they had just arrived, Aston waited a good long while before imparting...

"Gentlemen, I welcome you both to a crisp, bright November afternoon in twenty-first century London."

About the Author

Born in the year 1840 James Bartholomew Bass was raised for the first twelve years of his life as an orphaned only child in the Derbyshire workhouse where his mother lived and worked for a short time after her husband's tragic death in a mining accident until her passing during childbirth.

Soon after his twelfth birthday James ran away from the dour, oppressive workhouse life and made directly for London where, in the East End district of Whitechapel, he proceeded to live for the next two years of his young life relying on his natural guile and wits alone in order to survive.

During this time Bass met and formed what was to become a lifelong friendship with fellow street urchin Alan Tiberius Blackmore and whilst employing certain questionable, and more often than not quite illegal methods of securing their next meal and keeping a dry roof over their heads, the pair began to develop not only a keen instinct for survival but also coupled with an encyclopaedic knowledge of London and Whitechapel in particular, a problem solving acumen that honed their rapidly developing intellects and was supported by the pair's fearsome reputation for employing violence to achieve their goals.

Facing the unenviable choice of immediate transportation to an antipodean penal colony for life or joining the Army after being arrested and found guilty of perpetrating various misdemeanours in and around the city, the hapless pair opted for the latter and were pressed into service with the Prince Consort's own 95th Rifle Brigade.

After a distinguished career of fifteen years with the Rifle Brigade, a further five years spent with The Prince Consort's own Hussars Regiment then a further seven years as agents sequestered to Her Majesty Queen Victoria's special black operations unit CSF (Covert Special Forces), both men retired bearing full military honours in the year 1885 after serving in the second Anglo-Afghan war.

Having been highly decorated for services rendered to Queen and country and rising to the rank of Major, James Bass and his companion Commander Tiberius Blackmore were recommended by their military superiors for employment with the London Metropolitan Police force where they each took up the immediate commissions of Detective Inspector under the command and mentorship of their old Army colleague and close friend Detective Superintendent Francis William Abilene and were based in the Leman Street station house at the heart of Whitechapel.

Both Detectives became founder members of the organisation named The League of Ghosts and a series of novels chronicling the pair's many and varied exploits were adapted from the original journals kept by Detective Chief Inspector (Colonel) James Bartholomew Bass.